Praise for Blood Dawn

"Jason Bovberg brings his *Blood* trilogy to a close with an assurance of redemption in the midst of terrible destruction. The narrative steadily amps up the tension while delighting us with continual surprises along the way. This is an exceptional tale delivered with exceptional care, and it's a fitting and powerful conclusion to a not-to-be-missed trilogy!"
—Robert Devereaux, author of *Caliban* and *Oedipus Aroused*

"*Blood Dawn* ends with a bang, and a ton of heart! It's a terrific final novel in a trilogy so inventive and unique that it's all but impossible to compare it to other tales in the genre. But be sure to read these books in order!"
—Rob Leininger, author of *Killing Suki Flood* and *Gumshoe*

"*Blood Dawn* provides a slam-bang ending to a compulsively readable saga. It's even bloodier, weirder, and crazier than *Blood Red* and *Draw Blood*, bringing this wacko sci-fi/horror mashup to a satisfyingly splatter-drenched conclusion."
—Bill Braddock, author of *Brew*

"With *Blood Dawn*, Jason Bovberg has crafted a chilling end to his twisted world."
—Kirk Whitham, documentary filmmaker, creator of *Postcards from the Apocalypse* and *The Life and Various Deaths of Ambrose Bierce*

"I absolutely love the *Blood* saga—it's gripping, raw, and inventive. Thumbs up!"
—Jonathan Maberry, *New York Times* bestselling author of *Rot & Ruin* and *Code Zero*

"With *Blood Red*, *Draw Blood*, and *Blood Dawn*, Jason Bovberg—a master of tension—offers up a zombie epic for the new century."
—Alden Bell, author of *The Reapers Are the Angels* and *Exit Kingdom*

"You've been to the end of the world before, but never quite like this."
—Richard Lee Byers, author of *The Reaver* and *Blind God's Bluff*

"The *Blood* trilogy is must-read zombie fiction—familiar enough to keep you glued to the action, innovative enough to keep you guessing."
—Craig DiLouie, author of *Suffer the Children*

Praise for Draw Blood

"*Draw Blood* is a real nail-biter of a zombie novel that will delight die-hard fans and draw legions of new ones to the genre!"
—Jonathan Maberry, *New York Times* bestselling author of *Rot & Ruin* and *Code Zero*

"*Draw Blood* launches itself at you with relentless terror from the first page to the last. Bovberg, a master of tension, keeps the action taut and breathless, driving the story forward with a combination of excruciating dread and linguistic majesty."
—Alden Bell, author of *The Reapers Are the Angels* and *Exit Kingdom*

"*Draw Blood* is a terrific sequel, propelling the story forward with singular intensity—and a great twist."
—Craig DiLouie, author of *Suffer the Children*

"In *Draw Blood*, Jason Bovberg attains a new level of mastery, guiding us with assurance and control into the finely etched, moment-by-moment travails of his characters without once relaxing the tension. *Draw Blood* deserves the widest readership possible and consideration for top awards. This one's a keeper!"
—Robert Devereaux, author of *Deadweight* and *Santa Steps Out*

"Jason Bovberg one-ups himself with *Draw Blood*—this menagerie of grotesqueries is a faster, bloodier, and even more demented thrill ride."
—Grant Jerkins, author of *Done in One* and *A Very Simple Crime*

"*Draw Blood* combines the best things about the *Autumn* series, *Invasion of the Body Snatchers*, and *Night of the Living Dead* into one coherent tale. If you liked *Blood Red*, *Draw Blood* will definitely not let you down."
—Robert Beveridge, former Top 50 Amazon reviewer

"*Draw Blood* starts off firing on all cylinders and never lets up. It's a fresh take with all the best elements of the genre."
—David Dunwoody, author of *Empire* and *The Harvest Cycle*

Praise for Blood Red

"An epic addition to the genre, *Blood Red* delivers a nonstop, real-time experience of the End Times—replete with visceral terror, buckets of gore, and, ultimately, a redemptive humanity."
—Alden Bell, author of *The Reapers Are the Angels* and *Exit Kingdom*

"Jason Bovberg proves he's got the goods with a whole new kind of horror novel."
—Tom Piccirilli, author of *The Last Whisper in the Dark* and *The Last Kind Words*

"With *Blood Red*, Jason Bovberg infuses a post-apocalyptic tale with a sustained sense of genuine mystery; of having no idea what's happening to the world and the people around you, or why."
—Brian Hodge, author of *Whom the Gods Would Destroy* and *Dark Advent*

"Guaranteed to creep you out!"
—Robert Devereaux, author of *Deadweight* and *Santa Steps Out*

"Jason Bovberg's *Blood Red* is unlike anything I've ever experienced. It starts as a slow-burn freak-out and culminates in a series of horror-show set pieces that will forever be etched in my mind. This book made my skin crawl."
—Grant Jerkins, author of *A Very Simple Crime* and *The Ninth Step*

"*Blood Red* is a tour de f***ed-up!"
—Peter Stenson, author of *Fiend*

DARK HIGHWAY
FEAR THE ROAD'S END

FOLLOW ME!

facebook.com/jasonbovberg.author

twitter.com/jasonbovberg

REVIEW ME!

www.amazon.com/Jason-Bovberg/e/B00JJ36NNW

Wherever you buy my books, they can be reviewed!

LEARN ALL ABOUT ME!

www.jasonbovberg.com

BLOOD DAWN

BOOK III

JASON BOVBERG

A DARK HIGHWAY PRESS book
published by arrangement with the author

ISBN (trade paperback): 978-0-9662629-6-4
ISBN (eBook): 978-0-9662629-7-1

Cover art and design by Christopher Nowell
Layout by Kirk Whitham

For Barb
From dawn to sunset
and dream time too ... always

CHAPTER 1

"Felicia!"

She jerks awake atop her warm bed. The blue curtain is moving restlessly against a morning breeze, her small oscillating fan is rattling, and that horse-sized dog on the other side of the parking lot is already barking. Oh, what a lovely summer.

She peers over at her bedside clock.

6:17 a.m.

Felicia groans softly. Too early.

Nicole shifts next to her, their hips bumping. The tactile memories and flavors of their night together flicker through Felicia's consciousness, bringing a secret smile to her lips. She feels a touch of wine hangover, but not too bad. Very much worth it.

Someone called her name, loudly inside a dream—it wasn't Nicole, but it was a woman's voice—and now that dream is quickly fading. Who was it, in there? Was it Janet at the store? Possibly. But talk about a dream character acting against type! Janet never raises her voice or gets demonstrably angry, even when three of her employees (Felicia included) call in sick simultaneously, as happened last weekend. Felicia had felt the need to exude a little extra cheerfulness for the past week to get back into Janet's good graces, but the fact is, Janet is just too nice.

Fantasizing briefly—not for the first time—about central air conditioning, Felicia pushes herself up from perspiration-moistened sheets and enjoys the meager pleasure of the whirring fan's breeze against her face and upper body. Before Felicia moved to Fort Collins, she assumed her new home at the foot of the Rockies would deliver cool, fecund mountain breezes at all times, even in summer, but the reality was quite different. Summer brought some pretty intense, dry heat. The intermittent draft of the fan cools her barely damp skin, and she's grateful for the sensation.

This current apartment is on the second story of a shoddily maintained complex north of the drive-in and Hughes Stadium, in the older, northwestern section of Fort Collins, probably built before air conditioning was even imagined. She's lived here for about six months now, and no way would she ever again rent a second-level apartment with no A/C. In the summer anyway. And this is only morning. *Early* morning! She's already thinking of ways to escape the heat this afternoon. A movie at the $2 theater? A dip in the pool at City Park? Too many kids there. If only the apartment complex had a private pool! That hadn't been a priority in January, when she signed the papers, but now it feels like a tragic oversight.

Today is Friday, and it's her day off, and all she's done since the end of her morning shift yesterday is hang with Nicole. Nine hours at the store, followed by a ride home from her willing roommate—Felicia's Jeep is in for repairs, so she's relying on Nicole for once, getting carted around in that old red Honda Civic. Felicia smirks at the memory of their giggles at Wilbur's, trying to choose exactly the right cheap variety of vino. Hanging off each other, both of them knowing exactly where the evening would end. Nicole also gives the best massages in the world.

Neither woman has any illusions that they're engaged in anything long-term—or at least that's how they're fooling themselves. But it sure is fun getting playful together. Since the day they met in the CSU quad—Nicole new to the school and needing help from a Fort Collins native—they've simply clicked. They've been together for nearly nine months now, but who's counting? Meeting near the student center might have been a goofy one-off, except that they'd sighted each other again, later, walking near Aylesworth Hall, both rocking their cheap-ass earbuds and laughing when they acknowledged each other. That had led to lunch, which had led to music in Nicole's minuscule dorm room, which had led to plans to bike together for Fort Collins' celebrated Tour de Fat event. And *that* day had led hilariously to their first fumblings at Felicia's place, and suddenly Nicole was the most natural, enjoyable girlfriend she'd ever had. No weirdness, no hesitancy, merely a human connection.

Not to mention, Felicia feels like she might have trouble imagining her life without Nicole's talented hands (and fingers), and she's sure Nicole doesn't mind the non-dorm place to stay on the weekends. They both have their stressors—involving family, money, and the future—but they're having fun. No doubt about that.

Watching the muscles of Nicole's toned right thigh tremble in sleep, Felicia is thinking again about her dream. Something else happened in there, didn't it?

She cocks her head, stares at the stained popcorn ceiling.

Something weird.

She tries recalling what happened inside the dream, but as with any dream, it's elusive. It's like grasping at smoke.

But wait—she remembers something red. Like blood. Just a suggestion of that. Blood. Fingers grasping. No, not fingers. But something like that. Rooting around. And something like tendrils, red tendrils snaking like lightning. Or blood spilling in jittery fast-motion.

She shrugs herself away from these peculiar perceptions. They're starting to make her heart beat faster.

Felicia gently extricates herself from the bed, knowing that there will be no more sleep for her this morning. Which is a bummer, because she likes to sleep past 7 a.m. on days she's not working or going to class. Maybe even 8 a.m., if she's feeling indulgent. Nicole is an even later sleeper and probably has three more hours ahead of her. No sense waking her. Felicia looks down on her for a long moment, appreciating the view, and then pads out into the small living room. She has to admit, the relative coolness of the morning is nice. She goes straight to the front window and opens it up.

There are the two empty Pinot bottles that they bought at Wilbur's, upright on the coffee table. One of the glasses has about an inch left. The other is empty, angled against the sofa cushions, against a pillow. More memories flood her, and she smiles again. Ah, the couch. She begins cleaning up, grabbing their flung-away clothes, replacing pillows, and taking the glassware to the tiny kitchen. She tiptoes back into the bedroom and silently drapes the clothes over the desk chair, then returns to the kitchen to take care of the dishes.

That damn nightmare keeps strobing back at her.

Red.

Blood red.

Like a flash of crimson behind her eyes. And more to it than a splash of color. Something malevolent. No, not quite that. But disturbing.

"Knock it off," she whispers to herself, soaping up another glass and setting it on top of a dish towel to dry. She gradually loses herself in the monotony of her task.

When she's finished, she dries her hands and returns to the bedroom door. She peers inside, sees that Nicole hasn't stirred.

Felicia moves quietly through the room and into the bathroom, whispers the door shut. She turns on the shower and steps in. The cool water is a thrill against her flesh, and she enjoys the sensation for a moment before twisting the faucet to lukewarm. She washes her body slowly, her eyes closed.

She's thinking about what to do with her day off. She now has a vague memory of Nicole suggesting something about a hike—Horsetooth

Rock?—but today Felicia feels like escaping the heat rather than embracing it. If she were a shopper, of if she had any money at all to burn, she might suggest jetting down to one of the big malls in Denver, maybe Flatiron Crossing, and making it a day, perhaps catch a movie down there, but lately she's found casual shopping to be a depressing exercise, at least on what Janet pays her for part-time work. Why couldn't she have sprung from some disgustingly wealthy family?

Felicia has a year left at CSU, and then the real world looms. It might not have been that way had she not shifted her major from English to Business two years ago—much to her finance-minded mom's delight. Doing so had added an extra year to her regimen. That was okay with both her and her mom, who was and still is helping bankroll her education (barely). Because for the first time in her life, Felicia is almost feeling confident about her future. She's planning to run a health food store here in town. Somehow, some way. And as much as she admires Janet at the Food Co-Op for what she's accomplished, Felicia can think of several areas where she knows she could improve profits, and use social media to start drumming up more business. Social media is where it's at, any fool will tell you that, and although she would never say it to Janet's face, she knows she could run the store better than her boss.

Now, feeling the water course over her grateful skin, she lets thoughts of business plans and inklings of future marketing endeavors drift through her consciousness. She tries to ignore the tendrils of nightmare still slithering around inside her.

The touch of Nicole's hand, curling around to her abdomen, makes her jump.

"You're up early," comes her lover's soft voice.

"Oh!" Felicia giggles, twining her fingers through Nicole's. "I hope I didn't wake you."

"Fun night." Nicole leans forward to catch her eye. She has her crooked smile on full display—emphasized by the nose stud, the ratty blue string necklace, the shag cut of her short hair.

"Yes, and you're ready for more, I see."

"I could be persuaded."

"What the hell are you doing up?" Felicia asks.

"Well, heck, on a day off there's no such thing as too early."

Felicia smiles.

"Still up for Horsetooth?" Nicole asks her.

Felicia closes her eyes and makes a small, involuntary sound, trying to lose herself in the moment. She doesn't want to acknowledge it, but when Nicole's hand touched her, startling her, her mind went straight to the nightmare—the slink of the tendrils like reaching vines, burrowing roots. She had to forcibly constrain a full-body shiver.

"I was just talking myself out of it."

"Why?" comes the whisper at her ear.

"Heat."

"You can't take the heat?"

Felicia smiles. "Oh, I can take it."

"Come on, we need to work off that dinner."

"I thought we already did that. A couple times." Felicia takes a quavering breath. "But you do make a very persuasive argument."

"I should have studied law."

"I'm not sure they cover that kind of persuasion in law school."

"Purely extracurricular."

The women enjoy an extended moment of silence under the steady pulse of the water and other sensations. Felicia furrows her brow, concentrating.

"You know, I don't even have much of a headache," Nicole says, breaking the silence. "Usually the wine decks me."

"I have a little one, but I think ... I think it actually came from a dream." Felicia turns to face Nicole. She needs to see her there in front of her. "That's weird, right?"

She slowly runs the bar of soap up and down her roommate's arms. On Nicole's left shoulder is a tattoo of a butterfly, colorful and new, and Felicia uses the edge of the bar to trace the wings.

"Dreams are weird." Nicole is watching her expression. "Especially the headachy kind."

"Can't shake this one."

"What was it about?"

"Well, there wasn't really a plot or anything, but ..."

"... what?"

"... it was, like, perceptions. Something in my head, like fingers in there, searching around for something. Stirring things up. Weird."

"Ewwww."

"Yeah."

Nicole takes the soap into her slippery hands. "I have to call my mom," she says.

Felicia can't see Nicole rolling her eyes as she speaks of her high-maintenance mother, but she knows she's doing it.

"It's her birthday," Nicole reminds her. "Then we can go. Get an early start. It'll probably be crowded up there."

"Okay, yeah." Felicia can feel a small frown at her eyes. "Did you call to me this morning? Like, yell out my name?"

"What are you talking about? You're starting to creep me out."

Felicia is shaking her head.

"That dream still bothering you?" Nicole whispers. "Really? It's nothing else?"

"Nope, promise."

"Well, I can help with a headache."

"I'm sure you can."

Nicole does indeed help.

CHAPTER 2

In the Honda, winding up toward Horsetooth, around the reservoir, and twisting up and around toward the trailhead, Felicia is pensive. For the past few minutes, she has been catching glimpses of Horsetooth Rock through the trees—the geometrical blue spruces, the verdant Douglas firs, the majestic ponderosas, the otherworldly bristlecone pines—and feeling its presence up there like gravity. Now that she's up here beyond the city, she can't imagine that she might not have come. And yet …

Nicole has asked twice about her mood, but Felicia has merely shrugged. She's staring out the passenger window at the scenery, and for some reason she's recalling those long-ago days in her youth during summer camp up in Estes Park. There was a counsellor—Mindy was her name, Felica's pretty sure—who taught her pre-teen charges about the different pine varieties. How they had all touched the trees' needles, their cones, had tasted them on their tongues. Sticky and sharp. Had used them in tea around a campfire later.

Felicia is unsettled by the memories, which come at her with a strange power. She's hungry, for some reason, even though while dressing in their hiking gear she and Nicole had made a healthy meal of a new breakfast cereal that a vendor gave away as samples for the store last week. Some high-fiber thing with oats and blueberries. But it's not the cereal she's thinking of now, nor any thoughts of what her future store might stock, but rather a mountainside so green and succulent that it looks edible.

"Are you not into this?" Nicole asks. "You want to go back?"

"No, I need it."

"Well, cheer up, why don'tcha? It's fuckin' beautiful up here."

Felicia laughs and shakes herself out of her funk. At least, she tries to. In moments, Horsetooth Rock is looming ahead, closer than ever as they wind up the final mile, Fort Collins behind them and the small mountain town of Masonville to the southwest. The distinctive "teeth" of the rock—jutting pillars of weather-gapped stone—seem to suck at her, drawing her in. Below the rock, a fertile evergreen expanse of forest sprawls in all directions. Felicia can make out a couple of trails leading off in several directions through the trees, like the edges of paint strokes in a work of art.

The trailhead is busy this morning, as expected. There are a couple dozen vehicles already parked in the lot, and she can see the colorful dots of hikers making their way up the trail. With the Civic's hatchback flung up, Felicia and Nicole pull on their small hydration packs and help each other with sunscreen on their necks and shoulders. After a mutual thumbs-up, they've locked up the car and are on their way.

The hike up the gradual ascent feels good in Felicia's lungs, as if the deep breathing is cleaning her out, invigorating her. Energizing her. Blowing out the carbon, as her father might have said, years ago when he was part of her life. The clean mountain air and particularly the smell of pine is intoxicating today. She lets her eyes wander out into the distance, savoring the great swaths of timberland.

Ahead of her, Nicole jumps up onto—then off of—a large boulder in the middle of the path.

"You're thinking about that teacher, aren't you?" Nicole calls back. "Accounting?"

Felicia raises her eyebrows. "Actually, no. But now I am. Thanks!"

And it's the truth. She hasn't thought of that horrible woman at all for at least—what?—an hour? The cantankerous finance professor, who seemed to hold some kind of grudge against her, had consumed too much of Felicia's energy since posting the letter C in her final grade book, and she refused to dwell on the woman today.

"Just thinking. Really, I'm fine."

"Is it your dad?"

Felicia feels the itch of irritation but forces a smile. She appreciates Nicole's efforts to help, but if she asks another question, Felicia thinks she might simply sprint away into the trees and get lost among them.

As for her dad, she hasn't heard from him in over a year, when he called her drunk at midnight from Chicago, and even that felt unintentional, like a butt-dial. She can't even remember telling Nicole about him—probably whispered deep one night, half-asleep at the edge of a dream—but it struck a chord with her. Both their fathers were almost completely out of the picture.

"No. I'm sorry. It's—" The smile turns into a frown. "I'm not sure what it is. I'll snap out of it."

They both nod hello to a couple of older men making their way down the trail. One of them, wearing a ludicrously wide-brimmed sun hat and brandishing a walking stick, catches Felicia's eye.

"Watch for a rattlesnake about a quarter mile up," says the man with the hat.

"No shit?" Nicole says.

He nods, smiling. "Nasty-lookin' fella, but a little guy. On your left, a little ways after the horse trail branches off."

"Wow."

"Just don't step on him, and you'll be fine."

"I don't think I've ever seen one."

"He probably won't even move, but I wouldn't poke him with a stick or anything." The man smiles, and they continue on.

They don't spot the rattlesnake, but something continues to dig at Felicia's mood. She's decided it's not hunger, exactly, but she almost feels a little light-headed as she trudges up the path. As if she didn't get enough sleep, or she's still feeling the effects of the alcohol.

Something's out of kilter. But it's more than that. Her senses seem to be experiencing a greater potency than normal. The sun is overly bright, the sounds of her boots on soil and rock are louder, the smell of pine and earth is stronger. She feels as if she can sense pine sap exuding its aroma all around her, from individual trees, from the cells of their needles, and she comes to the odd realization that it's almost inebriating. Like the pine oil of extreme aromatherapy. Overbearing and yet nearly sensual.

"Are you all right?" Nicole asks her, stopping. "Hey, what's up? You look pale."

Felicia stops, too, shaking her head out of a strange vertigo. "I don't know, it's weird, I feel okay, I really do, but my head feels a little off. It's no biggie."

"You're hungover probably. You want to head back?"

"No, no, let's keep going."

The trees still seem to pull at her, and she's again reminded of her nightmare. When she closes her eyes, she can see those blood-red tendrils reaching out for her, and something deep inside her conflates the tendrils with pine branches, except they're willowy and undulating, wet, slimy, grasping. She blinks the imagery away, nearly barking out an involuntary sound, nearly staggering in her upward stride. She covers the moment by drawing out her water bottle and taking a long swallow.

The cold water calms her, focuses her. She manages a grin, latching back on to Nicole's conversation, forcing herself to take part. She adjusts her pack, taking deep breaths, and after a while she's enjoying herself, helping Nicole up steep ascents and around occasional expanses of mud, finding makeshift walking sticks, checking out wildflowers.

They talk about school, and they talk about books and music, and—again—they laugh at the odd coincidence that they each have a 17-year-old brother named David. They talk about goofy childhood memories and longtime friends back home, and they talk about sex and marijuana, and they talk about past boyfriends and girlfriends, how one notion led to the other. And an hour into the hike, Felicia is back to her normal self, smiling as she trudges through the final stretch toward Horsetooth Rock itself.

She experiences only the briefest sense of foreboding as they arrive at the foot of the formation, gauging how best to scale it.

They boost and pull each other up the rockface, passing a couple of hikers on their way down, finally reaching the flat top and joining a small crowd. They hold hands, staring out at Fort Collins to the east and then at Masonville to the southwest.

The sky is a clear cobalt blue, and there's a shared joy among the people atop the rock that makes Felicia feel very fine indeed. The young women shrug off their backpacks and find a place to enjoy some Co-Op granola, some salami, and an energy drink. Felicia doesn't voice this thought, but she feels that this is one of those moments we live for. She rolls her eyes at the notion that she almost skipped the hike this morning, because really she savors days like these. True to that notion, she settles back, palms anchored against rock, and closes her eyes, feeling the sun on her skin and a warm breeze on her cheek. It's a perfect moment, and she smirks, knowing Nicole is watching her.

Nine months is a long time. She knows that. Earlier, she thought rather carelessly that neither of them probably assumed this relationship was anything serious, but that was a little bit of self-delusion. The truth is, it's pretty damn serious. Maybe she simply doesn't want to wreck it.

It's only about four minutes later, as she's clinking her plastic bottle against Nicole's, that she hears voices raised in concern, coming from somewhere behind her.

"... see that?"

"What is it?"

"Over there."

Felicia twists to see what's going on. Hikers are pointing toward the skies above Masonville. And there's something up there, some kind of weather disturbance above the cerulean blue. It's faint, but it's there. Like heat lightning—flickering bolts of energy tinged with red. Her eyes lock on it, squinting. Her heartbeat thuds.

She twists back to look at Nicole, but Nicole shakes her head. "No idea."

"Have you—what is that?"

"I don't know."

She turns back. The energy is snapping in the blue, electric. It makes her shiver. She doesn't want to tell Nicole that it is fully recalling her dream now—she's definitely feeling that echo, but to admit it would feel silly. Wouldn't it? Her heart is a drumbeat now, and she hides the shaking of her hands by planting them on her thighs.

And then the phenomenon fades out, leaving clear blue sky. Felicia watches the crowd react: a slow, curious emptiness in their gazes, which are still turned skyward.

How can this thing, whatever it was, be connected to her dream? She tries to rationalize the parallel imagery while craning her neck in an effort to spot it again. Perhaps she'd seen but not *really* seen the same phenomenon in the skies yesterday on her way home from work—say, in her peripheral vision—and she dreamed about it last night before seeing it again today? She locks on to the notion of familiarity with this thing, because there is an element of that. Something intimate, something only for her. She's almost embarrassed to speak of it.

Especially with Nicole, who's shrugging off the weirdness and already rooting around in her backpack for her bag of trail mix.

"Did I tell you my mom's coming to town?" Nicole's voice is a singsong that attempts to dispel any weird vibes emanating from Felicia.

Felicia blinks and stares at her lover. Now *there's* a way to get her attention and break whatever paralysis she's feeling in her thinking.

"What?" she manages, swallowing off the end of the word.

Nicole nods. "Next Tuesday."

"But—" Felicia's breath is steadying, her pulse coming under control.

"I know."

"Staying with us?"

"Ha!"

"I guess that means no?"

"She always rents a car and stays at the Marriott." Nicole chews on some trail mix. "You know she likes to keep a safe distance."

The one other time Felicia met Tiffany Bryson, the woman proved to be not only condescending but also pathologically high-maintenance. She expected the former but not the latter. In fact, she found it hard to believe that someone as laid-back and—let's face it—gay as Nicole had sprung from Mrs. Bryson's loins. Felicia's first impression of Tiffany Bryson was that the woman was arch and unapproachable, although admittedly beautiful and funny in her way. One might even say Felicia's first impression leaned heavily toward *Christian conservative*. Felicia hated to resort to generalizations, but after only a few conversations, it became true that this particular generalization held true.

When Felicia had first met her on campus, it had been less than a year since Nicole had come out to her parents. By Nicole's account, her brother and even her long-distance dad received the news with a slow, almost warm acceptance, but her mother changed the subject. Nicole's relationship with her mother had never been warm, but ever since that day, it felt reluctant and bristly. The woman's visits from Atlanta seemed performed more out of a sense of obligation than ever.

"She's mostly in Denver for a business meeting, but she'll stay up here for two nights. I'm hoping she takes me shopping."

"Anything planned, or just winging it?"

"I don't have anything, but I'm sure she has a schedule."

Felicia nods, takes a handful of Nicole's trail mix, and crunches it thoughtfully.

The hikers around them have mostly forgotten about the weird light in the sky. Felicia warily scans the mostly brilliant blue expanse but finds nothing.

"I don't imagine she'll want to see me," she says, turning back to Nicole.

"She likes you."

Felicia gives Nicole a withering look. "My ass."

"Truth."

"That may be what you'd like to believe, but I'm pretty sure what she *really* thinks is that I turned you gay."

Nicole sighs. "Well, she hasn't mentioned you."

Felicia watches her girlfriend carefully. She's got that faraway look in her eye that tells Felicia that there's more to discuss but the words for that discussion aren't coming anytime soon. Nicole's relationship with her mom is complicated in ways that Felicia will never grasp, but despite all the frustration and hurt, there's deep love there.

"Should we—" Felicia starts, stumbling. "—should we take the initiative and make dinner for her or something?"

Nicole remains quiet, watching Fort Collins below them. Life is going on down there, happily oblivious to the first-world problems of a couple of college girls. If Felicia squints, she thinks she can spot her apartment building. She takes a long swallow of her energy drink, finishing it off, thinking that she might have said the wrong thing.

"Sorry," she says quickly. "I know you don't—"

"Hey."

"What?"

Nicole pecks Felicia on the cheek.

"I really dig you, you know that?"

Felicia feels warmth spreading across her face and can't help but let a smile take her lips, despite herself. Nicole has the ability, with the tiniest touch, to make her feel wonderful, and she's never really felt that before. And today more than ever, because with that single peck on the cheek, she has banished all weird dream imagery from Felicia's mind.

The two young women sit on the top of Horsetooth Rock for forty-five minutes before packing up and heading down to enjoy the final full day of life as they know it.

CHAPTER 3

Today, Felicia expects the early-morning wakeup.

The face of her clock radio reads 5:15 am, and it's playing an old REM song she loves, so she lets it go for a minute or two, until Nicole grumbles from the couch in the other room. Felicia touches the top of the radio, and it goes silent. She sighs inwardly.

It's Saturday, and it's time to get ready for a busy day at work.

She stirs in the semi-darkness, immediately feeling a blessed, relative coolness coming from the window. This heat wave has been the worst. She sits straight up and yawns, then casts a forlorn gaze at the empty side of the bed. On the mornings when Felicia has to rise early and head for the store, Nicole prefers to sack out on the couch in the main room. They were too tired last night for any hanky-panky, and Felicia wanted to at least try to get a sound night's sleep. Otherwise, she would probably be cranky at the store, and that's a persona she prefers to leave outside work. If she wants to run her own store one day, she knows that the identity she cultivates for that role will be all-important.

She maneuvers herself out of bed, steps naked toward the bathroom. Eyes still gummy, she twists on the water and steps in. No surprise shower visitors this morning, unfortunately. She washes herself beneath the spray and mentally prepares herself for the day, clearing the sleepiness away. In the midst of the shower, she frowns.

There were no nightmares last night, but the one from the night before still nags at her. When she closes her eyes, she can still feel echoes of those blood-red fingers, those tendrils, clawing at her. She snaps fully awake, eyes open, shivering away this feeling that has somehow found a stranglehold deep inside her.

When she's finished with her shower, she steps out and towels off, then dries her hair, forming it into a sturdy, dark ponytail. She applies light makeup, then returns to the bedroom to dress quietly in jeans and a white blouse. She opens the bedroom door and sees Nicole sprawled out on the futon, only barely covered. She tiptoes over and covers her fully with the light sheet, planting a kiss on her forehead. Nicole murmurs in half-sleep, twists a little under the sheet, and descends into sleep again.

Felicia smiles.

In the small kitchen, she wrangles with the door of the old fridge and finally extracts the green smoothie she made for herself the night before. Time to start making up for that evening of debauchery. She shakes it up, then downs it quickly, nods, and washes her glass.

After brushing her teeth, she grabs her keys off the hallway table and opens the front door.

"See ya later," comes a sleepy farewell.

"Kisses," Felicia says, and closes and locks the door.

In the parking lot, Felicia ducks into her car and sits there for a moment. She blinks. Her ears pop, and she moves her jaw around. What is that? There's something in the air, but what is it? Some kind of uneasiness ... some kind of throb, almost like a distant helicopter.

She starts up the motor and pulls out. Motoring through the brightening but mostly empty streets east, she takes the turns in a weird funk. Something isn't right.

Her eyes flick upward, and she notices some kind of strange cloud up there. She knows it must simply be dawn coloring the atmosphere, but it looks very odd—a dark crimson haze, unsettled, stormy. It's even darker in the rearview mirror, over the foothills. She tries to crane her head to peer back at it but can't get a good view through her rear window.

"What in the world ...?" she whispers.

The streets are quiet, as usual for a very early Saturday morning. It's not even 6 a.m. yet. But there's more to this feeling than the yawning drowsiness typical of her drive in to work. There's still that uneasiness. She feels her pulse throbbing in her neck.

As she waits to make the turn onto College, she watches a silver Acura make its way south. The driver, a 40s-ish man, is peering west, beyond her, at the sky. His look of edgy curiosity mirrors her own. Just as he passes out of sight, she half-recognizes him. What's his name? He's a customer, isn't he? Maybe. She's tempted to try a wave, but he's preoccupied.

When she makes her turn north, she watches him in her rearview mirror as he drives south. Yeah, he's a customer. She should know his name.

Felicia, not immodestly, attributes her success at the store with the casual friendships she can spark up during her transactions. It's a part of her personality, which gives her a leg up on most of her coworkers. She's easy with the customers and finds it personally rewarding to engage with them and learn a little about their lives. She's good at it. That's what separates her from someone like Janet—who has to work much harder at customer service, and it never feels quite genuine—and it's what's going to help Felicia ultimately realize her goal. That's what her teachers tell her, and she feels it inside, like instinct.

She has such a strong connection already with the community here. It's that connection that has made her feel as if she might make a go of her own store in Fort Collins. Some day.

But she should've remembered that man's name.

His daughter, too.

In moments, she's on Mountain and turning in to the tiny employee parking lot behind the store. The sour stink of piss drifts through her car vents, a reminder that the assholes and bums of Old Town nightlife will use any recessed space to find bladder relief. She *almost* considers it a weakness that the smell disgusts her, but she feels contempt for people who have no value for property and community. She herself has tried pressure-washing the concrete out here, but the smell is too baked in— the result of a hundred years of drunkards' bloated bladders—and there are always new alcoholics. Alcoholics who are perhaps also customers.

The rear delivery door is already open, and Janet's old-lady bicycle is locked up by the trash bin. The woman is devoted to her work, that's for sure.

Felicia locks up her car and makes her way into the store. Janet already has the industrial fan positioned at the rear door, blowing through the store, filling it with as much cool air as possible this morning, in anticipation of another very warm Colorado day. Unlike Felicia's apartment, the Food Co-Op boasts central air, but it's weak as hell—and expensive.

"Good morning!" Felicia calls over the din. She grabs her green vest off its hallway hook and shrugs it on.

Janet is fastidiously refreshing the bulk items near the back of the store. "Hey you!" she calls. She holds a big plastic bag of peanuts with something like distaste, scooping into the bin. Felicia knows this is Janet's least favorite task in the store.

"Want me to take care of that?"

"No, I've got it. I need you to look over the schedule. I can't abide it anymore. Trish dropped that bomb the other day, and I can't get my head around it. Give it 15 minutes, see what you can do."

Scheduling is a newly delegated task for Felicia, and she has embraced it as one more tiny step toward her business goal.

"I'm on it." She yawns. "How was yesterday?"

Janet isn't the greatest casual conversationalist, not the sharing type, but Felicia always likes to try.

"Oh, fine. Not crazy busy, but steady. Did you have a nice day off?"

Felicia smiles privately. "Wonderful."

Pleasantries over, Felicia enters the tiny office, storing her belongings in her cubby. The office door clicks shut, and she's alone. She gives the desk a hard look, sighs, then settles herself into her task. The schedule is already spread out on the metal surface. It's a chaos of scribbles and cross-outs and highlights—not to mention Post-It notes containing all the idiosyncratic time-off requests from the rest of the small staff. She's tempted to start over with a clean sheet, but she decides to at least get a grasp of it before starting over. She takes up her favorite mechanical pencil and begins.

Two minutes and seventeen seconds later, something happens inside her head.

It's a red yank, a twist of gray matter like a fleshy hook digging in and grabbing hold. She feels her head jerk. Her consciousness blinks out for a moment, then returns.

"Whoa, whoa," she whispers, dropping the pencil and grabbing the edge of the desk.

She focuses on the schedule's scrawls, blinks hard.

What was that? What the hell was that?

Her first thought is *aneurysm.* In a worried flurry, she recalls some long-ago newspaper article about some perfectly healthy student in Texas falling over dead from a spewing artery deep in his gray matter. A pulse of adrenaline courses through her, liquid lightning.

Then she recalls her nightmare, more vividly than ever, the grasping red fingers, the slithering grab. She swallows heavily. Whatever happened just now is the same thing. It's connected.

It's the same thing.

She's shaking. Whatever is inside her is still there. Something is inside her. She feels a pressure building.

"Janet?" Her voice is full of tremors.

In response, her boss warbles an incomprehensible, almost guttural sound, and Felicia hears the unmistakable sound of Janet slumping to the floor and the big bag of unsalted peanuts spilling out over the laminate floor.

It is the last thing Felicia hears before her mind goes red.

CHAPTER 4

Felicia's consciousness shrinks to a tiny crimson dot.

She is crammed down beneath something—*something!*—and she can't move at all. It's something heavy. So heavy. She can't feel anything. She has a dim awareness of her body, her limbs, but they're not responding. They seem ridiculously far away, the foggy distance like something in a surreal dream. She feels an impulse to scream, but instead she experiences something like suffocation. Anxiety builds like pressure against her chest.

What happened?!

She comes to a slow realization that she's not even seeing out of her eyes. There's light, but it's a red, splotchy glow, like the sun behind closed eyelids. She feels a disembodied panic. Then she feels what little consciousness she has slipping away toward a black void, and fear spikes somewhere. Everywhere. And then …

Black.

After an eternity, the crimson light flickers.

She's sluggish in her awareness, as if waking from a long sleep. A coma, perhaps.

How long has she been unconscious?

She can hardly think. She feels an almost utterly draining weakness. She tries to focus—and can't. What was she doing just now? Where was she? Why can't she remember what she was *just doing?*

That panic again.

Wait. Wait.

She can't remember *anything.*

Who was she with? Just now, who was she with? When she tries to concentrate, the effort drifts away from her. Janet. The thought comes to her like the touch of a dark mist.

There's a surge of recollection for home—the lumpy softness of her bed, her tiled shower, her refrigerator with the frost-ridden freezer, the blue futon, the television set, Nicole cocking her pretty head in mirth—and she reaches for all of it, but it fragments and breaks apart like crumbling soil.

I have to wake up!

Everything is sluggish. Something is crushing her. She feels not the weight of it but rather its personality, its color. Red. As if she is on the verge of drowning under a lake of blood. But the lake is a living thing, the blood pulsing under its own influence.

She realizes that the lake of blood is her own body, and she is no longer in control of it.

Is she paralyzed?

I can't move.

She doesn't even feel as if she can see out of her own eyes. There's something there, though, some kind of awareness of light. She can't move her eyes! She can vaguely see something in her peripheral vision: cabinets, a pegboard covered with papers, shelves of manuals, a computer, a rolling chair.

She was sitting on that chair when this happened.

Wasn't she?

Something is forcing her consciousness away from recollection. Steering it toward something new. Felicia tries to resist the pull, but she can't.

Something is inside her. Inside her head. She feels it like pressure, and now the feeling is like drifting to sleep, with a dense weight on top of all of her. Drifting into unconsciousness but retaining awareness, as if in a waking dream.

Is this the nightmare? This drifting red fog?

Her skull is alive with murmurings, with red whispers. There's nothing else. Was there ever anything else? She doesn't understand the whispers. They're slippery and weird. They slide through her, around her, grabbing, relinquishing, trying again. Seeking something.

There's only the need.

The need.

The pull of this new consciousness is irresistible. She has no choice but to heed it. It's utterly focused. On the *objective*. The objective is everywhere, it is close, and she must go to it. Physically go to it. She can't put it into words, she can't name it, but she can see it huge in her mind's eye. It is verdant in her awareness, lush and green, and she feels as if she can lose herself in it if she can only go out and find it.

And there's something else. She knows that once she finds this thing, and simply lets go of her consciousness as Felicia Stone, she will know a new luxurious awareness as one with this fertile garden.

Is this what heaven is? Has she died? She feels a burst of anxiety at the notion. Has she really died and gone to heaven? If she were to simply let go, would she fall into paradise? Just like in the Bible?

No, that's not it. Not with this pressing need, not with this nervous and desperate compulsion. Some dim part of her feels it like a sexual need—a lust. Something she needs to take care of *now*.

But she can't move. She still can't move at all.

And this need, this compulsion, it's not coming from her. It's coming from something else. This new awareness. It's not her at all. But it's something inside her. She sees dim shapes in her vision, large things looming, and she knows that this … something else, something larger than her … is also seeing these shapes. It has muscled its way into her vision, using her immobile eyes to see what it needs to see.

What it needs.

Vaguely, something in her innards clenches.

She feels infinitesimal.

Deep inside herself, Felicia forces herself calm.

What can she see? With her limited peripheral vision, what can she see?

The chair, mountainous above her. The dingy expanse of the ceiling. She's on the floor, staring up. Her vision lacks any kind of clarity, so everything is mired in a thick haze. Fluorescent light buzzes up there somewhere. Recognizing these things, she realizes that her eyes aren't even blinking reflexively. They should be burning from lack of moisture, but she can't feel them.

Everything is so far away! Hopelessly removed, impossible to reach.

Where is she again?

The word *store* comes to her, but nothing else. There are memories surrounding that word, but they're blurry and dark.

Felicia becomes gradually aware of another presence in the store, and it is like her—it is undergoing the same transformation, the same ordeal. She can see it in her periphery like something glowing. An energy flows from it, reaching out to her, just as her own energy reaches out to it.

It's a person.

She remembers … what? Someone falling, someone she knows. She doesn't remember falling herself, but she remembers the other person falling.

She senses some kind of whisper—no, not a whisper, but a sound inside like a voice, or is it an image? Her senses seem to overlap.

The door. She has to get beyond it. She has to get out.

Something inside her is pulsing, and it's not her heartbeat.

Something urgent behind her deadened eyes. The need for the objective is focused there, like something magnetized. Like a black hole, it seems to be pulling at her, and if she let it, it would swallow her.

Everything is an obstacle. These eyes, this body, these mountainous objects in her peripheral vision, this closed room.

She tries sending signals out to her extremities, tries moving a finger or a toe, tries moving her lip and of course shifting her eyes—nothing.

Exhausted, she gives up the effort. She drifts into the background. She feels like nothingness. She experiences the equivalent of her eyes rolling back, but some part of her snaps back to alertness. She's frightened of oblivion. Because she senses that's what awaits her.

Do her ears work? What is she hearing?

Some kind of oppressive humming. A broken droning noise, as if her eardrums have blown out and all she can hear is a hard, monotonous vibration. It's the soundtrack of need.

There's something else. Images coming not from her eyes but from the overriding consciousness. Images of crimson and lava. Sweltering desert. No moisture. Dry fire. These images lurk like memory, an undercurrent, almost comforting.

But now, atop these static images, are moving things, organic things, all angles like elbows, clacking and twitching. The small consciousness that is Felicia rears back at these images, unnerved.

Everything is chaos in her mind and body, and she can only wait it out.

What seems like hours later, she feels herself waking. Not from slumber but into awareness. With a jolt, she realizes that she could have drifted away into nothingness, into the black hole in the center of her head, and she would have simply been ... gone.

The muscle beneath her eye is twitching.

She can feel it happening, knows it's her head, her body, but she also feels a disconnect. Because she's not the one making it happen. And it's more than involuntary. She's staring up at a small cone of red light, and the sensation at her eye is there, but far removed.

Why won't this body work?

That thought blasts through her—or what's left of her—and she's unsure whether it's her own thought or someone else's.

That eye, though, that muscle ... she tries to push her awareness up toward that small crimson hole, which she now equates with her consciousness, with her waking life.

She strains toward the eye. *Her* eye. Keeps straining.

Another twitch.

And another.

It's happening rhythmically.

She encourages the movement, tries to build strength, to regain sensation. To somehow emerge into consciousness. Real consciousness.

She pushes hard, as hard as she is able.

The muscle keeps twitching.

A little more. A little more.

Long minutes later, a muscle at the edge of her mouth moves a millimeter.

A tiny, almost lost part of her experiences a distant thrill.

But she's so sleepy. She's exhausted. She wants to give up. She wants to drift out.

No!

She pushes at the twitch, encourages it, as best she can. Urges it to move again.

And it *does.*

She pushes again. *Hard.*

It moves.

She's doing this.

Right?

Either way, it doesn't matter. She pushes and pushes. Stares way up at that tiny red dot. Too far up there. She has to get back there.

Perhaps an hour later, her nostrils flare, and her energies are renewed.

It's already the most difficult thing she's ever done—moving a few inconsequential facial muscles. She wants to weep but can't. She wants to flail her arms and bang her head in frustration, but she can't even sense that her limbs are there, let alone feel an inkling of how to control them. She doesn't even know the ghost of a phantom limb. There's nothing except the reaching sensation of those tiny muscles on her face.

In her drifting mind, she equates these little muscles with fingers on a ledge. She sees dream imagery of her own fingers, stretched to impossible lengths, their tips barely grasping the tiniest fraction of the ledge while the rest of her dangles over a sucking pit. That ledge is her life. The tips of her fingers keep wrestling for better grip, keep trying to gain further purchase.

Door.

Right, the door.

The door she needs to get through, in order to reach the objective.

But her vision seems darker. More indistinct.

How long has she been like this? Is it night?

… help …

The word floats through her, at the edge of her cognizance, but she doesn't know how to process it.

She keeps pushing.

There's a moment, after interminable hours—or minutes, how can she tell?—when she feels several muscles around her eyes moving in concert, in the perfect sequence, and abruptly her eyes swivel to the right.

As a pulse of excitement ripples through her consciousness, the other awareness inside her crowds in, a heavy weight inside her skull, overbearing. It whispers in images, urgent sights awaiting her. It's like a language coming at her at machine-gun pace, battering her senses, but part of her understands it.

Her eyes are anchored in place, staring flatly at the door now, and those muscles in her face are still twitching rhythmically, and that door is important. There's the knob, she knows the knob, she knows she has to turn it to open the door.

She tries straining her head, all the muscles in her head, toward the door. The effort drains her almost completely. She drifts back—

No!

—and surges upward again.

Her eye swivels again, randomly, and her face feels alive with tics. She can feel them!

She falls back, completely spent, drifting. She now has a sense of how far back she can drift without losing herself altogether—there's a precipice from which she can't let herself plummet. She's empowered by this sensation of control, as small as it is. Like allowing herself to float on her back in water, utilizing the countless muscles along her trunk and limbs to maintain balance and barely remain buoyant.

She feels herself come into awareness. Her eyes twitch once more, swivel drily—she can't blink!—and stare toward the door. Everything remains blurry. Disembodied, she feels great concentration in the center of her skull, unprecedented focus, like tightness. Like pressure. An uncontainable need. It's a pulse, a rush.

Over it all, a great frustration vibrates.

What is wrong with this body?! she screams, loud, inside, soundless.

Nothing works.

Why?

There's a whisper of a thought under that one, incomprehensible at first, then twisting into clarity.

What went wrong?

She doesn't understand the meaning of the words, lets them scatter.

Not-Felicia focuses all of her remaining energy on lifting her head. At first nothing happens, and then suddenly there's a twitch. Her whole head shifts up, chin pointing at the ceiling, and then falls back to the hard floor. The movement is all of a few millimeters, and yet the sensation fills her tiny, exhausted soul with relief.

Her head jerks again, rhythmic. She didn't do that one. The movement is simply repeating, again as if involuntarily.

She drifts back.

She can barely think. Exhaustion has taken her to edge of nothingness. All her thoughts are tendrils leading into oblivion, and all of them are pulling at her, almost seductively. There's a caress to the sensation, almost like—

Her touch.

Whose touch?

I don't know. It doesn't matter.

The words dissolve.

She wants to give herself over to the touch, to float away into bliss, but that's not going to happen.

It needs me.

Another thought from out of nowhere. The words echo across a great expanse, come back at her as she settles back again, conserving energy. The energy at the center of her is pulsing outward now, its illumination crackling in all these new movements, and it scares her. It scares the tiny part of her that cowers beneath it.

Her shoulder convulses.

Instantly she's back to awareness, trying to see out of cloudy, barely moving eyes.

Both shoulders are moving, jerking backward for purchase on the floor. Her muscles won't cooperate. She reaches back, muscle memory flashing.

Images of desert. Hot, searing. Scrabbling. Swarming.

Columns of clay twined into crumbling architecture, bustling with angular activity.

But.

Hunger.

She's screaming inside.

She needs this to work. She needs this body to work. She must reach the objective. Which is beyond that door. She knows how exiting through that door will work. The key is the handle, and she knows she can turn it. She has studied it. But it's all for naught if she can't get this body to work.

With each passing second, more muscles cooperate. She bends back, willing the limbs into full motion. She knows how to move them, how to use them to escape this room, but they won't come fully under her control.

She squeezes her shoulder blades back—the musculature is working!

The motion repeats.

She's getting stronger.

This rhythmic twitching, it makes sense now. The rhythm is at the center of everything, and it is working. It equals persistence, and it equals power. Control is returning to limbs and trunk. And yet as power over her body returns to her, there is a distant pain. It's there, and it's strong, but it's also muted. Something is muting it, and so it doesn't matter.

How much time has passed? She has to get out of this room.

That's what matters.

She lies there, on her back, her muscles clenching, surging.

Getting stronger.

Until she hears a clatter.

She hears!

She was so intent, focused on the center of her being, that she didn't even notice her sense of sound returning. Her mouth opens in a crooked O of surprise, and her body goes still.

Beyond the door—the door she *must* get past—something is making a shambling sound, of limbs and frustration. Is it the objective? No. She can visualize the objective in her mind's eye, gigantic, luminous. Fecund, and healing, and glorious. It is something she must go to; it is not something that will come to her.

What is this noise?

It's the other body, the glowing energy that is a part of her. And when she extends her awareness outward, she can sense others in the vicinity, and more in the broader area, and still more in an uncertain distance. She can feel them, and they are all a part of her.

A web of souls.

The whispers are everywhere, and she understands that her thoughts and her actions are in concert with all of them. She feels a powerful kinship with them, a shared purpose. She takes a silent, unmoving moment to acknowledge them. They're in the neighboring businesses, in the street, in apartments all around.

She feels immediate empathy with the closest body's movement, and as if reflexively, her own body thrashes on the floor, the elbows knocking the tile, the shoulder blades banging, the heels flailing. From her mouth comes a raw gasp.

The momentum of her strained thrashing lifts the body in a severe arc, and she feels—not so distantly now—the knuckles cracking against the floor, the fingers angling for purchase. Sensation is returning to this body exponentially now. She hears the other body thrashing as hers is.

As she batters the body against two larger structures on the floor—the words *chair* and *desk* move through her compromised mind—she stares at the door. She can see through the eyes a little more clearly now, although they're still difficult to control. She keeps blinking as if to clear the vision, but the cloudiness won't go away. She can, however, see the door's handle, above some kind of boxy item in the foreground. She locks her vision on that handle. The handle that leads to—

The objective.

She continues to gasp with effort. She can't help it. The sound is like gravel from out of the dry throat. Her heels are thrashing against the desk now, and although not-Felicia distantly recognizes the jarring and repeated impact with the metal corners, it is immaterial. The bones and joints are sound.

Her arms slide back behind her, shoulder blades pinching, and she's propped up off the ground, favoring her left shoulder. The consciousness inside her trills with jubilant energy. Not-Felicia feels it like contagious laughter, overlaid with a surging purpose. She can manipulate this body to her purpose.

But why is this taking so long?

She should be out of this place!

As these thoughts pummel her consciousness, she hears further movement beyond the door—the other body moving now with full purpose. It moves directly to her door, and the glowing presence is vivid. Not-Felicia can sense its urge to help her, but the pull of the objective is too strong. She wants to call out to it, but nothing happens. Through blurred vision, she can see the shadow of its progress. It is moving toward the objective. Its mindscape is clear and clean, and it knows that it has a clear route.

The sound—of limbs jerking, hands and feet grasping at the ground—fades to the left. She hears a laborious sound of metal on metal, a slide and shift, and understands that the body is manipulating another door. She imagines herself doing the same. She has that knowledge.

After a length of time, she hears the front glass door open, and the body rushes out, toward—

The body is gone, and its mindscape fades into the distance.

The loss of contact sends her into a frenzy, kicking and flailing, and now she feels a full sense of control overtaking her. She rises to full bent-back height, stares through still-blurry eyes at the door. She knows how to manipulate that handle, but there's something blocking the door. She can't reach her hand over this obstacle and touch the handle. She shoves at the obstacle with her head, instinctively, and it rasps along the floor and lodges directly beneath the handle.

She pauses and stares at the obstacle, and above it, the blocked handle. The predicament doesn't make sense to her for a moment. She growls in her throat and glares, flexing her muscles rhythmically.

Her inverted head pushes forward again, shoving at the obstacle. It won't move.

What is it?

Human words whisper through her mind, but she can't grasp them.

Feeling a new confidence with her limbs, she heaves herself onto the obstacle itself—it's a wobbly construction of metal and plastic, and for some reason its name won't come to her. She balances her right shoulder on its black surface, and grasps the door handle firmly with her fingers. She twists the handle, but the metal of the obstacle prevents it from moving. A metal bar has lodged beneath the handle, preventing it from turning.

She screeches a hoarse gasp.

She stares.

Frustration boils in her blood.

She has knowledge inside her—not only about how to manipulate various types of door handles and how to identify most obstacles, but also a basic knowledge of the workings of this body. She knows how it has been bent to the will of her nature, and she knows how its life-giving functions have been altered to support the pursuit of the objective. She knows how the blood flows through its veins, and how its inefficient central circulatory muscle has been rendered dormant in favor of a more familiar mechanism. She has this knowledge, but she can operate the body only as far as it will allow.

She is confounded by this obstacle.

She ratchets her head on its neck, searching the darkness through the small, blurry eyes for another means of exit. There is none. No window, no other door.

She balances atop the obstacle and throws her body at the door, to no avail. She tries repeatedly, not caring about the cosmetic integrity of the body's epidermal layers.

After a long period of time, it's clear that the door will not be opened by force.

Not-Felicia can only perch atop the obstacle, stewing, the muscles along her trunk and down her limbs clenching and unclenching in rhythm.

Twelve hours later, she's in the same position, staring at the door, hunger clawing at her insides, and all the other bodies in the vicinity have gone.

CHAPTER 5

Her new mind dreams of voices, of distant mindscapes, as the body remains idle, conserving energy. Her eyelids tremble under a constant onslaught of stimuli and the occasional blasted directive from the atmosphere. Her body feels the urgency to respond, and each time a new directive invades her skull, her muscles twitch, and her bones strain. She aches to escape and contribute; the compulsion is all-consuming.

She has only the vaguest awareness of others in the vicinity now. There is one body to the southeast, a body that has achieved its objective on a singular target and is extracting the nutrient. In her mind, she can feel the relief, she can feel the rush vicariously. She is still part of the collective and understands the achievement. It's happening.

She waits.

Then, as if from under water, not-Felicia hears a crash of broken glass. Her body convulses and lurches up, aware. Her ears are hyper-attuned.

She feels as if she has been in stasis for days. The need is clawing at her now, fervent. A terrible thirst is consuming her. Her body is deteriorating, she knows. It is becoming weak. Soon it will fail because of its own limitations.

There are voices, and in the very next room she senses the bright, glowing presences of two human beings. Living humans! How can that be? Not-Felicia stares motionless at the door, beyond which she can sense closer movement.

"Go, go!"

"Are we clear in here?"

"No movement."

The words mean something to a tiny, hollow part of her, but they wisp away almost immediately under a general notion of threat.

There are more words, murmurs, then a heavy sound in the distance.

"Aw shit!" one of the voices cries.

"Nothing … nothing. Wait, wait, here we go!"

"What?!"

"Something collapsed."

"I think it was the restaurant on the corner, where BeauJo's used to be. That building. The FedEx plane might've clipped it. It's probably been smoldering all this time."

"We gotta get out of here, right? Like, now?"

"I still don't see any bodies, let's just get what we need."

The voices go indistinct.

Not-Felicia stares at the door.

What's happening?

The door handle jerks—right in front of not-Felicia's inverted face. She tenses, ready to leap. In a sliver of a moment, she can see inside the mindscapes of both humans. It is not as clear a view as she has of those in the web of souls, but the minds are open to her nonetheless. One is a figure of authority, trying to wrestle some sense of control over the situation; he is a focused, powerful being and a direct threat, carrying a weapon. The other human is a father, and at this moment he has his offspring on his mind, as well as a number of other surviving humans holed up … somewhere.

How have they survived?

The door flies open, and the obstruction clatters away. Light floods into the room. She feels a sting in her eyes, and involuntarily her eyelids flutter.

"Hey!"

A human being is standing there—against all reason.

It's a strange bipedal creature, tall and pale, and not-Felicia feels a sharp twang of fear. It's standing *right in front of her*, utterly weird. It's the authority figure, and it is wearing some kind of gray cloth over its skin, and it is holding two loose, bulky containers, full of obscured objects. Both of the humans' minds bloom with yellow fear, and she knows she has the advantage. She reacts instinctively.

Not-Felicia propels herself out of the room, directly on top of this creature. The male body goes flailing backward, screaming hoarsely. The items it was holding tumble all over the ground.

Not-Felicia's body is frail, but she instinctively tries stabbing at the human with her head. She knows she can cause harm this way. But the other human, the father, crashes into her from behind, and she sprawls onto her back, directly into a large obstacle.

The father screams, *"Why'd you open that door?!"*

Not-Felicia regains control of her limbs and attempts to leap back toward the doorway—the objective firmly in mind—but her incarceration has left her limbs lethargic. She pushes herself across the floor, wary but purposeful. She has to get outside.

These humans shouldn't be conscious and self-aware. What happened?

Something *thunks* into not-Felicia's side, and she shrieks.

Everything changes.

She has never known bewildering pain like this. It's a heat, centered at the impact point of whatever hit her, and it spreads rapidly, sparking and raging. She twists and trips, her vision kaleidoscopes, all of her muscles begin contracting in spasms. Her body is out of her control. She coughs, feeling her lungs heave and shudder. The coughs become screams, which launch from her throat, out of her control.

"Nooo-ooo! Noo! Neeeeee—"

Felicia falls heavily onto her back again, twisting and writhing. Pain engulfs her body, not quite like fire but more like electricity, and a great scraping pressure is building in her left shoulder. She has never felt such torture.

"Huuuuuurts!" she screams out of her cramping mouth.

The humans—

—they're people, two men, what are they doing?—

—clamber away from her. She half-registers their sounds but doesn't care about anything but the torture burning through her veins. Her shoulder is a glowing ember. Liquid springs helplessly from her eyes.

—tears—

Her foot catches some boxed merchandise on a shelf, knocking a stack to the floor. She's in a grocery store. Why is she in a grocery store?

It's the Co-Op.

She's at work.

At the thought, her consciousness expands like a balloon, filling her, and the sensation is that of bursting back to awareness, to breathing after near-drowning.

Thoughts ricochet as she squirms, and she sees that one of the humans—one of the men—is staring at her, and she knows this man, this father, he's one of her customers, but what has happened, what has happened to cause this pain, this all-encompassing pain that nearly blinds her? She blinks hard, feeling sensory information flood her like something boiling. It's too much, inside and outside of her! She whips her head back and forth. And now the man is leaving the store, and why won't he help her? Why is he going away? Because *he* has done this to her? *What's happening?*

Sound erupts from her in a throaty gasp.

Then the man, the father, is back, hovering over her, and she locks eyes with him. He's blurry behind inconceivable pain. She blinks hard, desperately.

"*Helllppp!!*" she cries.

The man takes hold of her flailing arms and begins to pull her toward the front door, and her skin and bones scream in chaos. She shrinks inside herself, cowering, while her body clenches in torture. Stuttered sounds are choking out of her mouth, but she has no control over them. Her tongue lashes against her teeth.

"All right, all right!" she hears from somewhere. It's the other man—

—*the policeman*—

—hurrying toward them. Felicia instinctively twists away from both of the men so that she can fall to the ground and be still—*for God's sake, be still!*—but the policeman takes hold of her feet, and her body goes swinging into the air.

Torment.

Her eyes bug and turn up in their sockets. Her jaw locks open, her breath caught deep in her throat. They're carrying her. What have they done to her?

"Christ, you and your daughter, man!" the cop yells. "Cut from the same cloth!"

Felicia feels herself approaching unconsciousness, black spots blooming in her vision, but the man's words bring her fluttering back.

The daughter.

The name comes to her like a whisper, somehow soothing— *Rachel*— the simple act of remembering. But no. She has read the name in the father's consciousness.

And this is Michael.

Is that possible, that she can see these things? How?

Then the names are gone again, and she's writhing in the men's grip. Now her voice comes back, and an ugly gasp discharges from her throat. She bounces on the rear seats of a large vehicle, screeching. She recognizes the interior of the truck as quiet and soft, but she is utterly focused on her pain.

Make it stop!

All she knows is agony. The truck gargles to life and soon it's rumbling across asphalt as she clenches screaming muscles. Her skull feels as if it has been hollowed out with a blunt tool. As if something has been pulled violently out—and yet residue remains.

What is that?

There's something inside her. She feels it like a crawling thing, something slippery high in her throat. Whatever it is, it's wounded and clamoring. Perhaps it is dying inside her. She retches at the thought, her throat screeching in protest.

The truck bounces and she moans. She opens her blurred eyes. Tears continue to stream from them.

Where is she? There are bright souls all around, scurrying. They are human beings.

Before shutting her eyes against the brightness, she catches glimpses of the corners of buildings and the tops of trees.

Trees.

The men are talking up front, but she can't hear anything above the din of pain. And it is that: The agony is like a great, insurmountable wall of sound, devastating her eardrums.

The truck bounces violently, twice, and it's all she can do to keep from biting her tongue off. Time bends and warps. The vehicle comes to a jarring stop, and the engine rattles to silence. There are voices, human voices. The first is female, but she can barely make it out—

—and then the voice coalesces into a contained and understandable stream of sensation, and Felicia realizes that she is not only hearing Rachel's spoken words but also her thoughts. Behind the voice, the mindscape is shifty and thread-like, like a smoothly skipping needle atop a wet record. Synaptic sparks effortlessly merge with one another, skipping off on tangents, reacting to stimuli, moving like a constantly forking river in fast-forward. But there are understandable wisps of thoughts there, and Felicia feels as if she is in tune with Rachel's chemical processes, with the electrical impulses in her brain. She can almost visualize them. She senses fear inside a multitude of anticipated worst-case scenarios, and she senses a black awe underneath everything that has happened to her.

But then pain blots it out.

"We heard some kind of explosion up that way," Rachel says to her father, giving clear voice to her fears. "Thought you were done for."

"Still alive," Michael responds. "I keep dodging bullets, huh? We have a passenger. Where's Bonnie?"

Gritting her teeth, Felicia focuses her inner gaze on Michael, whose mind is awash in relief to be back at the library, back to Rachel.

"She's with the—"

"Bonnie!"

Felicia tries opening her eyes again. It takes Herculean effort. She wants to wipe the moisture from her eyes, but none of her muscles will cooperate. She can see shapes, she can see the silhouettes of people. And then Joel, the policeman, bends close to her, becoming momentarily clear in her vision, and his mind remains rigid and orderly, and there's another man there, she sees his mindscape before his face looms close to hers, and—

—*he is a younger man, his name is Ron, he is unsure of himself, thrust into a leadership role in the group and regretting it, his mind veering toward the fate of his father, who lives alone in Laporte, and with whom he shares the same blood type, but who is wheelchair-bound and helpless in his isolated home, and Jesus Christ why didn't Ron try to go there when this first started, because now all he feels is a burning shame—*

What was that about blood type? When *what* started?

Felicia's pain is enormous, unwilling to let her see more, but she's startled by the sudden knowledge of this man's thoughts. How is she seeing that? It's as if, in his proximity, the thoughts have become hers. And when he pulled away, the thoughts faded. Her ability to do this thing—it should seem incomprehensible, and yet it feels a natural extension of her own thoughts, a part of her mind, perhaps, that was always there but that she hasn't turned to before.

She grits her teeth, trembling.

Just as she's losing her grip on consciousness, Michael calls out to the woman named Bonnie, "Prep a morphine shot!"

The words bring her back to the edge of awareness, but she still feels herself as deadweight, disassociated from her flesh.

"Someone at the store," Michael's voice says. "Go ahead and get that shot going."

There's a finger at her neck. "She's alive." It's Joel. "Probably dehydrated and starving ... multiple dislocations ... other internal traumas we have no idea about ... you know, the usual! But hey, at least she wasn't chewing on trees!"

She's being carried from the vehicle toward a large building. As if peering up at a tiny hole in a high ceiling, she tries to make sense of what's happening to her and where she is. She senses human souls crowded around her, and their mindscapes are whispering at her under the sharp weight of the pain.

No! Where are they taking me? I can't be here!

She has to—

Relative darkness envelops her, and then strong hands are settling her to the ground. She tries to move, to escape, but her body won't respond at all. She reaches out with all her will and finds nothing to latch on to. But then the ground seems to embrace her, and there's comfort there.

Yes, let me be still, please let me be still.

And then—

A blessed warmth spreads through her limbs and torso and head, fattening her throat but dulling everything, and now Felicia succumbs to unconsciousness quickly, as if yearning for it, and she dives deep and headfirst into blackness.

CHAPTER 6

Felicia is not sure how long she's out, but as she gradually surfaces toward consciousness, she has endured a nightmare of bustling activity, of thirst and roiling colors, of sucking wounds and crackling tinder. She cries out involuntarily, moving sluggishly atop some crude cardboard pad.

She's in the center of a musty, claustrophobic room, and through her still-blurred vision she can see the spines of books, desks, colorful though muted posters—*Good Readers Are Good Learners!*—splashed on the walls, and a black mini-fridge, which is humming to her left. She stares at it in confusion.

There are people all around; she can sense them like ghostly blobs in her consciousness, and when she turns her head to face them, they swim into better focus, as if she can geolocate them. Just like the web of souls in her awareness before, when she was ...

How ...? is her only thought.

Michael is closest, and therefore his mindscape is clearest.

He exudes a complex fear, not only situational but also a larger fear, something about ... what? ...

—he will be found out—

She stares at that thought, hovering there black and furtive. She can see so much around it, but his personality, his history, is obscured by this shadow. There's his wife—wait, two wives? Ah yes, the wife who died, what was her name? It's not there. Susanna is there, his current wife, and there is both love and grief there. She's dead. How is she dead? Is she infected? No, but she died during the infection—not like the others. How?

He doesn't know. There's a conflict there, and it appears like a color in a corner of her own mind.

How is she seeing this?

Impossible!

She also feels Rachel's strong presence close by, and another in her orbit, a young soul—

—*Kayla*—

—the two of them facing each other, sitting cross-legged on the floor, talking in soft tones, and the girl is weeping softly and nodding, images of her family large in her mind, especially her mother: kind, generous, smiling. Rachel's mind is filled with the face of her own mom, distant, dead for years but still powerful, indelible, and this is the topic of their quiet conversation—mothers—and now Felicia senses a strong wave of old sadness thrusting upward inside Rachel's head. Felicia feels this imagery pass over her like warmth, and she knows it's informing the conversation between Rachel and Kayla.

Felicia shifts her gaze again and sees others. A group of humans is knotted together beyond Rachel and Kayla, and she catches a jumble of thoughtwaves—

—*a man named Bill pondering the fate of his ex-wife, with whom he has been enduring a prolonged and nasty alimony battle, and actively hoping for her demise, and feeling as if he's won the lottery by remaining alive at the end of the world, and praying to whatever god remains that he can live to have another chance at everything …*

—*a young woman named Mai, outwardly rebellious but harboring great insecurities and fears inside, and glad she's with a group rather than alone, like she was for weeks before this shitstorm happened to her, left by an on-and-off-again boyfriend whom she repeatedly fucked over, even she admits that, she can't help it, and now she has to live with the guilt that she never apologized to him before he ended up sucking on a tree somewhere …*

—*a young man named Liam, watching Mai's every move, startlingly unconcerned about his situation as a survivor and what the future holds, wondering how to get into Mai's pants, he's the most eligible guy here, right? Might as well take advantage of the situation…*

The names and thoughts come at her fiercely, and inside the pain she tries to reconcile her ability to perceive these thoughts with what happened to her at the store. Something was inside her, something took control of her, something with a kind of psychic power—she felt it, she knew it, she remembers it. She doesn't doubt it. The fact that it happened makes her feel at once violated, as if raped, and altered. Because she has retained this … this clairvoyance, this telepathy.

She turns her head to the right and finds—

—*a shifty man named Scott, or maybe it's his very consciousness that is shifty, his eyes flitting from person to person, scheming, trying to figure out his way out of this, and he understands that none of these people matter except to help him get there, and it would all go away if he could only get to the painkillers in the fridge where they put those fucking bodies, but now someone is always in there with those monsters, especially that busybody Bonnie, and to hell with all of them, he doesn't need them, does he …?*

She pulls away, the thoughts sticking to her like tree sap.

Although the pain wracking Felicia's body isn't as severe as it was before, she can still barely stand it. Tears move helplessly down her cheeks, and she can't keep a stream of whimpers from spilling out of her throat even as the mindscapes shout at her, and she tries twisting her head away from them, but they're always there, around her—

—a desperately helpful man named Rick, an architect with precise, orderly thoughts, anxious to help the group but dealing with grief, like almost everyone, he understands that, thinking about his fiancé at home, who never woke up this morning, and whom he bolted away from when he saw the crimson glow in her throat, he can't shake the memory of sprinting out into the street, his heart sledgehammering against his ribcage, unable to control his breath, he will never forget that moment as long as he lives, and he can't stop wondering where she's gone, wearing the ring he kneeled to give her only weeks ago …

Felicia squeezes her eyes shut, harder, not wanting to see anymore.

But underneath everything, she still feels the hunger for—

—for the objective—

—what?

The need clutches at her, making her innards tremble and clench.

She's thrashing her head left and right now, moving her limbs restlessly, trying to escape the dull pain but failing at every angle. She's also trying to locate something, anything, familiar. Her brows knit with fear.

Then she's aware that one of the survivors has come close to her, but in the chaos of all of the mindscapes shouting at her, she doesn't recognize this person.

"You're okay," comes a whispered voice. A man.

Her head lolls in his direction.

"I'm Michael," he says softly.

"I … I …" she tries, but her mouth won't work properly. Every word is coming out strangled, as if there's a great swelling at the back of her throat. She blinks, attempts focus, but he's too close, and it's too dark. "Who …?" she manages, but then she sees him huge in her mind's eye—

—he doesn't deserve to survive this thing, does he? For God's sake, he even left all that money lying there, spilling out of the safe for anyone to walk in and find, in the same room as his dead wife. Rachel got her wish, didn't she? Jesus, he can't think that way. He ought to tell her, hadn't he? Take her there when this is all over, and please, please, at least let Rachel survive, his little girl, let her survive this thing. If he can save this woman from the Co-Op, surely he can save his little girl …

The mindscape is chaotic, confusing. But she has a memory of him that stabilizes the jumbled imagery. Memories from the store. This is the man who yanked her from the Co-Op, brought her back to herself. And she realizes now that this is the man she passed on the street earlier, in her car—when? How long ago? How did he find her?

"Are you in pain?"

She tries to form words, but her mouth is in the clutches of a prolonged cramp.

"Can you swallow a pill?"

She nods, whimpers.

"Wait here."

She manages to turn her head and glance through the open doorway. She squints and tries to comprehend what she sees. Tables of books? Beyond that, a messy checkout area and what appears to be great mounds of tossed-aside tomes. It's the library. For some reason, she's in the downtown library, and it appears to have been ransacked. The survivors' thoughts pull at her.

—a sweaty man named Brian, his perspiration mirroring his internal distress, knowing he's without his heart medication but too proud to inform the others, fueled by stuttering adrenaline, certain he's not getting out of this alive but anxious to help while he can, as long as he doesn't overdo it, and gnawing on the memory, almost constantly, of his grown son who lives in Loveland but whom he hasn't spoken to in eight years, and he desperately wonders what has become of him and his granddaughter ...

She searches for information inside these mindscapes.

Little pieces of memory, little jags of perception, from all of them.

—monsters—

—have to get through this, and then—

—she'll keep me safe, she will, she promised—

—will anything be the same, ever? I mean, how can this be happening? What's next?—

Swallowing a black knot of pain, she collects the thoughts and tries to make sense of them. Then she wonders, How come I'm not at the hospital? I need help. Serious help.

In a moment, Michael is helping her swallow six pain pills. She does her best to help him, reaching up one shaking arm, but her shoulder grinds in its socket again, and more quiet sobs escape her. The pain is literally blinding.

"Let me know if that doesn't help."

"Huuuurts," she mouths. "F—feels wr—wro—wrong."

"What feels wrong?"

She brings up a wobbly hand and touches her head, grits her teeth.

"You've been through a lot," Michael says. "Just keep as still as you can, let yourself heal."

She looks at him, imploring. "Wh … what h—h—h—"

There's a pause. "You've had an accident."

Amid the chaos of her senses, Felicia tries to focus her own thoughts. Her consciousness remains scattershot, but her memory is there. It's in splinters, but it's there. Her inadvertent incarceration in Janet's office feels like a shivery nightmare, but she knows it was real. Somehow, it was real. It happened. She was overtaken by something—controlled by a living presence—and it gradually gained control of her body, for some reason tearing her bones from their sockets, bending her backward as if she was a child's plaything. She knows these things because she can still sense the presence that was inside her. *Something was living inside her!* She can visualize the echo of its thoughts. The things that it tried to communicate to her, the impulses it wanted her to act on. No, that's not it. The things that it communicated to the web of souls that she was part of.

"Do you need morphine?" Michael asks.

She barely hears him.

As her body quivers with its myriad physical maladies, she narrows her thoughts on the thing that was inside her. It's almost as if a snake has slithered through her, leaving its skin behind. Except the skin is pulsing with lingering life. She feels it at a cellular level. And she can still feel the urgent need in those cells—as if it's her *own* need.

"What is it?" Michael whispers.

"They—they—they—" Her mouth can't make words! "They c—c …"

How can she possibly describe the need, the objective, the thing *they crave*, to a surviving human being? And even if she could clarify the unprecedented thing that has happened to her, how can she get her mouth, her voice, to cooperate with her thoughts? It's almost as if that small piece inside her, that remnant of *other*, is preventing her. Or trying to prevent her.

"They …" Michael urges.

Felicia closes her eyes, concentrating. "C—c—c—c—"

"They …" he repeats. "They what?"

Her body requires unconsciousness. It pulls at her. She feels her eyes closing, feels her thoughts drifting.

"No, no!" Michael's voice pleads, fading.

And she's gone, tumbling into blackness. At some point, a heavy blanket of numbness descends upon her, and she feels relief flood her.

She floats in emptiness.

As she eventually drifts back to the world, she becomes aware of imagery, of lingering foreign memory. She feels the ghost of the urgent need that possessed her before, she feels it strongly but from a remove.

The scratching, throaty insistence of it. Like desperate hunger. The power of it humbles her. She's never felt anything like it. Somewhere deep inside, she likens it to thirst. The most burning thirst she can possibly imagine—not only the thirst of one person fighting for survival but the thirst of ...

She feels as if she's grasping something, but as it begins to form, it breaks apart as she approaches waking life.

Life.

She comes out of her dream state in agony again. She works her jaw, still feeling that phantom hunger. Or *is* it phantom? She feels disassociated from it and yet aghast at its depth.

Michael is directly above her, watching her. How long has he been there?

Her jaw clicks, and she swallows a dry lump of pain. Something awful has happened to her throat, and the area above and around it. She should be in a hospital; she should be in surgery right now. She feels it innately. She also knows that something has happened to the world to make it impossible for her to get the care she needs.

She has sustained some kind of life-changing injury, she fears. But what? She's sure that something was inside her—a life form got into her mouth, or ear—but what was it, and what did it do in there? She shudders at the thought of some kind of ... insect ... burrowing into her and attaching itself leechlike.

What did it do to her?

It.

This thing inside her.

She knows what it was. Her connection to it was intimate. It was inside her, quite literally. Perhaps it still is. Yes, she knows it still is. At least, part of it is. There is something still in there.

She shivers at the notion. Her teeth won't stop chattering.

She remembers the visions she had. She saw what it saw. Is that it? Not quite. She read its thoughts. She *thought* its thoughts. Yes, she knew its memories, she knew its needs. Felt its thirst.

And she can still feel all these things.

She stares at Michael, tries to focus on his eyes.

"I—I—I ...."

She shakes her head angrily, stubbornly through the pain. Her thoughts won't gel, won't become cohesive. Frustrated, she reaches out and grabs his hand. The motion causes more pain, but it's manageable. She closes her eyes and concentrates.

"They ..." she says, swallowing and cringing. "... life."

"Life?" Michael repeats.

"D—d—dying."

There's some kind of commotion beyond Michael.

He squeezes her hand gently. "Life, death ... which one?"

Felicia shakes her head.

"Inside," she says, eyes shut. "D—d—dying."

He says, "And the trees have what they need?"

Felicia opens her eyes, thoughts sparking.

The objective.

"*Neeeeed.*"

"Pain relievers now?" Michael whispers.

Grateful, she nods, and together they manage to get some bitter-tasting liquid down her throat. She grimaces and lies back while Michael turns away.

"*Neeeed,*" she whispers again.

Unconsciousness takes her like a dream of nature, floating amongst the trees, and she's gone.

CHAPTER 7

She wakes to a pulse of negative energy. Her ears pop, and her eyes open, flooded with moisture. She takes in a sharp breath.

They're speaking to her.

They.

Around her, the humans are dropping to the ground, covering their ears. She hears the sound as they hear it—a gargantuan blast of thunder, incessant, like a meteor tearing a rift in the atmosphere, making the face of the earth cower. But inside the sound—to her ears—is a strange and elegant music. The notes are filled with imperatives, yes, but also beauty. Seduction. Her chest fills with heat, arching from the floor despite the pain of movement. She focuses on the dim tiles of the library ceiling, imagining that she can see the source of this music. The trilling throats and curved necks, the angled limbs, the piercing eyes.

But what she is seeing is the objective.

A new objective.

The humans.

The humans who were never meant to survive.

But they did—and they're a threat.

Music floods her, and inside the notes, inside the rhythm, is strategy. But it is only partially there, whispering at her. She understands it, but her hold on that knowledge is tenuous. And when the communication breaks up, and the skies fall silent, it leaves her like a fever breaking.

She exhales loudly, emptily. Then her eyes clear.

What happened?

A lingering sense of nausea pervades her consciousness, of something slimy having slid through her innards. Something foreign. Her lip curls. She comes to the realization that, in that moment of communication, she would gladly have killed a human being with her own hands.

She shudders.

There's an older woman on the ground outside the door—

—this is Bonnie, a woman made to help those around her, all her life, she studied it and she practices it, and now, after everything that has happened in the past few days, she feels that she is faced with her life's purpose, there's a reason she's still alive, and it is to ensure that these survivors remain survivors, especially the women and the girls, because if what she dreads is true, they are the key to the future of the human race, and although she is past the age to make a difference in that sense, she can surely help to make sure that others remain, and what greater good can she as a caregiver provide? Only occasionally is she cognizant of how quickly she has set aside thoughts of her husband and grown children, whom she knows are gone, she will think of them later, there will be time for that, for grief, when these plucky survivors have finally conquered this thing, but good sweet Lord, she doesn't know how much more of this she can take …

—and she's peering around, dazed. Bonnie and Felicia lock eyes for a split second, and then Bonnie is on her feet, heading toward what Felicia assumes is the front of the library.

In a moment there are raised voices, and beneath them Felicia can feel a low rumble.

It's them.

She can sense them. Coordinated and desperate. Coming together like the single organism they are, attacking this resilient band. Exploiting what it sees as a moment of weakness.

She pushes past the pain into a seated position. Survivors are running this way and that beyond the door, screaming. Felicia tries to stand, fails. She has to warn them. Right? Tears stream helplessly from her eyes. She tries again to stand and manages to get to her knees. She needs to find a window. All around her is the sound of mad scrambling, bodies scraping and surging. She can hear their gasps—

—and they are beautiful! Beautiful and fierce in their determination, and she can feel them, all of them, a roiling collective of alien souls, desperate, hungry, and they are approaching, they are so close—

She uses the corner of a desk to pull herself to wobbly feet, crying out in agony. Using the desktop as an anchor, she drags herself to the inner doorway, in time to watch through madly watering eyes a wave of bodies approaching the library, an interconnected mass of flesh like a tangible embodiment of the web of souls, churning, roiling. The surge of infected bodies stretches as wide as her vision, and she feels her breath stop in the middle of her throat, watching the inexorable approach of this thing that is at once impossible and beautiful. Then the bodies upon bodies slam against the thick windows. Bodies upon bodies, darkening the library.

Felicia stares into the eyes of the—

—strangers—

—once-human bodies glaring in. She wipes her eyes, tries desperately to focus.

They see her. She knows it.

She sees something in their eyes.

They know her.

She's one of them.

No, she is not.

She feels as if she might faint. She lowers her head, closes her eyes, and more tears stream out. All around her, a cacophony of sound, pandemonium.

The survivors shout at one another, alternately determined and hopeless. Felicia can taste the humans' fear. A battle has been brought to their doors, and they are woefully unprepared for it. They number a handful, and the strangers number in the thousands. This little band of survivors is going to lose. Each one of them can feel it. Each one knows that his or her death is upon them. They are no match for the unified threat that literally surrounds them, the writhing mass of former humanity whose objective, now, is to end them.

Felicia feels that new objective like an itch, a pull toward vicious action. She can strike from within!

She pushes that thought away.

No!

She brings weak arms to her head, trying to block it all out. But muffling auditory and visual stimuli only enhance her new ability, this outrageous curse—*is she dreaming it?*—and her entire consciousness seems filled with shards of thoughts, flitting sensory blips, every tiny moment that those around her are experiencing.

—*Kevin in primal survival mode, throwing his bulk at a melting window and firing his weapon into the wall of alien-puppeteered flesh, his mind a bleary glut of adrenaline and focus*—

—*the twins, Zoe and Chloe, their minds remarkably similar and single-purposed in their response to extreme stimuli, exhibiting intensive control over their survival, aiming a blood-packed tranquilizer rifle and a heavy AR-15 at the incoming bodies, calm in the face of ripped flesh*—

—*even Scott, his mind fractured under stress and chemical addiction, entering the fray, feeling the pull to action, defending his right to exist from these marauders, his mind a screaming gush of frustrated fury*—

—and as Felicia acknowledges the common consciousness of the strangers, the web of attacking souls outside the library, she coughs, recognizing nearly the same in the human survivors, the will to live, the *fight* to live, and she understands the mistake the strangers have somehow made.

The library is suddenly a warzone, exploding with violence. She wraps her arms more tightly around her head, muffling the sounds coming from everywhere. Gunshots, screaming, running, throbbing. It's too much. It's impossible.

She's about to fall. She carefully backs into the book-returns room. She doesn't know where she's going, but it doesn't matter, because finally she does fall to a heap beside the desk. There are so many voices, so many thoughts, so many mindscapes, screaming back and forth in the main hall that she can't get the sense of them. Closing her eyes, she sees those upturned faces considering her, taking the measure of her.

"No!" she moans.

She doesn't want any part of this.

She wants to be at home with Nicole—

Nicole!

—to be wrapped in her arms on a quiet Sunday morning, breakfast in bed, listening to music or binge-watching a TV show on Netflix. It's the first time she's thought of Nicole since she returned, and at the thought, blurry tears spring to her eyes.

The carnage seems to go on forever.

Finally, the clamor of warfare slows, and the library is left pulsing rhythmically with crimson light. Felicia can sense the strangers' directive inside it, the impulse to end the human resistance, and she also senses the human despair among the survivors, their hope dwindling, their exhaustion becoming resignation, their weapons beginning to empty of ammunition and fall to the ground. There's nothing more to do.

—can't possibly—

—it's over—

—so this is how I die—

She feels as if she has awoken at the end of a long, terrible battle, and she understands only partially why it is taking place. She's experiencing it in broken pieces, bewildered by not only her pain but also the barrage of mindscapes fluttering into and out of focus. It's beyond her comprehension, furthermore—as she, for a moment, clears her vision to behold what's happening—the reality of these formerly human bodies crammed against the outer walls of the library, their minds filled with the presence of the strangers, about to prevail.

And then she feels a surge.

It's Michael.

He's hurt.

Felicia feels his mind turn brightly toward Rachel.

—everything in their shared life hangs in the humid air: every mistake, every joy, every laugh, every tear. The image of Rachel in his hands, tiny and fragile at the hospital, surges forward, pressing at his eyes—washing over him and through him. Holding his hand at the mall, giggling like crazy at some shared game at the

arcade. Jumping into his lap at Christmas and hugging him hard. Twirling with him in the back yard under the evening sun, as Cassie watches from her chair on the porch. Eyeing him mischievously over a game of chess. Proudly sharing a graded essay. Crying with him, her head at his shoulder, at the hospital while Cassie lies dying. And yes, the yelling, the defiance. Waking to find her hefting that shotgun, there with him at the end. At the beginning. And shrinking now to a tiny dot, behind all this, is his crime. His betrayals. He was never destined to survive this thing. A peaceful warmth overtakes him—

"Oh no," Felicia whispers.

Something compels her to rise. Screaming, she laboriously gains her feet, and staggers to the doorway. She stares out, blinking madly to clear her vision of endless tears. She watches Michael preparing syringes with blood—

—O-negative blood—

—and then sprinting toward a melted-in window—a window that the strangers compromised with their inner energy, their heat—where the wall of flesh awaits. He thrusts his body out into the fray, using the syringes to deliver short stabs of blood, pumping bursts of it into every body he can reach, and the air is filled with screams.

Felicia feels the shock and pain among the strangers.

A brief, sharp shock.

But it won't be enough.

The survivors are doomed.

Unless …

Felicia strides forward toward her own window, which the bodies have also breached. Instinctively, she pushes outward with all her strength, all the strength she has, and she can almost see it as a physical force—her energy ripples outward in shockwaves, pushing the bodies back from the window and the wall. They tumble down and away like a child's playthings, lifeless, powerless, squealing. She reaches the wide-open window and stares out at the scene, a battlefield of bodies, both infected and turned back, human and stranger, agony and fury. The sky broils with activity, as if watching her, considering her.

What did I do? she whispers inside herself.

And a new emotion she feels among the strangers for the first time. Bodies scurry away from her, like a breaking wave.

Fear.

CHAPTER 8

"NOOO!"

Rachel stares at her father, her breath caught in shock.

She feels as though she's been slammed in the gut. Her face burns beneath a mask of blood, and her hands scrabble at the ground, her mind caught between instincts to embrace him and to scramble away from this horrible scene.

This can't be happening.

Just as she starts to choke, her breath returns in a rush, and she's screaming at her dad, tears in her eyes, splashing on his face. She grabs his shoulders and pulls at him, willing him back to consciousness, but his body is unresponsive deadweight. She wipes at his face, clearing it of blood.

"Daddy, no, please no, you can't go!"

One of the remaining bodies scurries past her, cranked hideously backward, and she kicks at it, furious. There are other bodies retreating from the library, but there's no more focus to them. They're merely fleeing. Did *her dad* do this? He did, didn't he? He saved them all, and he's killed himself in the process. Her dad is dying!

He's staring at her, but she can see his pupils dilating. She can see it happening, even as she pleads.

Suddenly she notices that he's raising a weak, trembling hand, and he touches her cheek, but then the hand falls away. She grabs at his fingers, and sobs cough out of her.

"Please don't leave me, Daddy, please!" she screams, straining. *"I love you, Daddy, I love you so much, please don't leave!"*

Rachel cups his face with her hands, turning it toward her. She leans over and clutches him into an embrace. There's no response. And then Kevin angles in next to her, enormous, settling her father to the ground and beginning chest compressions. Kevin is breathing heavily and yelling, *"Mike! Mike! Wake up! Stay with me! Mike!"*

Rachel's own breath comes in quick gasps, and black spots throb in her vision. Her dad's skin is going ashen.

Someone is holding her, and she thinks it must be Bonnie, but no—

It's Kayla.

Bonnie is dead. Bonnie is dead.

She reaches back at the girl, desperately, her fingers cramping, trying to latch on to life in the face of all this impossible death. Because it's surrounding her in an obscene diorama of crumpled bodies and spattered blood, anguished faces and spent ammunition. Smoke and trauma and tears. The haze in the air speaks of inconceivable loss. She has lost control of herself. She feels as if she is spinning, caught in black chaos, bewildered.

Death.

It can't be.

She mutters some kind of unintelligible sound, and it becomes a hopeless mantra:

"Daddy daddy daddy …"

Kevin keeps at the compressions, and he's still breathing in great, desperate gasps, and after long minutes he gives up, cursing. *"I'm sorry, Rachel, I'm so sorry, fuck!"* He stares out at the library grounds, his eyes glassy. Rachel feels as if she's seeing everything in her peripheral vision, and Kayla's arms clutch her, and suddenly they're suffocating her, everything is suffocating her. She pushes away from them, away from the sight of her father, bloodied and dead on the hard ground, heaps of broken and twisted bodies surrounding him like some death camp.

Except most of these are alive.

They're writhing and screaming, unable to move their broken legs and fractured arms. Their shoulders are dislocated, and their hips are twisted horribly out of true. Rachel claps her hands to her ears, staring in all directions, eyes wide and stinging. It's a landscape of horrors, and she's at its center.

Some distant part of her watches Kevin's meaty calves retreating into the distance, and she feels more alone than she's ever felt in her life.

She staggers up off the ground and somehow gains her feet, almost trips over several bodies as she weaves away from the library. There are other bodies around her—still infected, still crabwalking—scurrying away from her as she approaches them. She notices this only peripherally as she reels almost drunkenly. She braces herself on the hood of the Thompson brothers' truck for a dizzy moment, half-acknowledging the bright red swaths of blood along its side and splattered on its windows, then keeps going. Someone calls her name above the din of the bodies' wretched screams, and she can't summon the ability to respond.

Her feet find grass, and she keeps walking, dazed. She feels and smells the drying blood on her face, and she gags, wipes savagely at her cheeks with her forearms, but then she sees that her forearms are already painted crimson. A sob of revulsion erupts out of her.

She falls to the ground and begins methodically wiping her exposed skin on the grass. She spits on her flesh, loosening the already caking blood.

A small part of her knows that the blood is why those things won't approach her, but she doesn't care. A more overt part of her knows that she would gladly die right now, on this spot, rather than be a part of this hellscape any longer.

"Rachel!" someone yells again.

Deadened, she looks out on the lawn, out toward the street. The neighborhood far beyond the library looks halfway serene. Only a couple bodies, scampering and dragging limbs across the warm asphalt, disoriented. Most of them are headed west, gasping and seized by what appears to be fear. She doesn't care where they're going, she doesn't care about anything.

She's exhausted! She can't believe how tired she is. Her muscles are spent. She doesn't even think she'll be able to rise again from this lawn. She doesn't even want to. *Ever*. And with that thought, she lets her upper body crumple to the grass.

She stares at the blades of grass, so serene and all-encompassing in her vision despite the high-decibel fusillade of screams that engulf and threaten to swallow her. She wants to lose herself in these blades of grass. She wants them to speak of summer and playtime, of nature and sweet smells. Of lazy days and family, her mom laughing and reading on the porch and dad mowing their small yard, wearing his years-old grimy Broncos cap, and Rachel helping with the weeds or sunbathing in a chaise lounge with a book, texting nonsense with Tony or Michelle or Beth and grinning about stupid jokes and Internet memes. She wants these things so badly that she would die for them, right now.

Rachel falls unconscious—

—*her mind finding only lesser turmoil, shifty imagery of blood-slicked arms reaching for her, undulating, sliding against her flesh, coaxing her, opening her inside out, and there are no survivors, no one left, all that remains are the echoes of their screams, because they have all left her, they have all succumbed to the alien extremities, and she can see the ghostly souls of her friends rising, crimson, into the heavens, and they're not even looking back, and whatever is up there, it has finally won, it is taking what it needed from the start, and really the survivors never had a chance in the face of global apocalypse, they were powerless, and now the limbs are gently coaxing the rest of her from her shell, but then those limbs are ratcheting as if in pain—*

"… achel!" an urgent voice surges into focus. "Rachel? Are you okay?"

It's Joel, looking ragged and stubbly now in his rumpled and bloody uniform. He kneels next to her, touching her, making sure she's unbroken, turning her gently toward him. She feels his rough fingers at the skin below her eyes, one at a time, and he's staring at her, very close.

"I'm sorry, I'm so sorry," he mumbles, half-embracing her.

And then he's gone, as quickly as he arrived, and Rachel doesn't care.

In his absence, she stares up at a maelstrom. The sky roils with a dark energy, fierce but also scattered now, sparking like something failing. She feels her vision come into better focus, and she watches the phenomenon. Something is different. Where before the atmospheric storm had a dark, smoothly swirling menace, with its beams of energy surging toward earth, it now appears to be stuttering, and the energy is no longer flowing down with assurance but rather stuttering with uncertainty.

What have we done? she thinks in a rush.

It's a breathtaking sight, and she turns away from it. She closes her eyes tightly, tuning out the shrieks of the living and the dead. It's all too much. She can't bear it. She wants to return to that daydream of home, but now she can't even recall those images. They're gone.

She opens her eyes to find Kayla staring at her from ten feet away. Living corpses writhe and squirm around her, hissing at the blood on their skin, trying to get away from this place. Turned-back human beings cry in agony. The girl is sitting on the concrete path, an island of purity amid charnel-house horror. A look of concern for Rachel is plain on her pretty chocolate face, even with all the blood and gore surrounding her. The sight makes Rachel crumple again, but she feels a surge of love for this relative stranger, and she beckons her closer with trembling arms.

Kayla immediately gets to her feet, rushes to Rachel, and embraces her. Rachel pets the preteen girl's frazzled hair, feeling her shiver in her arms. It must be ninety degrees, and yet Kayla is shaking as if in the grips of hypothermia. Rachel hugs her tightly. By all rights, Kayla should be sobbing, but she's rigid and quiet and trembling.

Over the girl's shoulder, Rachel reluctantly watches the library.

Kevin has disappeared—back inside, perhaps—but she can see Scott and Mai meandering off to the north, wobbly, as if lost. Chloe and Zoe are huddled together by the main entrance doors, sticky with red sweat, crying with what appears to be a mixture of relief and nausea. Underneath the grime, they all look pale under the bright sun, surrounded by mountains of dirt-encrusted bodies and puddles of blood.

Rachel feels her vision broadening as if loosening itself from the tunnelvision of shock. There must be a hundred or more bodies left moaning and screeching on the library grounds, shoved up against the library's face and the melted-in windows, with more inside the building itself, piled up in mountains of hyper-extended limbs and bent-back spines. Rachel can hear their screams, rendered hollow by distance and library walls. They're the bodies of their attackers, made human again. The survivors stopped them, stopped a thousand of them. Maybe more. She's not entirely sure how they did it, but they stopped them. Repelled them. And the ones they didn't change back, they killed or sent scurrying away in retreat.

She doesn't want to look at her father's body—her head won't even turn in that direction—but she's flickering back on his final actions.

The images flicker.

Her dad throwing himself into the throng of bodies.

The sound of his scream as the bodies enveloped him.

What did he do? What did he do to push them back? To cause the skies to fracture?

She screams rage at the too-recent recollection. Her daddy was alive *moments ago!* Why did he rush out here? Why did he have to sacrifice himself? Why did it have to be *him?* She sobs into Kayla's shoulder, feeling younger than this compassionate little girl clutched hard to her chest. She lets the tears flow. Kayla simply holds her. Still rigid, still shaking.

Through her tears, Rachel manages to whisper, in a softly hiccupping voice, "It's all right … it'll be all right … I promise …"

She would like to believe her own words.

She's not sure how much time passes, but she loses consciousness again inside the embrace—

—and the limbs are still snatching at her but with diminishing force, and they are pulling up into the alien sky, her father rising with them as if curled in a crooked palm, and inside she is screaming at the crimson vortex, screaming for him to come back, come back to her, he can't possibly leave now that she has rescued him, it's not fair—

When she opens her eyes, it's as if she's awakening from a coma.

She surveys the scene, blinking in an exaggerated way to clear her eyes of tears. She doesn't want to wipe her blood-stained hand or forearm there.

The remaining Thompson brother—Pete is the name that comes to her rattled mind—is standing forlornly at the passenger-side door of his truck. He doesn't seem to know what to do. Perhaps they're all in shock, all of them except for Joel, maybe, whose police training might have prepared him better for what happened. But then Rachel shakes her head: Who could have prepared for this?

Pete is covered with drying blood, just like her, just like everyone, and he's hobbled by injury. Rachel doesn't know what happened to him, but there are pale blotches across his face and arms. He's limping, but he's a survivor. The surreality of what they've gone through, collectively, keeps coming back at her like the fragments of a nightmare. Pete is peering into his truck, repeatedly, as if hoping that his brother Jeff will materialize there, alive and boisterous, behind the wheel.

And then Rachel realizes that Jeff's body is still in the cab. She can see the man's protruding, meaty shoulder over the rim of the dash. Pete has been walking around the truck, catching glimpses of the corpse that was once Jeff, unsure what to do. Rachel sees now that there are tears in Pete's eyes.

She looks away.

She spots Scott, to the right, at one of the windows close to the main doors, and he's helping that girl. The one her dad brought to the library, the CSU student from the Co-Op. Felicia. She's standing on a makeshift ledge of concrete—what was once a bulky window sill—facing the horrors. Her hands are open, palms forward, and Rachel notices even from a distance the wide O of her mouth, and her turned-up eyes. Is she in pain? What is she doing? The questions dissolve inside her.

Kevin appears to Rachel's left, coming away from the library entrance. He turns blindly about for a moment, then spots Rachel.

Rachel pushes herself up, finding determination somewhere deep inside, and Kevin arrives breathless and red-faced.

"It's over," he gasps. "They've stopped, but it's a bloodbath in there."

She doesn't know how to respond to that.

Kevin offers his arm, and she accepts it, steadying herself. Her other arm is still entwined with Kayla's, and she helps the girl up from the ground. They move together, on unsure feet.

"Let's go," Rachel says, and her gaze moves unconsciously toward the blown-out window where she last saw Felicia. "We have to help."

Everything is numb.

Felicia is no longer at the window, which looks like a mouth with blown-out teeth. Rachel feels scraped out at her core, but some part of her awareness is drawn to that window.

"You sure?" Kevin says.

"We're going back in." Rachel clears her throat. "I need to. Seriously. Get me away from here, okay?"

At that moment, the gangly Ron comes jogging over. He looks haggard and about ten years older than he did an hour ago, with his bony limbs and slumped shoulders. He's not as drenched with blood as the others, for some reason, but he still appears as if he just stepped off of a battlefield.

"We need pain relievers, bad!" he says. "There's at least two hundred people who need help. It's terrible in there. I mean, it's bad out here—

" He casts his gaze around the bloodied vicinity. "—but it's absurd in there. I don't even know where to start. But what I do know is we need morphine. Whatever else is there. Anything and everything."

"We're out?" Kevin asks, looking like he already knows the answer.

"Hell, we were out before they attacked. Joel is rounding up a crew to get to the Old Town police station, the armory there, and arm up again, but what are we gonna do about those people? They're alive, and they're—" He slaps his hand to his mouth to stifle an unexpected sob and gather himself. "—they're … begging. They're desperate."

People need her.

A *lot* of people need her.

"So what do we do?" Kevin asks. He keeps glancing around, waiting for the bodies to attack again, but it's not happening. They've mostly crawled away, leaving this bloody aftermath.

Rachel feels herself convulsively swallowing.

"Isn't it over—?" Kayla pulls at her.

"It's not over," Rachel says, striding toward the entrance on leaden feet. "We need to help. Okay Kayla? Do you think you can help? Help them with—with me?"

She glances down at the girl.

Kayla is peering up at her with her large brown eyes. The compassion remains, but there's fear in there, and an exhaustion that mirrors Rachel's—bottomless and vast. Her eyebrows tremble, as if at any moment she will dissolve into little-girl tears. But she holds it inside. Somehow.

"Are we going back in the library?" Kayla says.

"Yes." Rachel watches the entrance, steels herself for the chaos of the lobby, not letting her eyes wander over to her lost father. "We have to … have to figure out what's next."

"No!" Kayla half-whines, clutching at her.

Rachel closes her eyes for a moment, and everything is suddenly assaulting her at once. She feels faint.

Kayla's protestations fill with a memory from her youth, of being with her dad at the fairgrounds near Windsor for a carnival. It's one of her earliest memories, a crowded night, a hot night, and she held his big hand tightly, squeezing through the rowdy masses, eating funnel cake and cotton candy, buying tickets for dirty little rollercoasters and all manner of spinning rides, and getting all giddy and sweaty. At one point, a giant smelly bearded man with a greasy handkerchief wrapped around his forehead inadvertently squashed her foot, and he only gave Rachel a passing glance, but she choked back tears for twenty minutes and never told her dad about it. She wanted to be brave under the clamor and chaos of the bewildering night, and perhaps because of her internalization of that little horror, the moment defined her nightmares for years later—the overbearing horror of something huge towering over her, a hulking threat to her soul, threatening to squash her …

She opens her eyes, blinking spastically, feeling that old night terror getting the better of her as its equivalent is now all around her.

"I can get medicine," Rachel says, halting her stride.

She's not quite sure where the thought has come from. All she knows is she doesn't want to go back in that library, doesn't even want to approach the entrance. Not now. She doesn't want to see—

"Where?" Kevin says.

"Where do you think?"

"The hospital? You want to go back there?"

"I … I don't *want* to go back there, no." She looks down at Kayla. "I *have* to. *We* have to."

Kevin looks around. "Is it safe?"

All Rachel can do is nod. She can't find her voice. She needs it to be true. She needs to leave. She knows her way around that pharmacy better than anybody. Why not her? She has to leave. Now.

Ron is spinning around, assessing the threat, but he stumbles, betraying his own inner turmoil.

"Those things are scattering." Ron points west. "But they all seem to be going that way. Toward the mountains. It's a miracle, really, but they're retreating. And none of them in the direction of the hospital. So there's that."

Kevin sighs raggedly. "Why don't we all get the hell out of here?"

The question is met with silence—and the chorus of agonized moans all around them suffices as an answer.

Rachel finds her voice. "We can't leave them. They're people again. They need help."

She takes her first good look at the remaining bodies around her. Some of them are managing to crawl fitfully along the ground, in search of some kind of relief, but others are incapable of movement, their limbs fractured and unusable. More than a few of them are vomiting bright red blood onto the concrete, their throats ravaged by splinters. In their eyes is a desperate fear and pain. Very few of them are even acknowledging their surroundings; they're too consumed by their own plight.

"I can help them," she says, getting control of herself but feeling a growing flame of anger and determination deep inside her. "I can do this."

"Jesus," Kevin says. "All right, I'm in. We have a tight window, or maybe we don't, but right now, we have an opening to gear up."

"I'm going with you," Kayla says, not even looking up.

"Even if we get medicine," Kevin says, "are any of them gonna be left alive by the time we get back?"

Kayla reacts to Kevin's words—and the situation in general—with visible unhappiness, and Rachel feels the tremble in the girl's shoulders increase in severity. She looks down on Kayla in time to see her lift one hand to her face to wipe at her eyes. This girl has withheld her flow of emotion until now, after all this, after the attack, after all this death, after comforting Rachel, even. She holds the young girl tightly against her, struck not only by the kid's empathy but also by her inspiring bravery.

"Let's go," Rachel directs toward Kevin. "We have to try, right? Let's stop talking and go."

The sky continues to rumble malevolently. It crackles like heat lightning, and the sound of it reminds her of some kind of broken radio broadcast. When she was very young, her dad—*her dad!*—owned a ham radio, and he would play with it some nights, out in the warm garage, involving her in his weird hobby. The sound coming out of the speakers as he eagerly changed channels, from static to static, was like this: broken patches of hissing and spitting—on a much larger scale.

Above the alien clouds, the crimson luminescence strobes in weird ways. Those columns of light from earlier—which Ron had insisted amounted to some kind of communication—are jittering and flashing unhealthily. Or angrily.

Her dad caused that.

—didn't he?—

Kevin has already taken off toward the library entrance, presumably to inform Joel that they're going. Rachel almost calls out for him, then realizes he wouldn't hear her over the din. She wants to go before Joel has a chance to stop her.

Rachel half-registers loud moaning coming from somewhere and wonders if it's a survivor or a turned human. Does it matter? She glances down at Kayla, finds the girl staring up at her.

"I'm not—I'm not good at this," Kayla whispers.

Rachel can't register the words. "What?"

"I'm good at other things, though." The girl's eyes move off in the distance toward her home across the street. "I'm good at reading and math. I get the best scores on my math tests." She's still shivering, in little bursts now. "I like to bake things with my mom. She showed me how to put M&Ms in cookies. I'm good at that, too. I was good at remembering to feed Gizmo, that was my guinea pig, but he died last year."

"I bet you were. I bet you're good at all that."

For some reason, the words from Kayla are calming Rachel. Perhaps the simple act of comforting a child.

"But I'm not good at this."

Rachel holds her and runs her own trembling fingers over her hair.

"You're better than you think, honey. Way better."

Then Kevin comes back out of the library with Joel at his heels. The two men weave through the mass of broken humanity and find their way to Rachel and Kayla. Rachel braces herself as Joel stops, while Kevin moves toward his truck.

"Hey girl," Joel says, somehow maintaining his veneer of authority in the face of bedlam. "You're sure you're up for it? It would be a big help for you to grab what you can over there and—"

"I'm on it," she says, curtly, pushing through the rising anger in her voice. "I have to get out of here."

Joel pauses, watching her. He places a strong hand on her shoulder, squeezes gently—an almost effortless show of compassion. "We'll have time to work through everything that's happened, I promise." His eyebrows are crooked with stress. "Let's clean up this mess."

She nods, dismisses his words. Then a thought occurs to her.

"Can you ...?" she begins, softening.

"What?"

"Can you do something about ... about ... my dad?"

"You want to take him to the hospital?"

"Will you ... put him in a safe place? Away from everything?"

"We'll take care of him. And after we take care of these people, we'll figure out how to treat him right."

Her mouth won't open. She looks into Joel's eyes.

"All right," Joel says. "Make it quick. In and out. Get to the pharmacy. I think between you and Kevin, you can identify a shitload of pain relievers. Bring 'em all. Ron's team is gonna start putting joints back in place and setting broken limbs as best they can."

"We'll be quick," Kevin says.

"While you're at the hospital, I'm gonna jet over to the station to sack the SWAT truck. That's essentially the armory over there. Mobile armory. I've got access. I'll bring everything here, might even bring the truck, if I can." He glances around, at once bleary-eyed and focused. "So, we clear?"

"Clear," Rachel says.

"Be *careful*." He stares her down. "Got it?"

"Yeah." Then, after a hesitation: "Joel?"

"Yeah?" Joel stutters in his step.

"That girl, Felicia." She has to practically shout over the sounds of misery coming from everywhere, and she feels him looking at her in confusion. "Have you seen her?"

"She was ... yeah, I saw her over at that window."

"Do you know what she was doing?"

He shakes his head. "What do you mean?"

- 67 -

"I don't know." She lets the thought float away on the wretched air. "But help her, okay? Make sure she's all right."

"I will." He mumbles something after that, but she can't hear it. "Be careful."

She nods.

"All right, let's get all this done while we have this opportunity, while those things are still stunned, and then … and then decide what to do next. See you back here ASAP."

He jogs back toward the entrance, and Rachel gets a glimpse of Scott, Mai, Liam, and Rick already at work moving bodies. Pete is dragging a woman's broken body, right there at the doors, and she's screaming like an animal. Rachel feels something like heartburn scalding her throat. She knows they must be laying the bodies out in a way to better help them, but she wonders how the crew can bear those sounds. All she knows is that if she doesn't get in the truck soon and start for the hospital, she might start running and never stop.

"Let's go," she tells Kevin and Kayla.

And soon they're bouncing over the grass and shrubs of the library grounds in Kevin's old truck, bumping down off the curb, and onto Remington, headed south toward Prospect. The world is still stuttering, and Rachel is numb and shaking, and nothing is over yet.

CHAPTER 9

The streets are utterly quiet, and the ghost-town nightmare reality of Fort Collins is revealed again. She can't be out here again, can she? On these streets again, entering yet another phase of a prolonged nightmare?

What time is it?

She peers around with gritty eyes, glancing into the smoky sky. Ash is drifting lazily, almost like light snow. A dirty orange sun, cloaked in crimson and smoke, is still high in the sky but heading west toward Horsetooth. She guesses it's probably nearly 4 p.m.

Holding tightly to Kayla in the passenger seat, she watches the scenery whisk past. Kevin navigates the silent, collision-strewn streets roughly, wrenching the truck this way and that, and at one point careening over someone's lawn to get past a tangle of crashed trucks.

"They coordinated against us," Kevin mutters. "They attacked us because there was a bunch of us all together. Right? Don't you think?" He shakes his head. "Jesus."

Rachel doesn't respond. As Kevin continues to theorize, she feels anger continuing to grow inside her, a red heat, a powerful itch to destroy the things that have destroyed her life. She feels blunt curse words at her lips but holds them back from Kayla.

"So you know what to look for, right?" Kevin asks as they approach Lemay. "What are we grabbing?"

Rachel bounces on the bench seat as Kevin takes the turn.

She tries to focus. "Pain relievers, obviously. I'm not sure how much morphine is left. Vicodin, Percocet, OxyContin? But also gauze, antibiotics, creams … topical stuff … rubbing alcohol, hell, Band-Aids, supplies for treating wounds." She squints, thinking. Her father's face keeps flashing at her. "If we can swing it, basic surgery tools—scalpels, clamps, even tweezers, you know."

"Right," Kevin manages to mumble. "Almost there."

They pass Wendy's and Culver's, then various medical offices, and then the dreaded hospital, all concrete and glass, looms on their left, past the burgundy footbridge to the parking garage. She seems to keep coming back to this awful place.

Kevin turns carefully into the parking lot in front of the hospital. He's watching everywhere. He pulls up to the all-too-familiar double front doors and stops, motor running. Now they're all watching the entrance. There appears to be no movement. Remembering, Rachel peers out her window to her right. At the edge of the parking lot are two rather large pine trees, and the bent-back bodies of two businessmen are attached there. By Rachel's foggy estimation, those bodies have been in those precise positions for three days.

"Let's roll," Kevin says, shutting off the engine.

For the first time, Rachel recognizes that he has brought along one of the rifles. As he hefts it and prepares to open his door, she asks, "Didn't we run out of ammo in the attack?"

"We scrounged some out of Pete's truck. Not much, but enough to hold us till Joel gets back to the library. I hope." He glances down at the rifle, which is specked with blood, like everything else in Rachel's reality. "I have exactly one mag left, so let's not get into too much trouble. Keep your eyes open."

He pushes out of his side of the truck, and Rachel follows suit. The three survivors quickly and stealthily enter the hospital through the cockeyed and broken front doors. Everything is dark inside. The generator must have died. Or did they shut it off? She can't even remember the events of a few days ago.

Immediately, they notice the sweet-sour, eye-watering stench of death. All three of them lift their hands and forearms to their face, trying to block the smell. It's powerful. Rachel knows all too well that there are still scores—perhaps hundreds—of dead bodies in this hospital, covered and given as much dignity as possible, but nevertheless unrefrigerated and untreated.

"What is that smell?" Kayla says with dismay. Her left arm reaches out blindly as if for support.

In answer, Rachel can only give her a look.

"That," Kevin says, "is exactly what the library's going to smell like in a couple days."

"Let's get this done," Rachel says, surging forward.

"This is gonna be fun," Kevin says, muffled.

Rachel pushes through the metal doors beyond the admissions desk, and the smell of putrefaction now hits her like something physical. She stops dead, and so do her companions.

An incredulous, horrified expression overtakes Kayla's face. "What—?"

Rachel has to urge her forward to get her moving again.

"Rachel …" Kayla breathes through her sleeve. "I told you I'm not good at this."

"And I told you you're better than you think." Rachel places a hand on her shoulder. "Let's be strong, okay?"

"This won't take long," Kevin says, his left hand drawing a magnum flashlight from his belt. Some distant part of Rachel recognizes it as one of the two that she and Jenny took from Target on that first horrible night. "Kayla, can you be the lightbearer?"

Kayla, one hand still crammed against her nose, takes the flashlight and directs the light ahead of them in a nervous jitter. The halls are ghostly, muted and smeared, making the hospital appear as if it's been abandoned for far longer than a few days.

"It's all right, kid, there's no one here but us," Kevin assures her.

The girl's big brown eyes consider him, then focus on the hallway again. Without the generator light, there's only occasional ambient light from windows in offices to the left. Rachel is glad Kevin had the presence of mind to grab the magnum.

At first, she barely registers the shattered door handle of the office that recently held her father, but then she does a double-take and stares into the empty room. Remembers her reunion with him there, the way she sunk inside herself. She hurries past. She sees the open door of the pharmacy on her right.

"Here we are."

The room already appears ransacked, but Rachel recognizes the mess. For the most part. She sees evidence of both Bonnie and Scott—Bonnie's desperate sense of order, and Scott's panic and theft—but most of all, she comes to the realization that she's out of her league. When she helped Bonnie on that first day, the older woman escorted her to one precise section of the pharmacy, where the morphine packets and vials sat in orderly rows. Most of that medication has since been swept quickly out into a box, probably by Bonnie herself, when the newly aggressive bodies attacked the hospital and the survivors were forced out.

Those rows of morphine are all but empty now, although she sees several packages toward the back.

"Kayla, can you see if you can find a box? Some kind of container? A pretty big one. Just whatever you can find. Dump something out."

The girl now has her forearm clamped to her nose. She nods, her big eyes shiny. Kayla hands Kevin the flashlight, turns, and begins searching.

"Be careful, stay close." Rachel exhales and focuses on the other shelves. She recognizes perhaps three medicinal names on the bottles and boxes in front of her.

"Uh, where do we start?" Kevin says, scanning the rows with the light.

"Looks like all the painkillers are together. Here we go … Oxycodone, Fentanyl, Bupre … Buprenorphine—?" Rachel points at a lower shelf. "—Amitriptyline, Gabapentin … let's grab everything in this general area."

Almost immediately, Kayla brings over three white U.S. Post Office bins, of all things. Rachel lifts out one of the bins and starts sweeping small boxes and bottles into it. She finds large assortments of salves and ointments after some scrutiny, and Kevin helps her find the antibiotics. In a small adjacent room that Kevin has to break into, they find boxes and boxes of sterilized, plastic-wrapped surgical tools, along with gauze and wraps of all kinds. They load up the bins quickly.

"Let's start filling the truck—Kayla, can you handle that? Just start dumping the bins in the back, then come right back with the empties. Got it?"

Without a word, Kayla takes a full bin and sprints for the truck.

"Let us know if you see anything out there!" she calls, immediately feeling a spike of apprehension for sending her off on her own.

But she knows the kid can handle herself—possibly better than Rachel can.

Kevin and Rachel do their best to raid what they can from the shelves, feeling an increasingly urgent need to get out of there. Not because of any physical threat but because of the psychic damage caused by the dark and the stench. Rachel's eyes have been watering for ten minutes, and her sinuses feel singed.

"What do you think happens next?" she asks darkly, breaking a silence.

"Those things?"

"Yeah."

Kevin is quiet, seeming to finish up his scan of the medical inventory. He exhales loudly through clenched teeth.

"I've been thinking about what happened." He widens the beam of the flashlight and trains it on a new bank of shelves. "What your dad did. He turned the tide, Rachel, he really did. I have no doubt about that. But it seemed like something scared them, too, something bigger. I mean, they went from super organized and confident to … scared as rabbits, just, you know, scurrying away. And it was instant. Something spooked them. Grab those bandages there."

Kayla returns with an empty bin, grabs another full one, and sprints away.

"Was it the blood?" Kevin goes on. "We were pumping them with O-negative for quite a while before they turned tail, right? How long? An hour? My sense of time is all screwed up, but it was a long time."

Rachel almost can't bear to listen, feels that pulse of anger growing stronger. She stays quiet, filling her bin.

"Was there a point where the blood finally had a … a collective effect that scared them?" Kevin says. "Enough to worry that hive mind, or whatever?"

That was her dad's plan, yes. She can visualize him attacking those things with his tranq rifle and then with syringes, wildly injecting the curing blood into the mass of bodies—

She shakes her head, blocking the image, feeling her eyes moisten. *Later.*

"Maybe it doesn't matter," Kevin interrupts her thoughts. "Maybe they're on the run for good now. But I doubt it. I think they'll regroup, and they'll come after us again eventually."

Rachel's gut clenches.

"I'll tell you what I don't want to do—and that's to regroup ourselves into a giant goddamn target again." Kevin pauses in his work, letting his words fill the small room. "I'm for gearing up with more weapons, more ammunition, some machetes and baseball bats, right, and all this medicine and supplies, enough food and water to last a while, and getting the hell away from Fort Collins. Just drive east and see what happens. We already know they want something in these trees, right? So why are we staying near the fucking *trees?*"

Kayla has returned from the lobby and stops short at Kevin's words.

"Sorry kid," he sighs. "But listen, even if that's not what everyone agrees to, it's what I plan to do. I'm done with this town. Now let's get the hell out of here, huh?"

The three survivors make their way toward the front doors, carrying the last of the bins.

Even after fifteen minutes, Rachel hasn't grown accustomed to the smell, and its power has her on the edge of nausea. It doesn't help that she knows exactly where these odors are coming from. She experiences visceral flash-images of Alan and the little neighbor girl, Sarah. Jenny and all the others. They're all here, piled in with innumerable other corpses.

Rachel brought death to many of those other bodies. She was the one who smothered dozens of human beings without realizing that life could return to them, given the right antidote. That's something that she did. She won't be able to wipe away that stain.

Her dad was fond of talking about karma, mostly in a joking way but sometimes seriously in his contemplative, not-quite-spiritual way, and those occasional pronouncements whisper back at her now.

You're gonna pay a karmic price for that one!

Jason Bovberg

She can hear him saying it, like he might have said after catching her playfully cheating at Monopoly—his voice, clear as if he's right behind her now in this stinking hallway, walking with her as they move farther and farther away from the source of the stench. As if making a pronouncement about her immediate future.

Rachel bolts roughly away from Kevin and Kayla, finding the closest open doorway—an observation room. She pukes onto the floor, turning her face to the far right and avoiding the box in her arms. She endures three hard bile-spiked convulsions, then takes a moment to spit out the worst of what's left.

"Sorry," she coughs wetly.

Her throat burns and her sinuses are ravaged. For several moments, she simply clutches the doorjamb—the box of medical wrappings trapped between her abdomen and the wall—and tries to balance herself. She takes in long, slow breaths through her mouth.

After a minute, she realizes she's shaking her head, back and forth.

She's not going to think that way anymore.

No regrets.

She suddenly feels as if her whole life has been one of capitulation. Giving in to her mother's illness, folding in on herself while grief had its way with her. Letting her lesser, self-pitying demons control her while her dad reached for a new life. Surrendering to baser impulses, pushing her friends away when they wanted to help in the wake of tragedy. And then, all too recently, second-guessing her decisions when the world exploded around her. She feels on the verge of capitulating again and not seeing the situation for what it is. She's about to fail herself. She can see it clearly, that moment on the near horizon when she will turn inward and fail herself, fail her father.

She can't let him die in vain.

These are monsters she's dealing with.

They're the ones about to pay a karmic price.

She spits foul saliva and bile onto the floor, clearing her mouth. She straightens up and turns around. Kevin and Kayla are watching her warily.

"Okay, let's g—" Rachel starts.

A concussion hits her.

She's aware of herself falling, her box clattering on the dirty floor, and in her vision somewhere, she catches stutter-glimpses of Kevin and Kayla also tumbling. Her head is filled with noise. She is already on her back by the time she realizes that the sky is roaring. She shuts her eyes tight and—

—*the red tendrils are pulling at her again, coaxing her, and it makes all the sense in the world to simply surrender and go limp, to let the warm limbs lift her toward her father, to take her too, to be with him again as if nothing happened, to start over. The red throat narrows and roils as if swallowing, and she feels her body giving up, but no! She won't let it happen, she feels Kayla close to her, and—*

—when she can open her eyes into a squint, she sees Kayla rocking on her side, hands covering her ears. She also sees one of Kevin's legs jerking in the air above Kayla's head. Everything is shaking under the sound.

"Stop it!" Rachel yells at the ceiling, but the sound dies under the thundering bray.

The walls shudder as if in the midst of an earthquake, the sounds of medical machinery clanking all around them. The roar lasts for perhaps twenty more seconds, then slices cleanly off, leaving an echo of itself in the air, leaving her ears ringing. Something made of glass shatters in the far distance.

"Jesus Christ!" Kevin cries.

"Why does it do that?" Kayla asks, her voice a timid warble. Her face is blank with confusion or shock.

Kevin is already laboring to his feet. "I don't even want to think about it. Let's get the hell out of here." He works his jaw left and right, trying to pop his ears.

"They're communicating," Rachel says, accepting Kevin's hand up. She immediately bends to gather supplies and throw them back into her bin. "They're up to something again. Already. Planning, maybe."

"Figuring out how to murder us," Kevin mutters.

"Kevin!" Rachel barks. "Dude!"

He gives her a glance, then Kayla an even more sheepish one. "Yeah, I'm sorry, Kayla. We're fine. Let's get in gear. They're doing something."

Rachel shoves at his shoulder, and he nods again, deserving it. Then she helps Kayla up, only to find that the girl is brushing her hands on her pants with something akin to anger.

"It'll be all right," Rachel soothes, giving Kevin a hard stare. "You're safe."

"But I'm not," she says. "I'm not." She eases up, sniffing. "Everything is worse. I shouldn't have left my house. I shouldn't've have left my room in the library. I was safe there. It was dark and quiet and safe. I was fine there till you—"

She catches herself, then buries herself against Rachel in a hard embrace. No tears, no sound, just holding her tight.

"I didn't mean that." She shakes her head furiously against Rachel's upper abdomen.

Kevin lifts his box and gives Rachel a look.

"I got her," she whispers. "Go ahead."

Jason Bovberg

He takes off through the double doors, into the lobby, and out to the truck. As the doors clatter shut, Rachel pets Kayla's wild hair.

"I'll take care of you, sweetie," she says. "I'll do everything I can to keep you safe. I promise I'm doing my best."

The words escape her naturally, easily, and she thinks of her mother then. The vividness of the image stuns her. It's warmed by memory, and it calms her. How many times did her mother say those kinds of words to her when she was young? She remembers her little conversation about both of their moms, back at the library.

Kayla nods against her.

"I know," she says.

At that moment, the truck starts up. Rachel takes Kayla's face in her hands, and looks straight at her.

"You ready to get out of here? Go back to the library?"

"Let's do it."

Kevin meets them in the lobby, then about-faces back toward the truck.

Everything seems to turn sluggish at that moment. At least, that's how Rachel will think of this moment in retrospect.

Outside, the skies stutter and roil. Crimson light seems to fall in shards from the ever-present clouds of smoke. Kayla has handed her bin to Kevin, and he is in the process of setting it in the truck bed.

That's when Rachel sees them: the two men who had been clamped to the evergreens on the other side of the parking lot. They're halfway across the asphalt now, and closing, scurrying in mad, bent-back gallops. She can see the insane yet single-minded purpose in their eyes. Her words choke in her throat. On instinct, she recoils, and wraps herself around Kayla to shield her. She yanks the girl back, away from the assault, away from the threat, and toward the front of the truck, down and away.

Now a hoarse yell of warning erupts from her, and Kevin reacts with a full-body jerk, twisting downward.

The bodies leap from the ground, snarling—

Thunder cracks, and everything is muffled.

Rachel feels a shower of shrapnel against her back and right flank, and she winces at the sting. A hot spray of blood needles her skin.

Silence.

Whatever happened, it happened in an instant.

Her ears are ringing.

"Sh—shit!" Rachel yells, on the ground now, lifting her head cautiously, wincing in anticipation of another blast. Where are the bodies? Where did they go? She searches frantically. She has the sense that someone saved them at the last possible second. Was it Joel, coming for them?

Kayla shivers beneath her, curled into a ball.

"You okay?" Rachel says.

Her voice feels far away, bass-heavy.

The girl nods against her shoulder.

Kevin is on the ground, face-down, trying and failing to lift himself. His big arms are shiny with new blood. There's blood everywhere, and Rachel quickly finds the source. The two bodies that assailed them lie motionless not far from Kevin, their limbs angled unnaturally, broad expanses of exposed flesh stained black and green. A trill of uneasiness travels Rachel's spine, and she lets go of Kayla to tend to Kevin.

Her eyes dart everywhere, not spotting anything. She feels utterly exposed.

Kevin is moaning and cursing. "The *fuck!* Where'd *that* come from?"

Rachel goes to her knees next to him, tentatively reaching for him, trying to help. There's gray matter on his clothes, and a single large bone shard is embedded in his shoulder. She stares at it with disgust. It's very clearly a piece of cranium.

"Oh God!" Kayla whines. She's anxiously wiping blood from the side of her face. "Is he hurt?"

"I think so." Rachel watches that piece of bone. "Kevin, you have a piece of skull in your shoulder," she says. She doesn't know what else to say.

He can't seem to hear her. He's pushing himself up off the pavement, or trying to. His hand slips once, twice.

Then he speaks loudly. "Everyone okay? Damn, I can't hear a fucking thing." His voice pitches louder. "Rachel?"

Rachel reassures Kevin with her touch, shifts position to get in front of him. She uses one hand to calm him. "Shhhh." The word devolves into a whimper, and she feels the urgent need to get him under cover, to get back in the truck and leave this godforsaken place.

Kevin's features are pockmarked with gore and bone. He blinks rapidly, wiping at his eyes. Rachel can't tell if any of this blood is his.

"What happened?" he yells. "Fuckin' *OW.*"

"I don't know."

"Huh?"

She gestures at her ear, shakes her head, and he nods, understanding.

"Did someone shoot at those things? Are there more coming? I can barely see. *Fuck!*"

Rachel studies their surroundings. She can't see anyone—not a soul. And no more bodies are racing toward them, but that could change at any moment.

C'mon, girl.

Just like her dad would say.

She yells in frustration, briefly, loudly, then shuts up. She closes her eyes tight, tries to shove out pessimism, she can't deal with all this—*Can things stop, for chrissakes stop, for a minute?*

Kayla stares at her with worry.

"Grab those bins and put 'em in the truck, Kayla," she says, and the girl moves unsteadily to do so.

Without ceremony, Kevin plucks the skull shard from his shoulder, sends it spinning into the parking lot. He inspects himself. His jaw still works rhythmically, now more forcefully. He's going to need attention.

Rachel spots Kevin's handheld radio, a few feet beyond him, closer to the truck, which itself is speckled with more gore. She goes to the radio, snatches it up.

Oh no.

Its face is shattered. She finds the Power and Send buttons and tries them anyway. Nothing. She inspects the exposed innards helplessly, trying to find an easy fix, a loose wire—nothing. It's done for. She tosses it the back of the truck, looks around.

The bodies on the ground—the ones that were clamped to those trees moments ago—are decimated and have already mostly bled out. Rachel can't make sense of them, of what has happened to them. The bodies' heads have been brutally ripped from their torsos. The flesh of the shoulders and chest has disintegrated, leaving a messy, hollowed-out shell. She searches the area for the heads, but there's no sign of them. She does see what appears to be more shards of skull, as well as mushy, purple blobs of gray matter. The heads have exploded as if targeted by a high-powered weapon. Simultaneously. Someone around here is an expert shot but had no apparent regard for the safety of three survivors.

"What happened?" Kayla whines.

"I don't know," Rachel says simply. "But I know we have to get out of here. We're completely in the open. We're in danger. Again." Her voice is flat and dry, resigned. "Different shit, different day."

Kayla whimpers.

Rachel looks at her own arms and clothes, which are dotted with spots of blood and brain. A few days ago, she would've gagged at the sight, but she doesn't even pause. She lifts her shirt and finds that her right side is inflicted with cuts of all sizes. She's bleeding—not horribly but enough to need bandages. From one of the larger punctures, she withdraws a bone splinter.

"Great," she says, dropping it.

She casts wary glances in all directions, including back at the dark hospital.

"We've got everything we need in the truck. We need to get back to the library. We can take care of Kevin there."

"And you," Kayla says meekly.

As if hearing them, Kevin shouts, "We need to get back! Like now."

He twists his head to look at her, make sure she heard him, and she gives him a curt nod.

"Kayla, get in the truck. Hurry."

While the girl scurries up into the truck, Rachel kneels next to Kevin and offers herself as a crutch. He's a mess. He keeps wiping at his arms, seemingly frustrated that he can't make a dent in all that red. Rachel has never seen him tremble before.

"I can't get it off," he says loudly.

"We'll take care of you at the library!" she tries. "Keep some pressure on that shoulder. Can you hear me?"

"A little," he says after halfway reading her lips. *"Fuck!"*

"I'll drive," she says. "Let's get you in the back."

With some grunting effort, she manages to help him up.

"I think I'm concussed," he says. "Just like my football days. Fuck. I'll shake it off. Wow."

Wobbly, he digs into his front pocket and pulls out his keys, hands them over.

"It's all you, Rach."

CHAPTER 10

Rachel has Kevin's keys in her hand, and now she's simply staring at them, breathing hard. Getting him into the back was a trial. The big man was on the verge of collapsing into unconsciousness. She fears that the concussion—if that's what it is—is a bigger deal than he's making it out to be. Her only basis of comparison is the concussion Bonnie diagnosed in her father, and that took days to recover from.

She realizes that she's whisper-repeating a rather foul word.

Kayla touches her forearm. "Are we going?"

"We're definitely going."

"You can ... you can drive us back. Right?"

For the first time, Rachel notices that the truck has a manual transmission, and she lets out a mournful cry, which echoes loudly in the confines of the cab. She stops and closes her eyes.

"What?!" says Kayla. "What's wrong?"

"Everything! Why did I bring us here?"

She cranes her neck to peer back at Kevin. He's flat on his back, and his chest is still heaving up and down. His large body is splayed perpendicularly across the corrugated floor, dots of blood spotting his clothes, mostly across his right side. He's holding his skull with his hands, his teeth gritted. She can't ask him to drive in his state.

Kayla only sits there, staring out the window, with that one hand still positioned on Rachel's forearm. "It'll be fine," the girl says, quiet, desolate.

Rachel glances out at the ground next to the car. The two bodies there are a horror show, torn apart, ghastly. Blood has pooled everywhere.

"I'm sorry, honey, I don't mean to—" Rachel covers Kayla's hand with her own. "You shouldn't have to be seeing this. You shouldn't have to go through this. But we're on our way, okay?"

Rachel can see now that Kayla is turning unresponsive. There's a dried tear track down the pretty girl's cheek, right along her nose. Rachel can't take her eyes off that tiny path for a moment. It looks like a scar that will remain there for her whole life. And as she watches it, something surges inside her, stronger than anything else she's felt over the past few days.

Rachel is now Kayla's protector, as surely as if she's her legal guardian. From what the girl has told her, her family is dead. Gone. The girl is only twelve years old. There is no one left for her—except Rachel. It is now her responsibility to shield this girl from harm. For the rest of her life. As long as that might last.

Rachel feels that she took on the role of protector in the library. She immediately took the girl under her wing and calmed her down, made her feel a part of something again. Yes, but it wasn't conscious; it was an automatic big-sister thing. She didn't understand what Kayla really needed. Now, out here in the open, having narrowly avoided death yet again at the hands of one of these beasts, it's hitting home.

Rachel scans the larger area. There are no moving bodies that she can see. No gasping human-monsters. No humans with high-powered rifles. No threat.

For now.

"All right, sweetie, I need you to watch outside for any more bodies, okay? Any people, actually. But stay as far down as you can. I'm gonna figure out how to drive this damn thing. You let me know if you see anything. Anything moving. We don't want that to happen again while we're sitting here."

Rachel has Kevin's weapon now, right here in the cab, and she's not afraid to disintegrate one of those bastards while it's still at a safe distance.

The library seems much farther away now, without the radio, without Kevin driving. She thinks of Joel and Mai and the others, hopes they're all right. Has something happened at the library, too something like this? Somehow, she doubts it. The image of Felicia comes to her, standing there at the destroyed book-returns window, looking powerful despite her injuries. Protective. Safe.

As Rachel prepares to turn the key, sending out a silent prayer to whoever's listening, she wonders what *has* happened here.

Those bodies went *down*. Someone destroyed those bodies before the bodies could destroy them. Is there someone out there with an entirely more effective, violent means for dispatching these monsters? What else would explain the destruction of the immediate threat like that? Why wouldn't that someone approach their fellow survivors first, rather than putting them in danger?

And what about that latest blast from the skies? It takes a moment for Rachel to remember that the sound directly preceded whatever happened on the ground. Does it mean anything? Was this attack orchestrated from above?

Probably, if the events of the past few days have meant anything.

It's what Ron said a couple days ago, and it rings true. Whatever the case, she has to report this back to the group.

If they're still there.

She ducks her head below the steering wheel and stares at the pedals at her feet. She hears her daddy's voice, and her heart cracks, but she heeds his words.

That left pedal is the clutch. You use your left foot on that one. I guess that's obvious. The other pedals are like the ones you use in Suzy's car. Gas and brake. Stop and go. Easy. But in this car, that left pedal is super important. It's what lets you shift gears here, see?

That first driving lesson is still so vivid in her mind—mostly because it didn't take. Despite her dad's patience with her frustrated screeches and the car's endless jerky fits and starts, the manual transmission was never easy for her. The violent stalls outnumbered the smooth thrusts into gear. And at a certain point, rather than continue to attempt to master the clutch, she gave it up. Flatly refused her dad's increasingly exasperated entreaties to at least *try*. But no, she turned down his offers of further instruction in the parking lots of City Park or Rocky Mountain High School.

What she would give now for another lesson from her dad!

At the time, though, she relied on friends to drive her places. Mostly Tony.

She presses the clutch to the floor and turns the key in the ignition. The truck roars throatily to life, rumbling like exactly the kind of vehicle Kevin, not Rachel, might drive. She pauses, gathering herself.

It's Kayla, again, keeping her grounded. She smiles at the girl looking up at her and then focuses on the rattling thrum of the engine.

"Ready?" Rachel says.

"You got this." Kayla's expression sparks something almost nostalgic, as if Rachel has been given a glimpse of what this girl was like before the end of the world.

Rachel moves the gearshift into what she believes to be first gear, then carefully begins letting out the clutch and pressing the gas. She feels tension at her feet, and the truck begins to roar, and then the truck judders forward and stalls.

Damn it!

She starts again, this time managing to hiccup the truck across thirty feet of pavement before stalling out. It takes her four tries to get the vehicle into second gear, and then they're descending the pavement onto Lemay and heading north, then west, toward the library.

"Watch those neighborhoods," she says, gesturing toward the deceptively silent street of Myrtle, and then they're passing Debut Theater and approaching Mulberry. After making the wide left onto Mulberry, she peers down Cowan. She doesn't see anything, but she can feel those inverted, gaspy glares coming from all the street's shadows.

Kayla watches everything outside her window open-mouthed. On the trip to the hospital, the girl was wedged between the two grownups, and mostly looked down at her lap, but now her dark curiosity is in full effect.

"There's no one," she whispers. "It's so ... it's like a movie."

Rachel has consciously avoided passing the Udall Natural Area, where the Thompson brothers said the mob of bodies amassed and eventually flowed from, on their way to attack the library. She'll approach the library from the south instead.

She keeps the speed at a cautious 30mph, taking turns with great caution, and worrying about stalling every time she weaves between abandoned and wrecked vehicles. Every car she sees is empty, at least one door flung open—sometimes as many as four.

"Why are there so many cars like that?" Kayla says over the engine noise. The barrel of Kevin's shotgun shifts over against her thigh, and she prudently rights it, holding it to the center console. "Like, with the doors open?"

"When people changed, when they could move again, they got out of their cars and ... just left them where they were."

Kayla nods thoughtfully. "They knew how to get out."

Rachel glances over at her. "I guess so. Somehow."

"They knew how to use the doors."

"Eventually, yeah."

Rachel is unsure what Kayla is getting at, but her words only reinforce Rachel's own meager understanding of what's going on with these bodies. There's still humanity in this flesh, despite the snarling, gasping, aggressive evidence to the contrary. It's as if the longer the bodies are under the sway of whatever presence has inhabited them, the more they let go of that humanity. Early on, right after the near-corpses regained locomotion, they were at their most vulnerable but also their most human. Now, most of them are long past hope of recovery—broken, ravaged, lost.

She gives Kayla another glance.

The girl has settled back into the bench seat, as if trying to retreat from the world. She's been scared to death for days, has had to endure so much. Rachel isn't practiced at comforting little girls, but she can channel her mom. And Bonnie. It's what she's been trying to do with Kayla all along. She loosens her deathgrip on the gearshift and places her hand gently on Kayla's thigh.

"We'll be okay," she says. "Just like you said, we got this. Right?"

Rachel tries for an encouraging glance but notices that Kayla's lower lip is trembling again. She's trying so hard to keep it together. Then Kayla mouths something that Rachel can't hear. Her brow is furrowed in fear.

"What?" Rachel asks.

"I want my mama," the girl says, barely audible.

"Me too, honey."

Kayla responds with a quick wet glance.

"I lost my mom a long time ago," Rachel barely whispers. "It was the hardest thing ever, in the whole world." Her vision blurs only for a moment, then she focuses on the road again, concentrating on the wide, mostly deserted expanse of Mulberry. "She just … *left*. It wasn't fair."

"She died?" Kayla's words tremble in her mouth.

Rachel nods. "Five years ago."

Kayla sniffs. "My dad went away five years ago."

"I'm so sorry, Kayla."

"He didn't die, he went away. I don't know where he went. One day he drove away and he didn't come back."

Maybe that's even worse, Rachel thinks. Worse than the agony of a dying parent must be a parent who abandons you and is then forever a dark mystery in your life, surrounded by anger and loss.

Kayla brings her knees quickly up, wraps her arms around them, shuts her eyes.

Rachel can see a new pulse of anger behind that closed-off face—a little-girl mirror image of her own. Perhaps Kayla didn't want to say what she said about wanting her mom, and now she's upset with herself that the words came out. Rachel understands the feeling, and it breaks her heart a little. The girl doesn't want to show youth or weakness. Now Kayla glances away as if ashamed. Rachel doesn't know what else to say. All she can do is squeeze Kayla's leg with some kind of reassurance.

Finally: "I know you miss your mom, honey. I miss my daddy."

Kayla sniffs, then nods quickly, her little head bobbing against her knees.

Rachel tries to find some appropriate words. This is what *she's* not good at. "What's she like, your mom?"

A sour look crosses the girl's face. "She's like … them."

Rachel feels stupid. "Before that, Kayla, I mean before all this."

"I don't know," she says, and Rachel can sense she's letting terrible memories overshadow everything. How can she blame the girl? But then Kayla says, "She tucks me in. She reads me stories. Books from the library."

The truck weaves through more collisions along Mulberry. Rachel keeps her eyes on the neighborhoods to their left and right, waiting for any signs of pursuit. So far, there are none.

"I know this doesn't help right now, but I'm not leaving you, okay? You and me, we're a team. And it's going to stay that way."

Kayla considers her.

"Okay." The word is barely a whisper.

Just as Rachel is beginning to calm down, cautiously optimistic about her driving, she's forced to slow down for a triple collision that's partially blocking the road at the intersection of Mulberry and Stover. Her attention is too focused on the silent homes crouching in long rows to the south—the splintered evergreens in their yards, the vehicles eerily abandoned with their doors hanging open, and what appears to be three distant bodies on the asphalt. She comes to a near-stop, forgetting about the clutch, and the truck stalls, coasting minutely.

"Oh crap."

She turns the key without the clutch, and a grinding sound assaults the cab.

Rachel lets out a little scream and lets the key slip from her grasp. "What did I do, what did I do?" Then she remembers the clutch. "Oh."

She's about to try again when Kayla grabs her shoulder.

"Look." The girl points out Rachel's window.

Rachel follows Kayla's gaze and sees three bodies barely visible at the base of a huge Douglas fir, perhaps forty feet away. The tree's lower branches have been snapped mercilessly to the side, and the bodies, two women and a teenage boy, are emerging like giant crabs from the trunk, which is stripped clean of bark. One of the women is wearing the sky-blue shreds of a nightgown like a tattered cape; the rest of her body is doughy and filthy. The other woman's jeans and red blouse are stretched and torn and sticky with sap, her feet black with dirt and angled impossibly, the toes obviously broken. And the poor boy is wearing only his white briefs; he appears positively alien in his human skin, the limbs askew, the movement jerky but somehow naturalized, the gait alien but confident. All three faces, upside-down and blood-ravaged, glare at them with singular menace.

"Can we go?" Kayla cries plaintively.

"Yes."

Rachel stomps the clutch and turns the key. The engine catches. Her knees are actually shaking. She can't do it. She hardly moves the clutch at all, and the truck leaps forward and stalls.

"*Crap!*"

"They're coming. They're closer. Rachel?"

Rachel snaps her gaze in their direction. The bodies are crawling off the curb and into the bike lane, and they're screeching at her from their ragged throats.

From the back, Kevin startles them. *We should—ow fuck—we should be going!*

"I'm trying!"

Rachel tries again, stalls.

The things on the street suddenly begin to gallop, and a spike of fear stabs her chest. Kayla emits a sharp whine.

The bodies are hardly even human anymore. In the split second before all three of them leap at the truck, Rachel sees tatters of bright clothing on their hideously distorted limbs, sees alien rage on their faces.

Then they're in the air.

"Duck!" Rachel screams, grabbing at Kayla's head and bringing her down onto the seat.

The triple explosions shatter the safety glass, showering Rachel's lap and shoulder with tiny fragments and beads. The world goes muffled once more. She stays on top of Kayla, her eyes tightly shut. There's something hot and wet on her face, and Rachel lets out a helpless, prolonged moan of revulsion. She wipes at it in a frenzy. It's gray matter. She holds her breath for fifteen seconds before her mind moves beyond hysterical nausea.

"Are you all right?" Rachel asks, sitting up and scanning all directions.

Everything is painted red, glistening.

What is doing that?

Kayla nods slowly, portions of her own hair and skin dotted with gore. She stares at Rachel's face and grimaces.

"You're—"

"Those things were attacking us!" Kevin shouts from the back. "They exploded!"

"I know." Rachel cranes her neck to look back into the truck bed. "You all right back there?"

"Oh, peachy." He gives her a bloody thumbs-up. "Can we please get the hell out of here? Those fuckers are all active again!"

"Well, how are they—?"

"We'll figure that out later, c'mon, let's go!"

She carefully starts the truck and manages to get it moving, jerking its bulk only a few times. Rachel doesn't even consider glancing back at the destroyed bodies in the street. Her heart pumps in a slow, hard syncopation. Her jaw is set.

It's getting bad again, isn't it?

Kayla peers through the rear window, eyes darting. Her trembling left hand keeps swiping at her face.

"I thought … I thought after what happened at the library … that it would be over." She sniffs. "It was supposed to be done. No more."

The attack at the library is still a jumble of images in Rachel's mind, and it hardly feels real. The survivors established a stronghold even mightier than the hospital, and somehow those monsters organized and pounced. As one.

As one organism.

They surrounded the entire library, folding over it like an organic blanket, pressing in, smothering, suffocating. Melting in thick-paned windows with the force inside their skulls, crawling through, and stabbing their infected heads at the exhausted survivors. And the monsters … they had all but won. They had beaten the ragtag crew, which could only await the inevitable in the crimson darkness. And then … what?

Fortunes changed. Did her father really save them? She has a strong feeling that Kevin is right: Although he certainly helped—maybe even turned the tide—something more powerful was at play.

Felicia.

The way the young woman stood there in the window, staring out. The feeling in Rachel's gut that it was Felicia whom the bodies were scurrying away from. Not so much the weak survivors with their tiny capsules of blood or their all-but-empty supply of O-negative blood or their remaining blood darts, but Felicia.

The one who turned.

They need to get back to Felicia. She should have attended to her right then; she should have found her and helped her.

"I won't lie to you, Kayla, it's not over." She returns her hand to the gearshift knob and changes gears to third, picking up speed for a fairly long stretch of empty road. "But we can't get pessimistic. Do you know what that means?"

"Huh-uh."

"It means we can't think the worst is gonna happen."

"But that's all that's happening!"

"I know … I know," Rachel says, scrambling. "But we're alive, right? We're still alive."

"Not all of us."

Kayla's words are starting to hurt, so Rachel shuts up for a moment. Then, she says, "I think we're gonna beat those things."

"What do you mean?"

"I mean, I think they're scared. Even more scared than us. I saw it at the library. I think what we just saw? I think that means they're desperate. They're scared of us, and they're desperate. They're trying everything they can."

"They can still kill us!"

"Not if we're careful. We have answers now."

"It's like every time we think of some answers, they do something different."

"Well," Rachel says, making the turn north onto Peterson, "I think they're running out of things to try."

Kayla watches her doubtfully, then scoots over, lifting her rail-thin legs onto the seat, and lets herself fall against Rachel. Her head rests against her shoulder. She doesn't say anything.

"I'll keep you safe," Rachel repeats. The words come out confidently enough.

She feels Kayla's nod. "I know."

Rachel clutches the steering wheel, crossing Magnolia. Her eyes are already on the library property, two blocks up on the left. From this distance, she sees no evidence of the traumatic attack. But as she gets to Olive, she begins to see the scrapes along the asphalt and on the curbs and concrete leading to the library—blood and sap and, when she looks closely at the ground to her left, what appears to be skin. She didn't pay attention to any of this when Kevin whisked them away earlier. She was in shock. But now it's all too obvious.

When the bodies came, they came from the east along a few avenues—between homes, circuitously along alleys—not only that inconceivable wall of monstrous humanity that flowed directly toward the library on Oak. She shudders to think what the asphalt of Oak looks like.

Perched on the edge of her seat, Kayla watches the library come at them.

"Do you see anyone?" she whispers.

Rachel shakes her head.

There are broken trees and trampled hedges leading toward the main entrance. The scene suggests vehicles running rampant over the landscaping, but Rachel knows it was the infected human bodies. Now, the way is clear except for the evidence of their passing. As she gets closer, she can see the hundreds of corpses that lay in mounds against the exterior library walls, spreading out onto the grounds, dotting the lawns to the north and south. Then the front of the library looms directly ahead of them.

Joel is apparently still away with Pete's truck, but the Hummer remains parked to the left of the entrance, along with two more vehicles from Ron's group.

Rachel manages to keep the truck running as she bumps over the curb and onto the lawn, weaving between bodies.

"Keep watching for anything that might hurt us," she says to Kayla.

"Uh huh."

But no further creatures approach. And why would they? This is the site of the things' largest defeat. When those human monsters were improbably turned back earlier this afternoon, the fear in their eyes was plain to see. They wouldn't come back here. At least, that's Rachel's hope.

Even before she glimpses any survivors, she's thinking again of Felicia.

And it's exactly at that moment when she sees the young woman back at the open and mangled maw of the book-returns area, staring out, as if awaiting Rachel's arrival.

CHAPTER 11

In a dark daze, Felicia half-watches Kevin, Rachel, and the little girl drive away in the old truck, across the battered lawn, off the curb, and onto the asphalt, on their way to the hospital. She's locked onto their tangled mindsets—extreme stress, echoes of fear, dread of a place that is already bursting with dark recollections. She thinks she can even catch snippets of their vocal conversation, but really it's the thoughts that lead to the words.

—*Kayla on the edge of shock, ready to fall into a nightmare sleep in childlike withdrawal from the horrors, her mind frantic with recent jags of imagery, and trying to shut them out by conjuring the face of her mother ...*

The images fading as the truck draws away.

—*Rachel experiencing similar flittering images, jerking away from them, comforting the girl, it's all about keeping the girl strong, even as Daddy is gone, Daddy is gone, how can he be—*

Their thoughts silencing with more distance.

—*and one last glimpse of Kevin's blunt thoughts as he begins to navigate the vehicle, watching the dash indicators, not letting the horrors and implications of the library attack distract him from his current purpose, thinking and not thinking of Michael and what he did, my god, this girl lost her fath—*

And gone.

The truck disappears from sight, and Felicia finds that she can't move. The cries and screams of the dying and maimed bombard her head, but that's only the beginning. If she directs her thoughts, she can discern each individual person's stream of consciousness, and every one of them is a study in confusion and agony. The scale is bewildering.

Her human instinct is to fall to the ground, curl into a ball, and wrap her arms around her head, but she's compelled to let all of the voices in. She feels the stain of her infection, a heat in the center of her head, and satisfying that heat requires that she absorb everything. As if these mindsets are part of her.

How is she seeing these things?

Beyond the horrific sights and sounds around her, it's the question that has absorbed her pain-wracked existence since she regained her humanity. She knows she is in the process of shedding her infection, much like a snake skin—she can feel the sticky residue of it, the organic warmth, it's still a part of her, but bits of it are falling away. Other parts of this thing that happened to her—they've remained very much a part of her, but they are changing, right along with the humanity that is seeping back. Almost as if it's altering her DNA, as if she can feel the strands twisting in new ways, in new directions. At times she imagines this new twist as some kind of instant evolution of her psychology. At other times … a mutation.

Her perspective keeps changing in that respect.

She has strong, tactile memories of her thoughts under infection. The way her thoughts threaded with those of the former humans in her vicinity. One of those had been Janet. Her mind melding with that of her boss, but in a way that ignored the soul that had previously inhabited the body. They had shared the same objective, and it was an all-consuming image of the nutrient, the chemical abnormality, the cellular aberration in the trees. They had also shared the consciousness of whatever it was that inhabited them, but at a remove. Ghost images, hard-wired and low. Insectile, clicking, tendril-wrapped.

When humanity had returned, she'd cried out not only in physical agony but also in inner tumult, losing—for the most part—that soul-deep connection with the rest of the inhabited. Although that sensation is reluctantly and slowly fading, she knows the experience of it will stay with her forever.

And in fact it is staying with her—and mutating into something else.

Her mind has been forever altered.

Synapses have fired along new neural pathways, and a new ability has manifested itself in a previously unused corner of her consciousness.

She can see inside not only the minds of the infected, but also the minds of the survivors.

Right now, however, she's surrounded by the agony of infected souls who have, like her, returned to humanity. She sighs, stands tall, lets her arms drift back, away from her body. Her head falls to her chest, and she lets the web of souls entangle her, not resisting. The voices coalesce into a screaming entreaty, and she pushes out, tentatively, with the intent to heal.

The screams subside dramatically, for only a moment, and then they slowly rise to their former strength, perhaps louder.

Felicia doesn't know what to do, how to help—or even if she should. She feels caught between two worlds.

The dazed survivors move in fits and starts, not knowing how to react to the deaths that have befallen them. Most of them are in the vicinity of Bonnie's body, in the south hall. A mere half hour ago, Felicia sensed the woman's lifeforce snuffed out, shortly before the end, before Michael leaped into the abyss toward his own demise. Felicia can feel the survivors' collective consciousness desperately trying to makes sense of the loss.

—oh no!—

—fucking Christ—

—not Bonnie! —

—oh my God—

And Scott on the periphery, burning brightly with high emotion, chewing the flesh on the inside of his cheeks, staring, but away from the bodies, any of the bodies, his mind aflame, refusing to accept this outcome—

—she didn't do that for me, she shouldn't have done that, impossible, it was an accident, a horrible accident, I didn't cause this, this isn't my fault, I didn't do that to her, she did that herself—

Before long, they're moving Bonnie's body, reverently, to a quiet corner, covering it with a brown blanket found upstairs in the staff area. Felicia doesn't know how she knows that without seeing them do it, but the knowledge is there. The sounds of despair—particularly from the young woman, for whom Bonnie had quickly become a mother figure—mingle with the agony of the turned bodies, which number in the hundreds. A number that is falling as, one by one, they succumb to their injuries. Even after the pain of the bloodchange, the return to humanity, they're dealing with much worse physical damage than she herself experienced locked in the storeroom. Much worse. In many cases, the wounds are horrific enough that death is inevitable.

The turned bodies see her, just as they recognized her at the end of the assault. They watched her with fear—she felt that. What is the emotion with which they're watching her now?

She senses souls winking out in her vicinity, and she's frozen in not only indecision but in pain. Her body is still rigid with it, despite the dwindling supply of pain relievers. All she can do is stand there, bombarded.

Joel and Ron are behind her then, raiding supplies, seeing where they stand after the assault. She feels Joel's eyes on her back, senses him studying her.

"How long will they take?" It's Ron's voice, and the young man's mind is filled with a shaky determination.

"You know where the hospital is, right? It's only about ten minutes away, and the streets are clear. Shouldn't take long."

"Is it a good idea, sending them out there? Letting that girl go?"

"Now's the right time. Those things aren't paying attention. And Rachel can take care of herself. I hope. And that kid, too."

"They're armed?"

"Yes."

"Not much left here," Ron says, opening the mini fridge. "In fact, pretty much nothing. I hope they're quick and nothing happens."

"Bring what we've got, let's do what we can. Get stuff to the girls."

"Roger that."

"Treatable inside, untreatable outside."

"Makes sense."

"We take and hour or two to treat who we can, and then we get the hell out of here before nightfall."

"Leave?" Ron radiates alarm like heat.

"This place is fucked—I mean, come on, you seriously want to stay here now? Look around. It's a warzone, and completely indefensible."

"We beat 'em here, we held 'em back."

"If they try again, we won't have the same luck."

A pause, then Ron says, "You're probably right."

They're on their way back out into the lobby area.

"We can bring Brian in here," Ron says.

At the mention of the man's name, Felicia searches, searches, and finds Brian in the south hall, on his back, Rick doing chest compressions and Bill checking the man's sweaty neck for a pulse. She can even sense Brian's mind—

—*jags of memory in nightmare flashes, bodies squeezing through gaps, gasping, and flitting further out to include his estranged son, anger there, vague, shouting, and damn if there isn't a bright light, something physiological, something inner rather than outer, resonating and rising from within, and the glimpse of it*—

—shocks Felicia out of Brian's mind, as if the light yanked at her, pulled at her innards. She knows that Brian is not going to survive.

Joel is directly in front of her, staring at her.

"You with us?" he barks.

"I'm ... here."

"Can you help?"

"I ... can try."

"How do you feel?"

She swallows, watching his eyes. They're like lasers boring into her. Behind those eyes, his methodical cop mind is thinking three steps ahead, like a hard-trained chess player, visualizing the layout of the library, anticipating where the rest of the survivors are, gauging the remaining threat and what kind of defensive tactics are available to them, as well as how much time they have. He has so much poise. He's strategizing about obtaining more weapons and going on the offensive now that the survivors seem to have the advantage. She wonders if he knows how they obtained that advantage. Does he believe that matters?

"I—I think the worst of it is over. It hurts, but I can manage it."

"Come on then."

She follows him out of the room and into the lobby.

Although she felt the turmoil occurring from the other room, she's stunned by what she sees. Bodies everywhere, most destroyed by rifle fire but many turned back to humanity by blood, tranq darts still lodged in their flesh, their screams adding up to an agonized roar. As they sense Felicia approaching, a relative hush fills the room, and the survivors pause in their frantic movements to determine its cause. They end up eyeing Felicia as she passes among them, just as many of those who have been turned back watch her with straining eyes before they resume their cries. Then everyone is in motion again.

"Girls, can you use Felicia?" Joel calls to the twins, Chloe and Zoe.

"Yeah, yeah!"

The young women are sweaty, bloody, shell-shocked, but they're absorbed in their task: looking for turned bodies that might have a chance at surviving. In the immediate aftermath of the assault—as the infected bodies began to retreat—these two went into emergency medical mode, searching for those they might coax fully back to humanity.

Joel goes off to his next task, and Felicia is left facing Zoe, who looks at her with wariness and exhaustion. Behind her red-rimmed eyes lies a controlled chaos—she's taking each moment as it happens.

"We're bringing bodies here, along this wall, see? You don't have to worry about that part, but when we bring them in, can you help us search the bodies for any bleeding wounds we missed? Use the towels there. Over there. That's all we have, so give pressure to what you can …"

Felicia nods. "Okay."

Then Zoe is gone, leaving a trail of jagging stress-thoughts and the sweet-sour odor of drying blood and body odor. Felicia sees Chloe out in the hot afternoon sun, sifting through the bodies, stopping at the ones that still move. Just as Felicia turns back to the small collection of bodies to the left of the checkout area, Ron whisks past, his mind seeking Liam.

Felicia closes her eyes, trying to find herself amid the commotion. She feels her body easing to the ground, her knees touch carpet, and she bears the brunt of human and alien voices battering her consciousness. What does she remember? She needs to focus on something.

Nicole!

What happened to her? Where is she? She experiences an alarming moment when she can't conjure her lover's face, or the sound of her voice, and she begins to shake. The voices threaten to overtake her mind, but she pushes them out and grabs at Nicole's memory—

—of lying next to her staring at the ceiling, touching here and there, talking about whatever, reminiscing about very different childhoods, laughing, singing off-key, listening to the oscillating fan sweep the room, trying on each other's clothes, dreaming of travel, the future, the future—

"Here's one!"

A new body drops next to her, a young boy to add to the several men and middle-aged women already here. His high voice is screeching like an animal squawk, and when he settles into place, he stops his braying noise, staring up into her face. He feels his inner exclamation—

You!

Caught between human and alien, caught between fear and gratitude. Then, as with the others, the pain clouds everything, and he's screaming again. But his mindset is there, anchored. His name is Perry. His strongest thought is of his dad—

—waiting that morning before the sun came up, because they were supposed to get up early and go fishing at the pond north of the city, their favorite fishing hole. He had his new, bigger tackle box ready, and all his worms writhing in the bucket, and he even got up before dawn all on his own, he was so excited. And every once in a while he poked his head into his parents' room and listened to his dad snore, waiting for the sun to rise, and when the sky began to brighten he did shake his dad's shoulder, and his dad stirred and grunted, and then—

Red.

Felicia looks down into the boy's pleading eyes. Can she help him? She feels him fading. The twins might not have seen it, because his limbs appear to be intact. His youth makes him appear more viable. But she knows he is close to death. His expression is wet with bloody tears, and he opens his mouth as if to speak, and that's when Felicia sees that his lips are torn, his teeth shredded from his mouth, his tongue a writhing stump. His throat is choked with pulpy, gargling blood. Pale and delirious, he faints away and succumbs.

She yanks herself from him, openly crying. Summoning strength to work past the pain of movement, she lifts him up and carries him outside to the growing line of corpses.

There are piles of struggling bodies outside, mostly crammed against the library's exterior walls, and she tries to close her mind to their pleas. Once afraid of her, they now see her as salvation. Why? What can she do for them? They grab at her in a final effort to cling to life—they grab with their dislocated limbs with their minds, reaching out psychically as part of the torn web of souls, tugging at her.

Felicia staggers, squinting. She hasn't been outside in days. The library grounds are sun-baked, sweltering. To her right, Joel and Ron are working at something inside a truck, and it takes only a moment for Felicia to understand that they're wrestling with a large body. The dead man is Jeff Thompson—a travesty of broken flesh. In a flash, Felicia can see what happened to him, the malicious bodies shoving their way through the cab on their way to the library doors and windows, crushing him, stabbing at him.

Jeff's twin brother Pete is standing at a distance, both watching and not watching. He's twitching with grief and anger while Joel and Ron move the body solemnly, talking strategy. Felicia can sense they're about to leave. They intend to determine whether the truck is drivable so that they can gather arms from the SWAT truck at the police station.

To her left, Chloe screams, *"Here! Here!"*

Rick goes zipping past her to help.

Felicia feels dizzy. She turns slowly back to the library, overwhelmed by the voices crashing into her. She needs to focus them, deal with them individually, and help however she can.

Just as she re-enters through the doors, she catches sight of Mai in the north hallway, beyond the book-returns area. Mai freezes as if caught committing a crime. Felicia stops, meets her gaze. Mai's mind opens to her effortlessly, almost like a scent, a hot odor singeing in Felicia's sinus cavity—

—could leave through that window and nobody would notice, could jet around the corner and be gone, grab a car and get the fuck out of here, shoulda done that from the start, and why the hell is she staring at me, freaky bitch, what are you looking at? And anyway, fuck her, I can sneak away and no one's the wiser, I can make it on my own, those things are on the run, I can go home, get my shit, and drive east, see what I find, there's no trees out that way, they don't want anything out there, maybe I'll find more people alive, sensible people who aren't into barricading themselves in a place that has a thousand giant windows, for fuck's sake—

As Mai is about to turn away, Felicia gestures toward her, catching her attention. Mai pauses, watches her curiously.

Felicia shakes her head—

No. Don't go.

—and pushes out with her consciousness, stirring Mai's mindscape. Mai stares, opens her mouth, then closes it. She disappears from view.

Felicia isn't entirely sure what she's done. Mai's personality is so strong that her thoughts appeared vivid and urgent to her. Or perhaps it was only proximity and focus. Felicia swallows hard, painfully, as she turns back to the bodies at the checkout area.

Chloe brings in another one, a teenaged female, naked, broken.

"See if you can help her," Chloe says. "I don't see much bleeding on this one. Check her mouth." She sets the body down carefully on the carpet, but the girl cries out harshly.

Felicia nods at Chloe, already focusing, and Chloe rushes away, out the door.

The girl's name is Abby, she can discern that as if it's written across her flesh in blood. Abby's mind latches on to Felicia's, smoothly though desperately, in confusion—there's an awareness that they're both still attuned to the strangers' web of souls, that they've retained this vital thing, and they're unsure how to use it as humans. They communicate this awareness in a mere sliver of a moment.

Abby shares something in common with the other three bodies lying in a row along this wall. Felicia looks down the row. A young man named Jake, staring at her with wet eyes, his hot breath moving quickly in hyperventilation, his face hastily bandaged. A girl called Sofia, eyes tightly closed, dealing with her pain. A boy named Oliver, also watching her, his mouth open, sap and splinters smeared across his forehead, his unruly hair stiffened into bloody stalagmites.

They're all young.

It's a common denominator that makes sense. Their bodies are more resilient, their bones and muscles more malleable. They stand the best chance of surviving what the strangers have done to them. But they're not superhuman, particularly when it comes to the vulnerable flesh of the mouth and throat. To say nothing of the stomach.

At that moment, Abby vomits up a great gush of bloody green mulch, coughing it out onto the carpet, her eyes letting loose a stream of tears.

Their mindscapes join in a chorus of—

—*Help me!*—

—and Felicia is all tentative gestures and indecision. What can she do? Why are they looking at her like this? She takes one of the towels—swiped from the staff room upstairs—and uses it to wipe Abby's face, taking care of the abraded lips. The girl is shaking and wide-eyed with pain. They don't share any words, but—

—*what happened? why did this happen to me? where's my mommy? who are you? WHO ARE YOU?*—

—Abby's frightened little soul blares at her, pure, simple, innocent. She can barely move her limbs. It's too much. Felicia stumbles backward as the young people stare at her. Their mindscapes are a clamor of hope and fear; they're caught between infected and eradicated, suffering the effects of both and not knowing who to blame or turn to. Felicia can't make sense of what she's sensing. There's too much to process.

She stands, steadies herself on the counter.

A hundred souls are shouting at her, and a hundred more are succumbing, facing a bitter, confusing demise. She watches them, one at a time, wink out like fireflies, their husks left strangled and shattered. Felicia has a dream-like conception of the web of souls she experienced while infected, and this is an atrocious parody of that, a web filled with clotting blood and screams. She pushes back at the fusillade of agonized voices, and then she's running back to the book-returns room.

"Felicia!" calls Zoe, arriving with a new body—a young man, straining and screeching. "Wait!"

But Felicia can't take it anymore, at least not yet. The pain in her joints and muscles and bones is growing again, and she reaches blindly for the bottle of Tylenol atop the fridge as she rushes past. She finds her corner of the room and tumbles to a fetal position, desperately swallowing five pills. She grinds her teeth, thunderstruck by the sensory overload.

Everything goes bleary.

The chaos continues around her, but they leave her alone. Or she won't let them in. She doesn't even know which is true.

Nicole! I need you!

Nicole is the only person she would let in right now. Where is she? What happened to her? She wants desperately to be with her. Did she survive? Is she still at their apartment, sleeping?

Felicia pushes tentatively outward with her mind, searching for Nicole. She feels as if she can sense her out there in Fort Collins, if only she could search in the right direction. She pushes outward farther, straining, seeing nothing. Tears stream down her cheek onto the carpet.

Help me! she whispers inwardly, echoing the bodies in the lobby, the bodies she herself can't help. Or won't.

It's a half hour later when she stirs from a ragged sleep and opens gritty eyes. People are still screaming, but not as many. Regret and shame burst through her, a blast of cold through her limbs. She swallows heavily, then struggles to her feet. She makes her way to the melted-out window and stares out at the library grounds. Survivors are still hurrying about their tasks, and Felicia catches sight of Mai, helping Liam. For a moment, their eyes meet, and Mai pauses, eyebrows knitted, as if considering a puzzle, and then she bends again to her task. Joel has taken Ron and Pete to the police station.

Fewer voices are bombarding Felicia now, and there's a sense of relief there, despite the fact that it means more death. She shakes her head, feeling a self-loathing as she acknowledges the relief.

Something occurs to her, and she snaps her attention southeast.

Rachel is coming back.

Something has happened. She senses Kevin in pain.

She steps to the shattered glass and peers out, one hand clutching the thick metal window frame. The truck is not in view yet, but she feels it coming, feels Rachel struggling with the transmission, feels her determination amidst fear and loss. And Kayla's.

CHAPTER 12

"Look at that," Rachel says, beholding the face of the library again.

It's a new perspective on the site of the survivors' last stand, and it remains a landscape of human agony. As she gets closer, she can hear the screams of the blood-converted—anguished and throaty and desperate. The mountain of bodies that Rachel remembers from the end of the assault has been diminished. Most of the bodies—the dead ones—have been dragged out of the way. She can tell they've been dragged by the vivid blood paths on the concrete leading away from the front doors. There's blood everywhere, reminding her of those final moments at the hospital a few days ago.

Rachel angles Kevin's truck to the right, avoiding the bodies still dotting the library grounds, and she acknowledges that Joel has moved her father's body. She can't see her dad, and for that she exhales her relief, then quickly looks away to the right and spots Felicia, who is staring in her direction, arms rigid at her sides, her posture unmoving. As she watches, Felicia's gaze moves toward the sky. Rachel cranes her neck to look upward through the windshield, sees only great clouds of smoke and what appears to be crimson atmospheric lightning.

What are you seeing? she wonders.

There are other survivors still hurrying about. A sort of triage scenario has taken effect, and now Rachel can see that at least a couple dozen corpses have been lined up along the library perimeter in the shade. Scott, all red-faced exhaustion, is hauling a body out through the library's main doors, toward a spot to the left. Mai is running in the opposite direction with what appears to be blood-soaked towels hanging from her fists. Liam is wading through the remaining mountain of bodies, apparently still looking for survivors. He is caked with both fresh and dried blood. Rachel thinks he's been crying.

He turns his head and spots her, gives a relieved wave with a dirty brown hand. He calls out to the others inside the library, gestures toward the truck.

Rachel pulls the truck in next to the Hummer and lets it stall. Her head falls briefly against the wheel, and she closes her eyes for a moment. A relieved tear squeezes out, slides down her cheek. She wipes at it, then looks to the right, toward Felicia again.

Felicia is back at the blown-out window of the book-returns area—eerily reminiscent of how she looked in the immediate wake of the attack. It's a strange sight, Felicia standing there, overseeing everything, as if challenging the state of the world. It's oddly disquieting, but there's something else there, too. Rachel feels it strongly. What is it?

Is it safety that Rachel feels?

It is. The reality of Felicia there—it makes Rachel feel safe.

"What is she looking at?" Kayla says, also trying to peer up through the windshield to see if something new is happening in the heavens, something they haven't seen before. But it's the same alien unrest.

"That's what I want to know." Rachel unfastens her seatbelt, cranes her neck to peer back at Kevin in the flatbed.

The big man appears sweaty and irritated but more awake and aware. He offers a half-hearted grin etched with pain.

"C'mon, let's get him taken care of," Rachel says.

Just as the two young women jump down from the truck—Kayla following Rachel out the driver's side—Scott and Liam come jogging their way. Scott, in the lead, offers a weak nod. He's obviously exhausted, his drenched red hair matted, his freckles standing out like pinprick wounds. None of the survivors have had much sleep in the past five days since everything began, but Scott has gone through his own hell.

"What have you got for us?" Liam says with something approaching desperation. "Whatever it is, we need it all."

The young man seems to have aged ten years since she met him a few days ago, when they all congregated at the library and hashed out a survival plan. He was still young and cocky then, a fresh survivalist shocked by everything that had transpired, but now he's been beaten down—exhausted, sleepless, nearly broken. His eyes are red, smeared, glassy.

"I'm swimming in supplies," Kevin says from the back. "It's all covered with blood, but hell, we're used that that."

"Did something—?"

"Kevin's hurt," Rachel says. "Concussed, I think, and shrapnel wounds."

"What happened?"

"I don't know, something new."

"Someone shot at us," Kevin calls. He tries to lift himself over the side of the truck bed. "Or tossed a grenade. That's all I can figure."

"Hey, slow down, man," Liam says, heading toward Kevin, who is gripping the truck's side wall as if to jump down to the ground. "Lemme give you a hand."

Scott joins in, opening the tailgate and lending an arm. Rachel has never seen him so quiet. Supplies are everywhere, spotted with dirt and bloody grime, making it seem as if Rachel careened and bounced recklessly back to the library.

"Attacked you?" Liam says.

"Some kind of attack, I don't know." Kevin winces through pain, his arms now draped over Liam's and Scott's shoulders. He's still working his jaw as if trying to pop his ears. "I'm fuzzy on that."

"What time is it?" Rachel asks. "How long till sunset?"

Liam looks confused for a moment, then checks his watch. "Almost 5:30. I think we have a couple hours."

Rachel enlists Kayla in quickly collecting the supplies and throwing what they can into postal bins. Rachel catches the girl peering off in the direction of the home, across the desolate street, that she shared with her mother.

"So, the attack, was it right after—?" Liam starts.

"Right after sky split apart again?" Kevin says. "Yeah."

"Well, we heard the same thing here—how could we not?—but it was a big nothing," Liam says. "No change in behavior that we could see. No attack. I wonder if Joel saw anything."

"And it was, like, coordinated—something killed those two things," Rachel says. "Expertly. And not only those, but a couple more on our way back."

"Did you get a look at anybody?" Liam asks. "I mean, did you see any movement around you? Cars, other people …? Something from above?"

Rachel jumps down from the truck bed, shaking her head, helping Kayla down.

"It just … happened," Kayla offers.

"Yep," Kevin manages. "Outta nowhere."

The group moves as quickly as they can toward the open, blasted front doors of the library, near which a few dozen bodies still lay piled, splayed, destroyed, some groaning, feeble, decimated. When Rachel glances to the right, she sees that Felicia has receded back into the library.

"What's the story here?" Rachel asks no one in particular. "What can we do?"

"Joel took Ron and Pete to his station to collect ammo," Liam says.

"He left not long after you did."

Rachel visualizes the sheriff's department. It's closer than the hospital, across College off of Mountain. In her previous life, she'd driven by the station frequently, almost every time she went to Old Town in Tony's car.

As they enter the lobby, Rachel is struck by the stinking humidity and the moans. Here is the hellborne chorus, mournful and anguished. As her eyes adjust, she can see that the entire lobby has become a makeshift emergency room, burdened with death. Lined up against the checkout counters are some young survivors, their bodies small and relatively unscathed. But corpses are still mashed along the east walls in piles, their limbs crooked, their faces frozen in outsized expressions of anger or fear, their skin thrashed and sticky with sap and splinters.

"*Jesus,*" Rachel whispers.

The still-living bodies are in extreme pain, writhing and gasping, and her heart plunges. She immediately regrets every spare moment she took in her journey to the hospital and back, every pause, every stall of the truck. These suffering people, the living corpses for whom they've used O-negative blood to expel the alien parasite, are human again, but in no way are they in the clear. Most are hideously damaged.

Liam grimaces at the scene, as if seeing it for the first time through Rachel's eyes. "There are more dying than living, and I don't envy those who might make it."

Kayla drops her postal bin and breaks from Rachel, sprinting off toward the north end of the library—where Rachel found her days ago.

"Kayla!" she calls, but stops herself.

She knows where Kayla is going, and she can't blame her. She watches her run, disappearing around a corner. Her footfalls dissipate, and eventually a door slams shut.

"Poor kid," Liam says, hobbling a little under Kevin's weight, still supporting him with Scott. "Will she be all right?"

"Yeah, let's give her some time. I'll check on her after a while."

"She handle the hospital okay?"

"Like a trouper." Rachel takes up Kayla's bin, moves both bins to the floor next to the checkout area. "What else?"

"I'm working with Scott and Mai and the twins to help whoever we can," Liam says. "Also, Rick and Bill. But those bodies we injected … the ones that turned back … they're dropping like flies. I think Joel tried to get Felicia involved, to help them out, but she's still too weak. She couldn't handle it. They're in so much pain, and we can't do anything. It's horrible. They're dying. Best we can do is give them some pain relief. The worst cases, we're lining those up outside. Viable bodies are inside."

Viable bodies.

Rachel catches sight of Mai hurrying through the library toward the book-returns area. The poor woman is working at top speed. Rachel knows she's about to join her in that task, and she's going to have to convince this poor kid clutched to her side to pitch in.

"Is Felicia okay?"

"I think so." He gestures. "I think it's tough for her somehow. Last I saw her, she was lying there in that little room, obviously in pain. I think she *wants* to help. She's getting there."

"I want to talk to her."

"Let's put Kevin over there," Liam says, gesturing toward the checkout area, where Rachel counts seven bodies, covered with makeshift bandages—break-room towels, mostly—shaking with wide-eyed agony.

The twins are there, wiping blood from the floor, preparing another area for more potential survivors. They look up, weary but eager to get their hands on the medication they've needed for the past hour. They rise as Liam and Scott maneuver Kevin across a tiled floor that is streaked brown with dried blood.

"Get the rest of those supplies," Liam calls back to Rachel, "and we'll patch him up."

Mai is suddenly next to Rachel, bloody rags hanging off her forearms. She manages to pick up Kayla's bin and rifle through it. She's been crying, although it's clear she's trying to hide it. It's not difficult to see the paths of tears through splotches of dried blood on her face.

"You made it," Mai says.

"Barely," Rachel replies as the twins descend on the postal bins. "We got every pain reliever we could find. Only a couple packs of morphine, but lots of other stuff that should help." She doesn't give Scott a significant glance here, but the urge is there. "Lots of cortisone and such. Creams. Wraps, splints. Two boxes over there, and a bunch more in the truck. Give me a hand with the rest, will you?"

"Yeah." Mai glances at Kevin. You all right, dude?"

"Never better," Kevin says, letting his head fall to the floor.

"Got a big box handy?" Rachel asks Mai, who bounds into the book-returns area and snags a large empty cardboard box. Mai follows her back out the front doors.

Hurrying across the open grounds, Rachel is better able to appreciate the amount of work that has been done in her absence. Corpses line the shady wall to the left of the main doors, in neat rows. Even now, Bill is dragging a body from the grass toward the stone wall. He doesn't look up. His cap is dark with sweat, his beard browned with dried blood, his face smeared with grime.

At Kevin's truck, the two of them are able to load up the remaining mail bin with the rest of the retrieved medicines, and the larger box with bandages and other supplies, then they turn back toward the library, walking as quickly as they can.

"I won't talk about what you don't want to talk about," Mai says.

Rachel glances at her, makes a small gesture of thanks. "All I know is we're still here at least partly because of what he did. I want to make the most of that. I want to survive. For him. We need to be smart about what's next."

"We've gotta go east," Mai says. "Like a hundred miles east. I'm not really into the idea of another sitting-ducks scenario near the foothills."

"It's not my idea of a fun time either," Rachel says.

"They attack again, we're dead."

"I know."

Rachel realizes that the library grounds are much quieter than when they left, almost in reverence. The truth has more to do with what Liam said: The bodies that initially survived, awakening to insufferable pain, are dying, and their screams are no longer adding to the chorus of human misery.

At that moment, Rachel notices Rick at the perimeter of the library property, apparently searching north and south on Peterson for any sign of aggressive creatures. Rachel can see a few dead bodies baking in the sun, particularly east on Oak, from which the wall of seething corpses flowed.

Rachel knows Mai is probably right. She has essentially echoed her own thoughts. This place is no longer where the survivors need to be. It's not sustainable as a stronghold. And now that the monsters are on their heels—for however long that might last—it's time to actively do something to survive. Still, there's a nagging voice inside her head—

What if what we've done here is to create a place that's safe by virtue of how we defended it?

Rachel glances warily at the sky, which is getting brighter with purple heat-lightning as evening approaches. Whatever is up there hasn't gone away. This is not over. They've repelled the beasts in what amounts to one skirmish of an all-out war. Those things will indeed regroup and try to find another way to snuff out the survivors. Rachel has the strong sense that the survivors' only chance to outmaneuver the alien threat is to remain at least one step ahead of them. And they're not going to do that by squatting here, at the site of a ruined bunker.

Striding through the front entrance, Rachel and Mai deliver the remaining supplies to the twins, who are already organizing everything atop three tables at the edge of the lobby. Both Zoe and Chloe watch Rachel hesitantly, peripherally.

"How are you doing?" Rachel asks them.

Up close, the twins appear as if they've been constantly sobbing for days—which is not far from the truth. They have endured a common nightmare as well as personal tragedies that Rachel hasn't even had time to ask about. Why hasn't she done that? These girls' lives have changed forever in unique ways, precisely as hers has.

"We're fine," Zoe says, finally turning toward Rachel, wiping her hair from her face. "How are *you?*"

"Not even going there," Rachel says.

"Glad to have you back," Chloe says. "Although this isn't really a fun place to be."

"I'm sorry we were gone so long," Rachel says. "I'm here to help."

When Rachel turns away from them, letting them do their thing, she realizes that the rest of the group is looking at her for direction. Even Scott. It's a disconcerting moment. She doesn't feel like any kind of composed, confident leader. But in the absence of Joel, she'll have to do.

"Uh … so I'd say we have the rest of daylight to do what we can here—does anyone not agree with that?" No one responds. "That gives us maybe two hours to finish this before we decide what's next. When Joel gets back, we'll figure out our next step, whether we stay or go, but in the meantime we find anyone here who might survive and try to take away their pain. That's why we went to the hospital to get all this stuff, so let's put it to good use."

"Are we safe?" Kevin asks from the ground. His voice is already slurring under medication. "Those things at the hospital were pretty determined to take us out."

"That was there, this is here. I don't think they're going to attack here again anytime soon."

"But you're not sure about that."

"No, I'm not." Rachel looks out on the library grounds and the streets beyond. There's not a soul out there. No movement. "We're safe for the time being. I know it. We've bought enough time to save some people and then get going. All right?"

"Let's do it," Liam says.

There are nods of agreement all around, only some of them reluctant.

"Let's keep Bill and Rick on the lookout, to the east and to the west," Rachel suggests.

"They're already on it," Liam says.

Rachel nods and turns. Heading toward the book-returns area to find Felicia, she seizes on a thought from out of nowhere, Rachel is darting her gaze in all directions.

"Wait … where's Chrissy?"

"I haven't seen her," Mai says.

"Oh God, she's not—"

"I don't think so." Mai twists in a tight circle, scanning the lobby.

Chloe and Zoe, across from each other in the lobby, pause and stare at each other for a full second, their faces mirroring a look of stunned shame. The shared look speaks volumes to Rachel. They've become so completely involved in their tasks that everything else has become secondary—including the well-being of their best friend.

"Shit, Rachel, I don't know where she is," Chloe says, hurriedly preparing a morphine shot. Her hands shake. "I didn't see anything happen to her, though. She was fighting right alongside us earlier, up in there." She gestures toward the north hallway, the kids' book area.

Zoe can't even look at Rachel.

"Seriously?" Rachel shouts. "No one?"

"Chrissy!" Liam calls.

"Anyone see her since the attack?"

Silence. Scott is shaking his head at the door to the book-returns room, and Liam is glancing around, too, checking his memory.

"Not since then, no."

"Nobody knows where she is?" Rachel breaks into a sprint toward the north end of the library, calling back to Mai. "I've got to find her. Check the other end, okay?"

CHAPTER 13

Rachel stares wildly about. There are masses of human bodies against all the front walls, and she gives a cursory glance to the closest, to the right of the front door. All she can see is a tangle of broken limbs and twisted torsos and hair. She starts moving north, out of the lobby, checking piles. She slips on tacky blood and almost sprawls into one of the piles. She touches an elbow tentatively, then flips over the corpse of a naked man. She doesn't see much in the way of distinctive clothing. Everything is torn, broken, thrashed.

She moves to the next pile, searching, searching.

Is this where she was fighting?

She remembers Chrissy with her tranq gun, firing darts into bodies. She preferred the humane route to the rifle. Rachel has a sudden, strong image of the girl's tiny, trembling hands grabbing O-neg-loaded darts from the box and hurrying through the hall. She went from here through to the kids' area, back and forth—she remembers that. Chrissy had looked so small and vulnerable as she ran, diminutive in the face of the claustrophobic, roaring horror bearing down on them.

Rachel enters the children's section. There are bodies here, too, less tended to, and Rachel feels an anticipatory lump in her throat. Her gaze darts back and forth, from body to mutilated body.

"Chrissy, Chrissy …" Rachel says, passing, breathing harshly.

—*her friend, meek little Chrissy, nearly killed at the hospital, nearly lost, and Rachel herself had picked her up, maybe injected a bit of confidence in the young woman … Chrissy always felt to her like a more timid version of herself— Rachel loved her, felt protective of her, but she was almost a cautionary tale, and now she was gone—*

There are four areas where Chrissy could feasibly be buried by bodies, mounds of ruined humans that have collected immediately below melted, blown-in windows. Rachel goes straight to the first, digging through them, her fingers slippery against still-wet flesh. She tosses corpses aside, in some cases shoving with her lower body, grunting and gasping, and at one point a large male arm comes loose from its shoulder socket in her hand, skin tearing and snapping like a sodden rubber band, and although somewhere deep she feels revulsion, she flings the arm away from herself, denying the sensation, and digs more deeply into the pile of bodies. Chrissy is not there.

It takes Rachel a moment to realize that Liam has arrived, directly beside her at the next mound of corpses. He's savagely tossing aside bodies.

"Not here," he barks, unceremoniously flinging a child's carcass against the far wall.

Rachel hopscotches to the next pile, begins shoving bodies left and right, and rolling the larger ones aside. It's only a tiny part of her that ponders such careless treatment of human remains: In any other circumstances, she would rail against her own behavior, but she can't deny the contradiction: Although they're human beings, they are also the remains of monsters that attacked her, attacked the entire group in a concentrated effort to extinguish them. They killed her father, killed Bonnie—nearly killed Kevin. They took Tony and Jenny and countless others. These bodies contained murderous impulses. And they might have murdered Chrissy, too.

Even as she digs, Liam is on to the next pile.

"Not here," Rachel calls.

There's blood everywhere, and only now does she realize that it's beginning to stink. Nothing like the hospital, but that sweet-rotten stench is going to overtake the library and make it uninhabitable within hours. There's already so much blood here that she can barely look anywhere without it overwhelming her senses. She staggers back from the windows, closing her eyes.

"Where is she?" she pants.

Liam pulls back from his pile, looking wildly around. He doesn't have answers.

"Could she be on the other side of the lobby?" Rachel steps into the long hallway, peering through the lobby, down into the darkened south end. "Mai! Anything?"

"No!"

"That's where we've been working all afternoon," says Liam. "It's pretty cleared out."

"Could she have—" Rachel is about to suggest that Chrissy might have run away, outside, away from here. Perhaps overwhelmed by the attack.

But then Liam interrupts.

"Look!" He's gesturing away from the windows.

The bodies are piled in an area where the carpet is inundated with blood—red, slick, clotting. Red footprints surround these areas like ghastly modern art. The farther removed from the windows, the less the carpet is stained by the assault. Rachel can trace the survivors' frantic paths from the lobby to the various warzones—those areas where the bodies destroyed the windows and gained entrance, squeezing and crawling through the gaps.

One pair of footprints—a small pair—meanders off into the darkening distance, alone.

A sudden feeling of relief floods Rachel, but she tamps it down. The footprints might be Chrissy's, but they might not be. They could be anyone's.

Where do they lead?

She and Liam race to follow the prints, but the bloody tracks quickly fade through the children's section and disappear near the elevators. Seeing a jerky curve to the trajectory of the remaining footprints, Rachel judges that Chrissy—if the footprints are indeed hers—scrambled through the inner hallway, toward the elevator and up the stairs. She glances up the two-tiered stairwell, then begins taking the steps two at a time.

Halfway up is a discarded tranq rifle.

"Chrissy!"

Liam is right behind her.

The second floor is a disaster of books and shelving, dim, sweltering, and claustrophobic. In the days preceding the attack, several of the survivors took great pains to shove bookcases against the big windows, letting books fall into disarray, and now the air is filled with a sweaty mustiness. Rachel strides blindly into it, kicking books aside.

"Check that way," she instructs Liam, gesturing to the north end, and he rushes into the shadows, calling Chrissy's name.

The community computer area is dead and ghostly to Rachel's left, the PCs looking like something from a forgotten time. To the right, the study rooms are dark and closed off, their windows black, opaque. Rachel circles around an information kiosk. Shafts of sunset light are searing in from the mountain west—or is it the alien crimson light that has come to define her existence?

She feels herself hyperventilating, knowing that a chunk of her sanity depends on finding her friend alive.

No more death.

The words rush through her mind—a desperate entreaty. She peels her eyes wide in the encroaching darkness. There are books everywhere, and the deeper she treads into the corners, the more the library seems to bear down on her, a monster all its own, ready to swallow her. The faces of those she's lost flash vividly in front of her as she stumbles deeper into the darkness, and tears blur the shadows. She blinks rapidly, trying to focus.

"Chrissy!"

The teen fiction area lies in shambles ahead and to the right. Rachel steps over a small landslide of books. Huge bookcases are angled crookedly against the thick-paned perimeter windows, and books are squashed between them and the glass, looking trapped, abused. Most of the books have tumbled to the floor, their covers bent, spines cracked, pages torn. Rachel wades through them as if through the detritus of a landfill.

A glint of something catches her eye.

A blinking eye, reflecting the fading sunlight.

Halfway buried in books, Chrissy watches Rachel from against the south wall. She's nearly lost in the pile, hiding, not wanting to be discovered. Eyes brimming with tears, she turns her head away as if ashamed.

"What—?" Rachel begins, approaching carefully. "Thank God, are you okay?"

Chrissy begins to shake her head violently. *"No ... no ..."*

"Liam, she's here!"

Rachel touches Chrissy's arm, and Chrissy flinches. In the half-light, Rachel sees now that portions of Chrissy's skin are pale and mottled. She's hurt; she's had contact with the inhabited bodies. Rachel isn't sure of the extent of it, but some damage has been done.

"Are you all right?"

Chrissy sniffs, doesn't look at her.

Liam arrives at a sprint, tripping slightly over scattered books.

"You found her!"

"She needs help, let's get her downstairs."

Chrissy lets out a small cry and twists her body away from them.

Rachel watches her friend's profile. "Sweetie, we gotta get you downstairs to take care of you."

Unresponsive, Chrissy closes her eyes, letting tears rain down on paper. She looks shockingly frail and vulnerable. She smells of perspiration and dried blood, and Rachel catches a whiff of urine. She settles back on her haunches.

"Liam, I think I need a little time with her."

He looks down at her, looks indecisive. Then, "Okay. Call out if you need me." He walks off, treading lightly.

Rachel settles down to her rear, letting a hand rest lightly on Chrissy's knee. At least her friend is alive. Exhaustion opens like a pit inside Rachel's chest, everything catching up with her. She feels as if she could fall unconscious without the slightest provocation—simply slump sideways and sleep for days. Instead, she merely lets her head drop to her chest, closes her eyes, and breathes in a careful, controlled rhythm as if she's meditating. She lets Chrissy get used to her presence, touching her, offering her strength.

Long minutes pass in the sweltering gloom.

Chrissy hasn't moved.

After a while, Rachel scoots over next to her and lies beside her so that she's looking straight into her eyes. She moves her hand from her friend's knee to her upper arm, where she can discern no injury. The contact seems to have happened on the forearms and the hands. It doesn't look terrible. Mostly incidental. She massages the skin lightly.

Chrissy locks her gaze on Rachel. There's an emptiness in the girl's eyes, a hopelessness that Rachel feels she can understand. She latches on to it, and suddenly everything washes over her—her failure to be strong at the beginning, the poor decisions she made when she thought she was trying for confidence, the times she wanted to help but might have made everything worse, her father's sacrifice—and she lets silent tears stream down her face and darken the pages of a book that lies splayed open on the floor.

There's distant commotion downstairs, and Rachel knows she should be helping, but she gives Chrissy long moments of silence, knowing it is what her friend needs.

Finally, a sound comes from Chrissy's throat. Almost a word. She coughs a little and blinks.

"I'm sorry," she says meekly.

Her whole body shakes uncontrollably, then settles.

"Don't apologize."

Another small eternity passes.

"I don't know why I ... why I ran. I couldn't help it. I didn't mean to—"

"Shhh."

Chrissy's expression goes from pleading to a tentative acceptance of Rachel's calming influence.

"Are you hurt?" Rachel asks.

Chrissy gives herself a half-hearted examination, twisting her arms back and forth, then shrugging. "One of those things—" Her lip trembles in disgust. "One of them touched me while I was kicking at it, like it was trying to bite me. It was a kid, Rachel, it could have been a kid from my street. Only a little older than my brother. He still had socks on, socks with stripes."

She stops talking, relives the moment.

"It felt like my skin was going numb. It freaked me out." She sniffs. "I fell backwards a little bit, and then …" She stops, looking Rachel in the eye. Her mouth trembles.

"And then what?"

"… then I kept going backward until I was leaving. Leaving everybody." She shakes her head, eyes closed hard, full of self-loathing. "I left you. I'm sorry."

Rachel feels a mixture of compassion and disappointment rising up in her. Of course she can understand the impulse to hide in a kind of amnesia. She herself has felt it. But she has not given in to it. She doesn't exactly feel pride for that realization, but she can't help but compare herself to Chrissy at this moment. She can't imagine abandoning her fellow survivors in a moment like that, but can she blame someone whose personal fears or failings led her to do that?

She scoots closer to Chrissy as if to embrace her, but Chrissy doesn't respond, simply lies there, deadweight.

Rachel flashes back on the aftermath of Tony's death, which seems weeks ago now. After a shudder, reliving the shotgun blast, she focuses on her mindset while driving back to the hospital to her unconscious father. She hardly remembers any of that. She'd been in a shocked daze. Stunned. Ready for everything to simply end, for whatever had taken hold of the world to get it over with already, to strike her down if only to put an end to the red chaos. Even after the relief of finding her father awake, Rachel descended into a pessimistic funk that lasted for days. In a sense, she *had* given up. She abandoned her fellow survivors, too. So who was she to judge?

"You don't have a *thing* to be sorry about," she whispers. "No one is gonna blame you for anything. We all do what we can, and that's all we can do."

After a pause, Chrissy impulsively surges forward and hugs Rachel sideways, pulling her against her. There are no tears, as if she has cried out everything she has, but the emotion is hot and close between them.

"It's all right," Rachel whispers in her ear.

Chrissy shakes her head. "It's not, it's not."

"Nobody's going to—"

"What about …" Chrissy pauses, swallowing, slicing off her words. "What about Chloe and Zoe? They're the ones I …"

"They're worried about you," Rachel says, mostly lying, but telling her what she needs to hear. Better that than the truth: The twins were so caught up in the aftermath that they weren't even thinking of Chrissy.

"They are?" Chrissy says with the voice of a child.

"Of course they are."

They listen to the sounds downstairs and watch each other for a moment as the darkness deepens.

"Is it bad down there?"

"It's not very good."

"Did anyone … did anyone die?" Her face implodes with quiet tears. The emotion is powerful, and Rachel knows the girl is blaming herself in anticipation of the news of any violence visited upon the survivors.

Rachel isn't sure how to answer. One by one, the faces of Bonnie, Brian, and then—vividly—her dad strobe in her mind, jagged, like photos ripped violently apart. But then she concentrates on her dad, smiling at her, his love gigantic, unconditional. She closes her eyes tight, tighter, wanting to keep that image close to her heart. Her chest convulses.

Chrissy sniffs, pulls back, and stares at her.

"Who?" she squeaks.

Rachel can't seem to open her mouth. Her lips won't work.

"Who?"

"It's not your fault," is all Rachel can say.

"Oh no." Chrissy dissolves again. *"I can't …"*

Rachel composes herself, pulls away from the embrace, wipes hastily at her face. She lets Chrissy cry for a moment, then begins to feel annoyance. It's hot up here, and there's the constant clamor downstairs of the others helping the formerly infected. She can't afford this time. The emotion startles her, and she finds herself able to consider it from the outside. It's as if she feels the urge to blame Chrissy for these losses but understands how wrong-headed that would be.

"Listen," she says, weighing her words. "You have nothing to apologize for. Truly. But I mean this as a friend: Get over this. The longer you stay here, the worse it will be for everyone."

"I want to go back down," Chrissy says, defensively, voice warbling, suppliant. "I *need* to help."

"I know," Rachel nods. "Just … don't dwell on this anymore. I mean, it happened, but you're human. We're all human. You're strong, okay? But it's time to get your ass back down there. Okay?"

"I want to clean myself up first."

"Take one of the flashlights and use the bathroom up here. There's still some water."

"Okay. Thanks." A pause as Chrissy sits up fully. She nudges aside a small pile of books. "I'll be down in a minute."

Rachel is already on her way toward the stairs, but she turns to face Chrissy, walking backward. "I know you will. And hey—"

"Yeah?"

"I'm glad you're still with us. Really."

A small wounded smile takes hold of Chrissy's lips, and then Rachel runs for the stairs.

CHAPTER 14

Rachel takes the stairs down two at a time, ready to dive into the bloody fray, anxious for this awful day to end. She needs a conclusion, for darkness to come, and then ultimately a new day to dawn, a day that does not hold the death of her father.

"Did you find her?"

The voice startles her, coming at her softly, barely discernible above the racket emanating from the lobby. It's Scott, waiting at the foot of the stairs, watching her come down.

"Yeah," she says, intending to fly right by him. "She's fine, She's shook up."

He makes an awkward half-step toward her, and she hesitates.

There's something haunted behind his eyes, and Rachel knows what it is, of course.

Bonnie is gone because of him.

She saw what happened at the edge of the lobby, in the frenzy of the attack, and he knows she saw it. Scott is bearing the emotional brunt of Bonnie's demise because she died in the act of pulling him away—in the act of saving him.

Selfless to the last.

Was Scott worth that?

He knows how much Bonnie meant to Rachel.

Standing in front of Scott, all Rachel can think is how much she wants to call for Bonnie. Right now. Rachel wishes urgently that Bonnie were still here in this miserable world, but she's gone. Rachel can't believe she's gone. The benevolent woman who took her under her wing days ago at the hospital, who reminded her so much of her own mother, who endured so much right at Rachel's side ... she can't be gone. But with her own eyes, Rachel watched her die at the hands of the monsters in the library lobby. Perhaps Bonnie is in a better place now—that's what they always say, isn't it? And maybe that's more appropriate now than ever before.

Rachel opens her mouth, closes it.

She wishes she trusted Scott more, or respected him even a little—not least of which because he sneakily hoarded (and, by all accounts, abused) morphine straight from the essential hospital supply when they needed it most.

And because he's generally just a dick.

Rachel dislikes him mostly for that latter trait. She saw it firsthand at the hospital when they first met, then later at the library. He hasn't grown on her.

"Listen, Rachel ... I'm sorry about your dad." He wipes his hair back over his forehead and stares at her.

She takes a deep breath, sighs.

Part of her, a small part, wants to fall into him for an embrace—that human contact in the wake of tragedy. Multiple tragedies. In the absence of Joel, this man would do. Even this man. She's not blind to how Bonnie's death must have affected him. There's even a part of her that wants to comfort him for that. But she can't quite reach out to him.

She feels herself nodding, not wanting to say anything, enduring the awkwardness of the moment.

Just as he reaches a hand out to her, she glances over to find a pair of eyes staring at her from the shadows of the book-returns room, shining eyes vaguely tinted red. Rachel gives a start, and Scott follows her gaze. There in the growing gloom, Felicia is staring at them.

"Oh ..." Rachel says, squinting to see the young woman more clearly.

Finally, Felicia's face gains clarity, and Rachel can see the troubled expression there. It's not the expression she expected, for some reason. Rachel recalls the sight of Felicia staring defiantly out at the sky from the busted-out window, corpses at her feet, looking for all the world like their savior.

Scott right behind her, Rachel steps toward the door. The hallway reminds Rachel of the hospital. There's so much blood that her shoes squelch in the carpet. It seems as if every place they go ends up drenched in the blood of the living and the dead. Mostly the dead.

She reaches the open doorway to the makeshift triage room.

Felicia has backed deeper into the room, toward a shadowy corner.

"How are you?" Rachel asks her.

No answer.

Rachel glances around. The first thing she notices is that a light rain is falling outside the blasted window. Then she sees five bodies lying supine on the floor. Two are obviously dead, and three are gasping, almost hyperventilating. One of them, the closest, is one of the former monsters that she remembers bringing back with a tranq dart full of O-neg blood, days ago, when they were testing the blood cure. It's a teenaged boy wearing a ravaged Broncos shirt.

His watery, somehow muddy eyes dart to hers when he sees her.

"Hel—hel—help," he whispers. The sound of his whispered voice is mangled. His eyes close tight, and a flood of tears squeezes out between the trembling lids, runs down the sides of his face.

She goes to him, bends down, places a reassuring hand on his shoulder. "Oh God, okay, yes, hold on." She turns to Scott. "We need pain relief in here right away."

"Right, yeah." His voice goes to a whisper. "He's been on a heavy dose of morphine since we turned him back, I'm actually surprised he's still—" He stops, then nods. "Give me a sec." And then he hurries toward the lobby, bumping the door jamb with his shoulder on his way out.

Rachel turns her attention back to Felicia, who's standing in the corner, in relative darkness, still staring at her. Her hands are extended outward at an odd angle, and Rachel's first thought is that there's still a remnant there of what inhabited her. It's in her eyes, mostly. A shadow of something. Felicia's limbs are trembling slightly, as if she's undergoing an internal struggle to remain human. At least that's how it appears to Rachel.

"Felicia?"

The woman doesn't respond.

"Are you all right?"

Nothing.

Rachel begins to approach her.

Felicia subtly shakes her head. No, she seems to be saying, warding off Rachel's approach.

"What's wrong?"

"I—don't—"

Rachel stands still, waiting. "Can I help you? What can I do to—?"

"I don't know if it's still inside me," Felicia says. "I think it might be. Everything is different. I—I don't know if I'll hurt you." She coughs. "I don't want to, but ... I don't know ..."

Rachel shifts her weight from one hip to the other.

"Why—why do you say that?"

"I feel ... wrong."

"How?"

Felicia's shoulders begin to narrow, and she glances toward the blown-out window. She appears to be considering something.

"I don't know what I've done."

Rachel takes a moment to study the young woman. Felicia is visibly shaken—to her core—and she's trembling, almost vibrating. Pain is evident in her features. But Rachel knows this woman. She has talked with her. She can recall conversations she had with her about school as Felicia rang them up at the Co-Op. These are memories from what she thinks of, in retrospect, as their window out of grief following her mother's death, before her father found Susanna, just Rachel and her dad finding their footing together in a new father-daughter dynamic, finding some semblance of happiness again, establishing new rituals ...

One of those rituals had been shopping together at the Co-Op, away from the usual stores they'd frequented with her mother. Because that was the most painful aspect of her mother's death, or at least the wake of it: the reminders. The thousands of places and people and sights and sounds and scents that were wrapped around the memory of her mom. Inextricably. All those things that resisted efforts to heal.

These thoughts flit through her head as she stares at Felicia, trying to figure her out. Shopping at the Co-Op—the memories there are good, despite the reasons behind them. And her memories of Felicia are fond.

Breaking her from the flow of memory is Scott, as he whisks in with some medicine for the boy. He squeezes past her and kneels to him.

"Do you remember me?" Rachel asks Felicia.

Felicia peers at her from beneath her misery, and nods slowly.

Rachel tries on a smile. "I'm glad my dad found you. Glad you're alive."

Felicia turns doubtful. She moves her mouth cautiously, then says, "I don't know if I am."

"What ... what does it feel like?"

Felicia's eyes are haunted, wet, vulnerable. She's working her jaw in a strange rhythm.

"I don't know." She swallows painfully. "It's like ... I don't remember the worst of it. But I can still feel something in there. Like it was a ... a nightmare, and it's leaking into real life." She brings up a shaking hand and touches her throat gingerly. "I don't know how else to explain it. I can—"

Rachel takes a step closer to Felicia, tries touching her arm to comfort her. Felicia flinches.

"You can what?"

Felicia looks at her. "Nothing."

"Is there anything I can do?" Rachel asks.

"I don't know." Her voice is on the edge of a moan. "I'm not sure what anyone can do."

"What do you mean?"

"I mean ..." She looks closely at Rachel, then glances away. "I don't know if I should be here."

"Why not?"

"What if I—" Her voice trembles, getting quieter. "What if I brought those things here?"

Rachel glances at her curiously. She hadn't thought of that. But as she considers the words, she comes to the conclusion that it can't have been Felicia who brought the monsters. The survivors had been the target for days before Felicia turned.

Rachel shakes her head.

"No, I think it's the opposite," she says. "I think you drove them away."

Felicia looks doubtful behind her blurred eyes.

But Rachel continues:

"When it was happening, I mean when the attack was at its worst, I thought it was my dad who turned the tide. I really did. And maybe he did have something to do with it—maybe we all had something to do with it, driving them back like that. The way he ... he ... he turned so many of them, all at once. But ..."

Felicia waits, her body seeming restless.

"... but I think it was mostly you. Something inside you. What you're feeling. Maybe they're scared of it. Maybe they're freaked out that we changed you back."

"But you've ... you've changed others. A lot of others."

"Yes we have, but they're all in bad shape still." She feels a catch in her throat. "It's awful, what's happened to most of them. To you too, but most are so much worse. They don't even know what's happened to them."

"Why?"

Rachel tries to explain what most of the infected bodies have been doing—at least, those infected bodies not barricaded or trapped somehow—but her words end up sounding silly.

Felicia shakes her head minutely. Her eyes have a faraway look.

"Do you remember anything?" Rachel says. "Anything from when you were ... well ..."

Felicia hesitates before speaking. "I remember feeling ... trapped ... frustrated ... alone." Her jaw works endlessly. "And I needed it terribly."

"Needed ...?"

"Needed ... needed ..." Felicia is searching for a word but appears confused.

"Something in the trees?"

"Yes." Felicia stares at her. "How did you ... know that?"

Rachel realizes that Felicia hasn't seen any of these bodies attached to trees, in their natural state. She's only seen them here, attacking. She explains what she's seen all over the city.

"Do you know why?" she asks her. "What is it in the trees?"

Felicia shakes her head slowly back and forth.

"You don't know?"

The afflicted woman gives a start, as if jolted from a trance. "I don't … I mean, it's like … I can visualize it, I have a sense of it … it's like a chemical, something totally unique."

Rachel notices that Felicia's eyes are full of tears—flooded with them.

"What is it?"

"It did something to me …" As she works her jaw, she brings up a hand to touch her face with trembling fingers. "…and I'm not sure it's getting better."

"Come on, let's get you some medicine," Rachel says, gently guiding Felicia. "Scott? Can you help?" Then, turning back to Felicia, "We scrounged a bunch. We can fix this."

"I don't know … I don't think anything on Earth can fix it."

Rachel stares at her. "I need to clean myself up anyway. We'll do it together."

In moments, she has Felicia seated in the center of the room, encouraging her to relax as she finds her a cup of water while Scott gives her an OxyContin tablet. Chloe has arrived with a morphine injection for the boy on the floor, as well as the two bodies surrounding him, but Felicia has refused the more powerful drug, insisting that others are worse off than she is. As the bodies relax, Rachel sits in a chair, directly in front of Felicia, handing her the cup of water with which to down the pill.

"Thank you."

"You *look* a lot better."

Felicia offers a painful shrug.

"Compared to when my dad brought you in here," Rachel says. She takes the plastic cup from Felicia and sets it on the counter behind her. "You were in bad shape. I wasn't sure you'd make it."

"Me neither. I'd—I'd rather not go through that again."

"I bet." Rachel watches her carefully, beginning to address her own wounds with some alcohol wipes. "What you've been through, what you did for us out there … Do you know what's going on in their heads?" she asks.

Felicia looks off in the direction of the lobby, then out the blasted window. She nods. "Yes I do."

Rachel gauges Felicia's expression. "It *was* you, wasn't it? They were afraid of you."

Felicia's gaze cuts so sharp that Rachel feels as if the woman is looking inside her.

"I'm still a part of them," Felicia whispers. "They … they feel that. But

I—I'm also not a part of them anymore. They feel that too."

Rachel considers that, wincing at the sting of the alcohol. "What—what was that like? To have it inside you?"

"An—an invasion. Almost totally p-pushed out of my own body."

"Are they really … alien?"

A pause as Felicia glances around again, as if she will be punished for what she is about to say. "I don't—don't want this to sound silly, because it definitely isn't. Whatever this is, it isn't from here. It is from out there. Up there." She gestures. "It is an actual *invasion*. Not only my body … but all those bodies out there. And more."

"You could feel it inside you?"

"It basically … became me." She pauses.

Rachel shudders. She finds a box of bandages and digs out a few, beginning to place them along her side.

"And when the blood cured you—"

"It didn't cure me." Felicia appears exhausted from talking.

"Then—"

"It's still inside me," she whispers. "I can hear them. It's almost like … some of it is still there. Like I have to cough it out. Like I need to have it removed. I don't know."

"Listen to me," Rachel says, pulling her shirt back down and taking hold of both of Felicia's hands. "They're afraid of you. You know that. I think you can help us. What are they afraid of? Can we use that again? Can we kill them? Get rid of them?"

Felicia stares at her blankly. "No," she whispers. Her voice is shaking so badly that her jaw seems unhinged. "There's too many of them. It's too big. I don't know what to do. I mean, there's fear there. I feel their fear. But I—I don't know why. I don't know what I can do."

"Okay, shhh, don't worry."

Rachel stands, watching Felicia, considering. "I'm going to help the others. Find me if you need anything. And think about it, all right? It's important. *You're* important."

Felicia has slumped in her chair, and Rachel can see her working to control her jaw, slowing it down. As Rachel moves away tentatively, Felicia brings her hands to her ears as if shutting out sound, although the screaming agony in the lobby is no more. The library has become preternaturally quiet.

What is she blocking out? Rachel wonders. *Me?*

There's a commotion outside the front doors, and through the open window, Rachel watches Pete's truck grumble up the path. The vehicle has sustained some damage. In the afternoon light, under light rain, the truck's left side panel appears to have been walloped by a fiery fist.

CHAPTER 15

Joel is at the wheel, with Pete at shotgun. The truck's motor guns and backfires as the vehicle bounces over the concrete lip at the edge of the grounds, but eventually the rusty behemoth comes to a hard, rattling stop, very close to the doors. Immediately, Joel flings open the door and steps down to the bloodied ground, Pete following his lead from the other side. Both their faces are stressed and haggard under the rain. A heavy, bloodied plastic bag lolls from one of Joel's fists, bulky and portentous.

Oh no, Rachel gasps inwardly.

Everyone in the lobby has approached the front doors to meet the men. Zoe and Chloe rush forward with Rachel in time to meet Joel and Pete as they make their way beneath the shelter of the library's massive concrete façade, shielding their heads with newspapers, their faces wincing.

"What happened?" Rachel calls.

Joel staggers through the doors and into the library, giving Rachel a hard look.

"Ron is dead," he says.

Stunned silence except for gasps from the twins.

Joel tosses the newspaper aside roughly, then winds up and slams the heavy plastic bag to the ground, scattering candy bars and protein bars across the entrance tiles. Rachel can feel everyone watching the food, hungry but dumbfounded.

Behind Joel, Pete is a shell of what Rachel remembers from a few days ago when she first saw him near City Park, blowing things up with his brother. There's no swagger left in him as follows Joel, limping, exhausted—even scared.

"Those fuckers are still ornery as hell," Pete says matter-of-factly.

"What did they do?" Mai says, wiping her bloody hands on her already stiff, blackened jeans. Her eyes are glassy with new moisture, and her voice is high and unsteady with emotion.

"They're using some kind of explosive."

Rachel looks sharply at him, then over at Kevin, who is sleepily trying to prop himself up on one elbow.

"They started after us at the station, a group of them," Joel seethes. "They telegraphed it! We saw them coming at the last minute, I mean *racing* at us, and we were able to duck into the truck, but they threw something at us, detonated something." He gestures back at the truck. "Blew out two windows. Ron took the brunt of it. Killed him instantly." Then he points at the scattered food. "That's what he was carrying. He'd just run over to the drug store."

Silence over the sound of steady rain, then:

"Where is—where's his body?" Liam says, deadened.

Joel doesn't answer.

Pete watches him, then says, "We left him there."

"You *left* him!" Chloe sobs.

"Yes, we left him," Joel says, hard. "*Okay?* We didn't have a choice. You think you'd take the time to gather up a dead body while grenades are going off all around you?"

"He's our friend!"

"Please, feel free to fetch him. He's right at College and Laurel, what's left of him anyway."

The twins are grasping at each other, crying openly now—tears of both grief and new fear.

"Joel," Rachel says.

"What?"

"Is that necessary?"

"Yes," he responds loudly. "Yes, it is. Because this isn't over. It's far from over. Goddammit."

"It was supposed to be over," comes a small voice toward the elevators.

It's Kayla. She's got a knuckle at her eye as if rubbing sleep from it. But Rachel knows it's exhaustion and fear.

In the hot, close library, the little girl's words seem to resonate, and there are several whimpers and loud exhalations all around. Rachel flashes back to a couple days ago, when Kayla bravely faced the room and spoke about what she had found out about conifer trees, theorizing about what these inhabited bodies might be seeking.

The girl doesn't have any more words, simply rubs her eyes and wanders over to Rachel, looking up at her. Rachel puts her arms around her.

"You okay, sweetie?" she whispers.

The girl nods. "I'm sorry I ran away."

Rachel shakes her head, dismissing the thought. "Shhhh."

Hugging Kayla tightly, Rachel looks more closely at the truck. The passenger-side window and part of the rear window are blown out. There's a gaping, blackened hole in the rear glass. Rachel gets an even closer look at the side panel, which appears blackened and pitted. There's no doubt in Rachel's mind that whatever happened to Joel is the same thing that happened at the hospital. Except in this case, the detonation probably occurred closer to the truck.

The twins are still clutching at each other, holding back sobs now, and Liam has fallen into a chair at the edge of the lobby, speechless.

"Why are you sitting down?" Joel says, taking on an accusatory, glaring stance.

"Hey," Mai says, stepping forward. "Take it easy, man."

"We're leaving." Joel glances around the lobby. "What's the status here?"

But before anyone can answer, Rick steps in through the blasted front doors to find all eyes on him.

"We've got a sighting to the south."

He's soaked and weary, looking around for something to wipe himself down with. Chloe breaks from Zoe, red-eyed, and looks hopelessly around for an unsullied towel, but there are none. Rick ends up wiping himself down with his forearms.

"What's it doing?" Joel growls.

"At first I barely saw it, it wasn't moving, just sitting there, watching. Then I caught a little movement, like it was reacting to Bill on the west side. It didn't see me."

"Fucking things are strategizing again," Pete says.

"Did they follow you?" Liam says. He's standing again, but he's glowering at Joel. "Did you lead them here?"

"You better lock that shit up right now."

To blunt the building anger in the room, Rachel fills in Rick on what happened to Ron. Rick closes his eyes and shakes his head. Rachel watches his jaw clench beneath a weary face speckled with dried blood.

"What are they strategizing?" Rick says quietly.

"I don't know," says Joel. "But I do know they're weaponized. Something new. You mind heading back out, keeping watch till we figure this out? Something is brewing. You and Bill be ready to sprint back here if you see anything, right?"

Rick sighs, straightens up. "You got it."

"Wait, take a radio. Liam, give him yours." Liam hands over the handset. "Pete, how about yours? Bill needs one too." From a deep pocket in his pants, Pete withdraws his own radio, hands it to Rick. "Give that to

Bill, clear? Radio in anything suspicious. *Anything.*"

"Right."

When he's gone, Rachel speaks up.

"Joel, we were attacked the same way at the hospital."

"Seriously?"

She recounts what happened at the hospital and fills Joel and Pete in on Kevin's condition—a concussion and minor shrapnel injuries, as a result of some kind of blast. And the same kind of damage to the truck.

"Kevin also said it was like someone threw a grenade at us," she says glancing over at Kevin for verification.

Kevin nods, eyes closed.

"What, like a human? Someone else threw something?" Joel says. "Not one of those things?"

"I don't know. All I know is something blew up, and we were all on the ground, including the bodies. Hell, I thought it was you at first, trying to protect us. But those bodies got the worst of it. Blown apart."

"Same here, yeah—blood all over the place."

"Is this something new?" Mai says. "Some new kind of weapon?"

There are glances all around.

"I can tell you that a roar came from the sky right before it happened," Joel grunts. "Just like before, exactly what happened before they attacked the library. You too?"

"Yep." Rachel nods, thinking desolately of Ron.

The group gathers closer together, exhausted, confused. People are sniffing, breathing unsteadily, scared. The air stinks of ozone and sweat, of smoke and rot, and although a heavy humidity still cloaks the library, the temperature at least is not as bad as it has been. Rachel notices that most of the survivors are watching the rain and the library grounds. The air is *expectant.*

"We have to leave this place," Rachel says, resolutely.

"Now," Joel repeats.

"He's right," Mai says. "We gotta get out of here."

"We need time, guys," Rachel says, scanning the lobby. "We can't act rashly." She thinks of her conversation with Felicia. "When they attacked us all here, they scrambled away. In fear. You all saw it. They're not going to rush us again so soon. I'm positive about that. We at least have time to gather supplies and do this right. We have to make sure these people can survive." She gestures to the victims of the library attack, the bodies that have only recently turned back to humanity.

"At the cost of your own life?" Joel asks her. He's rubbing one reddened eye.

"Hey, look," Rachel says, "I'm not disagreeing with you about the threat. What happened here—we're not letting that happen again." She angles her head and glances out toward the skies. "It *is* time to leave. But what's our plan? Where do we go?"

"East." Mai extends a long, shapely arm, pointing straight through the library's front doors.

"Just drive east?"

"It makes sense," Pete says. "Those goddamn things are obviously after the forests, so driving as far away as possible from the forests seems fuckin' reasonable."

"That's what I said!" Kevin calls.

"So, wait, why are we leaving again?" Liam says. "It's not like we're in the middle of the forest here. This is a city block."

"Dude!" Mai says. "You were here for this slaughter, right?"

"I mean, what if Rachel's right? What if the way we repelled that attack—that gave us a safe zone here? A place they're afraid of. This could be the safest spot in the city, regardless of the damage. They haven't even come close to these walls again, haven't you noticed that?"

"I'll say it again: Are you willing to gamble all our lives on that?" Joel counters. "Rick *just* came in to report one of those things out there, right now. This library could just as easily be the target of another giant attack, some kind of revenge. Something they're working up right now. They're obviously still aggressive."

"Joel, I'm on your side," Rachel says. "All I'm saying is let's do this methodically. Let's do this smart. I'm not just rushing out the door."

"Fine!" Joel looks around at the survivors one by one, takes in the situation in the lobby. "Christ! Look, it was—it was not a fun situation out there."

Mai punches Joel's shoulder. "It's fine. Now let's figure it out."

Joel can see the orderly rows of bodies, and Rachel is sure he can perceive the difference between the state of the library when he left and the relative calm now.

"Good work here," he says. "But we have to leave these people, you know. What are we doing with them?"

Chloe steps forward tearfully from the checkout area, massaging her wrists. "We can make it so they're comfortable for a few hours anyway. We can inject them with the pain relief we have, and we can add to that. These bodies need time to heal. We can leave them plenty of water and food. They can get better without us here."

"Are you sure?" Rachel says.

"Reasonably."

Zoe looks at her sister doubtfully for a brief moment, then nods. Rachel sees her working out the calculation: Either leave this place with the rest of the group or stay in this stinking lobby with these bodies, completely vulnerable to another attack.

"What happens to them?" asks Kayla, whose face is wet and tortured against Rachel's abdomen. She's gesturing at the bodies Chloe is referencing. "If we can't bring them with us, what happens to them? Will those things eat them?"

"They won't," says a woman's voice.

Rachel turns, startled.

Felicia is standing in the shadows near the book-returns area. She appears to have been there for some time, observing. Her eyes are on Rachel.

"Really?" Zoe says.

"Yes."

"How do you know?" Chloe asks.

Felicia manages a smile, but Rachel can tell that she's uncomfortable. "I used to be one of 'those things'."

"And so because of that, you can see ... you know what they ...?" Chloe says.

Felicia nods, eyeing the whole group. "I know how they think."

"So what should we do?" Chloe asks, and suddenly all eyes are on Felicia. "Do you know what's going to happen? Will they attack again?"

They're the questions Rachel put to her, but now she seems willing to answer them.

Felicia moves slowly from the shadows. "I'm not one of them anymore. I don't know what they plan to do now. I don't speak their language anymore." She swallows with pain. "I do know they never expected you to survive. That's the advantage you have over them. They don't know how to deal with you. They didn't expect to have to fight." Her brow is knitted, troubled. "What they want is in the forests. In the trees. You already know that."

"What is it?" Zoe asks.

"A chemical compound. It's hazy, but it is that. Something very specific and unique to nature on Earth. It's at the molecular level." Rachel can tell she's having trouble talking for so long. "I don't have the words to really describe it, but it's ... something that can't be produced in a lab or anything. It's the result of a very specific interaction. And they absolutely crave it."

Kayla glances up at Rachel with wet eyes. "I was right," she whispers.

Rachel smiles down at her. "Of course you were."

"So we leave them to it!" Mai says.

Joel clenches his jaw. "What you're saying, Mai, is we let them get away with everything they've done to us. What they've done to the world. They get what they want, and then they hightail it outta here, laughing all the way home?" He looks at Felicia. "Right? And of course we trust them to leave all those infected people alive when they're done with them."

Felicia shakes her head. "I don't see that happening."

"Exactly."

"Are you on our side or theirs?" Kayla says to Felicia.

The library goes quiet.

Felicia opens her mouth, closes it, then opens it again. "I'm on yours."

After a moment, Joel breaks a weighty silence.

"Are we safe here?"

Felicia looks at him gravely. "I don't think so."

"How much time do we have?"

She swallows painfully. "I honestly don't know. But they will never give up. They will use every weapon they have to destroy you."

"And now it looks like they have a new weapon," Kevin manages.

The sun is at the horizon now, what Rachel's dad used to call *magic hour*. Right now, Rachel would call it *decision time*.

"We're splitting up," Joel says, energizing the fear-clenched room. "We're splitting up and getting the hell out of here. I loaded up on radios, so we're good on communication again—at least as far as the range of these things." He takes the radio off his hip, gives it a cursory glance. "About fifty miles max, I'd say." He replaces it. "We send one group east to see if there are any answers out there, and I keep another group to go west, right into the thick of it—anyone interested in seeing this through and maybe stopping this thing. Bottom line is I'm not leaving town. I totally get it if anyone here wants to take off. Totally get it. But I'm staying. That girl right there might be the answer." He gestures at Felicia, who watches him doubtfully. "She's carrying something—something important. Maybe she knows what it is, maybe she doesn't. Either way, it's something we need to take advantage of. Hopefully with some help. I gotta see it through, see what about her is scaring the shit out of them. Cuz that's what she's doing."

The survivors peer around at one another.

"Mai," Joel says, "I suggest you head up the group heading east. Kevin is probably with you, and whoever else wants to join you. No hard feelings either way. No judgment."

"So we … pick a group?" Scott asks from the periphery.

"Or take off on your own, if that's what you'd rather."

Rachel can't help but hear Joel's ulterior message: *Remember how that worked out for you last time?* She all too clearly remembers his chagrined face peering out of that church window days ago, when they'd found him cornered.

Joel goes on. "Anyone wants to stick around and keep fighting, stay with me. But hey, I know that's asking a lot. So if you're gonna stay, you gotta be sure. No half measures. You're in, or you're gone. It's black and white. If you decide to go, you're going with half the weapons, and Godspeed. And I mean it when I say whatever group leaves is just as important as the one that stays. Both groups will be in search of answers, and we'll be communicating what we find. Again, as far as the range allows."

Joel stops talking, and as if in punctuation, a bolt of purple heat lightning jags across the eastern sky. Thunder arrives seconds later, more like a screech than a typical boom.

"What if they attack us as we try to leave?" Scott says, his voice breaking, betraying his fear.

"Like I said, all vehicles will be armed," Joel says. "I know that's not a huge consolation, but the alternative is remaining here, and being pretty vulnerable."

"Whatever these things are," says Rachel, "they're still reeling. You can feel it. It's like it's in the air somehow. They're not going to attack us outside—for now. But if we stay, they will."

"So we'll start with you, Rachel," Joel says. "You going east with me or west with the others?"

Rachel glances around at the rest of the group. "I'm with you. Those things have destroyed my life, so I plan to do the same to them."

"Fuckin' A!" comes Kevin's voice, still groggy.

Rachel glances over and finds that the big man is on his feet, approaching from the triage area, limping. He's patched up but still a bit wobbly.

"I mean, fuckin-A, yeah," Kevin says. "Let's fuck 'em up. But I'm getting the hell out of here. East. I'm with Mai."

"Jesus, Kevin, are you okay?" Rachel says. "You shouldn't even be awake."

"I'll be fine." He trudges toward them, looking the worse for wear. His right arm is thoroughly bandaged, and his head is wrapped in a bloody bandage. "And I'll be even finer once I'm outta here. I've had enough of this shit."

Joel looks around at the gathering. "Those of you going east aren't immune to attack. Same thing that happened to Ron could happen to you."

"Hell, same thing that already happened to Kevin," Rachel says. "He was lucky to survive, but he could easily be dead in front of that hospital."

"Amen," Mai says. "C'mon, let's get this thing in gear. Who else is with me?"

"I am," comes another new voice.

Chrissy is edging into the lobby from the elevator bay. Around her, several tables are crooked and leaning, their books having tumbled to the tile floor. The young woman braces herself against the corner of one of the tables, stepping over low mountains of novels. She keeps casting humiliated glances all around, as if attempting to gauge whether anyone will accept her back into their ranks.

"There you are!" Zoe says, rushing over to the diminutive teen, whose face melts with relief. "You scared the shit out of us!"

"I'm sorry," Chrissy says, "I'm so sorry," but she's quickly enveloped by both twins, smothering away her apologies.

"Shut up," Chloe tells her. "Jeez."

After a moment, Chrissy opens her leaky eyes and finds Rachel.

"Rachel," she says meekly, "I can't stay here anymore, I hope you understand, I have to go with Mai ..."

"Of course I get it," Rachel says. "But you'll still need to stay safe. We'll get back together when this is over. I promise."

Chrissy's gaze moves back to the twins. Chloe and Zoe have been whispering with each other, and now they embrace Chrissy harder, understanding but mournful.

Chloe stares at Rachel over Chrissy's shoulder. "Zoe and I are going with you."

"You sure?" Rachel says.

Both twins nod as if to say, *We're with you till the end.*

"It's not often you get a chance to save the world," Zoe says.

"You guys," Chrissy says in a small voice, and that's all she has to say.

Pete Thompson has been hanging at the edge of the group, wiping at his brow with meaty, filthy hands. "There's something in that rain," he mutters. "Kinda stings."

"Felt it too," Joel says.

"Well, I'm stayin' with ya," Pete says, looking up. "You couldn't drag me away. Those fuckers ain't gonna get away with what they did. What they did to Jeff. And now Ron. I wanna knock their goddamn heads off. Every last one of 'em."

"I'm with you too," Scott says to Joel, surprising Rachel.

Courage is the last thing that Rachel would have associated with this man. But there's no denying anymore that the events of this day—and the past few days—have conspired to make him a different person.

The entire group has paused to look at him.

"Seriously?" Joel says.

Scott's gaze moves from Joel's to Rachel's and back, and all he says is, "Yeah."

Joel shrugs and looks at Rachel. "What about the kid?"

"Kayla is with me," says Rachel. "No question."

Joel looks at Kayla. "You good with that, girl? I want to hear it from you."

"Yes." Kayla's voice is strong, and as she confirms her choice, she brings up her chin in kid courage, making Rachel smile despite herself. "No question."

Joel glances around and does a mental count. "Okay, that's eight of us staying. Half of the group. I'll take Rachel, Kayla, Felicia, Pete here, the twins, and Scott. Right? Anyone else? Speak up. Now or never."

"What about—" Rachel begins, but then—as if on cue—Bill staggers in from outside, drenched and cursing. He appears to be perhaps the most exhausted of all of them, pale and gaunt, with exaggerated bags below his eyes. Rachel hasn't had the chance to really get to know him, but he has been a tireless help at the library, purely trying to survive—and making sure the people around him survive with him.

"I had to get out of that rain," he says miserably. "There's a little bite to it."

"I get it, man," Joel says.

"Heard about Ron, man, shit."

"Yep."

"I'm not sure how much I have left."

"Rick told us about the body out there. Any movement?"

"No, it's just standing there, like it's waiting for something."

"Which is exactly what it's probably doing," Joel says. "Look, we're getting out of here. Soon. And we're splitting up—a group of us heading west, and another group heading east. You want to be a part of that?"

"Yeah," says Bill, his voice full of gravel. He's swiping moisture out of his grimy hair. "Rick and I have already talked about leaving, and I decided to head east. Him too. I can speak for him. Just makes the most sense to us. I don't know if that means we'll keep up with that group, but we'll probably be going in the same general direction. Stay mobile, look for others, maybe find some answers."

"Okay, that's fair," Joel says. "All I ask is that we stay in contact, share everything we find. Right?"

"Of course," Bill says, and Mai echoes the sentiment.

"I guess that leaves me," says Liam. To no one's surprise, he says, "I'll be going with Kevin and Mai. If that's okay with you?" he asks the big man.

"The more the merrier."

"All right, so that's it," Joel says. "That was actually pretty easy. We'll take the Hummer and Pete's truck, you guys have Ron's Subaru and that Chevy. I hope you don't mind that we take the more rough-and-tumble vehicles. Let's get busy divvying things up—food, supplies, weapons. Rachel, Mai, can you oversee medical, make sure both groups have a good supply, including blood, and leave enough here for these bodies?"

Mai nods and takes off for the book-returns area.

"Pete and I will take care of weapons," Joel continues. "We'll arm up the vehicles, make sure everything is locked and loaded. Chrissy, you and the twins are in charge of the food and water. There's plenty of boxes back there, pack them up and load them in the cars tight as you can. Liam, can you take over outside, do a perimeter sweep with Rick, see if there's anything threatening out there? Good. Take Bill's radio. Bill, can you help out with medical? I want to get mobile within thirty."

The lobby is abuzz with activity.

Rachel hangs back, Kayla still clutched against her. As the other survivors shout and scramble all around them, Rachel is left staring anxiously into Joel's eyes. For a moment, she can feel Felicia watching them, but then the young woman fades back toward the book-return area, a look of worry, or perhaps pain, on her face. Rachel closes the distance between herself and Joel and finds his hand. She holds it tightly.

"Sorry about what happened out there."

"Me too."

"We'll still make it."

Joel lets out a lengthy sigh. "This whole time, I've been making things up as I go. Reacting. It's gonna be satisfying to get on the other side of the equation. I feel like we have a chance with that girl. Felicia. Something about her. Something still inside her."

"I agree with you, but is that a plan?"

"I have an idea. And if I had more time, I'd be testing it in a controlled environment. Like right here. But that's not gonna happen. It's gonna have to be a field test. I think it's Felicia that's making us safe. They're afraid of her. But I have no idea how long that's gonna last. I'm thinking— hoping—she'll continue to ward them off. Just by being with us."

"She told me as much."

"So my idea is: We make more Felicias."

"Um … what?"

"Your dad and I saw another trapped body, another woman, up Remington, caught inside a VW bus—I don't know, the door must be jammed or something. I'm thinking we bring it down with a tranq dart, give it some blood, nurse her back to health as best we can on the run. See what happens. And maybe there's more out there like that."

Rachel gestures for Joel to wait a moment, then bends to Kayla, face to face. She wipes the girl's face of exhausted tears and smiles bravely at her. "I need you to go to your closet and make sure you have everything you need, okay? We're leaving in the truck in a few minutes, and I want you to make sure you don't forget anything."

Kayla nods.

"Everything will be okay, honey, I promise."

As Kayla runs for the closet, Rachel makes sure she's alone with Joel before she asks her next question.

"Joel," she whispers. "What if Felicia is the target? And by bringing her with us, we're putting ourselves in even more danger?"

He eyes her. "Have any bodies approached her here?"

"No. But it might be very different out there."

He sighs. "We have to assume she's an asset. And if it turns out otherwise, we let her go. Fair?"

"I can't imagine abandoning her on the side of the road," Rachel says, frowning.

"Yeah, well, that's getting a bit ahead of ourselves, right? Let's get the hell out of here, huh? I'm nervous as shit about this place."

"But what about a destination? Do you have something in mind?"

"Hadn't thought that far ahead." He gestures west. "That way?"

She pauses. "Okay, then one more thing."

"What is it?

"Like I said, I can't leave my dad here. I won't."

Joel gives a solemn nod. "I know. I remember. What are you thinking?"

"I'd like to take him home."

"And do what with him?"

"I don't know … take him back to his wife? Bury him?"

"We won't have time to bury him, Rachel."

"I want to at least take him away from here." Tears threaten to take hold of her, weaken her resolve. "I want to wrap him up and take care of him, even if that means leaving him in his bed for now. I owe him that."

"Okay, that's doable. That's on our way west." He gives her a comforting squeeze to the shoulder. "We'll take care of him. I'll get him wrapped up myself. In fact, I'll do it right now with Pete."

"Thanks, I appreciate that."

"Remember, I want to be on the move. I don't want to hole up anywhere again, unless it absolutely comes to that."

"Understood."

"We're gonna end this thing or die trying. I want to be clear about that. I think we've got an edge here to take advantage of, but I don't have any real answers. If you're coming with me, it's gotta be with that understanding. We're putting lives on the line. Including that little girl's. Can you handle that responsibility?"

Rachel stares him down as survivors bustle about around her.

"Yes," she says, and she curses herself for allowing her voice to break. "I told you, I'm with you." She lowers her voice. "I'm not running away. I'm all about finding the answers. Have been from the start. I'm going to see this through. And there's no way I'm leaving Kayla. She's safer with us and Felicia than anywhere else. I feel that."

Out of nowhere, Joel embraces her—more an encouraging, motivating embrace than anything—and she feels overwhelmed by his confident strength. At first, she's startled, but there's comfort there, and she loses herself in the hug for a moment. And then she understands that he's also drawn to her own confidence, finding strength in her, and at that knowledge she feels her back straighten and her self-confidence notches up. There's something else there, too, but she pushes it inside herself even as she reaches up to touch his broad shoulder.

At that moment, Mai hurries past with a postal bin full of medical supplies.

"Get a room," she says, in an emotionless voice, as if she's trying for a smirk but can't muster it amid the current circumstances.

Joel pulls back, ignoring Mai. "All right, let's get going, huh?"

"Right."

She watches Joel hurry out into the rain, calling for Pete to join him, and she feels somehow embarrassed. And angry with herself for the embarrassment.

Jesus, Rachel, knock it off. Get to work.

She shakes herself out of her fluster and jogs to the book-returns area, where Mai is already taking stock of the situation.

"So the cop, huh?" Mai says over her shoulder.

Rachel is shaking her head with an embarrassed flush. "You're right, he *is* a policeman."

"A little by-the-book for my taste, but I can see it, I guess."

"What happened?" Bill asks from the other side of the small room.

"Nothing happened!" Rachel says, irritated. "Good lord. So what are we doing?"

CHAPTER 16

Darkness is falling now.

Rachel can almost feel the collective heartbeat of the group. There's an intake of breath and then—

"Let's go!" Joel calls.

Bill and Rick pull back the double doors, and the way is clear to the vehicles. The rain is collecting in the gutters and making sizeable puddles on the grounds. The survivors' feet slap the wet concrete as everyone makes a beeline for their designated vehicle. Rachel's insides seize up as she runs. The grounds seem suddenly wide open in the evening dimness, reaching out into a malevolent nothingness.

Kayla's arm is wrapped around Rachel's waist, and her other hand is holding a flimsy newspaper over her head. The girl is crammed against her side, her small arm wrapped around her. The two groups of eight survivors huddle under their own newspapers, gathered from the reference area upstairs, near where Rachel found Chrissy. The survivors have protected themselves from the rain, for the most part, as they've filled the vehicles with everything they need. But some bare skin has been exposed, and those areas sting as if burned with a mild acid.

"What *is* that?" Chrissy cries.

"Who knows what's in that shit," says Pete, "what it's doing to us."

"One more thing, right?" Mai says. "One more thing to hurt us with."

"It's only rain," Kevin calls out, ready to get going. "Rain and ash from the foothills. Come on, let's stay positive here."

Joel has hold of Felicia, and he boosts her into the rear passenger seat of the Hummer within seconds. Rachel situates Kayla in the middle, next to Felicia, then holds the door open for Scott, who hops up and in. Then she hurries to the front passenger seat, climbing in as quickly as possible but feeling the sting of the rain on her arms. It's ashy and very slightly caustic, leaving vague black streaks across her skin. She wipes it off on her jeans, repulsed.

"Everyone groovy?" Joel asks loudly, slamming the door shut.

Through the rear window, she can see the cab of Pete's truck. Its windows have been partially fixed with cardboard and packing tape— it's wounded but still going strong. Pete is already behind the wheel, and Chloe and Zoe are talking to him as they fasten their seatbelts. The big man still looks morose, but Rachel supposes the presence of two pretty (if dirty) girls can only help his situation.

The Hummer fires up after the truck. Rachel doesn't even hear the other two vehicles start up, but they're quickly inching down the concrete path toward the street. The rain is a steady pulse on the windshield, and Rachel notices that it's the slightest bit thicker than the rain she's accustomed to. The moisture slides down the window a bit more slowly— almost like sleet, except that the temperature is quite the opposite of freezing. In fact, the innards of the Hummer are uncomfortably warm and humid, fogging the sealed windows.

Joel blasts the AC into the defrost vents to clear the glass, then flips on the windshield wipers, and the liquid slices away as if reluctant. The glass is more smeared than clear.

"That's weird," he murmurs. "Those things decide to attack, we're not gonna be able to see them until they're right on top of us." He pauses, then presses the gas. "Maybe that's the point."

"It's entirely within the realm of possibility that they're using this rain as a weapon," says Scott, looking down at his damp arms.

"We'll see," Joel murmurs. "One thing at a time, huh?"

The Hummer rumbles down the concrete, then lurches heavily off the curb north onto Peterson Street. Pete's truck behind them sticks close, taking the curb more carefully. Rachel watches it bounce on the asphalt, and she winces. She can hear the old vehicle creak from here, and she can even see the twins' scared, wary expressions. Joel makes a wide turn west onto Oak, toward Mathews.

Rachel turns and looks after the other two vehicles, heading east on Oak in the direction of Riverside Avenue, and she catches a glimpse of Chrissy's face plastered to the rear window, watching her. She thinks she's giving a small wave, but she can't be sure. Rachel wonders if she will ever see any of them again. She should've said better goodbyes. She feels a quick, sharp lump in her throat.

Shut up. You'll see them again. Soon.

The radio squawks.

"—is Kevin, wanted to wish you guys good luck. Again. We'll be listening, and we'll be in touch. Be careful!" His voice breaks apart in a squawk, then returns. "I don't think I said that before. Be careful. We've all been through too much for all this to end badly. Over."

Joel has already grabbed the radio. He thumbs it now. "Roger that, and same back at you. Take care, over and out."

And then the two vehicles in Mai's group—Ron's blue Subaru and what Rachel guesses is a late-model Chevy Malibu—are heading slowly east and out of view along the street from which the wave of corpses poured earlier in the day. She can see the evidence of the battle that took place here. There are large trees snapped into pale splinters, grass trampled to dirt, lumps of bodies scattered across the property— although she can't make out any blood from a hundred yards away. The rain has mostly washed away the evidence of the bodies' passage, but damage remains evident along the street, from uprooted trees to smashed and trampled mailboxes and mangled shrubs.

Then Rachel can no longer see that, as Joel makes the turn north toward Mountain. Scott and Kayla are watching the library recede, and she realizes that Kayla is probably also watching her home disappear into the distance. In the truck following behind them, Chloe and Zoe are also peering out through a hole in their busted-and-haphazardly-repaired rear window as if to bid farewell to this place. Rachel's own thoughts return to one of her final moments there before sprinting out the doors to the vehicles.

At the edge of the line of corpses was Brian, gray and gone, and at the sight of him, Rachel had emitted an involuntary gasp. Mai, next to her, had said, "I know. I think he had a heart attack." She sighed. "He had some nitro on him, and we gave him that, but … I don't think he was conscious again after what happened."

Even now, Rachel finds herself flashing back to the first time she saw Brian, guarding the library's front doors when she first arrived, and shoving them closed behind her. He was pale, she remembers, unhealthy and bulky. She never had a chance to talk to him, really.

Just minutes ago, she had bent down and placed her open palm against Brian's forehead and had thanked him. Another survivor, gone.

Felicia, huddled in the corner of the rear seat, is not looking back at the library. She's looking straight at Rachel, and the look of uncertainty in her eyes has only grown more pronounced.

"You okay?" Rachel asks her.

A slow nod. "I think so."

Beyond the steady downfall of strange rain, the darkening streets appear empty.

Rachel strains her eyes to make out any movement between homes, any bodies beneath the remaining upright trees, any suggestion of threat. And after what happened at the hospital, she watches for any danger— even from fellow survivors who might have an antagonistic bent. She's at once wary of getting too close to her window and somewhat comforted by the presence of the rain, which, if she's thinking optimistically, seems to be acting as some kind of cover.

To her left, the western skies are gloomy, but she can make out deep red flickering above roiling clouds. She realizes for the first time since it all began that the acrid smell of smoke no longer permeates everything. There's still the ghost of it, but it has markedly diminished, thanks in no small part to this downpour.

It should feel cleansing, but all it feels is weird.

The occupants of the Hummer are wary and subdued as the vehicle rumbles over the wet streets.

"Pretty quiet out there," Joel says.

"Do you see anything?" Scott asks from the back. "No bodies at all?"

"Nothing at all."

"We're not going west …? Or are you making a stop?" Scott says, staring straight ahead toward Old Town. There's a note of misery in his voice, and Rachel notices that all of his snark is gone. He's blank. Either from exhaustion or trauma or both, he's an entirely different person. And yet Rachel has no doubt that given a full night's sleep, he'd be back to his essential Scott-ness.

Joel glances back at him, as if he too doesn't recognize the new tone.

"Yeah, we'll be headed west—toward the foothills." He's still glancing all directions for any signs of movement. "But first we're picking up another passenger. At least, we're going to try."

Joel navigates around a knot of vehicles. Most cars, in the wake of the event, still sit where they drifted against curbs, but in this case several ended up in the center of the road, head-ons that multiplied.

In minutes, they're approaching an intersection that's clear of collisions, making Rachel wonder idly how many other survivors might have cleared vehicles out of the way or even taken some of those cars. Which leads her to wonder again how many people did survive—and how many of those are still in Fort Collins. In the first hours of the event, she remembers seeing quite a few survivors, in chaos, going about their own paths, but those numbers have dwindled, for whatever reasons. How many have fled, and how many have died at the hands of these monsters?

She voices these thoughts to the other occupants of the car.

"Obviously the smart ones got out of town pretty quick," Scott says.

"I don't know about that," says Joel in an even tone. "At least, I'd hope some smart ones stuck around."

"For what?"

"To beat these fuckers."

"Well," says Rachel, "we're still here, and we're smarter than the average bear. I'd like to think so, anyway."

"Plus," says Joel, "we've got Kayla, and she's probably the smartest of all of us."

Kayla offers up a half-smile from between Scott and Felicia.

"Should be coming up on the right—a VW bus." Joel leans forward, searching through the diminishing rain. "See anything?"

Rachel wipes at the fogged windshield on her side. "No …"

"I swear it was—wait, there," he says, gesturing. "I think that's it."

Sure enough, something resembling a narrow VW bus emerges from the rainy murkiness as they draw closer. It is a non-descript, faded orange vehicle, and it is leaning against the curb as if a tire has blown out, in front of a small business that Rachel can't identify.

Joel pulls up close to the vehicle and parks.

"Okay, Rachel and I talked about this earlier. When Mike and I went to the Co-Op yesterday, we spotted one of those things trapped in this bus right here. My plan is to turn it like we did Felicia here."

"To what purpose?" Scott asks, more curious than anything.

"To save a life?" Rachel retorts.

"More than that, though," Joel says. "We're seeing that the turned bodies might be able to help us. Once they heal."

Scott looks over at Felicia. "Wait, do you know something that I haven't heard yet?" There's eagerness in his voice. "Like, a vulnerability?"

Felicia rears to her left, wincing, closes her eyes. "I don't know."

Scott waits a beat, then turns back to Joel. "Are we confident in this plan?"

Joel considers his response, staring down at his service revolver, which he is checking to ensure that it's loaded. "No, we're not." He looks up. "But it feels right. I want to do this and then see where we go from there. Is that good enough?"

Scott looks at Joel, then at the VW bus. "Good enough for me."

The rain patters the roof of the Hummer, giving the evening a nervous soundtrack.

"Okay, ladies, keep an eye out for anyone or anything approaching." He looks around warily. "No telling what's gonna happen next, right?" He refocuses on the bus, then glances at Rachel. "Do you see any movement in the vehicle?"

"I don't see anything."

"All its doors are still closed, though. Still in there, I'd say."

"So what's the plan?"

"We need to get close enough to nail the body with the dart, and there's no way one of those things can make it through a car window and hit its mark," says Joel. "So we gotta open the door."

"Fabulous," says Rachel.

"Scott, you ready to be a hero?"

Scott takes a moment, then nods, seeming to weigh the question seriously.

Joel turns to the windshield. "It's not coming down as hard as it was before, anyway."

It's true—the rain has calmed markedly. It is no longer driving but rather a steady, light shower. The clouds still flicker with unearthly purples and reds, but not with the same ferocity. Rachel would even say that the energy of the luminescence has been gradually diminishing since she first noticed it after sundown.

"I'm gonna step out and take a quick look in there, then come back," says Joel. "Scott, you get that tranq rifle prepped and ready."

Before they'd left the library, Scott—left without a clear task—took up the task of replenishing the tranq canisters with O-negative blood. Without the benefit of viable bags from the hospital, he was forced to draw blood from Mai, the first to volunteer for it. He'd had time to arrange nearly two dozen canisters with new blood and anti-coagulant.

Now, Scott takes the tranq rifle from the rear compartment behind him and digs out a single small blood canister from the small cooler. He shakes it to make sure the anticoagulant is still effective.

Joel has the Hummer in Park, and Rachel's mag light is gripped in his left fist.

"Wish me luck," Joel says, "and Scott? Watch my back."

"You got it."

Scott thumbs his window down and scans the area.

Joel ducks quickly out of the car, the door clicking shut behind him. A humid rush of air swirls through the Hummer's cabin, along with the sour stink of smoke, which is stronger closer to Old Town.

While Scott scans the west side of the street, Rachel keeps her eyes peeled to the east, where Joel is now approaching the VW. The street is deserted. If anything is going to surprise him, it's going to come from between the businesses beyond the bus. These former homes have large, open side yards from which a body might spring quickly and savagely. Rachel can see it happening far too easily in her mind's eye.

The immediate threat, though, is supposedly in this vehicle, although even as Joel arrives at the driver's window and directs the beam of light inside, Rachel can see nothing. He sweeps the interior quickly, and as he moves to the rear, he gives a little jerk, then stabilizes the light. He takes a long look into the back of the bus.

"What is it?" Rachel calls, but he either can't hear her or is choosing to ignore her.

"Is someone in that car?" Kayla asks softly.

"I think so, honey."

Joel points at Scott and gives a beckoning gesture.

Scott opens his door and hops down with the tranq rifle.

Fiercely protective of Kayla—and all too aware of what happened to the little boy, Danny, as they approached the library days ago—Rachel observes the street with paranoid eyes, her peripheral vision heightened, ultra-aware. Her insides lurch.

Scott closes his door without incident, and then he hurries to Joel's side. Holding the tranq rifle upright in his fist, he peeks into the back of the bus. At that moment, Joel turns to Rachel and gives her a brief nod.

Directly behind Rachel, Felicia makes a small sound, a whimper.

Rachel barely makes note of it as Joel prepares to open the VW's side door. He grasps the handle and gives it a turn. It's locked. He shakes his head, pointing to the driver's door.

"Rachel?" Kayla says softly behind her.

"Not now, sweetie."

"Something's wrong with—"

"Hmm? Wrong with what?"

Outside, Joel opens the driver's door with some difficulty, and it scrapes open on a rusty hinge. The squawk of the metal is loud, and Rachel turns her head to scan the area again, as do the two men, to see if anyone or anything reacted to the sound.

When she glances behind her at Pete's truck behind them, she notices that Felicia is staring out her window at the bus, her eyes large, her body tense.

"Something's wrong with Felicia," Kayla says.

"Felicia?" Rachel says, alarmed. "What's the matter?"

Felicia's eyes swivel in their sockets, and her jaw drops awkwardly, her mouth opening at a slant. *"Wait,"* she whispers.

"What is it?"

"That—that woman in there," Felicia says in a rasp.

"Yeah?"

"I can—I can—sss—"

"You can see her? I can't see anything. Where—"

Felicia is shaking her head. "No, no."

Joel slowly reaches his hand around behind the driver's seat to unlock the sliding rear door. Scott watches the rear of the bus, apparently for any sign of attack.

Pete calls something from the truck behind them, and Rachel can't hear it clearly, but it sounds like, "Is it dead?"

Joel responds with something that ends with, "—count on it!"

The rain seems to be intensifying just as Rachel needs to see and hear what's going on. Her stomach aches with foreboding. She feels the sudden urge to open her door and scream a warning.

"Felicia, it's okay, settle down, they're all right," Rachel whispers.

The men huddle for a moment after Joel closes the bus's driver's door, and then Pete makes his heavy way toward the vehicle, casting long, searching glances into the distance with his own mag light, holding his rifle authoritatively in his big right hand. Rachel follows the path of his light. There's still nothing out there. Very quiet, except for the patter of the rain.

Then there's a clatter, and the rain is suddenly very loud, and Rachel is unsure what's happening at first.

Felicia has opened her door and is stepping down into the rain.

"Felicia!" Rachel yells. *"Wait! Kayla, stay there!"*

Kayla clambers backward, away from the open door, making herself as small as possible.

Before Rachel has a chance to think about it, she's stepping out of the Hummer herself, following Felicia.

"Wait!"

She feels the rain immediately, and there's something about it that feels cold—the slightest bit stinging, despite the warmth of the evening. More than that, she's now all too aware that she's out in the open, and vulnerable. A tightness clutches at her chest.

"What are you doing?!" Joel shouts.

Rachel reaches Felicia and grabs hold of her arm, but the woman is resolute in her approach toward the bus.

"Hey ... what's wrong?" Rachel tries, being dragged. *"Stop!"*

"Guys!" Joel says, motioning for Pete and Scott to watch the street until it becomes clear what Felicia is up to. The two men fan out north and south, aiming their weapons into the semi-darkness.

Meanwhile, Felicia has reached the bus. She plants her hands against the window and stares inside.

"Felicia, what is it?" Rachel peers in, too, much more carefully.

There's a body inside the bus, stretched out on its side, and the first thing Rachel sees is the crimson glow pulsing at its neck. The sight sends a shiver of disgust through her.

"It's not dead!" Rachel shouts. "We have to stay away from it!"

Felicia shakes her head slowly from side to side.

Before Rachel realizes anything is happening, the sliding door is opening. She spontaneously lets Felicia's hand go and goes tumbling backward against the Hummer. She doesn't want to be anywhere *near* this bus. She looks wildly behind her, making sure Kayla is safe, hunkered down inside.

Felicia bends into the bus, her hands touching the body.

Then Rachel pushes herself off the Hummer's fender, grabbing at Felicia fearfully.

"Be careful, don't touch the head, don't get near—"

Felicia turns to Rachel, looks her in the eyes, and Rachel stops talking. Felicia's eyes flash under the rain, a luminescence all their own that echoes that of the body in the bus. It's so faint that Rachel doubts it's actually there, as if her mind is playing tricks on her. But she feels immediately calmed under the drone of the rain, even as she becomes increasingly soaked from the droning precipitation.

Felicia doesn't say anything for a moment, but her jaw works, almost crookedly.

"Okay," Rachel says, even as she doesn't know why she's saying it.

"What is it?" Joel shouts. "What's going on?"

Rachel shakes her head, watching.

Felicia turns to the body in the bus again and lays her hands on the thing's shoulders. The body is thin, wasted away. It could be dead. Felicia pulls at it, as if curiously. The body doesn't respond.

"What's wrong with it?" Joel says.

"Is it pretending?" Pete calls from the rear end of the bus, peering in. "Just kill it!"

"*No!*" Felicia says now, forcefully.

Scott edges back, glancing in at the body as he circles the bus. "It's been in there for, what, five days?" he shouts. "Without water, any kind of food. It's no wonder it would be out of it."

"I wouldn't trust that thing as far as I could throw it," Pete says.

"Keep watching!" Joel calls to the men. "Could be a diversion."

Felicia is halfway inside the bus, her hands roaming the trapped body as if searching. The body itself has revealed itself to be that of an older woman, long gray hair spilled out over the floor. The mouth is open, revealing the alien glow, and the eyes are closed. It looks ghastly, pale and corpselike.

Rachel is transfixed and wary, but she takes another glance back at Kayla to make sure she's safe. The girl is crouched behind the Hummer's front seats, as if she wants to disappear into the floorboards. Rachel extends a palm, reassuring her, and Kayla nods.

"What are you looking for?" Rachel cries into the VW bus.

"I don't know," Felicia responds, barely audible.

Her hands inch toward the woman's face, and with a creaky jerk, the body wakes. The eyes open blearily, and a wheezy moan escapes the dry, peeling lips.

Rachel gasps.

"Shit!" Pete shouts, bringing up his rifle.

"No!" Joel yells at him. "Scott! Bring the blood!"

But now Felicia is on top of the body, her hands placed firmly on the woman's head. Rachel cringes at the proximity of Felicia's limbs to the glow, but she notices that the pulse of the red light has increased and become erratic.

At that moment, Rachel sees that the old woman is looking into Felicia's eyes with an expression of terror. The face is frozen in a mockery of humanity, the mouth twisted, a scarlet flush taking hold of the cheeks.

Scott rushes up.

"Wait, wait!" Rachel says.

The spark is loud inside the bus, brightening the interior with a purple flash, and the crimson sphere of energy inside the body's skull collapses in a sudden implosion. As darkness overtakes the bus, the old woman's moan turns instantly to a pained cry.

"Oh my God," Rachel says.

"What happened?" Pete yells, lowering the rifle and wiping rainwater from his brow with his forearm.

Felicia falls away from the woman, her limbs weak, unable to support herself. She crashes back into Rachel, and Rachel takes her full weight, preventing her from spilling to the ground.

"Help!" she calls, but Joel is already there.

His weapon holstered, he takes Felicia in his arms, easily lifting her. He gets her quickly out of the rain and into the Hummer's back seat next to Kayla. Felicia is conscious but bleary, her arms moving as if she's suffered a concussion.

"Her name—is Julia," Felicia whispers raggedly. "She—she—" She shakes her head groggily, as if at any moment she might fall over. "She was on her ... on her way to pick up her grandson ... to take him to daycare." Her voice is high and gaspy, the words diminishing into gibberish.

In the bus, the old woman continues to moan, and tears spill helplessly from her eyes.

Rachel stares at her, unable to process what has happened.

CHAPTER 17

It has stopped raining. That's the one bit of relief.

A moment ago, in the back of Pete's truck, Rachel helped Chloe administer a dose of morphine to the old woman, Julia, who responded by going mercifully quiet. Since being dragged from the VW bus, the woman has been moaning a loud, agonizing drone. After the injection, Rachel checked the woman's pulse and registered a deep kind of awe—understanding that for days, this woman has effectively been a corpse, with no vital signs. No pulse, no respiration. Whatever red thing had inhabited her, it kept her alive in an entirely different way. As the morphine began to take hold, they at least were able to get some water into her without her regurgitating it across the truck bed.

Now she's human again. As with Felicia, her essential human functions have returned, however reluctantly, and the woman will now have to deal with the obvious pain of rehabilitation. If Felicia could do it, then—hopefully—so can this former corpse.

Rachel is back in the Hummer, looking after Felicia herself. Since somehow turning that woman back, she has been at the brink of unconsciousness—pale, unresponsive, limp, and unable or unwilling to talk about how on Earth she knew the woman's name, let alone how she brought her back by seemingly a sheer force of will.

As they dragged Felicia back to safety, the survivors who had witnessed what happened in the VW bus exchanged bug eyes, wordlessly communicating their wonder. Something had happened, and none of them knew what it was, or how it was possible. They didn't know what to say. And the Hummer fell into a deep silence as they all digested this thing—this supernatural thing.

Joel seems to be working it through his mind. He's about to take the turn onto Mountain, and there, off to the right, is the Fort Collins

Food Co-Op—Felicia's store. Felicia herself is oblivious to the proximity, but Rachel notices Joel giving it a second glance. A wash of memories cascades through Rachel's mind, and she finds herself watching Felicia's slack face and the employee shirt she's still wearing.

"There it is," Joel mutters.

"What?" Scott says.

"That's where Michael and I found Felicia."

"The Co-Op?"

"Yeah."

Heading west now on Mountain, Joel runs over something, and Rachel can't help but wince at the soft, uneven feeling of the thump. She's almost certain he ran over a body. She doesn't even want to look.

Since she discovered that many of these bodies could be saved, she has clung to the idea that, as survivors, they should be striving to save as many of them as possible before resorting to annihilating them. She still feels the tug of humanity in that aspiration. But after all the tests, all the bloody episodes, all that has happened since they arrived at the library with nothing but a bunch of O-negative blood and a will to survive … she has come to realize that the vast majority of these spider-walking corpses are beyond redemption.

Not an easy thing to swallow.

Holding Felicia's hand with her left and Kayla's with her right, Rachel sighs and pushes back into the seat.

She's able to look back on everything that has happened now. She's not proud of herself. And some of the actions she has taken, these things she has done with her own two hands—they have caused irreparable harm. She won't give in to the impulse to come up with excuses, not even now, at the end of the world. Her dad always told her—she can hear his half-amused voice so vividly in her mind's ear—to be a decent human being. Above all else, be a kind and decent and empathetic person. He'd usually say this in the wake of her doing something stupid.

She's not sure she ever really understood the full weight of that instruction until now. But goddamn, she has tried. Does it count if you try your hardest to be a good human being, but the decisions you make toward that attempt are not sound?

Oh Daddy, she whispers inside. *Why aren't you here?*

His body is in the back of this very vehicle, snug inside a tarp. Joel himself wrapped the body, giving the job a formal and almost militarily solemn precision. She watched him from inside the library, through the rain, not dwelling on the details of her father's body but rather Joel's and Liam's careful movements and serious expressions. Her heart swelled for the two men.

Liam had found her right after, and she had thanked him as he'd toweled his head dry, still out of breath.

"Look, I'm sorry about what happened to him," he'd said. "He was a standup guy." He paused, appearing to search for words. Liam didn't know Rachel, really, or her dad. He happened to be thrown together with them under extraordinary circumstances—by virtue of them having the same blood type. Sheer coincidence. He was trying to be nice. He looked at a loss, standing there. "It's … ridiculous."

"I know," Rachel had said, focusing on her work, loading boxes.

"For what it's worth … I think your dad actually saved us. I think his plan worked."

All she'd wanted was to go deaf at that moment, to run away, to sob. She'd found the strength to nod, if only to make him stop talking, but she knows her reaction must have seemed rude.

Now both of her parents are gone, and she herself might be on her way to a similar fate. She has no idea what the future holds. Either death—the most probable—or something else. All she knows is that her existence is moment-to-moment. Has been for days.

"Where are we headed?" she barely hears Scott ask Joel.

"We're stopping at Rachel's house," he whispers, barely audible. "We're going to drop off Michael. If you have a problem with that, we can talk it over."

A pause.

"I don't have a problem with that."

"Good."

"We're going to bury him? Is that the plan?"

Rachel leans forward. "That's for later. But I do want to take him home."

Scott nods, looking down.

Joel glances back at her. "Don't plan on staying long, girl. If I sense any kind of danger, we're *out* of there. That's what I told Pete, and that's the agreement."

For the first time since the VW bus incident, Kayla speaks.

"Are we almost there?"

Rachel peers out the window at the homes flitting by. She watches for a street sign. After a moment, she catches a glimpse of the Philly cheesesteak place at College and Olive.

"A little longer," she says to Kayla.

"I have to pee."

"Can you make it 10 minutes?"

"I think so."

"You'll get to see where I live," Rachel says, then immediately guesses that it wasn't the brightest thing to say to someone who no longer has a home.

Kayla doesn't say anything.

After checking on Felicia again, feeling her pulse, Rachel leans over her and stares out the window. The streets are preternaturally quiet, devoid of any life. She would almost prefer to see one of those things spidering its way down one of these side streets, even rushing at them, than to see these barren roads. Even now that the survivors are on the move, away from the library, there's the sense that monsters are peering at them from hiding places, plotting their next move or watching for vulnerabilities. Even worse, there's the feeling that Fort Collins itself has been murdered—and by extension, the rest of the world.

Up front, both Joel and Scott are watching the streets as well, silent and wary. But it has been long minutes now since they found the old woman, and a sense of relative calm has fallen over the crew. She knows they're all cautious of that being a *false* sense of calm. Nothing that has happened so far has been predictable.

Rachel becomes aware of a soft sound in the silence, and she realizes it's the radio spilling static.

"Has anyone tried the radio?" she says, scooting forward.

Scott appears startled from his reverie. He looks away from the passenger-side window. "At the library, yesterday, yeah, but not recently."

He tries the knobs, turning up the volume and poking through the presets as Joel makes the turn onto Mulberry. Giving up on the presets, Scott finds the Seek button, presses it, and the digital readout scrolls endlessly through the FM dial.

"Try AM?" she suggests.

He switches the band and tries again.

Same thing.

He stabs the button off. "I'll try again later. That's depressing."

"I don't see *anything* out there," Joel mutters from the driver's seat, watching the dark businesses float by. "Not a goddamn thing."

"Where did they all go?" Kayla asks in a small voice.

"That's definitely the question, kid," Joel says.

Slowly coming into focus in the distance is a smoking ruin—the remains of some kind of collision?—near the corner where Mulberry meets Meldrum, below the Lincoln Center performing arts complex. As they approach, memories of her friends' productions with the youth troupe at Debut Theatre wash over her. Rachel had attended some of the plays in those days, before her mom started her gradual decline. She feels a distant pang of regret now for the way a lot of her friendships at that time dissipated. Rachel finds it hard to believe that she was once weak enough to let her entire life crumble like sand from her grasp.

How is it possible she lacked the maturity and strength to weather those times? She feels more regret for her own actions than for the machinations of fate. After a period of grieving, her dad brought home a woman. So what? He was human, after all. All she remembers now is an embarrassing teen rebelliousness, and it stabs her painfully knowing that her father was right about her all those years.

She feels the urge to glance back toward his wrapped body, which is right behind her in this big, unwieldy, stupid vehicle—inches away. If only she could wake him with apologies. She would do that. She would definitely do that.

"What is that?" Kayla wonders as they get closer to the wreck.

Joel approaches the smoking hulk warily and comes to a stop thirty yards short of it.

Pete pulls the truck up next to them, windows rolled down.

"What's up?" he calls.

Rachel thumbs her window down. "Not sure, hold tight."

Two cars are angled toward each other, not quite touching, and one of the cars is a blackened shell, completely burned out. Black stains have blistered the other vehicle's silver paint on its left side. Rachel counts nine bodies strewn across the asphalt—a horrifically gory scene that has become all too clear in the headlights of the survivors' vehicles.

"Don't look, Kayla, okay?"

But Kayla has already seen something and is curling into a trembling ball next to her.

"This is recent," Joel says, loudly enough for Pete to hear. "Look at the blood there."

Twin, bright red lakes of blood—fresh blood—have formed next to two mangled bodies perhaps ten feet from the vehicles. Both bodies appear to have been dismembered, and not neatly, either. They have been torn apart, decapitated. Rachel feels her gorge rise and looks away.

"Let's get the hell away from here, huh?" Scott says.

"I'm almost positive we're safe."

"I wish that 'almost' filled me with more confidence."

"Do you think this is the same thing that—?" Rachel begins.

"The same thing that attacked us near the station—same one that almost got you and Kevin at the hospital. Yeah." Joel lets his forearms rest against the top of the steering wheel as he cautiously glares around the vicinity.

"And you think we're safe from that?" Scott says, genuinely matter-of-fact. "How?"

Joel gestures with his thumb straight backward, toward Felicia, who is still dozing but now mumbling softly. "Her."

After what happened north of the library, Rachel is even more in line with the theory that Felicia is the key to something—something larger than the odd sense of safety that she engenders, and even larger than what she showed them at the VW bus. She's not sure that what Felicia did equates to actual salvation, in any way, shape, or form, but there's a certain amount of promise to her. Truth is, she'd rather be with Felicia than not. She's not even sure she would have agreed to this little mission without her.

"How?" Scott asks.

"Well, I don't know yet, Scott, but I think we're gonna find out."

"You have any theories? I mean, you think it's those things doing this?"

"Yeah, I do."

"How?"

"Get out of the car with me, I'll show you."

Rachel feels Kayla tense up next to her, and she lays a comforting hand on her thigh.

"I don't think so," Scott says.

"I'm gonna prove right now that we're safe."

The door opens, and Joel begins stepping out.

"Joel!" Rachel shouts. "Wait! Are you sure—?"

"I'm pretty damn sure, but—" He pauses, looks across the Hummer's vast hood. "Hey, Pete, just in case, you watch my back, willya? Honk if you—you know—if you see anything horrible."

"Jesus, Joel!" Rachel pleads, grabbing at his sleeve, which slips through her grasp.

"You got it," Pete says as the twins watch him bring up his AR-15 and maneuver it through his window to aim in the general direction of the scene.

Joel slips out of the Hummer. His service revolver is in his fist immediately, drawn steady and high. He signals to the occupants of the car next to them to stay put and remain quiet. Gaze darting left right and behind, he inches toward the suspicious wreckage.

Rachel's eyes are peeled, anxiously watching the surroundings. She knows Joel can take care of himself, and she's somewhat encouraged by the fact that the skies have been relatively calm. The attack at the hospital occurred suddenly, out of the blue, yes, but it was preceded and perhaps precipitated by some kind of cosmic roar. When Rachel glances skyward now, all she sees is a dissipated smokiness, backlit by crimson—as if whatever powerful presence was once there has receded but is keeping a watchful eye.

Or perhaps it's only wishful thinking that the presence is no longer powerful.

Joel makes it to the scene of the accident and kneels to examine something. He cocks his head, rises, goes to the first of the bodies. He stares at it with distaste, then goes to another body—what's left of it.

After that, he takes a look at two more bodies, then backs away from the wreckage.

When he climbs back into his seat, Rachel and the others wait for him to talk.

Finally: "It's so quiet."

"What did you see?"

"I think it happened in the past hour, probably. So it wasn't the same time as the library attack, and I think it's even more recent than the two attacks on you and me, Rach. They're still active, and I think it's safe to assume they're still targeting humans. Survivors."

"Okay, so …?"

Joel nods. "They're basically suicide bombers."

A moment of silence.

"What?" Rachel says.

"You're kidding me," Scott says.

"It's pretty clear out there: There are two bodies that were turned—it's obvious from what's left of them that their joints are popped. Skin abrasions from the way they walk. Dislocated limbs. All that sap and splinter and shit. And so on. Those are bodies in the worst shape."

"Could it be some survivor targeting them?" says Scott. "Like we were doing? Some kind of assassin?"

"Doesn't look that way. The damage to the bodies, the blood and bone spatter—it's all consistent with a detonation from inside." Kayla gives a sickened look, but he goes on. "If we were talking about a projectile from outside, or some kind of explosive like a grenade, you'd have a very different spray. And the collateral damage suggests suicide bombers, too."

"What do you mean?"

"From the looks of it, those *other* bodies were survivors, and they were the ones targeted."

"But targeted how?" Scott says.

"That thing in their heads," Rachel says. "That glowing … thing. They're detonating themselves."

"That's what I'm betting, yeah. Let's roll."

As they drift past the wreckage, Rachel steels herself and takes a long look. Immediately she's reminded of the aftermath of the attack on the truck at the hospital. After the roar from the crimson sky, those bodies at the small pines beyond the parking lot—those two businessmen—had become abruptly mobile. They had spidered toward them, and—if Joel's theory is correct—they had thrown themselves like grenades in an effort to destroy human beings. Rachel shakes her head, knowing Joel is right. Maybe a part of her knew it all along.

There are also two formerly infected bodies on the ground here, and

Rachel imagines them detaching from trees and doing the same thing to these poor people. She can barely glance at the targeted corpses. There are three of them. What, had these people been on foot? Shrapnel wounds dot their bodies, darkly red. Still fresh, but beginning to dry. Their faces are frozen in anguish, surprised in death, the corners of mouths down-turned, teeth showing. Rachel tears her gaze away.

As they pass Canyon Avenue, Rachel feels a spurt of adrenaline, knowing she's close to home. Just a few blocks now.

The sky is still on fire, but at least the raging fires of a few days ago have calmed. No longer churning great black cumulous clouds of noxious smoke, the fires have turned mostly gray, either nearing the end of their fuel or calmed by somewhat cooler temperatures, the rain, and no wind at all. At least that's what Rachel imagines.

She considers that. Since this thing began, there has been no wind or breeze of any kind. As if this presence—whatever it is—has not only destroyed humanity but all of nature. Is it possible? She hasn't seen any animals either. Insects, even.

"Rachel," Kayla whispers. "Are they going to kill us?"

"Shhh, no, honey."

"How do you know?"

Rachel feels a lump in her throat in anticipation of her lie. "Because we're so much stronger than they are."

But Joel's interpretation of the attack scene has filled Rachel with a new nervous energy. The survivors' plan so far has been ambiguous at best, and now the thought of confronting these things again—this collective menace—seems impossible. If the reanimated bodies are still attacking, as has become clear, is Joel's idea of going on the offensive still the best idea? Perhaps they should be fleeing east with the rest of them. Night is approaching rapidly, and that prospect too gives her the chills.

She leans forward to give voice to her fears.

"Are we doing the right thing?"

"What do you mean?"

"Should we be going in the other direction?"

Joel pauses before answering. He's watching the surroundings carefully. Behind them, Scott is fidgeting but doing his best to hide it, Kayla looks meek and drained, and Felicia seems to be on the edge of consciousness, coming to slowly.

Joel rolls his window down and gestures for Pete to drive up next to them. In a moment, the vehicle slides up, and they're face to face with Chloe and Zoe, peering out from the front and back passenger seats. More than ever, it's like seeing double, with their exhausted sunken eyes and their twin expressions of teeth-gritted anticipation. Both of their windows are rolling down.

"Hey," they say in unison.

"What do we got?" Pete calls from the driver's seat. "We almost there?"

"Not yet, a few more blocks to Rachel's house, but—that scene back there."

"Yeah?"

Joel tells them about what he suspects. His words are quick and efficient.

"I'm not turning back, man," Pete says. "Those fuckers took out my only brother. I want to go right to the source and burn 'em to hell."

"Well, that's pretty cut-and-dried."

"I'm serious, dude."

"I know you are, but what about your companions there? You gals still game for this?"

The twins look at each other, then back up at Joel.

"We never figured this was gonna be easy," Zoe says as Chloe nods. "You spend a little time with Pete, and you start feeling like you can take on anything."

The big man, startled by the compliment, blurts out, "Damn right."

As the Hummer idles, Joel turns his gaze to the occupants of his own vehicle.

"Look, the bottom line is this: Even though we're armed up and pretty well defended, it's still dangerous out here. Something's going to happen, I think we can count on that. I still think we have them on their heels, and I've made it clear that I also think we have an advantage in this truck. Two of them now." His eyes dart to Felicia, who is waking up. "I want to make sure we're all in."

No one speaks for a moment.

Finally, Scott says, "Yeah, Joel, we're all in."

"Okay, let's do it," he calls, loud enough for everyone to hear. "A few more blocks, then we'll hang a right."

He settles back and motors forward toward City Park.

Kayla squeezes Rachel's hand, and when Rachel looks down at her, she is surprised to find an optimistic expression on her face.

"We're going to win," the little girl says.

"Of course we are."

Rachel almost manages to keep her voice from breaking. Because at the moment, she's feeling far from positive about their course forward. She's about to say goodbye to her father and then hurtle forward into an uncertain future with only an indefinite plan for success against a gigantic, unfathomable threat.

In moments, they're passing Joel's wrecked police cruiser at the mouth of her neighborhood. The Honda Pilot that her dad rammed it with sits crookedly against it. The memory is a tough one, and she can feel Joel recalling it too. She remembers the bodies rushing toward them. She remembers escaping them by the narrowest of margins. Good God, they had come so close to meeting their ends. So close! The memory makes her shiver.

Next to Rachel, Felicia is murmuring more loudly.

"… she … she …"

"Hey, you doing all right? It's me, Rachel."

Felicia blinks and stares at her, then at Kayla.

"Is she … did she survive?" Felicia whispers, looking around.

"Yes, she did. I got some morphine in her, and she's in the back of Pete's truck. She'll be fine."

Felicia twists her neck to try to get a glimpse.

"Don't worry, she's back there, she's fine."

"No … no, she's not." Felicia appears overcome with sadness. She turns toward the window, and Rachel hears the bump of her forehead touching the glass. "I need to be back there with her. I can help her."

"We're making a stop, so we'll see what we can do, make sure she has everything she needs."

Felicia is silent.

Kayla reaches across Rachel and pats Felicia's right leg affectionately.

"It will be okay," she says. "We're going to win."

CHAPTER 18

Rachel's home appears ahead of her like a dream inside a nightmare. As they draw closer, she watches the familiar yard, the small porch, the cracked driveway. There's a corpse at the edge of the lawn—an unclothed young woman who has suffered some kind of head wound. Her limbs are askew at impossible angles. Did her father actually shoot this body during his escape, before he rammed Joel's cruiser? She remembers, years ago, him telling her about grandpa's gun—showing it to her with a sense of reverence, communicating its power—and she knows he kept it in a safe somewhere in his bedroom, although she has never seen it. The thought of him using that old gun to fire a bullet into someone is beyond her comprehension, but then so is this world.

Joel pauses the Hummer in the middle of the street, his eyes tracking the rows of homes. Nothing but heavy silence out there.

"Which one's yours?"

"That one."

He inches forward, still scanning.

"Two bodies there, you see 'em?"

"Yeah."

The second body, that of bloated Mrs. Carmichael, is now on her porch. Last time she saw Mrs. Carmichael, the woman was gnawing on the Bristlecone Pine in Tony's side yard. Why is she on her porch now?

"This all went down before we found your dad."

"Yeah."

"How do we look? Anybody see anything? Scott?"

The neighborhood is deathly still, under a troubling sunset, under the persistent white-gray of diminishing smoke. As Rachel scans the blackly broiling skies, she senses unrest but relative calm. The air coming in through the vents isn't as rank as it was a couple days ago, and it's blessedly cooler, by perhaps thirty degrees since the worst of it. Colorado summer evenings have always brought relief, and that holds true even now.

"Nothing out there," Scott says. "Not that I can see."

"Let's get this done," Joel says, lurching the Hummer to a stop and setting the transmission to Park, leaving the big vehicle to idle. He reaches for his door handle, then pauses. "Just to be clear—if anything happens, if we see anything aggressive, we're outta here."

"I know, I get it."

"Do I get to go to the bathroom now?" Kayla says.

"Yes, honey, you follow me close. Take this flashlight."

Just as Rachel hands Kayla one of the flashlights, Felicia opens her door and hops down to the pavement. In the dim light, Rachel watches her hurry, hobbling, to the rear of Pete's truck to check on the woman there. Felicia peers over the sideboards, reaching an arm over.

"What's she doing?" Joel asks.

"All I know is she wants to help that lady," Rachel says. "I don't know, maybe she—maybe she feels the kinship?"

"You gotta tell me something—what in the hell did she do in that bus?"

"Heck if I know."

"Think she can do it again, if we find more?"

"I'm not sure how much strength she has. Whatever she did, it brought her down for the count."

Joel nods, then turns to Scott. "You're on watch, okay? The whole time we're in there."

"Got it." Scott now has a rifle in his grip.

"All right. Rachel, you ready?"

She nods.

"You'll lead the way with Kayla, and Pete and I'll carry Michael through to his bedroom. Right?"

"Yes."

"You armed?"

"Yes." She has taken Joel's revolver and become accustomed to the heft in her grip.

"Let's do it."

Two doors open, and they spill out into the smoky night. Joel motions to Pete, who is watching from the truck directly behind the Hummer. He opens his door and drops out heavily. He and Joel go directly to the rear of the Hummer and lift out Rachel's father with a little difficulty. Rachel looks away and starts up the lawn toward the porch.

The first thing she sees is that the front door is slightly ajar—her dad must have left in a hurry. And during whatever frenzy he faced, Mrs.

Carmichael met her end right there on the porch. Her massive body is splayed out on its stomach, hanging halfway off the concrete and into the large rose bushes there. She looks as if she tried to squeeze underneath the white porch railing—maybe in pursuit of her dad?

Rachel stutters to a stop when she sees that Mrs. Carmichael's limbs are still twitching.

"Wait here, Kayla."

The little girl bounces backward, away from the porch.

"What is it?" Joel huffs behind Rachel.

Rachel steps onto the first step, and a ghastly wheeze escapes the large woman's mouth. Mrs. Carmichael's head, dotted with blood, twists to peer and scowl at Rachel as she tiptoes closer. The mostly unclothed body, its flowery muumuu tangled up near the armpits, roils fleshily but can't move more than a few inches. One arm is hopelessly stuck, immobilizing her.

Rachel gestures. "She's not dead."

"Rach, get out of there!" Joel shouts, coming to a realization a split-second before Rachel. "Now!"

Rachel springs backward off the porch, takes three stumbling strides, and a bomb explodes behind her, strobing the street red. As hot blood sprays her back and flank, she tumbles to the ground, both ears ringing.

"Jesus!" she yells, muffled, still rolling on the grass. She spins, watching for Kayla, sees her all the way back at the truck. Relief floods her.

A hand finds her shoulder and holds her still. She wants to get away, farther from the porch, but she's being held by a vice grip. It's Pete.

"Did you fuckin' see that?" he shouts in the aftermath of the concussion.

"Yes I did," comes Joel's muted voice.

"What happened?!" one of the twins yells from the truck.

"Rachel!" Kayla cries.

"Corpse blew up on the porch!" Joel responds, his eyes wide, scanning the vicinity.

"Blew up?"

"Head fuckin' blew like a grenade!" Pete says.

"Let me go!" Rachel writhes on the ground. "Is Kayla all right?"

"She's fine," Joel says, close now. "You took the brunt of that one. You hurt?"

His hands touch her back lightly, feeling for wounds. "Christ, I need one of those flashlights. Scott, can you—"

"Here." He hands it over.

"I'm fine!" Rachel cries.

"Hold still, girl."

"I'm not a girl!"

"Hold still, lady."

"Oh for chrissakes—"

The mag light is in Joel's hand now, and sudden light blinds her then moves down her body. She feels his fingers swiping at blood, determining whether it's hers.

"I don't see any injuries, actually," Joel says. "You are one lucky—"

"Jumpin' Jesus!" Pete says, standing up. "That thing went *off!*"

"Scott, stay focused, willya?" Joel says. "That blast was loud enough to wake the dead. Literally."

Joel helps Rachel to her feet, and she brushes herself off, feeling embarrassed and horrified in equal measure. She wipes at her neck and feels slick, fresh blood. She undergoes a full-body shudder.

"Gah!"

She glances up to see the twins rushing to her with towels.

"Damn!" says Chloe, voice warbling. "That was too frickin' close!"

"Here, let's clean you up," Zoe says, wiping her arms and back. "Did that thing really—"

Rachel nods miserably. She catches a glimpse of Kayla near one of the Hummer's big tires, watching nervously, holding her flashlight like a talisman that might ward away evil. Rachel gives the girl a shaky thumbs-up, mouths *It's okay.* Then she gestures at her to come back.

Behind the Hummer, still leaning over into the truck bed, Felicia watches Rachel almost impassively.

The blanket-mummified body of Rachel's dad lies between the Hummer and the truck, and her heart aches at the thought of Joel and Pete simply dropping him there. She looks away, then shrugs the twins away.

Kayla is back at her side.

"You're okay, right?"

"Yes, I'm fine."

Which isn't exactly true, but close enough.

Joel and Pete have surrounded Mrs. Carmichael's body, staring down at it with frank curiosity. The mag light aimed down at her has a slight tremble.

Rachel hears Pete say, "Lord have mercy!" The ringing in her ears is already subsiding.

She moves toward the porch, shielding Kayla from the sight.

Joel catches the movement. "You sure you want to see this?"

"Yeah." She clicks her jaw, and her ears pop.

"Oh my God!" Chloe says, stopping.

Mrs. Carmichael's head is gone, and so is most of the top of her body. Her torso is a parody of human flesh, torn apart from the head down, sloppy piles of yellow fat glistening in pools of blood across the porch. A great cavity reaches down toward her bowels, and the torn flesh is still bleeding out. There is no black scorch from an explosive, just splayed-open muscle, devastated bone, and sickly, veined adipose tissue. The window behind the mess is shattered, and brain matter is sliding down a glass stalactite still clinging to the pane.

Long moments pass before Rachel looks away from the red ruin, her gorge rising. Her mom's rose bushes are splattered with blood and pieces of skull and brain, and in a flash she sees that these bushes might have saved her life—or at least injury. They acted as a partial shield from the bone shrapnel.

"Let's finish this and get going," Joel says. "I think this is a pretty convincing illustration of the danger out here. I'm sorry we won't be burying your dad, Rachel, at least not now. But we can leave him here with his wife."

"I knew that going in," says Rachel, still shivering, still shaken. "Come on, Kayla, the bathroom is right through here." She kneels next to Kayla, facing her away from the atrocity on the porch. "It's right there, to the left, okay? Point your flashlight right there. See it? See that door?"

Kayla nods and goes inside.

Rachel turns back to the porch.

"Get back to the truck," Joel calls to the twins, "help Felicia with that woman."

"Right," Zoe says.

"Keep a constant eye on everything, got it?"

And the twins are off.

"C'mon, Pete," Joel says, handing Rachel his mag light.

The two men head for her father's body, and Rachel is left on the porch, still staring. She feels herself convulsively swallowing, not wanting to throw up. She has to concentrate hard to stop. And it's as much shock as the horrorshow on her porch, she knows. She closes her eyes, finds strength, and turns her back to Mrs. Carmichael to face the street.

Joel and Pete are already approaching with her father.

"Go ahead," Joel says, gesturing her forward. "Go, go."

Rachel steps into the house, followed quickly by the two men, and although she immediately registers the foul, unmistakable reek of Susanna's decomposing body, none of them comments on it. Rachel begins breathing through her mouth.

The house is dim, lit almost solely by her mag light, but it reminds her, once again, of the morning—less than a week ago!—when this all began. She'd awoken predawn that Saturday, enjoying the silence of the new day, eating her apple here in the front room. Her eyes dart to the coffee table to find the apple gone. No, there it is on the ground below the table, dried out, brown, a thin core. It's still there. Her throat fattens with a kind of longing for a too-recent past.

"Back here," she says. She clenches her teeth to keep them from chattering.

The men maneuver through the front room, into the narrow hallway, and find her dad's bedroom.

That's when she stops, and Mrs. Carmichael is mostly forgotten.

The reminders of her family, of her father, overwhelm her. In the sweep of the flashlight, she sees evidence of his passage here days ago, when he was alive, when he was simply going home to find his wife. When he was still a part of her life.

In a burst, the tears begin. They flood her eyes helplessly, surprising her with their ferocity. In the quiet room, she trembles and weeps, and she's embarrassed, and she can't help it, and she doesn't want to apologize. She knows the gory fate of Mrs. Carmichael is coloring everything— the woman's blood still feels warm against her back, smeared on her exposed skin—but she's desperate for this moment to mean something, and everything else angers her.

"I'm sorry, Rach," Joel says, and the words are strangely loud in the dark room.

Through blurred vision, she sees that her father wrapped Susanna tightly in their bedsheets. A surge of love flows through her, for both of them, for both her father and his wife. For Susanna. Imagining her fate and his grief, his loss. How he must have felt, losing two spouses.

Rachel gestures to the bed, and Joel and Pete carry her father there, laying him gently next to his wife. Rachel wipes at her eyes.

The two men step back.

"We'll be outside," Joel says. "Take a few minutes, okay? But not too long. We gotta get back on the road."

She nods.

At that moment, Kayla comes out of the bathroom, her nose crinkled in the flickering luminescence of her flashlight. She doesn't say anything, merely takes Joel's hand when he offers it and lets him guide her back outside. Wordlessly, Joel picks her up. Rachel watches him carry the girl away toward the front door, sees Joel whispering to Kayla, and Kayla turning off her light and covering her eyes, burying her head against Joel's shoulder.

Rachel steps back in to her father's bedroom, stops, sighs. It's almost impossible to ignore the high, sweet reek of decomposition, particularly as she sniffs back tears. The stench makes her eyes water still further. She wants so much to be able to ignore that smell—as well the knowledge that her father would soon only add to it. If only they had time to bury him properly.

"You're home," she whispers. "You're home now."

The words sound hollow and meaningless coming out of her mouth, but they will have to be enough. She's suddenly at a loss what to say. She feels depression still scratching at her soul—ever since her return to the hospital after destroying Tony—and a part of her would even admit that she would be willing to crawl into her own bed right now, just as her dad and Susanna are back in their bed, and pretend that none of this ever happened. She would sleep for twenty hours and wake to some new day, and wander to the kitchen to eat her morning apple and contemplate her life as dawn gave way to morning. And Susanna would wake sighing, her father not long after her, and they would try to connect with her, with Rachel, and this time she would listen to them with all she had, and hug them, and laugh with them. Both of them.

It takes her a moment before she realizes she's talking through her tears.

"*... miss you so much, Daddy, you can't be gone, you have to tell me what to do, why did this happen, why did this happen? Please wake up, both of you, please wake up, I promise things will be different, I'm sorry I was such a ...*"

She wipes her nose and eyes with her forearm.

She goes quiet.

She knows she has to go outside and join the others.

Something catches her eye.

The bedroom closet is open, and even in the dimness she can see that a panel has been opened in back, and the open face of a small steel safe has been revealed. She steps closer, squinting, training the mag light on the closet, wiping her eyes again. This must be the safe where her dad kept grandpa's gun. He must have grabbed it hurriedly and left everything open.

And there's something else there. For a moment, her mind refuses to process what the stark light has revealed. She edges closer and bends down. Stacked in the safe are neat, banded stacks of cash. She reaches down to draw one out. It's a thick packet of brand-new $100 bills. She reads the band. Ten thousand dollars. There are other packets of smaller bills, too. Her stomach does a somersault. There must be over a hundred thousand dollars in here.

"What the hell?" she asks the empty room, her voice almost a whine.

She re-examines the rest of the closet. Susanna's clothes have been swept aside, same with the drywall-and-laminate panel that hid the safe. It has been flung to the right and left there. Her dad did this—what— two or three days ago? Is that possible? He had opened this secret safe and taken the gun but left all this money for anyone to find?

Is this what you came back to do? Why?

The scene exudes secrecy, even shame. Haste.

Crime.

She lets the money drop to the floor, kicks it with her foot toward the steel safe, and slides the closet door shut with a bang. Then she backs away from the closet, casting glances from the door to the bed.

What happened here?

In a moment, she's rushing through the house and back outside, skirting past the demolished body of Mrs. Carmichael, giving it a resentful glare.

The relief of fresh air is tangible, but the afternoon is starting to fade toward evening. She jogs to the Hummer, which is still idling. She hurries around the great yellow hood and climbs up into the passenger seat. Tears are still moistening her cheeks, and now she feels a strange bewilderment.

Why are there untold thousands of dollars spilling out of a secret compartment in her dad's closet?

Her mind has begun to reach back to relevant memories, grabbing for anything that might make sense. Images of her dad from the past mingle with terrible, more recent memories of him in his dying moments, and she shakes them away, feeling grief rise up like bile, knowing that she shouldn't have to be dealing with any of this.

It's not fair.

She can't help but go back to the sequence of events that led to her and Joel racing from the hospital to find her dad. When she'd awoken that fateful morning at the hospital, bleary and hollow, he was gone from his room. When she'd asked Bonnie and Joel about him, they said they had no idea. It was Kevin who'd laid out the truth: Her father had left the hospital pre-dawn to return to their home.

"Why didn't you wake me up?" she remembers crying. She'd begun to gesture with her arms, and realized with some embarrassment that she still had her stuffed bear in her left hand.

Kevin only shrugged his big shoulders. "He asked me not to."

"He has a concussion!"

"He seemed pretty lucid to me."

"Did he say why he was going?" In her head, at the time, she'd added *without me.*

"He said it was something he had to do, and that he'd be back within an hour or two."

Outside the hospital's windows, Fort Collins had been silent. Rachel could only imagine his mission, three miles away. She knew her father would find Susanna and wonder why she was dead in her bed—and they had dealt with that. But now she knows he'd had another purpose— something entirely mysterious that he "had to do."

What else?

At some point before leaving to fetch him—Joel had even asked out of the side of his mouth, "Your dad always been the needs-rescuing type?"—the sky had opened up, once more, with an alien roar, signifying something new, some kind of change. As he'd been rooting around in that safe, had the bodies around him started becoming newly aggressive? Is that why he'd left things messy, unfinished, in his closet? At the hospital, in the wake of the roar, she remembers the bodies at the edge of the parking lot flinching. Had the corpses closer to her father reacted to the sound in a different way, immediately attacking? They were surely aggressive when she and Joel had arrived at this neighborhood to find him.

She'd been rightfully angry at her dad for leaving her at the hospital without saying anything to her, and she had at first blamed that head wound. He clearly wasn't in his right mind. That's what she'd thought at the time.

Now, slamming the Hummer's door shut behind her and staring at the house—with its splatter of dark red across the entire porch, with the skull-shot naked corpse at the edge of the driveway, with her father and stepmother side-by-side on their bed near a pile of mysterious cash— she feels again as if she might throw up.

Where did it all come from? What did it mean?

Her thoughts are hopelessly scattered.

Kayla has leaned forward from the rear compartment and attached herself to her left arm, nuzzling her wordlessly, and the contact spreads a modicum of warmth through her. She closes her eyes, pats Kayla's shoulder gently, tries to let the little girl work her magic, but it won't happen. Something inside her resists. She can also feel Felicia's gaze on the back of her head, and once again, it feels as if the young woman's stare is reaching more deeply inside her than her surface.

As the Hummer rumbles away from her home, Rachel watches the familiar façade recede behind them. Then she glances over at Joel. He's staring out the windshield, inspecting the homes to the left and the right. He looks over at her.

"You okay?"

"I think so, yeah."

"You think so?"

"Uh huh."

Shit, is the single word that she repeats inside. She can't afford for this thing—whatever it is—to distract her. She swallows, closes her eyes, grits her teeth, and urges it all away.

When she opens her eyes, she tells Kayla to sit back in her seat.

"Buckle up, honey, I'm fine," she says, lying again.

Felicia is alert, turned toward her window. She's looking at something.

"What is it?" Rachel asks her. "What's going on?"

"They're out there." Felicia whispers, gesturing with her head against the glass. "They were coming toward the house, and now they're following us."

"You've been watching them?" Joel asks.

No answer for a moment. Then:

"I can feel them."

Rachel stares out the windshield. At first she sees nothing, and then she finds them. Beyond the trees of the neighboring homes, moving in fits and starts behind low fences, their almost-indistinct crimson glows throbbing left and right, through the gaps in the weather-worn cedar. Vague flashes of red.

Joel glides to a stop, thumbs on the radio. "Pete, come in, you see our friends over here to the right? Over."

A moment of static, then: "I see 'em now, yeah, over."

"Just keep an eye on them, out."

He drops the radio into the center console, then seems lost in thought, watching, as the two trucks idle.

"They're restless," Joel whispers.

"Can we get the hell out of here?" Scott says.

"Now hold on a sec. Look at them. They're staying put. They're scared."

"They get enough numbers behind them, maybe they won't be so scared."

"I'm not sure that matters."

"You're betting with our lives again, sitting here and testing those things," Scott says reasonably.

Rachel watches Felicia. The young woman is motionless, save for the working of her jaw.

If Felicia is protecting them, Rachel is almost certain it's inadvertent. Felicia is still undergoing some kind of inner trauma, and a part of that struggle is wrapped up in what Rachel believes is an ability to actually communicate with those bodies. Somehow, in some way, the collective voice of this thing, this invading species, is still in her head, even if she won't admit it. And she's locked in an unconscious battle with it. Rachel gathers this not only from what Felicia has managed to tell her, but also from how Felicia seemed to instinctively know Julia's name, and the shift of her jaw, the look in her eyes, the way she moves.

And if that's the case, it's not only Felicia protecting the survivors.

It's the woman in the back of Pete's truck, too.

In which case, Joel's plan is working.

Kayla clears her throat in the middle of the back seat.

"We need to drive," the girl says in her small voice. "Can we drive now?"

As if snapped from a doze, Joel blinks and turns to her. "Almost, girlie."

He's watching the surreptitious movement beyond the fences. It's far enough away to not be an immediate threat, but Rachel can't help but flash again on the loss of Danny, before they got to the library. The horror of that moment will stay with her forever, and the thought of that happening to Kayla makes her break into a quivering sweat.

The radio squawks, and every occupant of the car except Felicia jumps.

"Christ," Joel whispers. He picks up the radio, messes with the volume.

"Joel, this is Mai, come in."

Joel grabs the radio. "Mai! Good to hear from you, go ahead."

"Well, we were attacked." Pause. "We're okay, but Jesus Christ. They're still active. Over."

"Where are you?"

"We, uh, we made it past I-25 on Mulberry, and we managed to gas up there. Siphoned a truck. There was nothing in the area, no movement at all, only a bunch of empty cars, and we thought we were safe, but as we got farther east, a swarm of them came rushing out of one of those neighborhoods and started ramming us." Her voice stops, and in the empty hiss of the spectrum, Rachel can barely hear other voices in the background. "We got a few darts into them, and they broke off like a wave, man, it was the weirdest thing, like the library. But a few of them jumped at us and—and they blew up, they just blew up!" Her voice rises and falls as if the vehicle is moving quickly over unsteady road. "We got windows busted out, some minor cuts and shit, but damn!" Another pause. "Anyway, that's what I'm calling for." Empty static for a moment, then: "Over."

"Glad you're all okay, Mai." He proceeds to tell her what happened on Rachel's porch.

"Sounds like they have a new mission."

"Yep," Joel says. "But it still sounds a little desperate to me."

A pause. "Hadn't thought of it that way."

"They're literally killing themselves to stop us."

"I guess so."

"You got enough supplies to take care of those cuts?"

"Yeah, we got plenty of that. It's pretty gross, though. It's bone. Blood and bone. You think that's all safe? That's not gonna, like, cause, I don't know—"

After a pause, Joel says, "I wouldn't worry about that too much. Just clean everything up as good as you can. We've got enough to worry about. You keep on heading east, see what you find, got it?"

"Got it, over."

"Take care of yourself. Keep in touch. We've got some bodies trying to keep pace with us, but they're keeping their distance. We're heading west, see what kind of trouble we can get into, over."

"All right, you guys be careful. Out."

Joel drops the radio into the console and lets out a sigh. Rachel can see him working through everything, despite the extreme fatigue evident in his eyes. His eyes flick upward, to the right, at a clear view of the western sky, where daylight is almost completely gone now. The jittery purple lightning continues, and the shifting columns of energy continue to pulsate. The alien presence is focused southwest of Horsetooth, seemingly between the sites of two diminishing wildfires. She can feel him tracing the route they must take.

Then he's talking.

"This is it. Moment of truth. Jesus, I could use a whiskey about now."

Silence hangs heavy in the cab.

"Back at the library, we knocked those fuckers back on their heels," Joel says. "They didn't expect that. We showed them we have some fight in us. But did you see them back there? They don't know what to do." He gestures toward the broiling sky, which ripples with deep reds, strobing and crackling. "*They* are not sure of their next move. That's what Felicia said, and I believe it." He brings his attention back to Rachel and the others, who are watching him with suspense. "So I think it's time we make a move."

CHAPTER 19

Joel motions Pete to come up beside the Hummer, and slowly the truck comes abreast of them. As soon as the vehicle comes to a quiet stop, Chloe rolls down the window.

"Yeah?"

Joel looks down at her. "Talked to Mai. They were attacked, like that thing on the porch. Those bodies are basically suicide bombers at this point, so we can count on that."

Pete leans over to catch Joel's attention. "Do we need to find another stronghold? Right now, we don't have nearly the munitions or the numbers to hold these things back, 'specially if they're massing up like they did at the library. Those damn things back there looked like they were about to swarm us."

"Never knew you to be one to fall back, Pete."

"Hey, hey, now, all I'm saying is if we seriously want to throw down with these things again, we better be prepared. All our munitions are covered up in tarps right now. They're not gonna do a bit of good like that. And what we have won't be nearly enough. Now, there's Active Arms down on College, or we could even try a pawn shop or two, find enough weapons to blow most of these fuckers back into space or wherever they came from."

Joel checks the rearview mirror, watching the restless monsters between fence gaps, behind trees, restless in their upside-down pacing. Rachel twists back and can barely see them, approaching the fence, receding, appearing ready to jump, as if daring the survivors to make a move—or daring each other to attack.

"I think our guns aren't gonna matter much anymore," Joel says. "I think our best weapons are Felicia and that other woman."

"What?" Pete says. "I don't think I heard that right."

"You know what I'm talking about."

Zoe speaks up. "Uh, that other woman is passed out in the flatbed, and a bit ago she was gagging from pain, even though we pumped her full of drugs. She's unconscious."

"She's still our biggest advantage, along with Felicia here."

"I'm still not following," Pete says.

"Even if they are, Joel, what do we do with them?" Rachel asks.

She watches Felicia, who still seems to be unaware of her traveling companions, her eyes darting from glow to glow along the hunkered-down row of '60s-era homes.

Joel ponders the question. Then: "The fact that they're human again seems to be enough to send shivers through them, so the question is, is that enough? What can they do that will downright terrify them? What can they do to end this thing? *Can* they do that? You saw what Felicia did back there. *She turned that woman back.* I don't know how, and I don't know why, but maybe the fear is as basic as that. Do they have the power to reverse this thing?"

"What, one body at a time?" Rachel says. "Or you're thinking on a bigger scale?"

Joel nods. "Right, from what I saw, Felicia has some kind of—I don't know—a need to change them back. She walked right over to that woman, all on her own. Not sure what that is, what the impulse is. But there's a desire there. And I think that's what's scaring them."

Rachel is clenching her jaw, imagining Felicia's weakness, let alone the state of the other poor woman, Julia. What possible good can either of them do, when the simple act of changing one old woman back to humanity sapped Felicia of all her strength?

Scott speaks up. "Are they scared of that woman back there as much as they're afraid of Felicia? Or is it the fact that Felicia has fully returned?"

"What do you mean?" Joel says, frowning.

"Is it only the *existence* of a person that has changed back—you know, lying there, unconscious but *human*—or is it the fact that we've found a way to really make Felicia one of us again, walking, talking ... back on our side?"

"You're thinking about how long it took to bring her back to relative health," Joel says.

"Yeah, because that took a long damn time. And she's not out of the woods yet, either."

"And we don't have the benefit of time. At least I don't think we do."

"Not something I would bet on," Scott says.

Joel wipes some grit from his eyes. "Regardless, we need to get moving. It's getting a little hairy. But I propose a little test." He turns toward the truck. "Pete, here's what I want to do. Let's get out of here and work our way west, then south on Shields. I want to see if we can find any more trapped bodies. There's bound to be some in vehicles. I've seen at least a few over the past few days. But here's the thing: I want you to go back and do a drive-by of those fences. I want to see how those things react to the proximity of that woman you've got back there."

Pete studies the fences doubtfully.

"Is that the best strategy we have?" he says.

"Trust me."

Rachel watches the small smile on Joel's face with a kind of wonder. How the man can muster a smile after everything that's happened is beyond her, and yet she can't deny that the sight of it brings her comfort. She remembers the way he'd sat up with her at the hospital, soothing her and encouraging her over her father's unconscious body, how strong and yet selfless he was. In the space of a week, they have lived through a lifetime of horrors and challenges, and they're still here. At least the two of them are still here.

She's willing to trust him.

"Yeah, trust him," she calls now to Pete.

Pete cracks a wary grin. "Well, all right, little lady." The grin disappears as he addresses Joel. "I ain't stoppin', just rollin' on by."

"All I need."

"You gals all right with this?" Pete asks Chloe and Zoe, who look into each other's eyes like the twins they are, communicating something. Together, they reach down to the floorboards and draw up the weapons they've held close since leaving the library. Chloe has the rifle, and Zoe has one of the tranq guns left over from the library defense.

Pete gives another shrug. "Once I'm done, I'll let you take the lead west to Shields."

"Check," Joel says.

The truck moves forward cautiously, and Rachel watches the back of Pete's head in the cab. He's looking in every direction, waiting for a move. Joel leans forward, searching the area. Nothing happens.

Pete takes a wide, slow U-turn, bumping up onto the yard of the Sanders home. The long fence on the south side of the house seems to have the most activity, and as the truck approaches, the movement becomes more frenzied.

"See that?" Joel says.

"Yes I do," Rachel says.

Kayla stands up in her seat, peering through the rear window.

The truck rumbles over the grass and passes within ten feet of the fence boards. Rachel watches closely for the crimson glows, the way they move. The small glows aren't exactly blinding or even distinct—in fact, she could probably be convinced that some of the light she's seeing is manufactured by her own fear-raddled senses. But as Pete brings his truck and its unconscious occupant close to that fence, she's sure she sees movement back there. The bodies behind the cedar slats retreat into what she judges to be the middle distance of her neighbor's back yard. There are no glows anywhere near that fence. The truck moves away, toward the street, and finally bounces gently down onto the asphalt. Pete pulls the vehicle next to Joel, this time on Rachel's side.

"They moved away," Pete says. "Did you see that? I could hear them, like, scurrying away. Goddamn animals."

Joel nods, calls across Rachel, "Let's not get too confident, but I'd say that was pretty conclusive."

"Really?" Scott puts in. "I could hardly see anything."

Joel glances back. "Lose your glasses?"

"Yeah, yeah."

"It was conclusive enough for me, anyway," Joel says, turning back to Pete. "Convincing enough for our next move."

"What's our next move?" Kayla asks meekly, now between Scott and Felicia, her words devolving into a yawn. The poor girl is bushed. Rachel wonders if she's had any sleep in the past twenty-four hours. Maybe when she holed up earlier at the library? If so, it was a catnap.

"You can try to sleep, Kayla. We're just driving. Scott won't mind you using him as a pillow."

Scott doesn't appear to know how to respond to that at first. "It's fine."

"How much blood do you have over there?" Joel calls over to Pete.

Chloe leans over and says, "We've got maybe a dozen of the canisters that Scott put together, and two units that we took before we left. Obviously we can take more at any time from any of us—I brought the equipment."

"Really? Clean enough to do that repeatedly?"

"We brought plenty of alcohol and clean syringes, yeah."

"And anti-coagulant," Zoe puts in.

Rachel thinks these girls will probably be trained for full-on phlebotomy by the time this whole thing is over—if it's ever over.

"Here's what we're going to do—or at least here's what I propose we do," Joel says. "We'll get to Taft Hill and then go south until we can make our way up to Horsetooth and into Masonville. Into the foothills. We'll see if we can find any more bodies along the way. If Felicia finds the strength to turn them, we do that. If not—tranq dart. Got it?"

"I ... I'd remind you that there's still a lot on fire up there," Pete says. "We were burning everything at the south side of the reservoir, and those flames took off, man. It's hellfire up there, very smoky."

Rachel watches Joel's jaw clench, and she feels her own heart tighten inside her chest like a fist. All those bodies—all those humans—burned to death, before they learned the truth that, at least in theory, they could be saved. Perhaps it is a naïve way to look at the situation, but it's the only way she knows how, having herself caused the death of too many for Rachel to bear.

"I've been watching those fires," Joel says, glancing up through the windshield at the almost totally darkened skies. "The flames have moved southwest. Mostly south. I haven't seen a lot of smoke coming north. The smoke we have seen has been from fires above us to the north. I'd be willing to bet that the fires have driven bodies south toward Loveland and also north toward Lory. What else do you see out there?" He nods toward the west.

The Hummer is pointed south. Rachel stares up at the roiling skies, at the jittery redness of the heavens. The power of the alien threat has diminished since its height during the library assault, but it's still there—an otherworldly throb. At first glance, it seems to encompass the skies, north to south, and west. But looking closely, she can see its essence reaching down into the foothills. And damned if the most vivid part of it is pulsing below Horsetooth—where Joel is looking now.

"They've massed over there," Rachel whispers.

"That's what I'm seeing."

"What?" Pete calls from the truck.

"The fires are burning southward, have been for most of this time," Joel says. "You guys were blowing everything up south of Horsetooth, right? Near Masonville?"

There's no malice in Joel's voice, more of a tired resolve, but there's still a fiery part of Rachel that will always resent that hillbilly attitude—embodied by the Thompson brothers—of blowing everything up and asking questions later.

Pete is slightly chagrined as he answers Joel. "Right, Jeff's buddy Trevor, he's the one radioed down when that wall of corpses was comin' down on us, he had a cabin down south of that general store at Stout, and he had his own armory there. He had fuckin' flamethrowers, man. We weren't just gonna let those—"

But he can see that excited tales of his exploits are falling on deaf ears.

It's a strange thing, Rachel reflects, to have encountered an existential threat—the most terrible of monsters—and to stare into its very human face. Maybe not for the Thompson brothers, but definitely for her. They burned thousands, but she's not guiltless. She has murdered human bodies. Even though those bodies were cranked backwards, bending their spines to the breaking point and dislocating limbs, they were still human bodies that this alien presence took over. Now, their throats are ravaged, their brains are perhaps forever altered by the presence of a sinister glowing orb—but the fact is, they can be changed back. At least some of them. Maybe only a fraction.

They *were* human, and they're *still* human, to a certain extent.

Rachel realizes that both vehicles have been silent for long moments, the occupants' collective imaginations seemingly latched onto the thoughts sledge-hammering their way through Rachel's mind.

"So why head down Taft Hill?" Scott says, as if to break the tension. "Why not head west from here, or even northwest on 287? That looks like as good a route as any, and we wouldn't have to weave our way through these streets."

"Because we need more bodies," Joel says frankly.

"Um," Scott says, unable to finish the thought.

"You think we need even more like Felicia and the woman," Rachel says, thinking out loud. "Power in numbers, huh? You think we can find more?"

"I'm sure of it. We've all seen the bodies out there, in the cars, like that woman. Stuck because of seatbelts or locked doors or crashed cars that they can't navigate, whatever. There aren't many of them out there, it's true, but they're there."

"Where do we put 'em?" Pete asks from the truck. "You want to stack 'em up back there?" He gestures to the truck bed with his big thumb.

"There's plenty of vehicles out there for the taking if we start piling up bodies."

"You really think this'll work?" Rachel asks.

"Can you think of anything better?"

"Let's go for it," calls Pete. "I wanna get the fuck outta this neighborhood. Looks like we got company again."

The glows have assembled behind the fence again, and the bodies are pacing restlessly, as if eager to get at them. They're wary of what the vehicles hold, and yet they crave the attack—at least, that's the way Rachel imagines it.

Joel nods and lurches the Hummer into Drive, scooting ahead of Pete. Soon, the two vehicles are heading west toward Taft, and the wide-open sky reveals the extent of the alien threat, a nightmare horizon that seems to exude anger and disease.

"Is she awake?" Rachel asks Kayla, as much to distract her from the view as to check on Felicia.

Felicia appears unconscious, her eyes closed, her head back, but then the head comes forward and the eyes open, bloodshot and teary still. Can those eyes ever be healthy again?

"I'm awake," she whispers.

"You are!" Rachel twists to face the young woman. "How's the head? The energy?"

Felicia gives a slow nod, wipes at her eyes, clutches her temples. "Still hurts."

"Have some more Tylenol."

Her head shakes back and forth. "Not yet—it's like I can't think clearly with that in me. Just makes everything fuzzy."

From the other side of the rear seat, Scott speaks up, leaning over. "Hey ... so ... we were just talking about you."

Rachel looks at him. "Maybe we can wait till she's more conscious?"

Scott ignores her. "When you changed that woman back—how did you do that?"

Rachel senses everyone in the vehicle tuning in for the answer to that question.

Felicia swallows heavily and looks at each survivor, one by one. "I don't know, I ... I just did. I pushed out, somehow. With my thoughts."

"How did you even know you could?" Joel asks.

She seems to think hard on that. "It was like—like she was calling to me. Like *it* was calling to me."

"It?" Joel repeats.

"We ... what I was like ... when it was in me ... the light inside."

"Like it wanted to change back?"

"Maybe."

"Do you still feel that thing inside you?" Rachel asks. "That light?"

Felicia is stone-still for a half a minute, then her head slowly nods.

CHAPTER 20

The streets are desolate and dark. In the headlight luminescence, Rachel can make out abandoned collisions, floating past like derelict ships in fog. She trains her flashlight on some of them as they pass, and so far all of them have been empty—cold and dark, doors flung wide, and layered with a thin grime of ash. Joel makes it a point to veer close to those he sees.

In the tense, monotonous silence, Rachel can't help that her thoughts are returning to her father. She's comforted by the fact that she has returned him home and placed him next to Susanna—despite what happened on the porch. It feels as if she has righted a wrong. She's more at peace with what happened at the beginning of all this. But she still feels the shock of her dad's death. It's not possible. Not after she saved him. It's not fair.

She can't help it, goddammit—what do those stacks of banded money mean? Why did her dad do this to her? To make matters worse, those wrapped bands of cash amount to little more than trash now, their value completely altered in a matter of days. They probably meant everything when her dad was alive, but they mean nothing now.

There's no getting around the fact that he'd fled from the hospital, had gone straight to that safe and had left it open—what, for her to find? Why hadn't he said anything about it? He'd retrieved her grandfather's gun from the safe, so maybe that was one purpose, but the money was key. It was scattered about, as if he'd handled it, as if he had intended to remove it. But to leave the door open—why didn't he slam it shut and spin the dial, hiding the money away again? Was he that hurried by the things outside? Was it that exact moment when they turned aggressive? Even if it had been, he'd surely had time to prepare himself and evacuate.

It's infuriating. A mystery. And she isn't sure she wants to know the answer to this particular riddle. She doesn't want to think of her dad—so recently alive—as a man with a black secret.

"Still with us?" Joel asks, glancing at her and startling her from her thoughts.

"Huh? Oh. Yeah, thinking about my dad."

He reaches over and touches her knee, lets his hand linger there.

"Look," he says, shaking her from a recollection that she can't seem to stop reliving, "I never was good at this part of the job, but I'm so sorry we lost him. I'm sorry you lost him. He was a good man, and he saved lives."

Rachel can only look up at him, feeling her eyes fill with new moisture. "I know."

"I'm glad we took him home," he says.

"Me too." *I think*, she adds.

They make the turn onto Taft Hill and begin the journey south. It's immediately clear that more vehicles are here, scattered, crooked against curbs, abandoned.

"There," says Felicia, startling everyone in the Hummer. Joel jerks the wheel.

"Where?" Rachel asks, straightening up.

But Felicia is already gesturing to the northbound lanes. There's a big station wagon there, sandwiched between a silver Subaru WRX and a green, late-model BMW sedan. Rachel isn't sure she would have noticed the faint, telltale red glow unless Felicia had said something, but now she can see it in the darkness. It's throbbing, barely, in time with the red throb from the heavens.

Joel crosses the center line and moves toward the station wagon. The high headlamps light up the station wagon like the sun, and shortly it's clear there's a body slumped in the driver's seat. The Hummer comes to a jolting stop. Joel signals through his open window for Pete to fall in line.

"Felicia, are you—" Joel begins, but Rachel stops him.

Felicia appears catatonic in her seat, her eyes nearly rolled up in their sockets. She is fainting away.

Rachel touches the young woman's leg—no response. "Wake up, Felicia! What's wrong?" She touches her face as her head lolls gently against the seat. "She's unconscious."

"We'll have to use the blood," Joel says, frustrated.

One aspect of his plan is falling apart. Felicia's energy is still bottomed-out.

Behind them, Pete maneuvers his truck so that its headlamps face due north, in the direction of any potential followers. The light disappears in the far distance—no bodies have tracked them. Rachel can't see any movement of any kind.

"Can we reach it?" Scott asks, leaning forward from the back.

"I think so, if we approach from the front. See that gap?"

"Yep."

"Careful everybody," he says. "Scott, you follow me in with the blood, all right?"

"What if that damn thing explodes?"

"I don't think it will."

"You don't think?"

"Remember, the first woman didn't."

"Why not?"

"Frankly, I think it's because she was on the verge of death. These bodies are stuck. No energy, no food or water of any kind. They're dying. Weak."

"But to be clear—"

"Right, take all precautions. Don't leave yourself in plain sight. Don't give it an opportunity."

"Let's do it then."

"All right, we'll do this quick and easy."

The Hummer idling roughly, Joel and Scott open their doors and jump down to the asphalt. Rachel sees Pete racing over from the truck. Behind her, she can make out the twins poking their weapons out their respective windows, watching the homes and yards around them for any movement. These battle-tested young women are a far cry from the scared, whining teens she remembers picking up from the side of the road less than a week ago. They're warriors.

The three men are a study of efficiency, impressing Rachel with their speed and strategy—particularly considering Joel and Scott were practically mortal enemies not forty-eight hours ago. Joel carefully peers into the interior while Scott shines his flashlight in, illuminating areas where the Hummer's headlamps can't reach. Immediately, Joel backs away and gives a thumbs up. Then he points to the passenger side of the vehicle. The men hustle around. Joel grabs the door handle and gives it a try. He shakes his head, moves to the rear door, tries the handle. No dice. He mimics smashing the window, and the other two men give a nod in the darkness.

Kayla has crawled away from tending to Felicia to the center console to watch. Rachel can hear the girl's breathing—rapid, a bit fearful.

Rachel's eyes keep flicking from home to home, from vehicle to vehicle, watching for movement. There are perhaps thirty cars and trucks along this section of Taft Hill, angled into lawns, crushed against the facades of homes, and one is even overturned on its back—a red Toyota whose passenger door is flung open, its driver long gone. But behind any of those vehicles might be bodies poised to attack. In the darkness, she can't see the telltale glow, but that doesn't mean anything. It could be hidden behind—

Crash!

Joel has smashed the passenger-side window and is scrabbling for the door lock. In moments he has opened the door and swung it open. Rachel can't see much from her vantage point, but she watches the men huddle there, yanking at something. Then she realizes that they have pulled the seat forward to reach into the back seats, which is where the body must be. Finally, Scott rears back and fires his tranq rifle, and there's a flurry of activity. The vehicle rocks and jolts. The men wait for the blood's effect, reaching in to wrestle with the newly animated body. Then Rachel hears the distinct gasp—that hoarse, alien groan, almost as if the body is fighting to preserve its invader and not give way to humanity's return.

Kayla watches, fascinated and horrified.

"It worked," she says softly.

"Yeah."

Rachel feels movement behind Kayla and glances over at Felicia, who has awakened abruptly, her back arching against the seat. The young woman's eyes are now wide open, staring in the direction of the three men at the car.

"Hey!" Rachel calls. "What's the matter?"

Felicia doesn't register the question.

"She knows what's happening," Kayla says. "She can feel it."

Felicia appears to be hyperventilating, but gradually it slows down.

The men outside are still struggling with the new body, but then the struggle is over, and Rachel assumes the body has gone unconscious. At the same moment, Felicia falls back to her seat and lets out a tumultuous sigh.

"Her name—is—Linda," she says in a clipped tone, stunned. "She couldn't get out, either. She was trapped. She—she—" She stops for a moment, hyperventilating. "So much pain." She brings her hands to her ears as if to shut out the sounds of the woman gasping, but Rachel is sure the worst sounds are coming from within. Such a strange thing.

The men begin dragging the body toward the truck, directly in front of the idling Hummer, and that's when Zoe begins shouting.

"Over there!"

Zoe is pointing north, to Rachel's left, where two bodies are lurching toward them, hideous fleshy crabs, their glows pinpointed at their stretched throats. There are two others behind them, but they are more tentative—at least, that's Rachel's first thought. More likely, they're injured or hobbled in some way.

The men drop the body, which falls limp on the asphalt. Rachel can

Jason Bovberg

see the woman now, dark-haired, gaunt, agonized in unconsciousness, her limbs angled in wrong directions.

Thirty feet away, the animated bodies become vivid in the light of the truck's headlamps, ghastly and quick now. They've launched into a full-on assault. How have they become so fast? It's as if one more day has made them all too comfortable inside their human shells. Rachel feels herself leaning heavily backward into her seat.

"Kayla," she says automatically, protectively, and she reaches back for the girl's hand. "Don't watch."

Kayla takes her hand but makes no sound.

Joel's shotgun booms, and the body in front—that of a housewife, cotton gown mostly shredded around her naked body, bloody sap pasted down her long neck, her mouth gaping but destroyed—blooms into a flower of blood, spraying the front of the Hummer and dotting the asphalt with crimson chunks. The corpse falls away in a heap.

Pete fires his AR-15 madly at the second body, which has closed half the distance.

"Fuck you!" the big man yells, rushing forward into the fray. "Drop, you motherfucker!"

The bullets hit their target, but they fail to slow the body enough. Pete leaps forward, defiantly, still firing, rage across his features.

"Pete!" Joel yells, grabbing at the big man's shirt. "PETE!"

"Oh no," Rachel whispers.

"Get down," Felicia says, almost matter-of-factly.

Rachel presses herself down into her seat, ducking and shutting her eyes. "Get down!" she repeats, loud, and feels Kayla drop behind her.

There's a hideous boom—fleshy, muffled—and the windshield blows in with the force of a grenade. Rachel feels coated with wet warmth.

"*Shit!*" Her ears are muffled again, and she's yelling. "Are you okay!? Kayla, are you okay? Felicia!?"

She works her jaw, hearing nothing. She risks a look back. Felicia and Kayla are there, aware and awake, crouched on the seat. Felicia's expression is one of extreme distress.

"Rachel!" Kayla screeches. "Your hair!"

Rachel reaches up to touch her hair and finds it slick with blood. It's not her own. She feels no wound.

She sits up, retches, peers carefully through the open maw of the destroyed windshield. The safety glass is melted in like a gooey web, and the hood beyond it is dark with blood and gore. A beefy dismembered arm rests squarely in the middle of the big yellow expanse, and Rachel is sure it's Pete's. She covers her mouth with a trembling hand.

"Fucking hell!" Joel shouts, rising into view from their right. "Goddammit!"

He reaches up and angrily swipes the dismembered arm from the hood.

"What happened?" Rachel calls, her eyes on the bodies—thirty feet away—that still hesitate on the periphery of the headlamps' light.

"Scott?" Joel calls. "You okay?"

"I think so," comes Scott's miserable voice.

"What happened?" Rachel says again, louder.

"Pete is dead," Joel says.

"No!" cry the twins in ragged chorus.

"We have to leave," Felicia says from behind her.

Rachel is about to repeat the words to the two men outside, but she's interrupted by the clamor of Chloe and Zoe exiting the truck and appearing brightly ahead of her in the Hummer's light. Both of them have readied their weapons and are staring down the ratcheted-back bodies, which have stuttered to a stop.

They're watching the girls, Rachel marvels. *They're judging the threat.*

Collective memory.

Of course this makes sense, considering what Rachel has seen up to now. But she wonders if this is evidence of a general fear of the survivors, or a fear of the weapons—more specifically, the blood—or a combination of everything, not to mention the presence of Felicia and the other bodies that have changed back.

Joel is still cursing, but Rachel sees that he has noticed the showdown in front of the Hummer.

"Let's go, Scott, now! Let's get this body in the truck. Can you handle it?"

Wordlessly, Scott lifts the woman by the shoulders and follows Joel past the Hummer and toward Pete's truck. They toss the body into the back somewhat unceremoniously, then scramble back for the Hummer.

"Help!" Zoe calls out, and Rachel sees other bodies massing at the north end of the headlamps' light.

"Oh shit," Joel says, "let's go." He's grabbing at the twins' arms.

They whip around to face him, and Rachel sees that their faces are wet and red with savage tears.

The bodies aren't moving. Even in growing numbers, they exhibit fear. They're still tentative.

Joel yells something at Scott, and Scott nods, corraling the twins back to the truck, and the three of them climb in. The Hummer's door swings heavily open, and Joel shoves himself inside, cursing repeatedly. He hands his weapon over to Rachel, and she takes it wordlessly. He shoves the vehicle into gear, and they lurch forward.

"Take this, you asshole!" he cries, intending to send the closest bodies under their wheels.

"Joel, don't!"

"Oh, I've heard enough of that!" Joel yells. "They aren't human!"

"No, not that—you saw what they did!" she responds loudly. "They get under us, they might detonate!"

Joel breaks and pivots the Hummer away from the growing horde, teeth gnashing. "Shit!" he brays, acknowledging that she's right.

Rachel watches the gathering bodies through the melted windshield. They have backed away from the Hummer—fearful of the occupant in the rear-left seat?—but they haven't fled, either.

The sight takes her breath away. There are perhaps twenty bodies out there now, all bent back upon themselves like huge, fleshy insects. For the first time, the word *swarm* occurs to her—not only because of the insect connotation but more because of how quickly the bodies massed, like wasps to a threat. She got a similar sense during the library attack, but that was different. During that siege, the monsters attacked as one strategic force, the bodies interlocked and attacking relentlessly as if they comprised a single, malevolent entity. Now, they're individuals, tentative and even fearful, but still defined by that collective consciousness.

"Holy shit," Joel whispers.

"Turn around and get us out of here," she says.

"Workin' on it, sweetheart," he says, tearing his own gaze away from the bodies.

Scott maneuvers the truck into a U-turn, beginning to turn south again, and the vehicle's lights flash across more tentative monsters, poised and watching. They're keeping their distance, but they're watching.

Joel cranks the Hummer's wheel then, backing away from the cluster of vehicles and straightening up to follow Scott and the twins. He punches the gas, and Rachel watches behind them as the bodies simply remain standing in the middle of the street, watching after them as if curious.

"Jesus Christ," Joel says, barely hiding the sneer from his trembling mouth.

CHAPTER 21

Five minutes later, they're approaching Elizabeth Street, and they can no longer see the bodies behind them. Although some began to give uneasy chase, most appeared to recede back into the night as the survivors pulled away.

The radio squawks.

"Joel, are you there?" comes Scott's tinny voice, breaking up slightly over the speaker. "Have we had enough? I'm—uhm—asking that honestly. We don't seem to be quite as safe as you thought we'd be, do we?" The radio cuts out briefly. "Over."

Joel stares at the handset resting on the dash, then finally picks it up and stabs the transmitter button. "Look, obviously—obviously they strike when we're vulnerable, when we're away from the vehicles. Hold on, let me think."

He releases the button. Rachel can see that his hands are shaking, and he's slightly slumped over the wheel. A far cry from the memory of him commanding a bloody war zone inside the library, racing down corridors while firing his rifle mercilessly at the windows, where gasping corpses were slithering through melted glass. That memory shifts to her dad, surging forward into the mass of bodies, vomiting and injecting blood wherever his own body could reach, and she angrily shakes it away.

"They came out of nowhere," Joel says to her now.

"Which they'll probably do whenever we stop."

Rachel can sense his growing frustration. He knows this nighttime journey isn't what he anticipated—but she also knows he left a lot to chance when he started.

He sighs loudly through his teeth.

"You didn't expect them to attack?" Rachel asks him.

"Well, you saw how they were, back there on your street."

"We let you get too far from the truck, from Felicia," Rachel says. "Don't you think?"

Joel considers that. "I don't know. Fuck, I don't know."

Rachel watches Joel for a moment, then takes the radio into her hand. "Scott, we're going ahead with the plan. We do have to be more careful about leaving the safety of the vehicles. They're still scared of us, we have to remember that. Over."

A pause. Rachel glances back at Felicia, who nods at her almost imperceptibly. There's something different about the woman's eyes now, she realizes. It's as if Felicia can communicate through them, through the power of non-verbal suggestion. Rachel feels an urging there, almost as if Felicia is swaying her—Rachel's—actions. It's subtle, but it's undeniable. Rachel watches her curiously.

"Roger that." Scott's voice sounds resigned, with only a slight edge to it. "Out."

Rachel drops the radio on the dash, then turns fully to check on Kayla. The girl has curled into a ball directly behind Rachel and has fallen into a kind of desperate, shock-induced sleep. Rachel extends her arm to delicately brush the hair from her face and pet her cheek.

Next to the girl, Felicia has leaned forward to stare through the broken windshield at the rattling truck, which Scott is winding laboriously around collisions.

"I need to be with them." Felicia's voice is so soft, Rachel barely registers the words.

"What?"

"I can help them," she says. "And—"

Her face twists into some kind of understanding. There are tears there, but then again, there have been tears in her eyes since she re-woke to humanity.

"And what?" Joel says.

"I can help better if ... if we're all together."

"Help those things or help us?" Joel asks, knee-jerk.

Felicia doesn't respond to that, merely stares at the truck. Rachel can't see the bodies in the flatbed, but she knows they're there, and she also knows they're suffering unimaginably.

Rachel asks, "Are you sure?"

"I need to be there."

"Joel, can we make it happen?"

"But we need her in here, Rachel. You *just* suggested we're safer with her in here. We drop her in that truck, and we—"

"Then they tailgate us like crazy, and we stay as close to Felicia as we can." She studies Felicia's face. "She can nurse them to help faster, and that way they're more of an asset to us."

Joel gives her a glance, then flashes his lights at Scott ahead of them. Scott's brake lights appear immediately, and Joel pulls to the right of the truck. Rachel glances all around, watching the lawns and homes that line Taft Hill. She can see the King Soopers grocery store up on the right and imagines all the water and food inside. No chance to run in and grab anything. Not now. There's a supply in the back of the Hummer, but it won't last.

Joel leans out his window and talks to the twins. Rachel can see the bottom of Scott's face as he scoots over to see Joel.

"You're getting another passenger in back," Joel says, gesturing to the flatbed.

As he speaks, Rachel becomes aware of miserable groaning coming from the back of the truck, where the two recently changed bodies lay. Felicia's expression is now one of even deeper despair.

Rachel leans in next to Joel and looks down on the twins. "We need to get morphine in the new one, probably both of them."

"I can do it," Felicia manages, watching the truck. Her limbs are moving restlessly. "May I go?"

"Of course," says Joel, gesturing his hand in a *whatever* motion. "Go on ahead."

Felicia pushes her door open and manages to step down from the Hummer into the street. Kayla helps her shut the heavy door. At the truck, Chloe is holding a small vial of morphine in her hand, along with a syringe. Rachel catches only her profile, but she can see that the young woman is still crying copiously over Pete, inconsolable.

What are we doing? is the question that is reverberating inside Rachel.

Felicia approaches and takes the medicine into her hands almost delicately. Despite her flowing tears, Chloe manages to speaks to Felicia, probably instructions—but Rachel can't make out the words. Then, Felicia goes to the flatbed and, with some effort, climbs in over the gate.

"She's vulnerable back there," Joel says. "Totally open to attack."

His voice is right in Rachel's ear. She realizes she's still essentially in his lap, staring out his window. His breath is sour but masculine, his presence large and comforting. She looks into his eyes, lingers a little too long, then backs into her seat, embarrassed.

"Sorry."

"Considering what those things are doing now, I'm not sure we ought to leave them out in the open."

Rachel watches Felicia settle in between the two bodies. Her movements are careful, empathetic.

"Out of anyone in this little entourage, they're the safest," Rachel says. "And they're stronger together. Better for us."

"How do you know that?"

Rachel lets the question hang.

I don't, she thinks. *But it feels right.*

There's no movement out there—yet. All the surrounding homes are dark, though, so dark that anything could be lurking in those shadows thirty yards in any direction. But nothing is sprinting at them. And in the diffuse red glow of the rear brake lights, no bodies are approaching, even cautiously.

"So ... go?" Scott calls up to them.

Joel looks down at him. "Let's do it. I'm gonna take the lead. Stay glued to our ass, right? You've got all our best defense in your bed back there."

"Roger that," Scott says, and Joel pulls ahead.

Homes drift by on either side of Taft Hill, completely dark, haunted. Although they contribute to the feeling that Fort Collins has become a ghost town, their yards and fences and darker places still suggest active menace. All the survivors are on edge, expecting an attack from the shadows at any moment. But the attack doesn't materialize, and so a sense of cautious calm takes hold of the Hummer's occupants.

They creep past vehicles left abandoned, their doors flung open. All empty.

Long minutes pass.

Fifteen minutes. Twenty.

Kayla begins lightly snoring in the back again, stretched out on the rear seat.

Homes drift by, islands of darkness.

Against reason, despite the thrumming of her veins, Rachel finds herself dozing, too, and her gritty, drowsy thoughts drift back to her own home, where the bodies of her father and his wife, right now, lay decomposing in the humid night. Where a mystery presented itself to Rachel and proceeded to lodge in her skull like a spur.

Daddy, an inner voice whispers sleepily, *what were you up to?*

And she's not only mystified by what drew her father to their home—without telling her he was going—but more urgently, by where all that money came from, and why he apparently kept it a secret. He must have had his reasons. Right? Was the money a secret from her, or from Susanna as well? Is it possible he'd headed up some kind of illicit endeavor?

Was her father a thief?

She would laugh under any normal circumstances. Her father was one of the most straitlaced, honest people she knew. One time, years ago, he had been jogging in the pre-dawn morning and stumbled on a $5 bill on the sidewalk in front of a home three blocks away from their house. Although it was too early to disturb the family living there, he returned with a reluctant Rachel a few hours later to try to find the bill's owner.

At the door, an eight-year-old kid listened to his story, confused, staring at the cash. The boy's mother finally arrived at the door, confused, and stared at Michael and Rachel with alarm. She took the money and shut the door with a curt word of thanks, and Rachel's father was left a bit bewildered, walking back home.

Rachel always considered that a mostly crippled attempt to teach her a lesson of honesty.

She thinks of the thousands of dollars secreted away under his clothes, behind a false wall, and utterly fails to reconcile the image with that memory of the returned $5 bill.

Perhaps it was part of an inheritance she didn't know about—from her grandfather, perhaps. It was all stashed in there with his gun, after all. But then why wasn't the money in a bank?

She shakes her head minutely, returning her shivery attention to the darkened street ahead of her, the warm breeze wafting in over the Hummer's blood-stained hood. A hood stained with the remains of Pete Thompson, whose truck rumbles behind them.

She finds herself zeroing in on conifer trees, but she sees no bodies attached to the ones she finds, only—here and there—the evidence of chewed bark in the form of ravaged trunks and small piles of vomited splinters, saliva, and sap. Bodies were definitely here, but they have moved on to some other destination. Are they in the vicinity still, aiming to attack, or are they assembling somewhere for another purpose? She imagines Joel is wondering something similar. Then:

"Looks hairy up ahead," Joel says, breaking a five-minute silence. "Hang tight."

The intersection of Taft Hill and Prospect looms ahead. Several vehicles appear to have collided. Abandoned, doors flung open, they're all that remains of the fateful morning when the world changed. Joel clicks on the Hummer's brights to reveal still more vehicles, illuminated in the otherwise near-pitch-blackness of the smoky night. A school bus lies on its broad right side, snugged up against the traffic-signal pole on the southwest corner. Rachel wonders briefly why a school bus was on the streets at 6 a.m. on a Saturday morning—*a weekend field trip? a sporting event?*—then her attention moves to other vehicles appearing in the headlight beams. The lingering smoke and ash render the beams almost solid, with sharp edges. It's like a scene underwater, reminding her of documentaries she's seen about deep sea divers. Silent, eerie, murky …

"I don't see anything," Rachel whispers.

"Yeah, me neither, but it's awfully crowded around here."

Joel's eyes dart left and right, as if gauging their route out of the intersection—should they need to escape in a hurry. Rachel spots several avenues through the wreckage, but they're narrow.

Scott's truck rumbles behind them, its six cylinders older and louder than the Hummer's. The truck's weaker headlamps sweep after theirs like a yellow after-image, like an echo.

Glancing back, she can barely see Scott in the truck's cab, a faint outline of his silhouette, hunched over the wheel, driving carefully. And beside him, the twins, their heads swiveling wearily left and right as they check out their surroundings. Rachel can't see Felicia and the other turned women in the flatbed, but she knows they're there, and she knows—hopes?—that Felicia is easing the others' pain.

She hopes something else is happening back there, too. Something that, perhaps, she wouldn't understand. Something to prepare them for whatever will come.

She locks on Scott's silhouette for the briefest moment.

Was he worth saving?

Her gaze lingers on the faint sight of him at the wheel, and she guesses that everyone is worth saving, no matter his or her mistakes. Even Rachel had been saved by her father, and she doubted she deserved it. But she can't help thinking that, given the trade-off of Bonnie for Scott, a weighing on the proverbial scales would have tipped far in Bonnie's favor, and now the thought of her gone brings a fresh wave of melancholy for not only Bonnie, but her father, and even Susanna, and the rest—all those people.

Everyone is worth saving.

She twists back around.

"… through there …" Joel is saying, gesturing to the left.

Rachel sees a generous path through the wreckage, and Joel rumbles through it, approaching the center of the intersection.

It's about that point where Rachel begins to feel unsafe again. Something trembles in the air—is it her mind playing tricks on her, or is something atmospheric happening? Carefully, she leans forward, hand against the dash, and peers up into the nightmarish sky.

"You feel that?" Joel whispers, startling her.

"Uh huh."

"Me too," Kayla says with a yawn from the rear.

Joel brakes the Hummer to a stop. "What *is* that?"

"What?"

"You don't hear that?"

Rachel listens hard, trying to discern anything over the sounds of the engines. Then it dawns on her. It's the moans of the women in the truck, and Felicia's voice is among them. She's calling to them. At that moment of awareness, Scott taps his horn.

Before she even knows what she's doing, Rachel has opened her door and is jumping down to the intersection's concrete. Joel calls after her, and her veins throb with hot blood. She runs toward the truck, seeing the twins' eyes pop as she approaches.

Their window is open. "Something's wrong back there," Chloe calls back to her, red-eyed, gesturing. "I was about to—"

"I got it."

At the flatbed, Felicia is in the process of standing up on the corrugated floor, steadying herself on the back of the cab, and staring off to the left. One of the women behind her has propped herself up atop the wheel well and is also staring in the same direction, her face a mask of pain and effort. The other woman—Linda, the most recent—is still unconscious on the floor.

"What is it?" Rachel cries.

She can't believe she's out here in the open. What compelled her to—?

"Over there," Felicia says immediately, her voice clipped, and the woman next to her voices non-verbal grunts from her own wounded throat—ragged, awful sounds that remind her of Felicia at the library less than two days ago. Felicia is gesturing to the east.

"All right, hang on." She jogs back toward the Hummer.

Kayla has been calling to her. "Rachel! Rachel! Come back!"

"It's okay, I'm here."

"Come back in here."

"It's all right."

She climbs up to the Hummer's cab, standing on the running board.

"What's going on"? Joel asks, an edge to his voice. "You trying to get us killed?"

"There's another body over there," Rachel calls up to him. "I don't know if they sense it, or ...?"

Joel gives glances in all directions. "Get in."

Back inside the Hummer, Rachel scans the car wrecks as they drift past them, angling farther to the left. She's watching for the telltale red glow of the infected, but it's hard to make anything out in the glare of the headlamps. The emptiness is frustrating and terrifying at the same time. She feels as if a body might leap into the windowless cab at any moment, so she pushes back into the seat and clutches her trusty magnum flashlight. The steel is slippery in her grip, and she keeps adjusting her cramped fingers around it.

Just as she glances in her side-view mirror, she sees Felicia jumping down from the truck, staggering into the street, and taking off, her stride hobbled by her injuries.

"Joel!"

"Oh Jesus!" Joel barks as Scott taps his horn again. "What the hell is with these *people*?!"

Joel shoves the Hummer into Park, gives the surroundings another glance, and flings his door open. He jumps down to the pavement.

"Girls, come on out with the weapons!" he calls. "Stay with those women, guard the trucks. Rach, bring the flashlight. Scott, you be ready to peel on out of here. Honk if you see something."

Felicia limps quickly to a knot of silver vehicles and turns right, disappearing in a flourish of silvered ash.

"Felicia!" Rachel cries, still at the Hummer.

She glances into the back seat.

Kayla is watching her with big eyes. "Don't go," she whispers.

"You'll be safe."

"No!"

"I promise. I'll be right back."

She steps down into the intersection.

I'll be two seconds.

"Wait!" Kayla's voice fades behind her, and Rachel screams inwardly, drowning it out completely.

The headlamps of the vehicles throw startlingly narrow beams—particularly the newer Hummer—and once she steps beyond the conical luminescence, a nightmarish darkness envelops her. Rachel feels her heart begin to palpitate. Shadowed by other vehicles, Felicia is gone.

Rachel stabs on the flashlight, and an O of light bursts against the silver fender directly in front of her.

"Rach, hold up," Joel says. "This is stupid! We have to get her back in that truck. Immediately. We do not want to get stuck out here."

"Working on it."

"There!" Joel shouts.

Rachel spins and directs the flashlight ahead of her. "Where?"

"Left!"

Just before she twitches the light in that direction, she sees the pinpoint of red—it's a flash, actually, a pop. And she knows that pop.

Felicia has already turned a body.

Revealed in the magnum's light, Felicia is bending into the open window of a small Toyota. Safety glass litters the asphalt like diamonds. Rachel and Joel sprint to her and gather around her. Rachel helps her extricate the body of a little boy, bedecked in Captain America pajamas, from a car seat. He can't be more than three years old. Returned to humanity, he begins crying—a raw, ugly bray.

"Christ, it's a kid!" Joel yells.

"Oh my god," Rachel whispers.

Felicia is mumbling again. "… Philip, his name is Philip … he was going on a … a trip … going to the airport …" The words go faint.

"Let's get him back, *now, now!*" Joel shouts.

But Felicia is shaking, the boy held tightly in her arms. She's not moving.

Rachel holds the light on the boy's face, and the circle of illumination vibrates. A strong feeling of foreboding overcomes her. She spins around once, twice, trying in vain to spot something, anything, in the peripheral pitch-blackness. Something is out there, she's sure of it. The magnum jitters in her grasp.

A gasp sounds to her left, and Rachel jerks her head that way.

"Come on!" Joel insists.

"We aren't alone," she calls back behind her, where Joel is already nervously backing toward the Hummer, whose headlights seem terribly far away.

She trains her magnum in that direction. Felicia is bent over the child's body. She has brought him to the ground, and his small chest is heaving in a jerky motion as if trying to expel a foreign object.

A gunshot cracks far behind them—Scott.

The truck's horn begins to blare, then goes staccato, then goes silent.

"Shit *shit*," Joel says. "Let's go!"

When he and Rachel turn back to Felicia, she's standing again— ghastly pale and corpse-like in the flashlight's harsh white, her face an ethereal visage, drawn and bleak, desperate. She hardly looks human— swaying, eyes red-rimmed, mouth open in a twisted circle. Her eyelids flutter, and her limbs go weak. Joel leaps forward to grab her as she's falling.

"Fuckin' great," he says. "Grab that kid, let's get the hell out of here."

Rachel doesn't hesitate. She takes up the child, against her chest, and the boy bleats into her neck like a wounded animal, a terrible cry that claws at her soul. She doesn't even want to look at this child's face; she can only too clearly imagine what she will find there, and the fact that he is an innocent boy, relatively new to the world, makes the anger pulse in her again. Hard.

There's movement everywhere, and she finds herself wincing in anticipation of another explosion of bone and gore—targeting her, or Joel, or Kayla.

Kayla!

Why did she leave her alone? What could possibly have possessed her to leave Kayla alone? She curses savagely at herself.

The flashlight's beam wobbles in front of her, illuminating Joel's back intermittently and flashing against the metal surfaces of the vehicle graveyard that the intersection has become. Joel carries Felicia's deadweight like a rag doll, her arms flopping to his left, as if unhinged. He's drawing away from Rachel, and she's gasping to keep up, the boy's shifting, mewling weight loading her down, nearly causing her to stumble.

Behind her is the scraping sound of unnatural chase, the quick-drag and collective gasp of frantic creatures, hungry for blood, desperate for the destruction of their enemy. Because that is what she and the rest have become.

The enemy. The last of the enemy.

Impossibly, she picks up her pace, thigh muscles burning, lungs straining, and the bright headlamps of the Hummer come into clear view. There's another rifle blast, and now she can hear Scott screaming, enraged and terrified. One of the twins yells something, indistinguishable words, and then a muffled blast sends a shockwave against her left side— not enough to throw her off stride but enough to shower the pavement with slick blood.

The scuffling sound behind her grows insistent, and with a cry of anguish and exhaustion, she halts and about-faces, hyperventilating, swinging the flashlight around. Seven or eight creatures are twenty strides behind her, and they come to an insectile stop, their spider-like limbs assured on the asphalt, their bodies almost entirely inhuman. Rachel's lips twist in disgust. And that's when she realizes that these creatures *aren't* breathing—not even using their human bodies' lungs for aspiration. They're poised there like malevolent statues, unmoving save for slow, anticipatory positioning, angling for their next attack. They look more foreign than ever, more angry, more calculating. And yet they have stopped.

The fear remains in their eyes.

Rachel follows their upside-down gazes, the trajectory of their wide-open, dilated pupils.

They're watching the boy.

They're scared of this boy. Or awed by him.

Mayhem reigns behind her, toward the Hummer—guns cracking, survivors yelling, a motor gunning—and yet she has a group of infected bodies in fearful thrall simply because she's carrying a three-year-old boy.

"Rachel!" Joel yells, too far away.

Impulsively, Rachel jerks a few steps toward the bodies, and as one, they gasp from their throats, recoiling.

"Rachel! Now or never!"

And now she can hear Kayla calling her name, and Rachel emits a small cry. She turns heel and begins sprinting again, and the group of bodies hurls forward, galloping in pursuit. She whimpers in fear but keeps sprinting, and now they're so close, they're so close, *too close,* and without warning a head explodes behind and to her right, spraying her and throwing her against the side of a Toyota van, and she ricochets off, not breaking stride, remarkably not dropping the boy. Her right ear feels completely gone, numb, and she shakes her head, gasping.

"*Kayla!*" she screams. "*I'm coming! I'm sorry!*"

BOOM!

She's knocked off her feet and goes to one knee, nearly flailing across the asphalt but catching herself with one hand on the side mirror of a crooked Jeep. She experiences a nightmare flash image of the boy rolling away from her across the asphalt, leaving her fatally vulnerable to these things. She clutches him tightly as she spins against the vehicle, her back to its front tire, and stares at her pursuers.

They've scrambled to a stop once more, meeting her gaze.

"*No!*" she shouts.

She sees the combination of anxiety and malevolence in their eyes, hears the throaty growls emanating from dysfunctional throats. She risks a glance toward the Hummer and truck and sees Joel there now, backlit, arriving and dumping Felicia into the truck bed. The commotion there has stopped.

Everything is centered right here.

Rachel finds her feet, lifting the boy reverently in her arms. The monstrous gazes are still watching the boy as if curious, and then shifting to her as if to size her up. Rachel looks into the eyes, one by one, wary, wincing, expecting the next explosion. There are five of them, and another approaching from thirty feet away—she catches the movement peripherally. Their movements are poised and fluid, their eyes black and unreflective, dead, dolls' eyes.

"C'mon, Rachel ..." Joel calls from behind her. "You're almost there."

Rachel pushes off the Jeep, walking backwards, and the monsters inch forward with her, dark and creaky with their bent-back limbs, bone scraping bone. Rachel registers the sound with more horror than disgust. Then one of them emits an involuntary dry belch, and it's enough to make Rachel bolt. She turns tail and sprints for Joel, seeing him ahead of her, holding a tactical shotgun now, and she sees him as some towering savior. She rushes directly toward the headlights. At the last moment, she angles left toward the passenger side and as she clears the bumper, Joel sprays lead into the alien assault, and the gasps turn into throaty shrieks, and there are the muffled thumps of ruined bodies rolling on asphalt.

Rachel twists to watch the bodies fall. Joel is there, but Chloe, too, with her tranq rifle. Most of the bodies fall dead at Joel's hands, but Chloe hits the final one, and it slides across the ground, coming to a rest at her feet. It convulses silently for a horrid moment, then finds its lungs and coughs wretchedly, expelling sap and splinters and blood, like a drowning man saved from a lake of mulch. Its scream is ragged and unending.

It takes a moment for Rachel to realize that she's screaming, too.

The back door is already open, and a sniffling Kayla is already there, reaching down for her. Zoe is there out of nowhere, taking the boy, and Rachel, sobbing, jumps up into the Hummer, thighs burning like acid, and takes Kayla into her arms, whispering, *"I'm sorry, I'm sorry ..."*

The vehicle jolts into motion, and Rachel hunkers down with Kayla, her beautiful brave girl, expecting a blast to finally bring an end to everything, but it doesn't come.

"It's okay," Joel says, his voice clipped. "They're staying away. They're not coming any closer."

Rachel can't stop the helpless tears. She can't stop. She convulses on the seat.

CHAPTER 22

The Hummer creeps south on Taft, approaching the dark and empty intersection at Drake. The Safeway looms on the right, barely visible. Before Prospect, Rachel had thought of Safeway as yet another possible stop for food and water, but now she can't imagine stopping this vehicle again. Ever.

"Christ, I thought we were going to be smarter than that," Joel murmurs, his hands shaking as he moves them from the wheel to the stock of his rifle, which he has placed next to him against the center console, smoking and spent. "Why aren't we getting smarter?"

"It's done," Rachel whispers. "We're still here."

Kayla is curled tightly against her, her body tense but her eyes closed. Her pretty, innocent mouth is open and slack. Rachel thinks the girl is actually sleeping again—increasingly desperately to be unconscious.

Joel glances at her in the rear-view, his eyes hollowed-out with stress. From this angle, she can see a vibration at his chest, his dirty shirt stiff with blood and sweat.

"All that for a kid?" he says.

At first, Rachel thinks he's referring to Kayla, but then she realizes he means the boy.

Philip.

Rachel closes her eyes and bends forward onto her knees, letting Kayla's head fall softly against the seatback. Rachel is warding off the shakes herself, and now spots are appearing before her eyes, shooting off like sparks in all directions. She feels as if Joel's trembling fear is fueling her own. He can't exhibit that kind of fear. He's the leader of this crew. He's a policeman, for God's sake.

"Shhh …" she whispers. "Yes, all that for a kid."

Rachel composes herself and glances out at the black night, then searches the dash for a clock. There isn't one, or it's broken.

"What time is it?"

Joel brings his shaking wrist close to his face, then returns it to the wheel.

"Jesus, it's after midnight."

"That's it? It feels like three or four in the morning."

Since leaving the library, Rachel has felt unmoored in time, drifting through a nightmare reality in which darkness and light shift and contradict. She shakes her head, trying to dislodge the grittiness from her eyes.

Joel shakes his watch again. "Maybe it is," he mutters.

Rachel watches his profile—haggard and drawn, mouth open, a few days' worth of beard, residue of blood and sweat. In the rearview mirror, his eyes are wide and red-rimmed, moving back and forth from the road ahead of him to the view behind him.

"Something's wrong back there," he murmurs.

In all the commotion, she had practically forgotten about the truck behind them, following closely. Now she registers the shift of the headlights.

"What is it?" She twists to peer back at the truck. "What now?"

Her insides roll over with dread. She can't handle something else right now.

"He's swerving."

The truck is indeed moving jerkily. She can't see into the cab from this vantage point, but as she's searching, someone leans on the horn— two long blasts.

"Shit." Joel pulls over to the curb, glancing all around. "Here we go again."

He waves an arm out his window for the truck to pull up alongside the Hummer, and immediately the truck barrels over there. Rachel watches for a threat out her window, squinting at the almost total darkness— rendered even darker by the absence of the truck's headlights behind her. She sees only vague shapes, nothing moving. She tries to listen for any sound out there in the blackness, but she can hear nothing over the thrum of two motors—

—until the twins begin yelling into Joel's open window, talking over each other loudly.

"Slow down, slow down, one at a time," Joel says.

"It's Felicia, she's going crazy," Zoe says.

"What do you mean?"

"She's screaming."

Rachel scoots over and searches the dark truck bed, but she can hardly see anything. The only illumination comes from the soft glow of the truck's cab. She can barely see a gray roil of bodies.

"I'm going," she tells Joel, still gripping Kayla's limp hand. *"We're going."*

"Rachel…" Joel says, exasperation in his voice.

"Kayla and I will trade places with the twins." She pats his thigh. "Behave yourself."

Rachel nudges Kayla gently. "Come on, kid, we're switching to the truck."

Kayla stirs from a surprisingly deep sleep. "Huh?"

"Come with me, Kayla."

The girl moves up, barely alert, instantly and groggily worried, makes a small sound in her throat.

"Are we clear?" Rachel asks Joel.

Joel sighs, scanning. "As far as I can see, yeah. Careful. No more than a minute, then we're rolling again." He calls down to the twins. "You two are riding with me, come on around."

"Scott's hurt," Chloe calls from behind Zoe as they step warily out of the truck.

"What?"

Chloe raises a finger—*hold on!*—then races around the front of the Hummer, climbs up into the passenger seat.

As Rachel shuts the rear door, she hears Zoe say, "He got hurt at Prospect, I don't know how, he won't say. He doesn't want to let on, but he's hurt."

"Did one of those things…?"

"I don't know."

Rachel takes Kayla's hand. "Come on, honey."

As she takes the two or three steps to the truck, she watches the open surroundings, her heart thudding. She doesn't see or hear anything. Yet. Just a darkened suburban corridor.

The truck's passenger door is already open, and she scoots Kayla into the middle. "Buckle up." Beyond the girl is Scott, looking pale and ghostly.

"Are you all right?"

Scott looks over at her, doesn't answer. He moves his hand minutely, and she can see that he is injured along his side. There's dark blood there.

"Jesus, Scott, what happened? We have bandages, we have to fix you up."

"Not yet."

"Then when?"

"When we're safe."

"We wait that long, you'll be dead."

"Bonnie didn't stop for a Band-Aid." Seemingly against his will, his voice quakes with an emotional perseverance, then he shakes his head as if embarrassed. The mention of Bonnie instantly gives his words a mortal weight.

Rachel swallows, watching him.

"I'll drive," she says. "Kayla will help you get bandaged up. Right, Kayla?"

"Okay."

For a moment, it appears that Scott's pride won't allow him to move, but then Joel cuts in authoritatively, calling out from the Hummer.

"We've got company—ten o'clock!"

Sure enough, there are two bodies in the far distance, their bodies bent, their limbs crooked. They're hanging back, though. Their position suggests that they're gauging the human threat.

Scott maneuvers himself into the center of the cab with what appears to be great determination. He winces but doesn't complain.

"Rachel…" Kayla whispers, one hand clutched to the aged dash. "Are they going to hurt us?"

"No." Rachel watches the bodies for a moment. "We're all right."

Then she swings her magnum to the north, through the broken back window, beyond the truck, adding her flashlight's cone of illumination to the muted crimson of the brake lights. There's a body back there, much closer, and it's watching her.

Oh shit.

Rachel freezes.

It's the body of a man, skinny and bony, naked. The upside-down head swivels like that of a huge praying mantis. The image is reinforced by the green stains all over its body. It seems to have crawled through a pool of fresh, masticated mulch. The limbs twitch, scraped up and knocked out of joint. Its mouth is wide open around a silent gasp, and the teeth appear broken and battered.

From the truck bed, a hand touches Rachel's arm, and a spike of fear hammers her spine like a sledge.

It's Felicia, in shadow. Rachel can see the whites of her eyes. Felicia is staring at the man, too. It's at that moment that Rachel understands that the man isn't staring at her, but rather at Felicia. Her hand is warm on top of hers—calming.

"What is it?" Joel calls from the Hummer. "Let's go!"

"Shhh! Wait! It's okay."

Rachel can see the bodies in the truck bed more clearly, the two other women and the boy. They are serene—even the boy. The women are watching over the tailgate, observing the naked corpse as it judders and sways. Is it watching them, too? The boy is nestled in the corner, against the left side of the truck bed. The tracks of tears glisten down his face in meandering paths. His eyes are flooded with moisture, but they are watching Rachel, recognizing her. Through his mouth, he inhales and exhales in a shaky rhythm.

Felicia's eyes, also moist, are locked on the body behind them.

"What happened?" Rachel whispers, but Felicia doesn't hear her. "Are you all right?"

"I can really feel it now," Felicia whispers.

"Feel what?"

"Their fear." She isn't moving, still watching the boy.

"What do you mean?"

"They know what we're up to."

"*We* don't even know what we're up to."

"Oh ..." Felicia whispers. "... yes we do."

The body behind the truck is whining. The sound comes raw from the ragged throat, but it's an uncertain, warbling whine. The body takes two shambling steps closer—a great, wounded insect—and then it begins to cough-sneeze through its gaping mouth, as if it's choking on something wet. A raspy gargle.

And then ...

Even in the red glow of the brake lights, Rachel sees the spark of the light. It extinguishes itself with a pop, and the body crumples to the ground, lifeless. Felicia's body relaxes suddenly, too, but she remains upright. Barely. She braces herself against the gate, the muscles of her arm straining.

"Holy—" Rachel says. "Did you see that?" She searches for someone, another witness, to what she beheld, but Kayla is buried against her side, shaking her head minutely, and Scott is dealing with his own issues.

Felicia did that—she's sure. She did it from a distance. She noticed Felicia visibly crumple at the precise moment it happened. How? How did she do that? A tingle of amazement raises goosebumps on her flesh.

In the truck bed, Felicia drops to the floorboards, almost in slow motion.

Joel is still barking. "Let's go, goddammit!"

Rachel pulls at some of the cardboard in the rear window, tearing it away. She pushes herself up, angling her face into the gap. "Are you all right?"

Felicia looks up at her with drowsy eyes. "I'll be fine."

And Rachel sees something in those eyes, there in the deep dark. There's a red glow that remains in Felicia, and it causes Rachel's breath to catch. She looks deeper into Felicia's eyes and can't help but see the barely-there glow as crimson residue of the poor woman's ordeal. Whatever has happened is because of that inner glow—the remains of the alien infestation of her skull. If she wasn't sure before that Felicia is the key to their continued survival, she is now.

Rachel drops back into her seat, stunned.

"We're okay," she says, mashing the clutch and grinding into first gear.

She can't see Joel in the Hummer's driver's seat, ahead and to her right, but she senses his glare. He pulls out in front of her, and she follows haltingly, Kayla jerking on the bench. In her peripheral vision, Scott is still and almost contemplative. Kayla watches him with concern.

In front of her, Joel swerves carefully around a small wreck directly in front of the darkened Safeway, and Rachel follows his path precisely, sticking close to his bumper.

"Kayla, I want you to do something for me. For Scott."

Kayla turns to her and shows Rachel her hands, which are slick with blood. "He's hurt."

"I know, so I want you to talk to Felicia through this window and ask her for bandages." She reaches back and tears more of the cardboard away. "Felicia?" she calls hopefully, knowing that if the young woman is mobile again so quickly after what happened with the old man, then that can only be good news for the survivors.

Kayla scrambles to her knees on the bench, facing backward into the night. Her small right hand takes hold of Rachel's shoulder, and Rachel can feel a tremble there.

"Felicia?" Kayla repeats out the window, softer.

"Hold on, girl," Rachel says, taking a slow arc around an abandoned minivan.

At that moment, Felicia's face appears ghostly in the rearview mirror. Rachel can no longer see the redness inside her eyes, but the exhaustion is clear. Something has been taken from her again—but not as much. She's not devastated, as she was when she turned the earlier bodies back to humanity.

Kayla is energized now by her task. She speaks loudly and clearly.

"We need bandages for Scott. He got hurt. Medicine, too."

As Felicia's face fades from view, Rachel bends briefly to Scott's side to investigate the extent of his wound. He nods at her, ghostly pale, and she lifts his shirt. Blood is slippery and glistening against his flesh, and after a few seconds she spots a ravaged entrance hole—enough to make her stifle a gasp. Whatever pierced his flesh, bone fragment or other shrapnel, it left a significant injury. Blood squirts over her knuckles.

"Scott," Rachel says, "you need to put pressure on that wound. Hang tight."

She guides his hands to the wound as he nods his weary head.

Felicia's hands push supplies through the small rear window, and

Kayla takes them eagerly, unwrapping them. Rachel keeps one eye on the rear of the Hummer, motoring south past Drake, and another on Kayla, who readies a large white bandage.

"Use the paper towels to dry the area as best you can, then put that on him, and wrap those long bandages around him. He'll need to lean forward."

"I can do this."

"'Course you can."

As Kayla busies herself with cleaning the wound, Rachel watches the road and occasionally glances at the rearview, catching glimpses of Felicia, who attends to the women and boy as if nothing special happened on the street moments ago.

Rachel keeps close to Joel's bumper, tailgating him, still believing innately that Felicia's influence—as well as the others'—is strongest with proximity. She envisions it as both a protective and healing shield. Whatever Felicia managed to do moments ago, that shield appears to be growing, possibly because of the number of turned bodies they have accumulated, possibly more because of Felicia's growing strength, but either way, Rachel remains glued to the Hummer's rear.

Darkened rows of homes and entrances to quiet neighborhoods drift past. She knows exactly where they are—she has many memories of traveling these roads—but her mind is still back there at the Safeway grocery store, where she and her mom would go for bakery items on some Sundays, so long ago now. A different life.

Her mind goes fuzzy again. She could easily doze, right here behind the wheel. It's been too long since she's slept. Her eye sockets feel hollowed out.

It's too easy to let her mind drift into memory, when she would go to that store with her mom as the effects of the disease (and treatment) became pronounced. Her mom had taken to hiding her balding scalp with a pretty blue scarf that she and her dad had picked out together, but it couldn't hide the gaunt, etched face that cancer and chemotherapy had conspired to inflict on her. Rachel remembers that face more from photos now than from actual memory, but the recollection is bloated with grief. The pity radiating from the bakery personnel, the sorrowful apologies that such an awful ordeal had befallen her, the sighs that accompanied the goodbyes. Rachel has a strong image of their bagged items between them in the car, a grease mark on the side, as her mom drove them home silently, with wet eyes.

She startles out of the memory, jerks the truck back into her lane, glances over at Scott. Kayla has managed to place the bandage fairly neatly over Scott's wound and is in the process of wrapping his midsection with long strips of gauze, applying pressure to the entire area. Scott has leaned forward and is in the midst of a prolonged wheeze. His face is locked in a determined grimace.

"Doin' good," Rachel says, and he manages a nod.

His eyes keep drifting closed, as if he's about to lose consciousness. She needs to keep him awake.

"Who did you lose, Scott?"

His eyes open, and he turns to her, halfway frowning. He swallows, looks away, then back again. "My folks." He winces. "They lived in town. We weren't close." He goes quiet for a while, and Rachel glances over at him to see him concentrating better. "Still, it was the first place I went when I woke up. They have a little house over on Mountain. You know the story: No answer at their door, and I found them in their bed. Unresponsive." He grits his teeth. "And yet something was happening inside them. I could see it right away."

Ahead of them, Joel takes a tight arc around a ghostly collision, and Rachel follows as closely as she can. She doesn't want to ram the Hummer for fear of messing with this old truck's antique engine.

"I panicked, didn't know what to do," Scott goes on. "Eventually I ended up at the hospital. Home turf. I wanted to help. I really did." He glances down at his side, places his restless hands on his thighs, then looks away, out the window. "I have no idea where my folks have ended up. I'm sure they're gone. My dad was an asshole anyway." His voice is matter-of-fact.

Rachel looks over at him, doesn't know if she should give voice to the first thing she thinks.

Scott catches the look in her eye. "Hard to believe, I know."

"I wasn't going to—"

"Yeah you were."

She can't help it—she's thinking of her own dad. The image of his slack face flashes at her, twice, hard, but she won't let it take hold of her consciousness. That's for later. No, she's thinking of him alive. Of everything he had to apologize for. She thinks of her mother and of Susanna, and how awful all that was. Her dad made mistakes, of course, but he was never an asshole—even though she'd shouted that very word in his presence on more than one occasion. Yes, they had their share of screaming arguments, in which she did all the screaming. *She'd* been the asshole the whole time.

That was the subject matter of her life only last week, and now it means next to nothing. Regret starts to flow through her veins like ice water.

She's about to cry, so she changes the subject.

"What about your mom?"

Scott's expression says he's done talking, but when he looks into her eyes, he softens. "She was so peaceful there in the bed. Like I could wake her up and everything would be fine. She put up with so much shit. So much shit. She didn't have a good life. But in the end, she was at peace. I'm sure of it." He focuses on the road coming at them, searching, then pauses. "That's gonna stay with me. Finding her like that."

Rachel nods.

Scott is wide awake now, chewing his lip. "I see what you're doing, you know."

Rachel half-smiles.

"Nice work," he says, wincing again.

Rachel looks behind her, through the window, shining the mag light back there. The older woman, Julia, is sitting up against the rear gate, staring at her. She appears vastly improved—a good sign. Her eyes are haunted, and her mouth opens and closes, as if testing an injury to the throat. Felicia did the same thing in the library, Rachel remembers, but it took her longer to become so aware. Linda, the younger woman, is writhing in agony still, her teeth gritted despite morphine, her eyes flooded with moisture, dealing with her transformation. As for the boy, Philip, he is mostly blocked from Rachel's view, but she glimpses a small, pajama-clad leg. She can make out a morphine mewl coming from his poor mouth, down and to her right, and her own jaw clenches in response. She can't even imagine the pain.

At least they're human again, she thinks.

However, she can't help but acknowledge that large piece of her that is looking down on these rather pitiful human beings—these almost mortally injured survivors, these hobbled wounded—and feeling futility. Does Joel really think these people can make a difference? Felicia has proven that she has some kind of power over the monsters, yes, and even Rachel feels the snap of hope when she considers what the woman can do, and has done, but there are obviously strong limits to that power.

Just as she's swinging her head back to the road, Felicia's head jolts to attention.

"Wait!" she says. "Wait!"

Rachel checks her distance from the Hummer, then looks back again.

"What, do you see something?"

A kind of nervous passion takes hold of Felicia's features, and she searches the distance to the southwest, her eyes squinting.

"*Nicole,*" Felicia whispers.

"What?" Rachel says. "Who?"

"I see her," Felicia says softly. "I see them. All of them."

Whatever color that remained in the woman's cheeks has drained away with the mention of that name. Nicole. Rachel's mind somersaults.

"Who's Nicole?"

Felicia keeps staring west. "She's up there, she's with them. Oh my God, they're all there."

"But who—"

And as Rachel continues to shoot glances back at Felicia, she watches the woman's face gradually turn from passion to unease to cold calculation. Rachel isn't sure if it's the glow of the Hummer's tail lights or whatever remains inside Felicia, but a crimson luminescence is still throbbing in the poor young woman's slack mouth. More than ever since leaving the library, Felicia's allegiance appears mysterious. Rachel decides to keep this thought to herself, but she feels a real anxiety that Felicia might not be the hopeful turned-back beacon that the survivors all hope she is. Either way, Felicia has been forever changed by her ordeal, and it's heartbreaking to watch her expression shift from hope to desolate cunning—whatever the cause. But more than ever, it feels like a leap of faith to trust in her as they approach the alien epicenter.

After passing more silent, darkened homes, tailgating Joel, she glances back again to find Felicia's gaze still locked on whatever she senses to the southwest.

"Thanks Kayla," comes Scott's struggling voice.

Kayla has been helping him with his bandage, making sure he keeps it tight against his side. His face is sweaty and pale.

He and Rachel share a glance as Kayla settles back into her seat.

"I know you would never worry about me," he says, managing a thin smile, "but don't worry about me."

"You're gonna get through this."

"Huh," he mumbles.

"What?"

"You've never lied to me before now."

"Oh, knock it off."

The night comes at her relentlessly. Joel keeps tapping his brakes, driving cautiously through the mostly empty streets, and Rachel begins to feel impatient. Scott is dying next to her in his seat, and Felicia is suddenly hyper-aware of the survivors' destination. But there's more to it than that, Rachel understands. She feels as if she's sensing some kind of collective need to get this done. And her instincts are telling her that this feeling is coming from the survivors lying in the rear of the truck. There's a sense of readiness, despite their pain and suffering.

The readiness mirrors her own.

Rachel taps the truck's horn once, twice, and the Hummer brakes to a stop in the middle of the road. Rachel guesses they're coming up on Horsetooth Road now. All around them are quiet homes, and she senses no movement anywhere. Rachel pulls up next to Joel and leans out the window to peer up at him.

His window is down, and his head is already hanging out. "What now?"

"Felicia is on to something."

"What do you mean?"

"She's sensing something."

"Sensing something?"

"I think she can take us directly where we need to go."

Joel glances back in Felicia's direction, although the woman has dropped out of sight into the flatbed. Rachel sees doubt in his eyes, and he gives voice to them.

"This whole party's over if she has the wrong motives," Joel says, echoing her own thoughts.

"She doesn't."

"You sure?"

"You were the one banking on her earlier, right?"

Joel doesn't answer.

"You up for following a girl who can barely drive stick?" Rachel asks him.

Joel turns to the twins next to him, and Rachel leans over to see them, too. They glance over at her miserably as Joel asks them, "Any objections?"

The twins shake their heads.

"Get on out there, girl," he says, nodding forward. "A former corpse with a sixth sense is good enough for me."

She nods, then wrangles the truck into first gear, turning to Kayla and Scott. "Let's go."

CHAPTER 23

Felicia senses Nicole like a vague, pulsing dot in a live satellite image, red and quivering in her western periphery, but alive and *there*. Amidst the chaos of the other souls—that's how she has come to think of them—she feels the pull of Nicole like gravity. Only a moment later does Felicia grasp the impossibility of actually arriving in front of her, of facing her, of getting to her through the throngs of infected bodies. Of even having the opportunity to bring her back.

Rachel works the gearshift into first. Felicia catches a hint of the urgency of the young woman's mind, coupled with the edgy exhaustion they all feel.

Rachel lurches the truck forward, swinging the giant yellow monstrosity around in front of them. "Let's go," she says inside the cab.

Felicia's body jerks with the sudden movement, but all this is happening mostly in her background, as her focus is on the west. She can't help but turn her head that way. Her lover is really out there, not dead, still a part of this nightmare reality, a bright spot amid the churning, alien mass that has occupied her violated brain for the past few days.

Now, she can't even focus on the two women and the boy, who are in varying stages of their return. She is in the midst of caring for them, feels deep sympathy for their plight, and now she can't focus on them. She can't turn away from this.

Since she herself returned at the hands of Joel and Michael at the Co-Op, her mind has been inundated by the presence of the web of souls. She has wisps of memory of her time under the sway of the strangers—that's the word that occurred to her first, the moment she turned—but they feel more like the remnants of a nightmare than a lived experience. Even so, inside those wisps of memory is the sense that she had her place in that web. Upon leaving it, she felt an overwhelming loss. Like a soul ripped from its host, leaving her with only the gasping memory of the host's warmth. She has the perspective to see that now.

But even as she experienced the loss, and regained her humanity, she realized that she had also gained something.

Something stayed with her.

Awareness.

Though she's no longer part of the web of souls, she can see it. And she can sense each individual soul. And not only those souls. Every soul.

Not many of her thoughts over the past few tumultuous days have dwelled on Nicole and her whereabouts, but now she has rushed to the front of Felicia's brain. When the truck takes the turn on Harmony heading west, Nicole becomes an even brighter spot in her mind's eye, as if acknowledging the fact that Felicia has seen her.

Felicia blinks and turns. The two women and the boy are in three separate stages of healing. Julia, the woman from the Volkswagen bus near the library, has come a long way from when they first found her near death in that cramped, furnace-like vehicle. She has no doubt that Julia would have perished in that car days ago were it not for the infestation. The strangers' presence turned her body into a nearly invulnerable host, replacing the supremacy of its fragile animal systems with a kind of energy new to the human species. It's an energy that Felicia understands instinctively, having been under its sway, but she has struggled to find words to describe it.

The truth is, it scares her.

Ever since Michael brought her back, she has been in fear of what she's gone through. She still doesn't understand what the infestation did to her—and what it is still doing to her.

When she looks at Julia, through eyes that have been irreparably damaged, she sees herself as she was two days ago: blind, enduring unutterable pain, and in the midst of psychic mayhem. Felicia feels as if she's still in the grip of the latter, but at least she knows now that she has become human again. In the early hours, she wasn't even sure of her allegiance.

And that's what scares her the most.

She doesn't want to admit it to herself, let alone Rachel and the others, but she feels as if she might—she could—change back at any moment. That's how powerful the infestation was.

It makes her shudder every time she thinks about it.

She can feel the presence of the strangers in her mind, ready to grab at her, ready to rip her apart, and yet so far she has been able to keep that presence at bay. But oh, the retribution in store for her if it becomes known to the strangers what she is doing.

Julia was only the first.

The other woman, Linda, is younger, darker, still in the early throes. Felicia and the twins have pumped her full of morphine twice since rescuing her earlier in the night, but she's still the equivalent of a trapped animal, jerking and grunting. Felicia secured her in a blanket near the right wheel well after the twins helped her set two dislocated limbs, but Felicia can do little for her internal injuries except for pain relief. It was the same with her, at the library.

Since snatching her from the back seat of her vehicle, Linda has been weeping inconsolably—probably not even understanding why. Felicia has been soothing her as well as she can. Sympathy blooms inside her as she has never before felt.

The little boy is another matter. Even when Felicia first sensed Philip, she knew there was something different about him. When he turned back to humanity, he peered straight into her eyes, and she beheld the crimson within them, and she knew that he saw it in her, and somehow they were one. They fed off each other.

He didn't even express very much pain in the turn. He screamed, to be sure, and he needed pain relief, but his protestations amounted to little more than typical toddler pain. He bounced back more quickly. Indeed, he was already the furthest evolved of all three of the bodies they'd saved. When she looks at him now, she sees an abused little boy, yes, but he's resting, healing, conserving energy. She can sense his resilience and vitality like warmth against her skin. She can also sense that, like the rest of them in the rear of the truck, he has retained the crimson stain.

She's sure that this boy, this Philip, means something—far beyond what his size suggests. And she knows, deep down, that he has fueled something inside her. She feels stronger, more alive. And she feels a new power inside her.

"They're doing well," she says when Rachel repeats her question.

"Do you think it's working?" Rachel shouts through the window. "This whole thing—do you think it's working?"

Felicia hangs on to the left side wall, turning into the warm breeze, toward Nicole.

"I do," she says simply.

Gauging the red pulse off in the distance, she feels a connection to her former humanity. She has felt an inkling with Michael and Rachel— her former customers at the Co-Op—but now the feeling has burst forth with the recognition that Nicole is still alive in the world. She's out there, she's close, and Felicia is going toward her. She holds out little hope that she can save her, but at least she will see her again. Her love. Her life. It remains.

Rachel nods, then turns her attention back to Kayla and Scott, helping the girl with something as she continues to follow Joel in the Hummer.

Felicia knows Rachel's mindscape. The young woman has been through her share of pain. Felicia senses great loss—the memories of her mother are wrapped in melancholy gauze, beautiful and bitter at the same time. She gathers that the loss preceded the apocalyptic event by a number of years, but the emotion surrounding it remains strong. Rachel has also watched friends die, recently, and even helplessly. And of course her father, Michael, who sacrificed himself for her.

Yet despite his sacrifice, there is mystery surrounding him—

Oh Daddy!

—inside the young woman's mind. Rachel has discovered something about her father, and she is full of questions. Doubts. Fears. Something to do with money. Secrets. And it's causing Rachel pain. Pain she knows she'll have to deal with. Felicia wishes she could help her, but she doesn't know anything about their relationship. It's not her place.

She doesn't even know how to broach the subject. Or even how to suggest that she has this new, impossible ability. She has admitted to Rachel that she can sense other infected bodies—their locations, even the state of their minds—but she has stopped short of telling her that the ability extends beyond the infected.

She feels the exhausted strength of Joel, who is fueled largely by adrenaline now and increasingly frightened about the end game—though he would never admit to that fear. She gets a strong sense of young Kayla's bright, goggle-eyed, innocent terror, tempered by her immediate attachment and even love for Rachel. Felicia has spent time with the resourceful twins, and even though she couldn't help them as much as she would have wanted, she knows the pain they both feel, in almost precisely equal measures, for their lost parents and friends. And she has seen inside Scott's insecure mind, has pondered the way it has veered from darkness to light, then back again. She knows his pain, and she understands the severity of his wound—can even feel it, a phantom stab in her own side when she focuses on him.

This ability, too, scares her.

Makes her feel … *alien.*

Nicole pulls at her, and she knows they're traveling in the right direction, and her heart fills with dark hope.

Face thrust forward into the wind, she closes her eyes and lets Nicole's soul work on her, tug at her. It's like falling sideways. For a moment, she manages to ignore the pain that still wrenches at her throat and her sinuses, ignores the throbbing soreness in all of her limbs and in her spine, and focuses on her lover—her face, her voice whispering to her to hurry, please hurry, even as Felicia knows she's supplying these words herself.

After only a few seconds, her attention is snatched to her right.

Three bodies are galloping fluidly across a greenbelt adjacent to the road, chasing them from afar. Felicia sensed their proximity as her vision became aware of them peripherally. Before she calls out to the others, she watches them. Their movements are almost graceful. There's a beauty there. She recognizes their beauty. How can she think that way?

Look at them! How they have evolved in so short a time!

It's all part of the objective.

As she watches them, she can't help but recall her own infestation. The details are foggy, but the hammering horror of that time resonates still. The cracking limbs, the straining, the immediate possession at her center—overwhelming! But even as she coped with the reality that she was trapped in the Co-Op office, she heard the whispers into her subconscious, the soothing *voice*—not in her tongue but understandable all the same—that calmed her and ensured her that the pain would ease and that adaptation would come.

Gazing at the sprinting bodies, she realizes that adaptation has been almost fully realized in them. This is what she would have become had Michael not changed her back. These bodies are no longer human. They are strangers in the flesh. She still has flash-imprints of the strangers in their own form, on their own world, and this is what they look like.

Nightmares in the flesh.

"Rachel!" she calls, trying to put strength into her still-broken voice.

"Yeah?" comes Rachel's voice over the rumble of the truck's motor.

"We're being followed."

"Where?"

"To the right."

Rachel searches out the passenger window. "I don't see anything."

"They're there."

"Are they getting close?" Rachel shouts through the window. "As close as before?"

Felicia is watching the charging bodies carefully, caught between mesmerized and fearful. The bodies are dashing fluidly over sidewalks and grass islands, leaping from asphalt to cement curbs, and their heads are swiveling as if tracking the vehicles. Or are they watching her?

As she has recaptured more and more of her humanity, Felicia has felt her consciousness turning outward, following a period of weird self-awareness of herself as *other*. She remembers feeling a truly vicious anger, an incomprehensible rage and failure, and it took her a long time to recapture herself as a human. It took days. The knowledge of that confuses and embarrasses her.

She sensed some of that in the human beings here with her in the truck bed, when they too turned—at her hand!—but it's fading with time. Fading along with the healing. And they are turning back to humanity faster than she did. Michael turned her with blood, but she turned these humans back with the force of whatever lingered inside her. That, too, distresses Felicia—whatever remains.

She can also sense the minds of these galloping bodies, albeit in a more distant way. The objective is clear in their minds—a singular, gleaming purpose—but these three are among the many dispatched to face those who survived.

She focuses hard on the lead body, feeling its urgency, its single-mindedness. It's so powerful. And the one thing she doesn't sense there is the knowledge that it can, at any time, detonate the orb of energy at the center of its skull. It is not in control of that. Its objective, divorced from the overall objective of the web of souls, is to get as close as possible to the targets—and then something else—

—the strangers—

—is pulling the trigger, exploding the orb in desperation. In anger.

She hasn't been able to see those coming.

And she knows they will keep coming until the unexpected threat is eliminated. But Felicia can sense the uncertainty. It's the same uncertainty that first gripped them at the library when Michael thrust himself into the horde, when Felicia herself rose from the floor and faced the wall of corpses.

"Felicia?" Rachel shouts again.

"They're keeping their distance," she says. "They're more afraid than ever."

"What?" Rachel calls, not quite hearing her.

"They're afraid."

"They're afraid of you?"

"Yes."

The word catches in Felicia's ravaged throat, making her cough. She winces with pain. She has been medicating herself since she turned, and has been trying to ingest less and less pain relief with time, but she has never felt such unrelenting pain in her life—as if she has swallowed fire, as if the center of her head has been burned out, as if all her muscles have been whip-snapped.

But it's that thought that nearly does her in.

Me. They're afraid of me.

She has suspected something incomprehensible happening inside her since she turned Julia in the back of that Volkswagen bus. Something simultaneously pushed and pulled at her as she approached that bus. For whatever reason, she resisted the thing pulling at her and instead went to the woman—the force that pushed at her. The woman with the long gray hair had seemed a corpse, but her soul all but shouted at this kindred soul, begged her to help her. The thing pulling at her no longer had sway over her. It no longer had its vice-like grip over her own body and spirit.

So she went to the woman, not even knowing what might happen.

And she had turned her.

Felicia doesn't know how, she doesn't know why—but she turned her.

She looks at Julia now, and finds the gray-haired woman glowering at her. Felicia can sense the woman's mindscape as surely as Julia can sense hers: There's a wave of itching doubt flowing out of Julia's mind now, as she grapples with the lost power of her alien conviction. The objective remains, but the motivation is gone. She's no longer under the strangers' sway, but she's having trouble reclaiming what she was.

Felicia gets it.

Because she still feels it.

Linda and Philip will get there. Eventually. And in the meantime, there is a power in their skulls that they don't understand. A power that is somehow helping the survivors.

"They're afraid of me," she repeats, her words drifting away on the warm night breeze.

She knows Joel and the others have been anxious for her to embody this persona—as savior—but she has resisted.

The notion terrifies her.

She eases herself away from the window and positions herself against the side wall, watching the creatures. She can hear them, barely, gasping, grunting. Their footfalls occasionally slap the concrete sidewalk between islands of weedy bluegrass.

Her mind is bombarded by stimuli. Philip's little-boy simplicity— troubled slumber and discomfort. Julia's morphine ache, and Linda's glower as she considers her plight and occasionally falls back on her probably dead family. Kayla's empathy atop exhausted fear, attached to Rachel with a poignant anxiety. Rachel's determination over all else, including bleak thoughts of loss and confusion surrounding her father, Michael. Scott's weakening as his lifeblood seeps away—a strange, chaotic man at the edge of death.

Farther away, behind them, Joel's determination mirroring Rachel's—and not for the first time, Felicia catches whiffs of something else mirroring Rachel's mind, and it brings a tiny, involuntary smile to Felicia's lips.

Felicia turns her lips down, discouraging the smile.

Amidst all that, the cacophony of whispers and static that is her new reality, the thousands upon thousands of souls out there, human and stranger alike. And Nicole, shining like a beacon, due west.

Another involuntary smile, and Felicia grits it away.

She won't be happy yet. She won't allow herself that.

As she watches the three galloping bodies, she focuses hard on them, and as one, they swivel their heads toward her, as if responding to her. She can read their malicious thoughts not only in the sounds of their gasps but also in the patterns of their thoughts. It's a red, collective rage. She knows that rage, remembers feeling that rage. It's a rage that brings even more tears to her ravaged eyes.

The lead corpse, its limbs flailing madly as it runs, is named Devin. Felicia can see flashes of his life before the infestation. Swimming, family, occasional marijuana behind the house. Computer games, aspirations to entrepreneurship similar to her own. All of that nearly blotted away. Behind him is Melanie, her shorter limbs struggling to keep up. Felicia can sense deep friendships and a broken family, an abusive boyfriend, and a love for art—all of that buried beneath the savagery of her imprisonment. And bringing up the rear is the snarling Jonathan, an older man with long white limbs, his mind throttled by the strangers but hanging on to a devotion to his spouse, and a passion for model railroads.

Human passions, human experiences.

All three of them nearly naked, straining backward in their puppeteered bodies, limbs nearly torn from sockets, joints screaming, throats raw, skulls aglow with alien light.

Felicia's hands are locked onto the lip of the side wall.

She targets her thoughts on the rushing trio as it bobs and weaves warily, closer and then farther away from the trucks. She knows the bodies want to attack. They're itching for an opportunity—when the larger power can then detonate the source of their new lifeforce.

She won't let them.

She swallows and closes her eyes.

Thrusts out.

A trio of electric pops, and the bodies immediately fall and slide across grass. Screams erupt from their ragged throats, and the sounds dwindle away behind them.

Felicia slumps against the side wall and feels herself slip helplessly to the grimy floor of the truck bed.

"Felicia?"

It's Kayla's voice, far away.

"Are you all right? Rachel, something happened to Felicia, she's ..."

The sound of Kayla's girl-voice muffles and fades.

CHAPTER 24

As Felicia surfaces back into consciousness, she wades through an array of images from her human life—random memories from her CSU classes, mornings with Nicole, even blips from her childhood with her mom. She wakes with the feeling of these memories rushing at her insistently.

The truck is slowing, its rumble softening.

Kayla's voice is still there, as if it never went away.

"... waking up, she's waking up now, she's ..."

Groggy, Felicia finds the strength to sit up. The night is still deep-dark, and she squints over her persistent headache to take in the surroundings. How long has she been out? She feels a responsibility now to protect this crew from harm, and by passing out, she has shirked that responsibility. And following that up is the guilt of betraying what she became—however briefly. In the midst of that conflict, she makes a frustrated sound in her throat, wincing at the pain, and focuses.

She neither sees nor senses any malevolent bodies following them, or even near them in these neighborhoods. There are bodies there, outliers clinging to trees in lawns, bodies that never made the trek into the foothills, satisfied with what they found—but for whatever reason, they aren't antagonistic. They're remaining where they are, even as the survivors whisk by, heading toward the strangers' terrestrial epicenter.

When Felicia turns her gaze west, she feels Nicole's presence like a solid thing, something she can reach out and grab. They're so close. She feels again that blast of anticipatory joy at the prospect of reuniting with her, despite her probable wrecked state—

—*the memory of their night together, before everything fell, their bodies entwined*—

She has no doubt now that they'll find her. They *have* to. She has an almost irrationally strong conviction in her new ability. But she also knows the thing that has a stranglehold on her lover, and she has seen the effects of that stranglehold. She herself has felt only a fraction of those effects, and she was close to death. She's under no illusions.

Before she sees the roadblock ahead of them, she feels Rachel's reaction to it as she drives toward it. Alarm, dread, pessimism. Then the mass of vehicles becomes increasingly obvious in the truck's headlamps, and Felicia knows in a red flash that the strangers constructed this obstacle themselves, using groups of infested corpses to push the heavy, stalled vehicles into place.

Rachel lurches the truck to a stop and turns off the engine. She swears, a blunt word.

The Hummer pulls up to the right of the truck, and Felicia is suddenly looking up into Joel's eyes.

"How you holding up?" he asks her from his open window before turning to take in the full breadth of the roadblock. "Shit."

"I'm better," Felicia says. "More human."

She can sense Joel's anxiety about this new situation, the fear of being trapped. His policeman's mind is working through escape routes and other options—she can see the math of it, and—again—she admires the way the synapses fire. In front of her, Rachel's mind works similarly but without the structure.

"Can you watch things while we clear this out?" Joel says, his eyes flitting from Julia to Linda to Philip. "I mean, you can do that, right? You can feel them getting close."

She nods carefully.

"Thought so." He studies the wide jumble of cars and trucks that have been jammed together.

The road drops off on both sides of Harmony at this exact point, precipitously, to allow the progress of a small creek. The road here is essentially a squat overpass above the water. This was strategic in the extreme. There's no getting around this makeshift vehicle blockade.

"Anything we should worry about on the other side of that mess?" Joel asks her.

Felicia focuses on the road beyond the vehicles and senses no immediate threat, save for the massive glow farther out toward Masonville, where Nicole's bright soul vibrates among hundreds of thousands.

"I don't think so," Felicia says.

He lowers his head to peer into the truck's cab. "Rach, I'm gonna start shoving at those cars with the Hummer. Looks like there's two rows of them, but shouldn't be a huge problem for this beast. Watch my back, okay? All of you, especially you, Felicia."

The twins hop out of the Hummer on the passenger side, each holding a weapon at the ready. Felicia feels their exhaustion and desperation but also their collective strength. She also catches a whiff of the anguished pride both twins feel. They know they're doing their part in this battle.

The twins step over to the truck, nodding at Rachel and Felicia and gazing at the dark neighborhoods surrounding them.

They've made it to the edge of the foothills, Felicia realizes. They're on Harmony now, west of Taft Hill, before the winding rise up to Horsetooth Reservoir. The roadblock appears to have been hastily cobbled together with vehicles abandoned on the road and others from nearby rural properties. She even spies a tractor. They're surrounded by more wide-open land now, compared with that of the city proper.

Joel butts the Hummer up against a seemingly vulnerable spot and edges forward. A late-model Chevy and a GM truck begin a dragging slide, but then they impact further vehicles beyond those, making the job more difficult. Joel guns the engine, and then they too begin to slide reluctantly. After agonizingly long moments, the Chevy begins to buckle and tip, and the Hummer strains. Joel backs off, and the Chevy lurches back to the ground. They all hear Joel's loud cursing.

"What is it?" Kayla asks.

"Looks like that one car won't cooperate," Rachel says. "Maybe it's stuck on something."

While Joel tries to shove at a new spot, Felicia takes a moment to check on Julia, Linda, and Philip. They're all conscious and alert. Felicia crawls over to Julia and finds her staring out into the night, defiantly. Her only real movement is her jaw, which jerks spasmodically. Felicia senses her pain.

"Need some—?" Felicia begins.

"No," Julia says, gritting her teeth.

"But …"

"No."

Felicia nods and turns to Linda, who is already watching her and nodding. She needs the relief of the morphine. As Felicia bends to the task of administering the medicine, she eyes Philip, who is watching through the truck's cab as the Hummer pushes at the row of cars. He's standing motionless, and Felicia detects very little fear in his mind—mostly curiosity. Some bewilderment. It's as if he's awakened from slumber into a darkly fantastic alternate realm. His young body and mind are so resilient! In some ways, too, he's a little kid again, fascinated by trucks and tractors.

Felicia carefully fills a syringe with 10mg of morphine and injects it into the muscle of Linda's upper arm. Almost immediately, the woman relaxes, her eyes closing, tears of relief squeezing out and flowing down her cheeks.

"It'll be all right," Felicia whispers.

She settles the woman against the side wall and looks once more out into the night. She senses no movement in the vicinity. The heavens remain restless with red light and rumble with almost constant crackling thunder, but it's distant ... restrained. When she was infected, she could read the skies—even through the ceiling of the Co-Op—as if the strangers were speaking solely to her. She heard messages in the wind, in the atmosphere. Not anymore. She can't tell if there's a gathering of strength happening, or a weakening.

At that moment, something takes hold of her senses.

The breeze has shifted east, and the odor of death wafts over her.

The others detect it, as well.

"Whoa," Kayla says. "Do you smell that?"

"Yeah," says Rachel.

It's been over five days since the strangers descended on Earth, and the neighborhoods of Fort Collins are filled with the corpses of human beings who escaped infestation but perished in other ways—because they got too close to those infected, because their bodies couldn't handle the infection, because they were killed by survivors—and those corpses have begun to decompose. Neighborhoods are choked with them. Is that what the survivors are smelling now?

"Over there," whispers Philip, gesturing with his small arm toward the wall of vehicles.

Felicia goes to him. "What do you see?"

He doesn't answer, but at that moment, the Hummer comes to a stop. Joel has mostly pushed his way through the barricade, tipping four smaller cars onto their sides, and Felicia understands why Joel has had trouble moving the barricade.

Beyond the vehicles lies a great mound of human bodies, bolstering the vehicular barricade with a massive row of dead flesh. Thousands upon thousands of pounds of deadweight. Joel slowly backs away from the metal mass, and as the cars settle to the ground, random limbs begin flopping to the asphalt as bodies pour into the gap.

"*Oh no!*" whispers Rachel, her hand moving to her mouth.

"They moved them there?" Kayla says. "They dragged bodies there to—"

Rachel nods. "I think that's exactly what happened. Oh my god."

Joel hops down from the Hummer and approaches the truck, his face ashen. He anchors himself against the hood and doesn't seem to know what to say. Felicia feels waves of horror radiating off of him, an inability to process what he has seen.

"I—I don't—"

"Have they trapped us here?" Kayla says. "Is this a trap?"

Joel looks to Felicia.

"I don't see anything," she says, sensing the air. "Still nothing."

"Can you … can you get through that?" Rachel asks Joel.

"Oh Jesus." He spins around, as if searching for some better option. "That would be … Fuck, Rachel. That's horrible. The kind of thing that would weigh on a guy, you know?"

"You want me to do it?"

Joel glares at her.

The survivors are at a loss for words, but Felicia can see them working through other ideas, devising alternate routes, and discarding them. On either side of the road, hardscrabble earth dips sharply into water—too much for even the mighty Hummer to surge through—and acres of other obstacles. She knows they could backtrack north to Horsetooth and find a way up to the reservoir that way—she feels Joel entertaining this same thought—but she's sure the same kind of roadblock awaits them there. This dumping ground of corpses was planned days ago, possibly when the strangers first understood that a small contingent of survivors remained in the area, and wasn't simply tossed together overnight.

"We don't have a choice," Felicia says, breaking the uneasy silence.

They all look at her.

"I know it's awful, but we have to drive through it. We don't have the time to do anything else." She pauses, clicks her jaw, swallows. "We can't move those bodies one by one—it would take too much time, in the open like that. That's what they want. And we can't go around them. Right now, they're thinking of other ways to end us. And they'll win. We have a window of opportunity, but that window is going to close."

It's the most she's spoken since she changed back, and the effort nearly does her in. But a new urgency is upon her—not only because of Nicole's pulsing soul in the distance but also because she can feel the ebb and flow of the strangers' machinations above her.

"Window of opportunity for what?" says Joel.

Felicia can sense Holocaust comparisons flowing through Joel's mind, and the fearful reluctance that has taken hold of him. For the first time, he has really considered the possibility that he, and all the rest of the survivors under his watch, will end up an anonymous corpse in a pile.

"I mean," he goes on, "I know where we're headed is right. *I feel it.* We have *some* kind of opportunity here, but what is it?" Despair touches his voice, making it drop in volume, in confidence. "We're still alive, and we've won some battles, but is that enough? Look at that." He gestures toward the multitudes of bodies. "What's after this? What's waiting for us as we get closer?"

Felicia watches him scan the area as he ponders his own questions.

She's not sure she has all the answer for him—not the solid, confident answers that his police mind requires, anyway. So she tells him what he wants to hear.

"I can end this."

"How?"

Joel's immediate response takes her aback. The truth is that she feels a growing power and knows she is a threat to the strangers. But whenever she has used this power, this strange energy, to extinguish a corpse's infection, the act has bled her dry, has sapped her of all energy. In the past 30 minutes, she cured three of them, and the act drove her unconscious. And she still has no idea how she's doing it. Nevertheless, she has aspirations to drive the infection out of as many bodies as she can. Once they reach Masonville, she plans to let loose, but she has the strong feeling it will be the end of her. She's willing to make that sacrifice.

"I don't know."

"Yeah, that's what I thought."

"You have to trust me."

"I do, Felicia, come on, there's just a lot we're leaving to hunch."

Rachel cautiously steps out of the truck, leaving it idling in neutral. She glances this way and that, watching the deep shadows for movement. Even as Felicia ponders Joel's words, she can sense the turmoil in Rachel's mind—the paranoia about everything, the horror she feels for the mountains of bodies behind the wall of cars, the confusion that remains surrounding her discovery in her father's bedroom, her fiercely protective notions surrounding Kayla, and now—

Scott.

Scott is dying, but Rachel is holding it back from the others.

Now Rachel is watching Felicia.

"Joel," she says, "you've seen what Felicia has done. What she's doing for us. It's more than trust." She turns to face the policeman. "There's no other way."

"You seriously want to bulldoze through those people? You?"

"We're dying, Joel."

"What do you mean?"

"For all we know, this is the end of the world happening right here." Rachel is backlit by the trucks' headlamps, which are pointed due west, raining harsh light on the piles of dead bodies—a small silhouette against atrocity. "We're running out of time, and we have a chance to do something about all this shit, but we have to get up there. We have to get beyond this. Can that Hummer do it, or not?"

"Christ."

"She's right," calls Zoe, off to the right, prowling the shadows with her long weapon. "We can't let anything they do get in the way of what we have to do."

Joel ponders that.

"How am I suddenly surrounded by so many bloodthirsty women?"

"You mean smart chicks?" Chloe calls from the left.

"Obviously, yeah."

"They're banking on your empathy," Felicia says. "They're counting on your to be the policeman you are."

"She's right," Rachel realizes. "They want us to care for each other as individuals rather than as ..."

"... as parts of a shared consciousness," Felicia finishes.

"Even when those bodies are dead."

"They consider that a weakness."

"Can it do it?" Rachel says again.

"I think so," Joel says. "The thing's a tank."

"Let's do it, then."

Joel shakes his head as he approaches the Hummer, and pauses at the open driver's door, bending his head, gathering his wits. The twins are facing out into the darkness, but they're casting worried glances toward the barrier.

Felicia has been monitoring the area with her senses, and she has felt an odd emptiness, reaching out almost as far as she can extend. She can feel Nicole out there, and the attendant mass of infestations around her, but it's as if all the closer bodies have disengaged from their tasks and headed to higher ground, leaving the survivors to this patchwork barricade. Peripherally, she's also aware of Scott's consciousness, dwindling.

Like Rachel said, the survivors are dying.

One by one.

Joel climbs quickly into the Hummer and slams the door.

"Are we driving over them?" Kayla asks meekly from the truck's cab.

"We are, honey," Rachel says, shifting the truck into gear. "If you need to, cover your eyes."

"They won't hurt, right?"

"I promise they won't."

Felicia watches Kayla bury herself in Rachel's side, then her gaze flickers toward Joel's Hummer, which is poised to break through a wall of flesh.

Then Rachel herself bows her head into Kayla's neck, closing her eyes.

The Hummer begins creeping in reverse. Joel wants to get a bit of speed up. She can almost visualize his thoughts—not too much speed, or the impact might affect the integrity of the Hummer's front end. He comes to a stop behind the truck, and they can all see his teeth-gritted solemnity. He revs up the Hummer and then doesn't waste any time: It bursts forward, roaring, its huge tires bludgeoning the asphalt, three tons of blunt metal thundering its way toward a mountain of human corpses. Felicia senses the collective intake of breath among the survivors, the squeezing of eyes shut. And then the big vehicle crashes into the first vehicles, sending them catapulting in both directions and tumbling away with twin symphonies of shattering metal and glass. In the immediate aftermath, the two cars behind those skid screeching out of the way, and then Joel is pummeling over bodies, squashing and crushing.

Felicia feels tears squirt helplessly from her eyes, but she can't look away. Distantly, she hears Joel screaming in rage.

Bones crack, heads split like melons, blood pools like oil.

The Hummer rocks atop a sea of flesh like an ocean vessel, tipping to port and starboard, and Joel hangs on to the wheel with his ropy-muscled arms. The tires slip and spin, spraying strips of bloody flesh everywhere, including the truck's windshield. Felicia feels bits of human meat dot her hair, and she ducks farther down, weeping.

For an eternity, Joel surges through the flesh by sheer source of metallic will, and finally the bloodbath is over. He has left unprecedented carnage in his wake, and Felicia knows the survivors—all of them—will never be the same because of what happened here on this street. Rachel is the first to think it, Felicia senses. Even compared with everything that has preceded this moment, everything in the past week, this is somehow the worst thing. The most horrible thing.

The Hummer limps out of the mess, something wrong with its inner workings. It comes to a bumpy stop, and Joel takes a moment to study his new surroundings, finding nothing but empty road and foothills rising up. Then he rests his head on the wheel.

Felicia slowly rises to her full height in the truck's flatbed, surveying the scene, wiping flecks of bloody flesh from her face. Then she bends toward the truck's open rear window.

"Keep her head down," Felicia instructs Rachel, who nods furiously into Kayla's hair.

"Stay down, sweetie," comes Rachel's whispered voice.

"I will."

The twins both have their free hands over their mouths. They have backed all the way to the truck and are staring at the Hummer with glistening eyes. Zoe is weeping.

"We have to get past it," Rachel says, rising as she makes sure Kayla remains secure against the truck's bench seat. "Right now."

Wordlessly, the twins hop into the flatbed Ford, and Rachel grinds into first gear.

"Felicia, how's it look out there? Any threats?"

Jason Bovberg

"Quiet," is all she says.

Then Rachel begins to roll forward, and her headlamps render the bloodbath clinical—every inch of destroyed flesh laid bare beneath the unforgiving glow, a vivid charnal house of ripped flesh. Just like Joel, Rachel lets loose with a string of obscenities, the words thick with despair. Felicia tries to block it all out, even the interior screams flowing from the rest, by focusing hard on Nicole, who is beyond this ridge, waiting for her.

She narrows her thoughts on the time before the end, entwined with her lover on her hand-me-down couch in her cramped apartment, in the heat of the summer with the fan on, the buzzing fan oscillating and cooling their damp flesh, the worries of the school year past them, their futures bright and giggly ahead of them, and nothing but slippery fun days and nights for now. That was all for now, and that was enough.

In her heart, a sharp ache stabs at her.

A sob shakes her from her reverie. It's Zoe, right next to her. The young woman has slapped her hands to her ears, unable to take the crunching sounds of bone and flesh beneath the weight of the truck. Her rifle is on the truck bed, sliding in the grit.

Rachel becomes aware of the skies, which are in heightened turmoil.

Is it because they are closer? Because they are approaching the center? Are the strangers reacting to their proximity? Their continued survival?

Are the skies roiling because of her?

Finally, the truck bounces clear of the smeared human remains and gains traction on the asphalt. Ahead of them, in the jittery yellow light of the truck's headlamps, the Hummer is parked aslant in the bike lane, looking injured. Its sideboards and tires are red with blood. Rachel drives toward Joel in a daze—Felicia can feel her mindscape like a numbness.

The foothills lay before them in deep darkness, the winding road reaching up and away toward Masonville. Hordes of bodies await them up there, amassed in the forests, feeding the strangers above. Great columns of light rise in shivering, crimson beams. Felicia watches the phenomenon, knowing that she once understood the communication in that light. She once understood the language.

Not anymore.

The light quivers, as if with rage.

As if watching them.

Something is happening.

The survivors barely have time to take in their new surroundings and emit final shaky sighs before the heavens erupt with crackling thunder.

And in the distance, a hundred enraged bodies begin racing toward them.

CHAPTER 25

"They're coming!" Felicia screeches through the constant pain in her throat. "They're—" she begins again, then stops, because everyone has seen them now as the rushing bodies appear from under the crush of sound.

The bodies rumble like angry bugs down the slope, graceful and alien, their clothes mostly gone, their skin red, enflamed, war-torn. Their faces are ravaged by their hungry assault on bark, gooey and obscured by sap and splinters. Felicia knows instinctively that their trajectory is informed as much by extrasensory communal intellect than by human vision. And yet how fluidly they rush at them, like birds, like insects with a singular intent.

Even Felicia, herself recently one of them, feels her chest seize with terrified awe. She is shocked where she stands, not having anticipated the approach. Had the horror of the barrier blocked her attention from the strangers? And they had taken advantage of that? Or had they tricked her?

Survivors gather around her in panic, also silenced by terror—she can feel it like a vibration—and for a moment Felicia too can only watch the horde approach.

Is her ability waning?

The bodies are a hundred yards away, scrambling, gasping. They're coming from all westerly directions, their throats glowing red, their shared purpose clear.

"Joel!" Rachel yells, grabbing at Kayla protectively.

No way Joel can hear her over the roaring motors.

"Felicia?" Rachel cries, scrambling, and Felicia can read her overriding thought—

What do we do?!

Ahead of them, the Hummer lurches and goes dead. Rachel stares at it, and even Felicia can feel the yawning pit of hopelessness open up in the young woman's center.

"Something's wrong with Joel's truck," Kayla says.

"I see that," Rachel says.

Chloe and Zoe nervously scrabble at the weapon reserves, taking up new rifles, touching hands briefly, acknowledging the threat, bracing themselves.

"Love you, sis," Chloe whispers.

Zoe acknowledges this with a nod and a nervous half-smile, then turns to face the onslaught, now fifty yards away.

Rachel has steeled herself, too, taking hold of the wheel and surging forward toward the Hummer, coming up alongside the massive vehicle.

"What's wrong?" Rachel screams.

"Axle's broken or something!" Joel calls.

He's already jumping down from the cab and leaping over the truck's side walls.

"Get movin'!"

Rachel guns it, letting the clutch go too quickly, and the truck jerks and stalls. Felicia nearly stumbles off the truck bed to the asphalt—a strong grip on her ankle prevents her from that fate. She looks down and finds Linda has saved her. The woman's face is scrunched in gasping pain, but she has saved her.

"*Jesus, Rachel!*" Joel shouts.

The silence fills with the sound of galloping, grunting bodies. The hills jitter with their luminescence. There are so many of them, a buzzing network of souls, and Felicia can only barely sense their humanity, so lost are they under the strangers' influence. A thousand alien souls, screeching and gasping, their eyes turned up as their straining bodies dash over grasses and weeds and wildflowers. Their mindscapes flow against Felicia like a red tide, feral, angry, terrified of her but determined to strike.

Joel has registered a flash of panic. Everyone is yelling at once, crouching, shielding themselves behind the metal of the truck, and Felicia hears the motor turning over, a sound like an old man coughing. It catches just as Joel is about to leap back out of the truck bed, shove Rachel aside, and take control.

"You got it?" he gasps into the cab, and she nods, and he falls back next to Philip, who is looking bewildered, as if he's recently awakened from a nap.

The truck heaves forward, and the scrambling bodies swarm as one toward the truck, closing in, veering in a new course like a flock of birds eyeing prey.

There are too many.

The thought quickens Felicia's pulse.

"Get down!" Rachel cries at Kayla, at everybody, because the things are upon them.

Joel fires savagely into the fray, as do Chloe and Zoe. All three of them are braced against the truck's side walls, their eyes barely over the rim. The twins are screaming, mindless, as their weapons unleash death and cure alike, and bodies begin to crash to the earth—but not enough of them.

"Felicia!" Joel yells. "Help! Please help!"

Even as Felicia pushes out with her mind, she shields her face with her forearm, protecting herself. The wave of bodies surges forward, and she hears the rat-tat-tat of twenty of them snapping back to humanity— the sound of flashbulbs, of paparazzi—but in the wake of those, as the bodies fall violently to the dirt, three or four more bodies explode like grenades, raining shrapnel against the truck.

Energy drains from Felicia like gushing water.

She staggers down next to Philip, who eyes her with little-boy confusion. His arms scramble for purchase on the truck bed, sliding along rust and dirt. She breaks the contact with Philip and peers again over the side. The next wave of bodies is upon them, leaping—

The truck fishtails, pauses alarmingly—

The passenger door swings open, and Scott staggers out, spinning, holding his side, falling to one knee and then crying out savagely as he lifts himself back up. He is ashen, delirious. Felicia is the only one who has seen him, and abruptly she senses his purpose. Everything stutters to slow motion. His eyes lock on hers for an eternity, and his mind is laid plain.

—*Never thought I'd get out of this alive*—

—*Take them the rest of the way*—

—*I wish I could've been*—

The words jitter away as he uses the last of his strength to run toward the bodies, and then his mindscape fractures under a clamor of ferocity as twenty bodies swarm him and explode at once. The shockwave of the blast is a visible ring of energy, sweeping out and buffeting the truck with a harsh wind. His final word arrives in her mind like a stuttered shout.

—*better*—

Felicia can barely protect herself from the spray of blood and bone and meat that follows. She weakly closes her eyes and lets her head loll to the left, but she feels the hot wetness of gore against her right ear. When she opens her eyes, they sting, but she can see Joel and the twins surging back to awareness, reacting to what happened.

"Was that—?" one of the twins starts.

"That was Scott," Joel finishes grimly, gauging the vicinity for further threat. A coordinated wave of them has swept behind them and are giving chase.

"Why did he...?" someone yells.

The truck careens up the long switchback. Scott has bought them precious seconds. Yet another wave of bodies circles ahead, waiting for them.

"Reload!" Joel calls out.

Felicia sees him glaring at her, and feels the blunt shout of his thoughts like a shove—

—*Now? You're failing us now?* —

—but she can barely move. She feels nearly paralyzed, not by fear but by an almost complete absence of energy. Even the clamor of souls around her, both survivor and infected, is muted and dwindling. Her chin rests heavily on the side wall, jarring and bouncing as Rachel navigates the twisting road, taking them ever higher up the switchback. Weapons explode all around her, but the sounds are distant, hollowly booming. Everyone is shouting.

Felicia drifts as in a dream ...

... to the time she and Nicole drove this road together, the day before the invasion, on their way to Horsetooth Rock, laughing in tune with summer, blaring silly '80s music in the warm confines of Nicole's old Civic. Felicia driving, Nicole's pretty bare feet on the dash, the color on her toes flaking now but still there—and Felicia remembers painting them, so meticulously as Nicole laughed, ticklish, lazing around the apartment the weekend before. Spotting four or five rigid deer on the right side of the road, studying them as they passed. Going only occasionally quiet when the realities of their lives intruded, and shaking those thoughts away and getting lost in the music again, and in the vivid details of a bright Colorado summer morning—the crisp, dry, deep blue of the high-altitude skies, the hillsides dotted with a rainbow of wildflowers, the satisfying crunch of tires on gravel as they motored into the Horsetooth parking lot, the sensual swab of sunscreen on each other's skin, the donning of wide-brimmed hats, and an adventure ahead—

Felicia surges back to consciousness and flinches.

She staggers backward on painful limbs, away from the side wall, all her muscles clenched.

What's happening?

A cacophony of sound and fury, swirling all around her.

And over it all, the call of Nicole, more urgent, she's there, waiting for her, if only she can find her way.

Rachel is calling Felicia's name repeatedly.

The truck shudders through the switchback's tight right turn, too fast, nearly tipping. The survivors in the rear hold on for dear life. Felicia feels a throb of dread radiating from all of them.

"Here they come!" Rachel calls, straightening the truck into the lane and gunning it.

Felicia peers out into the dark wide-open, angling her head around the cab, and sees the bodies coming to a coordinated and poised pause, in wait, their red throats pulsating, and it's almost as if Felicia can read the luminescence, like a language forgotten over time.

Joel and the twins reload frantically, sweat pouring off them in streams, making everything slippery.

"Don't get sloppy!" Joel calls. "Make every one count!"

Felicia feels another swell of energy, understanding the source now. On the filthy, rumbling bed of the ancient truck, Julia and Linda have crawled to her and grabbed hold of her lower legs, bracing her. Flesh to flesh. Julia, eyes still streaming, face twisted in agony, has a stranglehold on Felicia's calf, and Felicia feels the woman's lifeforce gushing into her, a hot blast of energy. On her other side, Linda has hold of her ankle, and Felicia follows the younger woman's arm up to her shoulders, and to the face, to find her staring at her with pale earnestness, her long gray hair undulating against a backdrop of rust. Both women stare at her, giving their energy to her, pushing it into her.

Felicia clamors to her feet, grabbing at the cab window for support.

"I'm here," she manages.

"Thank God!" Rachel yells, buzzing with purpose. The young woman has an overriding need to protect this crew and especially the little girl cowering next to her

Standing at the edge of the truck bed, Felicia faces the threat head-on, the souls of Linda and Julia threading through her own, those of the survivors bright and resonant. The sky is a black-and-crimson kaleidoscope, enraged. The truck barrels forward, and a hundred more bodies scramble forward, gasping, leaping over ridges and sprinting directly at them. Felicia beholds their webbed mindscapes like one raging organism, scattered though they are. And then they're upon them.

"Down!" Joel says, yanking in his weapon and falling to the bed. The twins fall simultaneously, covering themselves as best they can.

At that moment, Felicia pushes outward with all her strength.

The closest bodies fall like wounded prey, raining to the earth as one, battering the sides of the truck, their orbs of light extinguishing with a collective, crackling thunder that pulls at the survivors' eardrums, an implosive force. The bodies scream in new pain as they become human, and a dozen of them are trampled as Rachel adds her own scream to the barrage, not slowing, not easing up, and the truck pitches and swerves, and the survivors in the rear grunt and gasp, nearly flying out.

"Keep going!" Joel yells needlessly, as they can all hear the engine straining. "It's not over."

Amidst everything, he manages to wink at Felicia as she eases herself back to the truck bed, not completely sapped of energy this time but feeling a new wave of fatigue. The other women, Julia and Linda, appear similarly worn out, bowing their heads, closing their eyes, but they're still affixed to Felicia, hanging on as if their lives depend on it—and Felicia knows they very well could. Their collective energy keeps flowing up into her; she feels it like liquid warmth, healing her, strengthening her, filling her—

—and she knows it's another remnant of the infection, it's something else lingering, the sense of communal power, the cooperative clout—

Rachel takes the next hard left, farther up the switchback, and now bodies are hanging back, wary. As the truck makes the final push toward the top of the ridge, the bodies merely watch them, their throats throbbing in time with the pulses from the sky. Felicia sees a throng of them fall back into the distance, then she turns back around, catching her breath.

Chloe and Zoe have both fallen weary to the ridged truck bed, staring at Felicia with shattered wonder. Their minds are clear, and twinned: *Did you do that?*

Felicia's head slowly nods.

We did.

The truck crests the ridge, and Horsetooth Reservoir is laid out in front of them, black and slick. The road is dark and empty as Rachel propels them forward, along the rim, the weak headlamps wobbly and uncertain; the sound of the motor echoes out over the watery expanse. There's no activity here. The weedy scree and low-lying shrubs of the gently rising cliffside to the left is treeless groundcover, no place for infected bodies. There are only a few pines dotted here and there, gnawed upon and abandoned. And neither is the water to their right any place for these infected bodies. The bodies are still vulnerable to most human frailties, particularly drowning.

Felicia feels this knowledge instinctually, like something learned long ago.

No, the bulk of the bodies still lay ahead, beyond the reservoir, about two miles along this road. Every one of the survivors stares at the light show in that direction. With proximity, it has stretched beyond comprehension. The columns of light are syrupy, solid things, miles wide, utterly alien.

"Oh my God," one of the twins murmurs behind Felicia.

The luminescence flowing into the sky is a great pillar of shining energy that pulsates like a living being. Felicia feels it pulling at a small part of her, and there is a yearning there—something she's missed out on. She considers that emotion, that ache. It's distant and broken but still a part of her. A small bit of her still wants to be among them again, achieving the common objective.

But then a sneer takes her mouth. What they did to her, what she would have become had she not been locked in that storeroom ...

She shudders, glances behind her.

The twins are on their knees atop the corrugated truck bed, holding hands as they watch the skies, their faces an uneasy combination of dread and incredulity. Their weapons are in their opposite grips, ready.

Julia, her hands still clutching Felicia's leg, has backed up against the cab, and her eyes reflect the crimson lightshow. In the two women and boy Felicia turned back, Felicia senses what she herself feels. Not only that horrible yearning to be a part of that alien collective, but also self-disgust in the wake of that yearning. The power of it, the strength, even in the midst of existential thirst.

"You okay?" Joel says from the right wheel well, where he's perched, watching her.

Startled, glancing over at him, she considers that. "Better."

"Will it be enough?"

She clears her throat, winces with pain. "What do you mean?"

"Do you have enough left to ... to face what we're about to face?"

His expression is full of doubt, and it makes her insides shiver with anxiety. She feels this doubt, too, and she feels other things that she dares not tell him about. In her bones, she knows at any minute she might fall, drained of energy, to the corrugated floor. She also knows she hasn't fully escaped the sway of the strangers.

"We can do it," she says, wanting to repeatedly assure him.

And assure herself.

Her gaze drifts away, toward Nicole, who's inching ever closer. But she can still feel Joel's doubt. He's reading the fact that she's looked away as insecurity, and so she darts her eyes back to his, challenging his perception.

He's nodding now.

"We won't be able to do this with only these weapons," he says.

"I know."

There's a pause, and he sighs heavily with exhaustion—she can smell it wafting off him, the odor of sweat and blood and fatigue.

"I trust you," he says. Those are the words he uses, but she senses a different thought behind them.

We're counting on you.

Felicia knows he's reluctant to put voice to those words—with good reason. There's too much responsibility there. She can barely handle it.

And it's just as bad, sensing that thought rather than hearing the words.

Then Joel turns to watch the yellow headlights shiver in the red-tinted night. He's thinking about Rachel in the driver's seat, forcing himself to ponder more pleasant things than alien invasions and reanimated bodies and whatever lies beyond this final rise. He's thinking about a future that he knows will probably never come to pass. A future with Rachel, rebuilding, with Kayla, perhaps, finding a life amid ruin. A fantasy that blips like a brief dream and then sails away on the wind of the truck's roar along the edge of the reservoir.

"We're going to do this," Felicia says to him. "We're going to beat them." As these words leave her strained throat, she knows they sound weak.

He considers her, smiles thinly.

"Don't worry," she whispers.

Rachel makes the wide turn past the little general store that marks the edge of the reservoir's south bay. For a moment, the truck's headlights illuminate the small sign that says *Stout, Colorado*, in recognition of the town that was drowned by the reservoir when water filled the valley nearly seventy years ago. That bit of history fascinated Felicia when she first heard it, and she remembers telling Nicole about it on their own drive up here, so recently that the memory practically shouts at her.

"What are we about to do?" Chloe says, her eyes on the crimson columns radiating down on Masonville. "Are we actually going into that thing?"

Felicia senses new emotional turmoil in both the twins, compounded by weariness, and now Zoe stifles a moan.

"I mean," Chloe goes on, "are we about to ... to die?" Her hands are shaking uncontrollably on her weapon as she reloads it. "There aren't many mags left. Ten?"

"And we're almost out of blood." Zoe's voice cracks, and she clears her throat. She wipes her hands on her bloody jeans for the umpteenth time. "We've got maybe a dozen darts."

"It's okay," Felicia says, her gaze focusing west on the bright spot among thousands. Nicole is waiting there for her. It's too easy for her to imagine that her lover is alive around the bend, waiting with open arms, with a gasp of awe that they've both survived. She glances back at Zoe. "We won't need that anymore."

Zoe sniffs, nods. There's something like bleak resignation in her expression. She's sitting against the side wall, weapon loose in her lap, her palms up.

Felicia pushes into her mindscape and senses despair. The girl has interpreted Felicia's words to mean that the truck is barreling into a suicide mission, and that their weapons will be inconsequential. Zoe has accepted that fate. But she also holds a thin trust in Felicia. A desperate trust. They all harbor it. Is it unearned? They saw what she did at the library, what she did do to the other occupants of this truck bed—the two women and the boy. They have felt safer with her. Can she earn that again? Or will she fail them?

As if to punctuate that thoughtwave, Joel reaches over and takes her hand.

"You got this," he says. "You're doing great."

Gripping the metal side wall of the rusty truck, Felicia closes her eyes and concentrates. An entirely different lightshow kaleidoscopes in the blackness behind her eyelids, and Nicole remains its brilliant center. Beyond her and surrounding her, a hundred thousand souls jitter in unrest, a great agitated swarm. And the closer she gets to the concentration of strangers, the more clearly she can read their collective sensations—the hunger, the single-minded drive, and the suffocated humanity.

A humanity that is almost completely gone now, beneath the spine-cracking sway of the alien infection.

The truck makes the final turn toward the Horsetooth trailhead, and Felicia opens her eyes.

The survivors emit a collective gasp, and Rachel jerks the truck to the left, braking briefly, then forging ahead.

Across the sprawling mountainside to the right is a Boschian landscape of twisted humanity, bodies interlocked with one another, a massive throbbing collective lifeform crushing the forestry, moving sinuously among the thousands of splintered trees, merging with them, taking from them. Against the larger evergreen specimens, humans are piled into pyramids, reaching high into the stiff branches, searching with their mouths, attached ten and fifteen feet high, scraping and sucking. Their collective crimson energy ripples skyward, crackling, pulsing. As soon as Felicia sees the roiling mass of infected humanity with her own eyes, she experiences a harsh, involuntary cough and wheeze. The web of souls is an overwhelming force, bludgeoning her senses, thousands of voices screaming in her ears, a trillion synapses firing at once.

She stumbles to her knees, and then—as Linda and Julia also succumb to the sensory maelstrom—to all fours on the corrugated metal of the truck bed. She feels the overwhelming urge to drop, prostrate, to the floor.

"Felicia!" Joel cries, pulling at her upper arm.

But Felicia feels herself curling into a fetal position.

It's too much!

The voices bombard her mind—and she realizes that they are aware of her, *all of them are aware of her,* and the strangers above are conscious of her malicious intentions, and those of the rest of the survivors. She has a devastating sensation of all those bodies turning to face her, intent on destroying her.

They have been lying in wait.

Even Nicole.

Now the truck jerks to a stop, and Felicia, unable to move, is vaguely aware of the survivors shouting. Joel attempts uselessly to lift his weapon while pulling at Felicia. She knows he's counting on her, counting on her desperately, but the import of that floats away like a speck of ash. He's yelling at her, but the sound is a muffled nothing. Julia and Linda have wrapped their arms around their heads, having let go of Felicia, and all of their collective power has dissipated.

There is only the clamor of infected souls, almost completely given over to the strangers, and they are cramming her head with noise. Nicole is banshee-shrieking at her, a nightmare screech communicating all the desperate greed and hate of the presence entrenched in Nicole's skull, controlling her like a meat puppet. Felicia cowers under the bray, tears flowing from her squeezed-shut eyes as her own memories of Nicole are obliterated, piece by piece, moment by moment, like photographs blackening and curling in fire.

"*Nicole,*" Felicia whimpers on the truck's floor.

She lets her body go limp, understanding that her world—the *entire* world—is ending. She relaxes on to her back, her muscles relaxing, and finally she stares straight up into the purple sky, up through the vortex, up into the rippling throat of the column of crimson fire, and her eyes go wide, emotions bloat her throat, there they are, *there are the strangers*, a billion twitching limbs pulling at the rising energy, hurrying its upward flow, insectile antennae, an insatiable kaleidoscope of biological need, drawing up, taking, storing. She can hear their collective hunger like throaty entreaties, underscored with a shattering anger—an anger born of fear, the fear of ultimately failing this interstellar quest for a single complex nutrient, a quest that has so far failed on many levels, in so many galaxies, and the dread that this green planet, so far away, after so many distant and frantic searches, is their final hope—*and it is dwindling.*

Knowing all that, understanding the plight of the strangers, the few survivors in this truck still mean more to her than this entire alien species.

The sky opens with an earth-shattering roar.

Felicia hardly notices.

A starburst has opened in her vision, and she feels the pulse of a new power—at least enough to raise herself up. She blinks, stares around at the bleary, beaten faces of the survivors, cringing in anticipation of the end. She sees that Linda and Julia have overcome their own terror and have added their energy to hers, reattaching themselves to her lower legs with trembling hands. Felicia welcomes the incremental surge of power, rising through her legs and into her chest, and she struggles up to face the alien collective.

The mountainside is alive with infected humans, disengaging from their hungry attachments to target the survivors once and for all. Their collective sound is that of an echo-chamber swarm of wasps. They begin scrambling down the mountain.

Rachel grabs Kayla, smothering her, protecting her.

"Close your eyes, honey," she whimpers, and even Felicia can hear it over everything.

Here they come, Felicia breathes.

CHAPTER 26

Rachel watches Felicia falter, sees her face jerk with indecision and doubt, and it is at that moment when Rachel realizes—finally—that her luck, the luck of all the survivors, has run out. It's simply a twitch of Felicia's lower lip that sends Rachel tumbling toward blackness. She feels herself going limp, even as her peripheral vision fills with frenzied alien movement, human puppets.

Next to her, Joel clutches the side of the truck, watching the approach of their doom. He snatches a quick glance at Felicia, barks something desperate at her that Rachel can't decipher, and then the corners of his own mouth tic down in hopelessness.

Above them, the atmosphere swirls in turmoil. She feels as if she is at the base of a mighty tornado, doomed to be ripped up into its violence, torn apart, obliterated.

Rachel grabs Kayla, clinging tight.

"Close your eyes, honey," she whispers to the child.

When the thunder crashes from above, it seems to physically press her into the truck's bench seat. Rachel hugs Kayla as if she's her last hold on her own humanity, and Kayla herself has gone rigid, staring up into the eye of the nightmare tornado, as if daring it yet again to cross her. Her little body is wiry, squirming, and Rachel holds tight, protective at all costs.

She grits out a harsh scream against the onslaught of sound, but she can't even hear her own roaring voice.

From her place in the cab, she can squint her eyes open to see the thousands of bodies across the mountainside, and all of them are twitching away from their trees, their bodies stuttering, reacting to the thunder from above. As one, they turn their insectile heads to face the pitiful band of survivors at the road's edge.

Rachel squeezes into a tight ball around Kayla, her thoughts breaking into shards. *What have we done?* she thinks wearily under the chaos. *Why are we here? Why did we think—?*

Felicia behind her is still standing at full height, even under the buffeting onslaught.

Rachel's head blunts into a muffled silence. Energy crashes out of her. Her eyelids flutter, and—

—*the face of her father looms before her*—

She recoils behind desperately closed eyes.

—*and her father is shouting at her, an image too easily summoned, but no, his eyes are filled with love and concern and fear, it's not anger, and for some reason she connects his expression to that money, all that damned money, what did it all mean, Daddy? Why are you gone, and why did you leave a mystery in your wake, when despite everything I love you and need you more than I ever have …?*

The questions stab out from her in the space of a millisecond.

—*and her father listens impassively now, and there are stutter-images of her mother, so faded now, as if her only memories of her now are conjured from old photographs, rendered brittle with time, caught in another era …*

"Mommy …" she feels herself murmur.

—*and the face of her mother transforms from still image to flesh, coming alive with color and resonance, and*—

Rachel's eyelids flutter spasmodically.

—*her mother smiles, and Rachel can feel the blood-warmth of the gesture, like fresh tears on skin, and inside the vision she explodes with tears, yearning for the time, years ago, when she would curl against her mother on the couch, watching TV, or run toward her across the patchy lawn and embrace her, both of them in their colorful gardening gloves, the smell of soil in the air so strong that it felt as if roses might bloom spontaneously everywhere …*

—*but her mother only smiles, glancing down*—

Rachel realizes that her mother is looking down at Kayla, as if from one world to the next, and Rachel curls against the girl more tightly, protecting her with her whole body as the thunderous approach of the bodies intensifies, ready to engulf them. Kayla's flesh trembles with sweaty heat, as if adrenaline is seeping from her pores, and she's screaming into Rachel's shoulder.

—*and Rachel turns from gloomy past to fading future in an instant, and it's Kayla's smile she's seeing now, an older Kayla, an impossible Kayla, the Kayla that perhaps a small part of her believed she was protecting all this time, a Kayla whose future lay in her incapable hands. That Kayla will never happen, and neither will the future that Rachel occasionally glimpsed in rare moments of optimism, a future that she never deserved, surely, but that still reared up like flashes of bleak hope at the back of her head during humid nights at the library, in the wee hours, holding the scared girl as she cried for her lost family. Joel coming to her in the night and holding her and comforting her and the girl both with his large confident hands, and could Rachel be blamed if Joel was a part of that imagined future? The image of her first encounter with Joel, in the center of Old Town as it burned, immediately protective and in control, and somehow their fates aligned, and so of course she imagined the trajectory of that alignment continuing along a straight line toward a future together, and now that straight line has ended in a terrible blot.*

Kayla is tugging at her.

"Rachel!" Kayla says. "Wake up!"

Rachel opens her eyes, feeling a surge of alertness.

The girl is grabbing her arms and shoulders, urgent.

"What?" Rachel cries.

"Look!"

Rachel wrenches her gaze upward.

Felicia has risen to full height, and her mouth is open, emitting a crimson glow into the pre-dawn. Light escapes her like a scream rendered into luminescence. Everyone is reaching over to Felicia now, wanting to help her, emulating the strange touch of the turned bodies, the way they have clung to Felicia as if to share their energy.

And then Rachel herself grabs ahold of the woman's upper arm, through the open rear window, in support of her impossible power, and Kayla does too. And Joel is there, staring into Rachel's eyes, holding on to Felicia and Kayla and Rachel, holding fast to the lot of them in the rusty bed of a besieged truck. And the twins, teary and sweaty and terrified, dive in to the pile, holding on to tight, adding to the chorus of defiant screams. Rachel feels her throat go scorched, and she doesn't care, it's her end anyway, and she screeches out her rage and rebelliousness again and again.

Just as the edge of the horde reaches the truck, she and the rest of them flinch down, and she sees the face of the boy, the little boy they turned back. He's clutching Felicia, and in the squashed blackness of the truck bed, his residual glow seeps out from his little mouth, not inspiring fear but rather dark hope.

CHAPTER 27

Felicia stands to full height.

When she does so, she's aware of the hands on her flesh, everyone around her but particularly the small hand with the forceful heat. It's that of the boy, Philip, who is looking up into her eyes with a look of resolve on his innocent face—

—*this little boy, powerful in his innocence, resilient in his youth, new to the world, already mostly healed from the infestation, unaware of his own strength except in his determination to be among them, to add his lifeforce to those of the survivors, to band together against the threat surrounding them and return to his sane life of parents and toys and laughter, oblivious to the fact that he never will. His mind is small and emergent, but it is buzzing with the potential of all humanity, and Felicia eases into its blankness and lets it overcome her—*

Power floods her, and she can't help but cry out raggedly, helplessly.

She lets the power fill her, and then she unleashes it across the mountain.

The pulsing orbs in the throats of a thousand infected humans extinguish in a crackling wave, spreading up and away across the mountainside, leaving the bodies to fall to the soft earth, screaming in pain. A dozen batter the truck's sides and gate with a clatter. A multitude die instantly, their bodies too far gone, their injuries too severe to overcome. Felicia feels their mindscapes evaporating, so fragile, like candle flames blown out, and she mourns every single one, the emotion only fueling her outpouring. She pushes harder, harder still, and the wave of alien expulsion swells, choking the crimson throat above her. The energy column shudders and sizzles, breaking apart in a crackling shockwave.

The survivors awaken around her, numb and shivering, peering around at one another. The truck bed is an entwined mass of beleaguered human beings, still clutching at each other desperately for strength—abruptly and unexpectedly alive in the face of certain death. Stunned and shaking, Joel breaks away and laboriously reloads his weapon, then holds it at the ready, barrel trembling. He peers up squinting into the broken sky. Crimson shards of light fall away like a failing prism—Felicia feels as if she half-understands facets in the geometry but senses that understanding crumbling. She hyperventilates as she strains.

Rachel cautiously peers up and out, her eyes filled with tears, Kayla trembling beneath her.

"What happened?" Kayla whines into the sudden absence of activity. "Are we dead?"

Felicia continues to push, fueled by the survivors around her, and it's their collective energy that continues to engulf her with positive energy, filling her up and exploding outward, repeatedly. She gives over control to the three of them, letting their energy work through her.

"Fucking hell," Joel whispers, watching the orbs of energy. "I think it worked."

The twins can only watch, their weapons loose in their grip, as the end approaches.

Beneath the falling skies, bodies writhe across the forest floor, a sprawling expanse of human ruin. Decimated trees tower above the many-hued flesh, leaning as if in pain, considering the creatures that have stressed them. Their lower branches are bent and snapped, their trunks scraped of bark and sap. Heaps of bodies are everywhere.

Philip is clutching Felicia's left leg tightly, his little face clenched in concentration, and as his lifeforce flows through her, an unflinching healing strength, Felicia senses the moment Nicole's infection ends. She hears her lover's scream, deep inside, feels her return to humanity. She can sense it halfway up the mountain, amidst a hundred other abruptly changed souls, writhing in the dirt.

Felicia struggles against the arms clutching her, aching to jump down into the sea of bodies and wade toward her lover, but the survivors are still holding strong, nervous about letting go. She bends down to speak into the window of the cab.

"I need to go up there." She gestures.

"Go where?" Rachel asks, not understanding anything but a fierce and cautious relief.

Felicia doesn't know how to communicate what she needs. All she can do is blurt out Nicole's name.

"Who?" Rachel asks, bleary.

"I need—"

"Finish it!" Joel shouts at her, and she barely understands him over the screams of anguish all around. "Finish it first!"

In anguish, Felicia funnels another burst of energy outward, and she can see it radiate like a concussive pulse. It ripples up the mountainside and into the weakening crimson throat. Another roar comes thundering down at her, but it fragments into weak bursts. Felicia roars back, yet again, her actual voice tiny in the turbulence of sound, but her vigor gigantic. Luminescence continues to fall in shards to the earth, collapsing and impacting as if with weight. At the same time, alien souls shoot skyward, crackling out as they traverse the deep blackness of the night.

Nicole is alone.

She's still there, her energy weak. Felicia can sense her pulse, and her pain.

Sobbing, Felicia pushes upward and outward again, as if belching fire. Her mouth opens, and energy pours out in yet another healing wave, climbing the mountainside, and more humans fall to the dirt, screaming in agony. And now it's a series of waves, expelling the alien infection, crisscrossing the mountain and scattering down the slopes, down the foothills, and into the city.

More.

She screams forth yet another wave of energy, and strobes of lightning tear the fabric of the alien column, the insectile limbs jerking spasmodically and finally going rigid, becoming dry husks and instantly crumbling. And a cancerous blackness overtakes the alien throat, burning, and Felicia can hear the screams of the dying strangers, and she no longer holds empathy for them. Nicole is alone among the dead on the mountain face, and Felicia screeches her defiance and rage.

She feels her energy waning, but it is enough, she knows.

The atmosphere is full of death.

As is this mountainside, and the city below. And as she pushes out another blast of energy, she sees the shockwave begin to reverberate against some kind of distant perimeter, far away, some kind of barrier, and it's at that moment—somewhere at the back of her awareness—that she comes to a startling realization. It's as if she barely has the capacity to acknowledge it. But in that moment she knows that the world will survive.

She never considered the possibility.

The strangers never let her see it.

The edge.

She turns, wobbly on the corrugated floor, and lets the realization stun her and bring her back to herself.

"It's over," she says aloud, but she can't hear her voice. She repeats the words, louder. "It's over."

Joel stares upward with open-mouthed awe as the pulsing throat continues its collapse, breaking into ash and smoke. The structured column of energy and crimson light is almost completely gone, giving way to a blackness dotted with stars. Ash drifts down like gray snow.

"Holy shit, lady," he says, still staring upward. "You did it. You fucking did it."

"I need to go over there," she says again, and finally Joel looks down at her, sees the black trail of ash and tears down her face. She lifts a weary arm to point up the mountain face as the hands of the survivors gradually let her go. The human beings in the back of the old truck shift as if waking from a long slumber.

"Why?" Joel asks.

"My friend is up there," she says.

"This truck won't make it up there."

"Come with me?" Felicia says. "Please?"

Joel takes a moment to watch the side of the mountain, the thousands of humans in twisted agony, calling for help, and Felicia can sense he's at a loss. How can one man, or even the five of six exhausted survivors in this truck, make any difference at all in the face of all that? Then he gives voice to it.

"What do we do?"

"We can help them."

"How? How on Earth can we help them?"

"We're out of everything," Zoe reminds them, swallowing, returning to full awareness. Her own eyes are wet, and her cheeks are streaked black with ash. "They're dying."

"The radio," Felicia says.

She senses it crackling to life, and she understands now that the strangers had been blocking the communication for hours. Even that, they had controlled and stopped.

Joel looks at her quizzically, and at that moment Rachel staggers out of the truck, two-way radio in her fist. A familiar voice is stuttering over the speaker, quick-paced words that are unintelligible under the din coming from the mountain face.

"Kevin's on the radio!" Rachel calls. "He says people are alive!"

"What?"

"He's barely coming through, but they're finding people."

"Where?"

"I'm not sure, but I think he said Sterling." She's staring all around, in disbelief that the nightmare is actually coming to an end. "He's breaking up."

"That's it? They only made it that far east?"

"I think that's the edge of it," Felicia says.

"The edge of what?" Joel says, his head snapping toward her.

"The edge of everything."

"But this thing …" Joel says, then stops. "Wait."

Rachel watches him come to the same realization she has come to. Felicia can see it in Rachel's mind as well as Joel's: the awareness expanding from their first moments under the sway of the infestation, the belief—fed to them psychically?—that the phenomenon was worldwide, that all observable evidence pointed to the conclusion that the alien infection gripped the entire planet and not merely a section of it. Felicia grasps only a vague sense of this, as if her own mind is only now opening to the possibility.

Had Kevin and Mai's crew come upon an actual barrier? A forcefield of some kind? Had they found people looking at them from the other side? People observing the invasion from the outside but unable to interfere?

Static continues to pour from the radio, with only snippets of Kevin's voice coming through. Rachel tries to connect with him, repeatedly, but Felicia can no longer wait. She has to go.

"Help is coming," Felicia says. She can sense emergency response gathering at the perimeter. "Now please take me up there."

She begins to climb down from the truck bed, but Philip won't let go his grip. Felicia kneels and touches him warmly.

"It's finished," she says to the boy. "You did wonderfully."

He peers up at her, his wet eyes innocent and pure. He smiles at her. She knows he will be fine. Philip relaxes his grip and turns to the two women at his level. Both Linda and Julia are returning his tentative smile, weary and wracked with pain but finally—impossibly—optimistic.

Joel and the twins hop down to the ground, still keeping a wary eye on the surroundings.

"Is it really over?" Chloe asks, but no one answers.

The hills are still agitated with misery, and it seems very far from over. But as the survivors take turns gazing into the sky, they know that at least the worst is behind them. As dawn approaches, brightening the eastern horizon with muted fire, the phenomenon above them continues to dissolve into ash clouds and diminishing crackles of otherworldly electricity. The alien threat is gone, perhaps slain.

Is it possible?

They will survive.

"You won't need those," Felicia says.

The twins look at the weapons in their grips as if they don't make sense, then stow them in the truck bed. They blink and cough, and then begin to hastily stockpile morphine syringes in their boxes, as much as they can carry.

"You go, I'll stay with Kayla," says Rachel. "And Kevin!"

Felicia begins running and stumbling away from the truck, toward the mass of bodies in the trees. Nicole is up there, less than an eighth of a mile up the slope, the image is so clear it's as if she has binoculars trained on the spot. Resolute now, she races past twisted bodies into the trampled wildflowers leading to the forest's edge. It's old-growth pine mixed with Aspen—ponderosa pine and blue spruce, lodge pole pine and white fir. The strangers were after it all, and something in particular about this area. What was it? She can't see it clearly at the moment, doesn't care to, but increased awareness of the alien objective is possible only now that they're gone, and Felicia doesn't know why. Did they withhold information from their human hosts?

She shakes her head away from all that, and makes her way past the larger conglomerations of bodies. Approximately half are already dead, and the other half are writhing on the ground, teeth gritted, muscles thrashed, bones broken, joints blasted. Uniformly, their mouths and faces are scarred and bleeding and slathered with splinters and sap. The landscape is a deafening chorus of agony.

"Be careful!" Joel calls from twenty feet behind her, his voice nearly drowned out.

Felicia pays no heed.

The twins have slowed, wandering through the first of the screaming victims, trying to find the worst off so that they can administer what little pain relief they have. Immediately, they are kneeling next to two separate bodies. Two of thousands.

Their mindscapes fade behind Felicia's progress.

Nicole.

She's closer now.

Felicia weaves through the tapestry of human misery, the screams raining against her ears.

She can sense them watching her, knowing who she is, registering her passing even as they persevere through hideous injury.

It's her!

Felicia stagger-runs, gasping, her own injuries complaining, but she presses on. New tears stream down her face, not only in anticipation of her finding her lover but also in recognition of those in need whom she is passing without even acknowledging.

Surrounding her in all directions, pine trees have been gnawed into their deep sapwood layer. Every tree is surrounded by mounds of sticky, bloody sap and masticated bark and cambium. Next to each pile lay countless bodies screaming through horribly injured mouths, teeth cracked and gone, tongues swollen and torn, lips thrashed beyond repair.

Nicole's soul rears up bright and wounded in her mind's eye, and then Felicia is upon her, zeroing in. She stops, panting, searching all around. Misery everywhere.

Where is she?

Then a familiar birthmark on a naked, ruined shoulder. A butterfly.

Nicole is curled up, face clenched. She is obliterated, her bones broken, her naked flesh ripped. She's convulsing and coughing.

No.

Felicia bends to her, places her hand on the hot, bleeding skin. The skin she has loved.

Nicole is still unclothed from sleep. She never had the chance to wake up to humanity and dress herself and enjoy another second of life. She is shaking uncontrollably, but she reacts to Felicia's touch, knowing it's her. Nicole's wet, sap-encrusted eyes meet hers, but they are mostly unfocused, unseeing. Their bond has become inner.

Outwardly, Nicole is whimpering in her failing human shell, bleeding out from all kinds of horrific wounds. But the two of them share a flood of imagery, most strongly at the point where Felicia touches Nicole's unblemished skin—at the upper arm where the butterfly tattoo remains, bright and hopeful; at her back, where the vertebrae are red and inflamed; and at her stomach, where Nicole's belly button trembles beneath shallow breaths. The touch is hot, feverish from the body's immune system shifting into useless overdrive but also from the rush of sensory memory. Felicia's fingertips burn.

—*You found me!* —

—*I found you*—

—*I knew you would*—

Felicia carefully embraces her lover, knowing exactly where not to touch her. She knows Nicole's body as if it is her own, and the knowledge brings a flood of new tears.

She will not be able to save her.

—*and they're back to the moment they met on campus, their paths crossing at a moment of pure chance, Felicia new to the school from California and Nicole also new but offering help as a Fort Collins native, filling her in on the best hot spots, the best local brews, the best hikes in the area, and making a casual date the next day at Starry Night to share more tips, and by the end of that tea on College Avenue, knowing that one thing was going to lead to another, and the tightness and rightness in the pit of the stomach at the prospect of the immediate future, and as the summer days wore on, fitting together like puzzle pieces in more ways than the physical, and Felicia's reluctance to move to northern Colorado evaporating like moisture at high altitude, and*—

Nicole begins to shudder more violently, and Chloe is already there at her side, preparing a syringe with a full dose of morphine, but Nicole is laboriously shaking her head, and Felicia waves Chloe away.

"Are you sure?"

Felicia nods, and Chloe hurries away.

—and the memories begin to thin and weave like tendrils between them, like strands of DNA, and Felicia can smell Nicole's essence within the memories, and even as the body flatlines, the soul remains under Felicia's touch, moving into her through her fingertips, and Felicia feels a wave of pure love envelop her—

Nicole's body goes limp against Felicia's breast, but Felicia hardly notices. The mountainside and the survivors fade into nothingness, and all she knows is that Nicole's essence remains inside her, alive and soaring, and she holds on to it tightly, not wanting to let it go.

"Felicia," comes a voice.

As in a dream, Nicole begins to drift inside their psychic connection, ethereally, and Felicia is amazed to find that rather than dissipating outward, Nicole is moving deeper inside Felicia, becoming a part of her, and she has never felt anything like it in all her time on this planet. It's both sensual and spiritual, beyond anything earthbound, and despite the scale of death and suffering all around her, Felicia can't help but erupt in beatific laughter, if only for a moment, as Nicole nests in the deepest part of her.

"Felicia!" says Joel, louder.

She opens her eyes, still clutching Nicole's corpse.

"She's gone," he says.

Felicia shakes her head, gently sets her lover's body to the soft earth.

"No, she's not."

She turns away from the horror of Nicole's body to find Julia approaching, carrying Philip, and Linda bringing up the rear, limping but healing quickly somehow, much more quickly than Felicia herself did at the library. Felicia takes only a moment to marvel over the boy's quick recovery before she sees it with her own eyes: Most of the bodies around them are succumbing and their souls are drifting toward them, ghostly apparitions floating in the pre-dawn and merging with Linda, or Julia, or Philip, or Felicia, it doesn't matter, and Felicia senses all of them, absorbs their life stories, their memories, their passions, and they become a part of her, and to Felicia it's the most enriching sensation she's ever known. Whereas this alien notion of a web of souls frightened her, it is now an expression of humanity that is more human than anything she's experienced.

The mountainside is alive with wandering souls.

"It's beautiful!" she cries.

She can feel Joel staring at her, incredulous, but it only barely registers in her consciousness. Perhaps someday he'll understand what has happened.

Felicia is not sure how much later they all hear the chopping blades of three military helicopters approaching the site. Time seems to bend and stretch. But soon the urgent machines are sweeping in from the brightening east, and Joel is racing down the ruined mountainside, into the clearing, to wave them in. But Rachel is already down there at the road's edge, Kayla right alongside her, anchored to her side, and they are both waving their arms in thankful arcs, and Felicia can read the enormous rushes of relief in both their minds as the wind from the great metal blades blast their weary faces, which are laughing and happy despite the crushing death in their midst, as if they too know what is becoming of the infected souls.

Joel arrives at the road's edge, and without hesitation, before the copters land, he embraces Rachel, lifting her into the air, and they kiss and laugh, and Kayla hugs both of them in turn, dancing around them, and Felicia suddenly has a glimpse of their future together as a makeshift family, and although the glimpse is one of deserved joy, a slow sadness takes hold of her.

At that moment, way down below, Rachel drops from Joel's embrace and spins, searching for Felicia among the wounded trees—almost as if she has heard her thoughts—and she finds her, and Rachel's expression also becomes one of sorrow, and Felicia smiles warmly for her.

The helicopters land on the road some distance from the truck, and five armed men jump from each one, approaching Rachel and Joel. They are animated in their gestures, shouting at them as Joel responds, nodding. Rachel begins to gesture toward the mountainside, beckoning Felicia and the others to return to the road, and Felicia looks away, toward the bruised dawn, where—in the distance—more helicopters are approaching, medical helicopters from the looks of them, their blades making spirals of the lingering smoke.

She realizes that she, Julia, Linda, and the boy—those who returned— are the only ones experiencing or even seeing the absorption of souls. She is overwhelmed by the voices and personalities and lifeforces that are being released from their human forms and finding homes inside her, shrinking to an essence and nestling in the deep dark, becoming part of her.

With a start, she recognizes that although most of the human beings are giving in to their injuries, some are not. She can see these bright souls, still shining but suffering.

She can identify them.

Felicia grabs Zoe's hand, then Chloe's, and she drags them from new survivor to new survivor.

"This is Joanie, she'll make it, help her," she instructs Zoe, who hastily prepares one of the few syringes remaining, administers the medicine, then tells Chloe to run down to the truck and get bandages for open wounds.

Joanie the divorced schoolteacher, trembling, looks into Felicia's eyes.

—*Thank you!*—

Thirty feet away is Herb, a real estate broker with four kids and a beautiful wife who succumbed to the infection, and he is choking on his own blood. Zoe turns him over, and Herb coughs out the worst of it, then inhales wretchedly. In seconds, he is breathing easier under the warmth of morphine, but he is still bleeding from slashed gums and the open maws of lost teeth. The man is weeping softly, but Felicia hears his words flow over her.

—*You did it, you're the one, thank you, thank you*—

And she's shaking her head, *No, not only me,* and sparing another glance at the survivors at the road's edge, she moves on to the next body, a young woman named Tricia, whose confused thoughts center on her boyfriend Trent, whom Felicia knows is lying on a patch of ground north of Hughes Stadium, dying at this very moment.

Then Lawrence, an older man in shredded biking attire, his helmet still attached to his head and possibly the thing that kept him alive.

And on and on like that until the mountainside is buzzing with military and medical activity, blue triage and trauma tents set up as far as the eye can see, Felicia and the others leading the first responders to the bodies that have the best chance to survive. Death is still rolling across the mountainside, but there are new survivors among them, and at first the responders are mystified and suspicious about Felicia's ability to direct them to the bodies most in need, but before long they are relying on her—as well as Julia and Linda, and even Philip—to find those bodies.

Act now, ask questions later is the ruling philosophy.

But there are untold thousands of people to wade through, and an increasing number are corpses. As souls continue to drift toward Felicia, the responders are beside themselves with panic and disbelief.

"What happened here?!" shouts a young National Guardsman based out of Kansas who has dealt with emergency scenarios only in simulations. He has repeated the phrase three times as he has moved from body to mutilated body, helping to enumerate them lower down near the road. An Army contingent is already in sparse command there, leading the endeavor.

No one is answering the boy from Kansas. Instead, they are bending to their grim tasks.

It will be many days until the dead are properly reckoned with. Felicia and the others will not stop helping until the final bodies are discovered, and all those who might survive are on their way to recovery.

But she will occasionally stop to gather strength, to huddle with the others who have been brought back, and share their energies, and communicate in ways that only they can. This new ability, this power, will never stop being a source of wonder to her. And somewhere deep inside she understands that because of it, the world will never be the same.

She pauses at one point, breathing with her human lungs, and stares off in the direction of dawn, where the black dots of further military copters approach, and she acknowledges the new day.

At that moment, her thoughts move to Nicole, with whom she's shared a few sunrises, but she doesn't dwell on her destroyed human shell—rather, on the bright soul embedded inside her, and she can smell her scent, and she can hear her laughter, and she can even see the mischief in her eyes. Just before she bends again to her task, she sends a final thought to her lover.

I saved you.

EPILOGUE

Rachel opens the curtains of the front room and looks out on the quiet street. It's 6 a.m., exactly three months since the apocalyptic event that befell not only her hometown of Fort Collins, Colorado, but also Denver, Greeley, Loveland, Cheyenne, and all the other cities and towns within the irregular circle that described the circumference of the alien invasion. That's the term the media actually used.

Alien invasion.

The focus of the attack was almost certainly Roosevelt National Forest, according to research foresters and plant physiologists who had swept in with the government to diagnose the event. Felicia tried to explain it to her in the aftermath—the focus on the chemical makeup of evergreen forestry. Felicia sees it clearly in her mind now, too, as if she has wiped the stains of age from an ancient text—about the way the pine uniquely recovered in the wake of moderate-intensity wildfire. That chemical interaction, in conjunction with the amount of time between repeated injuries, is what the strangers had craved. Whatever had been visited upon Earth during that week had been about survival. Survival in the wake of fiery devastation.

Scientists debated endlessly about that chemical interaction, wondering why an advanced civilization had been unable to synthesize what they needed for themselves—wherever they came from. Why had it been necessary to forcibly take the chemical from another world?

The answer was that the aliens had been dying—had, in fact, been drifting from their destroyed home. A thousand other drifting pods held the hope of encountering other potential worlds, programmed to send hibernating souls into promising regions.

The event took the lives of more than four million human beings, as well as countless animals, forever altering the mountain region. Even most of those who survived were loath to stay, preferring to evacuate the blasted region and relocate in other, less devastated climes. Who could tell whether it might happen again? Denver became a lost city, as did dozens of other cities and towns.

But not Fort Collins, as far as Rachel and her new family are concerned.

This is where they belong.

And Rachel knows, somehow, that they're safe now. Maybe it's the proximity to Felicia, or maybe she simply feels it in her blood.

She about-faces from the window and brings her apple to her mom's favorite chair, watches dawn brighten the day. There are still rose bushes in the yard where her mom planted them, and they are still in the redwood planter that her father built for them, and they are no longer tarnished by the blood of Mrs. Carmichael.

Directly opposite this window, across the street, is the window to Tony's house. She has memories of crossing directly over there to be with him—memories she can recall so clearly that they barely ache yet. It has been difficult to conjure the memories of Tony from before the world ended, but now, despite herself, they flood her. Their young dates, walking to Old Town. Their first fumblings, the taste of fast food in their mouths. Hormones and her braces. The knowledge that her dad never thought much of Tony, and in the midst of Susanna, Rachel's reaction toward Tony, becoming closer to him, knowing the effect it had on her dad. Her dad didn't voice this very often, but of course he would have preferred someone a little more clean-cut for his only daughter, a relationship not borne out of across-the-street convenience but rather out of shared academic excellence—or something like that.

She still mourns Tony, and what happened to him—that will never go away—but he seems a part of a different life. A different reality.

Funny how an apocalyptic event can pave the way for a father's vision for his daughter to come true.

She takes a bite out of her apple, thinking about Joel and Kayla. She thinks about them all the time, yes, but this morning she's thinking about them in terms of the weeks following the event. Rachel and Joel married quietly in a nearly empty courthouse in order to officially adopt Kayla, who was left without any family in the wake of it all. Rachel's thoughts about her husband and daughter are so strong and proud and ebullient that she frequently weeps, but today she is fine to be away from them. This is her once-per-month ritual, and it is hers alone.

With their money from the government, they have purchased a large home in Old Town and have partnered with Felicia to re-open the Fort Collins Food Co-Op in one of the surviving sections of Old Town— actually, in the space formerly occupied by the Stone Lion Bookstore and later Beau Jo's Pizza. She's proud that she's helping Fort Collins rebuild. The twins, Zoe and Chloe, have also stayed in town, and they're spearheading the downtown library project, renewing and rebuilding the place where the battle turned. The government money gave that a big start, too.

As for her father's secret money, which has been instrumental in all these projects … the government doesn't need to know about that.

Rachel has stayed here at the house, alone, on five occasions since everything happened. It has become her way of remembering and honoring the way her life was before. But the first time she revisited this house, it was to direct medical personnel inside to remove the bodies of her father and Susanna and begin the processes of respectfully laying them to rest. That was two days after the aliens' ending.

The next day, she ventured inside the still-stinking room to retrieve the mystery money from her father's open safe and hide it deep inside an innocent corner of her own bedroom, behind her old games and dolls. It remains there to this day. Well, what's left of it.

She hasn't given a lot more thought to where the money came from. She will never know the answer, so why bother? Whenever she begins to ponder it, she recalls the moment Felicia came up to her one day at the Co-Op, putting her arm around her. At that moment, Rachel had been lost in thought, staring out onto the streets of Old Town, thinking about that cash. Thinking about what her dad had been doing, piling all of that up for no discernible reason. Had it been crime? Something shady? He'd kept secrets from her. These thoughts were not new, and they had been festering since her discovery.

Felicia had leaned into her. "Hey."

Rachel had smiled. "Hey yourself."

"He saved it all for you," she said. "For your future. He was trying to get it to you. That's obvious, right?"

Rachel had stared at her in shock, and Felicia had simply walked away, back to work stocking the store with government-purchased foods.

"What?"

Felicia had only winked at her over her shoulder, almost solemnly, and nodded.

Rachel had watched her go, her mind rapidly trying to connect the dots. Had Felicia known what she was thinking at that moment? Rachel and Joel had become convinced that Felicia was privy to the thoughts and feelings of those around her, resulting from what she had gone through, but they were never sure of the extent of that ability. Did she see glimpses of actual thoughts? Vibrations of feelings? Rachel had asked her point-blank one time, and Felicia had dodged the question, talking in vague terms and not wanting to delve too deeply into painful memories.

Rachel never said another word about it, to Joel or Felicia or anyone. Her dad had left her the money for her future. It was that simple. And her future is now.

She takes another bite of her apple and sighs, lost in the silence.

When she thinks of her future, she mostly thinks of Kayla, that beautiful kid. But she also thinks of her new business partner, Felicia, and what she has become. She doesn't spend a lot of time at the Co-Op, even though Rachel knows that was Felicia's own dream of the future. She is far more often in the company of the *alien survivors*, as the media has dubbed them. There are more than a thousand of them living in the southeast part of town, over by the abandoned Mormon temple. Felicia is occupying a ranch-style home in that neighborhood, a home that has become the center of activity for these survivors.

There's something brewing over there, and Felicia hasn't been exactly forthcoming about it, but she exudes optimism and energy when she talks vaguely about the shared-experience bonds the community feels.

A week ago, Felicia—under the influence of some cheap wine— spoke to Rachel in measured tones about Philip, about how he and other saved children might embody the next step in the evolution of the species, but then she stopped talking, as if she realized she was saying too much. It was an odd moment, full of portent, and it made Rachel flash back to the scene at the edge of the forest, when the military had finally and firmly established its stronghold in the Event's aftermath. Army personnel had detained the exhausted survivors till late afternoon, and waves of government interrogators had questioned them endlessly. Medical and science technicians had run them through the wringer, too, quickly separating Felicia and Philip, as well as Linda and Julia, for further scrutiny. In fact, Rachel hadn't seen those four until several days later when they were ultimately released to family. She had hugged each one of them and sent them on their way to teary long-distance relations, and they had all glanced back at her, acknowledging what they had gone through.

She had never heard another word from anyone—least of all Felicia—about whether anything was found inside them. Any remnants of the alien infestation. Whatever was there was ephemeral.

But Rachel is convinced it's there.

And that no longer scares her.

The phone rings, and Rachel stares at it there on the wall. The same phone where she attempted to make that 911 call on the first day of the event. She knows it's Joel. He's the only other person with this number. She hops out of the chair, finishing a big bite of apple.

"Hey J," she says into the old familiar receiver.

"Hey girl, knew you'd be up."

"Just having breakfast."

"Figured." He clears his throat. "So how are things going?"

"Feeling good. Like maybe I won't need to come back here much anymore."

"Lot of bad stuff happened there, but I wouldn't blame you if you felt the need to go back now and then."

"I know."

"You up for some real breakfast? Kevin is helping the twins get Lucille's back up and running. He says there's biscuits happening."

Rachel looks at her apple, then tosses it in the trash can by the wall. "I'm in."

"Meet you there in twenty? Your daughter is salivating at the prospect of real food."

She smiles at the thought of Kayla. "I'll be there."

They hang up, and Rachel sighs easily, walks into the living room. She casts her gaze about, taking it in. Then she walks back to her bedroom, looks around. It seems so small! She thinks her dad would be happy about how clean it is. She laughs at that thought, throwing a kiss at her stuffed bear, front and center on the bed. She closes the door and goes to her father's bedroom. She reverently closes this door, too, as if shutting the ornate door of an elaborate and worshipful tomb.

"I love you, Daddy," she whispers.

Then she exits the home, onto a desolate street, and the October trees are yellow and falling, and a crisp breeze is in the air.

Acknowledgments

Big gratitude to my family, as always: to my wife Barb and my kick-ass daughters, Harper and Sophie, who are growing up way too fast and gearing up to face a world increasingly populated by villains—perhaps even tougher to face than the ones in the *Blood* saga! Like Rachel and Felicia in my girl-power saga, all of the women in my life are up to the challenge and provide daily inspiration. To the ever-enthusiastic cheerleaders among my family and friends—you know who you are!

Major shout-out to Rob Leininger for his help getting this book in shape. Rob's powerful neo noir *Killing Suki Flood* is one of my favorite books of all time, and I'm amazed this hero author took the time to mentor the likes of me. It goes without saying that *Blood Dawn* is better because of him.

Thanks to Kirk Whitham, James W. Powell, Mike and Rebecca Parish, Justin Bzdek, and Doug Powell for their sharp observations during the early reading phase, and to Christopher Nowell and Kirk Whitham for the cover art, design, and layout. And finally, cheers to the authors who took precious time from their own writing schedules to read this book and provide excellent cover blurbs: Robert Devereaux, Joshua Gaylord (Alden Bell), Robert Leininger, and John Dixon (Bill Braddock).

About the Author

Jason Bovberg is the author of the *Blood* trilogy—*Blood Red*, *Draw Blood*, and *Blood Dawn*—as well as *The Naked Dame*, a throwback pulp noir novel. He is editor/publisher of Dark Highway Press, which published the controversial, erotic fairy tale *Santa Steps Out* and the weird western anthology *Skull Full of Spurs*. He lives in Fort Collins, Colorado, with his wife Barb and his daughters Harper and Sophie. You can find him online at www.jasonbovberg.com.

Made in the USA
Lexington, KY
11 June 2017